BY THE SAME AUTHOR

Frog
Frog and the Sandspiders of Aridian
Frog and the Tree of Spells

To

FRASER

[signature]

EARTHLAND

JOFFRE WHITE

Matador
9 Priory Business Park,
Wistow Road, Kibworth Beauchamp,
Leicestershire. LE8 0RX
Tel: 0116 279 2299
Email: books@troubador.co.uk
Web: www.troubador.co.uk/matador
Twitter: @matadorbooks

ISBN 978 1788037 389

British Library Cataloguing in Publication Data.
A catalogue record for this book is available from the British Library.

Printed and bound by CPI Group (UK) Ltd, Croydon, CR0 4YY
Typeset in 12pt Aldine401 BT by Troubador Publishing Ltd, Leicester, UK

Matador is an imprint of Troubador Publishing Ltd

To the class of 1960 –
In the blink of an eye, how far we have come.

1

DREADLOCKS

The world came rushing back on a relentless tide of sound. Screams pierced Savannah's ears. Shrill cries echoed inside her head like sharp fragments of pain. She forced her eyes open, pushing apart her half-drugged lids. Her pupils struggled to focus as the rest of her senses sluggishly kicked in.

A soft heat pressed cloyingly against her face, and a stagnant smell invaded her nostrils; a mixture of rotting fish and bitter salt caught in the back of her throat causing her to retch sour spittle. Hot tears seeped from her eyes and tracked dirtily down her sleep-reddened cheeks.

Warily, she pushed herself up and onto her hands and knees, and a moment of panic made her body tremble, as the soft ground seemed to disintegrate between her fingers. She frantically wiped at the warm, clammy grains, which eagerly stuck to her skin.

All the while above her, the horrific screaming continued.

Suddenly, amongst the cacophony of noise, she heard a voice.

'Get up! Get up!'

Hands roughly and urgently dragged her onto her feet.

'Move it!'

Amongst her confused and ragged thoughts, the voice registered no gender. Through damp tears and clinging strands of fine, blonde hair, her blurred vision slowly focused; she blinked to take in stark cinematic snapshots of her surroundings.

Grey sky.

Slate-coloured, foam-crested sea.

Murky and grey sand dunes.

Bleached, tufted grass.

Scattered remnants of shredded and torn clothing.

An old, lace-less work boot.

The face of a child's doll stared vacantly at the sky. Its eye sockets empty and hollow. What remained of its synthetic, golden hair was stained with dark, dried human blood.

Savannah forced herself upright and her legs quivered unsteadily like a newborn calf. She stared out across the banks of an estuary. A shock of confusion hit her, and then a wave of anger washed over it as ragged thoughts assembled a memory that prompted a question.

How could they let this happen to their own flesh and blood? To their own daughter?

The screaming swooped and echoed above her like a discordant chorus of agonised souls. Not screams of distress, but vicious, angry screams.

She looked up. Seagulls, but these seagulls were massive predators. The mutated results of escaped laboratory experiments, crossbred with nature's original creations. From beneath grey and white plumage, their sharp, bladed talons snatched at the air like jagged scythes. Oversized beaks, hooked and perfectly made for tearing and rending flesh apart, opened with the sound of each piercing scream. Their wingspans of over two metres beat violently at the air while their black, soulless eyes, stared down at her.

The voice, louder this time, cut into her fear.

'Don't just stand there. Get moving! I can't hold them off for much longer. Too many of them.'

She turned to face her mysterious rescuer.

Bright green eyes met her dark blue ones. A figure roughly her height stood there. Chocolate brown dreadlocks tumbled down to shoulder length, and framed a sharp-featured face that was distorted by hues of green and brown camouflage paint.

As with the voice, she couldn't quite decide if the person was male or female. Even so, she guessed them to be about her age – sixteen, or maybe older. Their attire consisted of rugged black combats and an old flying jacket of brown leather, which bore the scars and creases of previous adventurous exploits. Thick-soled boots dug into the sand. A tattered green, red and orange sash of defiance hung from the waist of the lithe figure. These were the tough, hardwearing clothes of a Diss – a dissident, a rebel. Their hands were wrapped in fingerless gloves, one of which held her firmly by the arm; the other gripped a large, dull-metalled catapult.

'Who are you?' she managed.

'Introductions later, that's if we both survive this. Just keep up with me.'

Then, without warning, she was pushed aside, and she watched as nimble fingers hastily loaded the catapult with a large, steel ball bearing. The thick, black elastic stretched back in an instant; tension and energy trembled along its length. With a "phizzzing!" the metal ball launched into the sky.

A strong hand clasped around the back of her overalls, and projected her onwards, almost lifting her feet from the ground.

'Run!'

Adrenalin coursed through her veins to fuel her into action.

She stumbled, mildly cursing. Her hands scrabbled at the sand, her feet frantically dug into the dune, and she pushed herself forwards and upwards.

'Good. Keep going. Don't look back,' the voice encouraged.

Savannah had spent most of her life being disobedient, and to be told not to look back was too much of a temptation. As they both clawed their way to the ridge, she turned a glance. The ball bearing had hit its target, and one of the gulls lay convulsing and thrashing on the sand as it desperately tried to stop half a dozen or so of its flock from tearing it apart, adding its own screams of pain and fear to the vicious refrain.

She watched, spellbound, as the creature was engulfed. Beaks and claws ripped at feathers and flesh. Blood splattered out onto the sand like thick crimson raindrops in an otherwise monotone scene. Other gulls hovered overhead; amongst them, one enormous bird caught her gaze. In an instant, it decided she was easier prey. With an effortless flap of its wings, it launched itself in pursuit.

'Oh, great,' said her would-be saviour. 'Now we've *really* got to run.'

'Where?'

'There. Head for that clump of dune grass.'

She couldn't see what sanctuary the small patch of grass would give them. It nestled about fifty metres ahead, maybe more. The gull, however, was now half the distance behind them, and gaining.

'Oooooh! Hell!' she screamed as she launched herself forward. Her legs pounded, kicking up sprays of sand.

With about twenty metres ahead of her, she still couldn't see shelter. The cold chill of fear ran down her back as a savage screech exploded overhead. With ten metres to go, the figure next to her let out a loud, piercing whistle, and the ground opened up in front of them; a trapdoor to safety hinged upwards, cascading rivulets of sand in its wake. The head and shoulders of a shadowed figure emerged, a crossbow aimed in her direction.

'Jump!' commanded a man's voice.

She tucked in her elbows and barrel rolled towards the hole. Just before she fell into shadow, she had a surreal, upside down vision of the pursuing gull; the bird's eyes bulged in shock as the steel shaft of an arrow protruded from its throat, and a red stain of blood spread through ruffled white feathers. Involuntarily, the enormous wings folded upwards, and it plummeted towards the sand with all the grace of a collapsed parachute.

A short fall took the wind out of her as she landed awkwardly on a sand-covered floor. Two bodies tumbled after her in a tangled heap; the trapdoor closed like a coffin lid, shutting out the riotous and carnage-induced screaming. For the second time that morning, Savannah found herself on her knees, gasping and retching. She wiped a gobbet of gritty spittle from her mouth with the back of her hand.

'Damn, that was almost fun!' remarked the dreadlocks, kneeling beside her, hardly out of breath.

Leaning back on her heels, she pulled in gulps of air while her eyes adapted to the subdued light. She was in a low ceilinged cave, the sides and roof shored up with thick black, rough-hewn timbers. To her left, at the dark entrance to a narrow tunnel, a man, also wearing the tri-colours of the Diss, sat on his haunches, fulfilling his role as a silent sentinel. He held a small, flaming torch, which flickered like a nervous sprite, and sent shadows skittering around the claustrophobic burrow.

Dreadlocks crouched in front of her at eye level, and displayed a set of white teeth, neatly framed in a broad smile. 'See, you can really run when you have to, and you're fast too – for a city girl.'

'I'll take that as a compliment,' she replied. Adrenalin clouded over the recent horror and boosted her confidence. 'So, what do I call my saviour?' she smiled.

'Tanis,' came the reply. 'Tanis Kane.'

'I don't want to be rude, Tanis Kane. Only, it's your

voice. I can't tell if you're a…' Her face reddened as she stumbled nervously over the words.

'A boy or a girl?' finished Tanis, enjoying her embarrassment. 'Don't worry; I get it all the time. I'm *definitely* not a girl; and just for the record, I'm nineteen, and a man.' He emphasised the last word without a trace of chauvinism.

'Well, it's nice to meet you, Tanis Kane,' she replied. She held out her hand. 'Thanks for saving my life. I'm…'

He cut her off, and there was no offer of a handshake.

'I know who you are; in fact, I know most things about you. It's been my business for the last six months.'

All she could do was utter a surprised, 'Oh!'

'I see you've got your brand,' he continued matter-of-factly. He tentatively eased aside the collar of her overalls.

Savannah put her hand up to touch the tender area of skin on the side of her neck. Her fingers gently traced the raised swelling, she felt the outline of the letter T: the brand of the Transported – a mark she would carry for the rest of her life. The thought of her unconscious body being violated in such a way caught her breath. A shiver scuttled down her spine like a sliver of melting ice. Dark images of unwanted hands on her flesh floated into her mind like the remnants of a bad dream. Thankfully, another voice interrupted the onset of Savannah's brooding hysteria.

'We need to go,' a man's voice came out of the shadows behind Tanis, and was insistent. 'We have to get back to Turnpike, before dark.'

2

CATALYST

Decades ago, the catalyst for society's breakdown and final collapse was an abrupt, global financial meltdown. Overnight, the flow of currency ceased. Banks and financiers closed their doors. Access to wealth and influence became a privilege – you either had it, or you didn't.

In the towns, the countryside and the cities, social warfare erupted. People took to the streets with a mixture of organised and anarchic demonstrations. Politicians argued, the army was deployed and eventually patrolled everywhere. Curfews were enforced.

Then, nature struck the final blow; a colossal solar eruption on the sun's surface sent out the biggest geomagnetic storm ever known. It hit the earth with such intensity that it enveloped the atmosphere with shifting curtains of sickly green and venomous red light. A nightmare version of the aurora borealis.

Within twenty-four hours, anything reliant on electrical power or charged impulses failed. Magnetic polarities were reversed, which resulted in permanent damage to everything from a simple handheld battery torch, through to the world's largest power grids. Computer terminals fell blank and lifeless. Blinking cursors became as extinct as dinosaurs.

The World Wide Web, mobile communication, radio, power-charged weapons – whatever needed an electrical impulse – were saturated by gamma rays, and rendered irreparably useless. Transport systems died in transit. Planes dropped from the sky and ships floundered at sea. Orbiting satellites and space stations crashed earthwards to burn up in the atmosphere; their scorching trails of debris patterned the sky in cosmic death throes.

In an instant, the electronic era came to an end.

To minimise the risk of core meltdowns and radiation seepage, governments enabled emergency protocols and shut down their nuclear facilities. This action, however, was not universal, and two rogue nations, in a bid to take advantage of the global shift in power, did not enact their safeguards. Consequently, parts of Asia and the Middle East suffered from widespread toxic irradiation, which eventually wiped out whole populations and rendered those areas of the planet lifeless and lethal. Manufacturing and production ground to a halt. The maintenance of water and power supplies ceased. Society fragmented into the survival of the fittest.

The class divide brought poverty, rioting, and finally, segregation. Loose change was useless, and paper money so insignificant that it was burnt in protest. Other commodities and possessions of previous value became worthless – a Van Gough or a Mercedes sports car would not feed or protect you.

In a mad frenzy of frustration, rebellion and wanton destruction, buildings and property were looted and destroyed, and all attempts to preserve public law and order finally failed.

The world became a dangerous place for the weak, the sick, and the pacifist.

Those with high intellect and influence – the politicians, scientists, doctors, architects, physicists, engineers – enlisted the protection of armed guards and soldiers-turned-mercenaries. Some commandeered huge aircraft carriers and military vessels, eventually converting them back to steam power and transforming them into floating havens: modern arks designed for the survival of their exclusive occupants. They took to the sea, and made their plans to create a new realm, a new empire far out in the ocean, away from the troubled landmasses.

Of course, they needed someone to do their bidding, and so they enticed desperate survivors from the old world, with promises of a new life, a safe future. They named this work force Servanti, and with the blood, sweat and tears of their oppressed generations, a new state, a gigantic floating city was constructed.

Now, the colossal structure, home to thousands, exists as a huge buoyant metropolis, anchored to the ocean floor. This is the territory of Opulence. This is the realm of the ruling classes – the self-styled Fortunata.

The Servanti live in the lower levels of Opulence, in their own clean, comfortable, but minimalist container style homes. A separate community, these are the working classes, who earn their place on Opulence with relative social freedoms, but whose purpose exists solely to wait on and provide for every need of the Fortunata who, in contrast, reside in their luxurious, ornate towers, with sky and sea vistas.

Twelve elder statesmen, known as the Masters, hold the ultimate power and influence. They make and enforce the laws, and the laws are *always* in their favour. Their identities are a closely shielded secret. Their rulings are governed by a select Fortunata Council, whose duty it is to enforce all instructions. There is no crime, other than that committed in the name of the Masters, by the repressive Transportation Police.

All, whether they be Fortunata or Servanti, live in the shadow of the Transportation Police. They search out criticism or careless indiscretions directed against the Masters. Freedom of speech or expressions of political discontent are luxuries that no one is afforded. With swift brutality, the Transportation Police seek out, restrain, and escort away those who have been deemed guilty of disloyalty.

The balance of the population is managed by stealth, and on the whims and decisions of the Masters, who ensure the numbers of the Servanti is always maintained for the Fortunata's benefit, and that the Fortunata are always grateful.

You lived and died here as long as you acted with compliance, diplomacy and exercised influence. When that ran out, you were Transported to the old world.

To Earthland.

3

SAVANNAH

Savannah Loveday was a child of the Fortunata – the privileged. Her family line stretched back to Franklin Loveday, the founding father of Opulence.

Somewhere in its lineage, every family has a rebel, a wild-child. Savannah was such a rebel. She openly questioned the ruling Masters' decisions, particularly when any of the Servanti lower classes found themselves in danger of Transportation. It was only because of her family's history and standing that most of her embarrassing episodes of protest were forgiven and conveniently shielded from publicity. Had it been any other individual, they would have been punished with Transportation without any hesitation.

As she grew through childhood, she developed into a headstrong adolescent; her parents' strength and will to control her became less and less effective. She would spend more and more time in the company of the Servanti. She would encourage others to question the methods of the Masters, and she began to call for equality, and for an end to Transportation. Those who sympathised and agreed with her thoughts would not reveal their opinions, aware that the Transportation Police and their spies were never far away. Always watching. Always listening.

Of late, she had increasingly become a source of annoyance to the Fortunata Council, and not all members felt she should be protected by the Loveday family's heritage.

Finally, there came a time when she witnessed several Servanti families, including young children whom she had become particularly fond of, being arrested and Transported. Their offence? – questionable loyalty to the Masters, an accusation brought against them from an undisclosed source. The cries of the offspring as Transportation Police roughly manhandled them, had angered her so much, that the next day she was caught defacing a statue of the Founding Fathers. She had carved across one figure's chest, the words – **GREED KILLS**.

Transportation Police took her into custody, and her parents were summoned to an emergency meeting of the Fortunata Council. Tiberius, her father, noticed that many of the older members were not present; the majority of those gathered on this occasion were a younger, new generation of Fortunata, who liked to be known as the Élite.

Enough was enough, they decreed. Savannah was to be Transported; and if her family obstructed the ruling, then they would be stripped of their personal fortune. Tiberius protested, and he demanded an audience with the Masters, confident they would overrule the decision.

With no regard to his position and heritage, he was

firmly instructed that any further objection would be taken as an act of defiance, and consequently, he himself would be subject to immediate Transportation.

Self-preservation did indeed run deep in the Loveday family's veins. In fear, he capitulated and denounced Savannah with unreserved compliance, while Corda, her mother, stood in silence, her head bowed.

When informed, the real grief would be that of Savannah's younger sister, Beth. At fourteen years old, she was more level-headed than Savannah. She had never shown the same defiant inclinations towards the system, preferring to accept it as it was, along with the privileged world she had been brought into. She was self-centred, but in an innocent, amiable way. She did not agree with Savannah's opinions or actions, and had no aspirations to change their world, but her love for Savannah was as deep as any sister's could be.

Voicing loud bravado, Savannah was restrained and escorted to a Transportation Centre, and detained in a small holding cell. Everything was dull steel: the walls, the ceiling, even the narrow bench, which she perched uncomfortably upon as she stared down at the scuffed, black-tiled floor. Its unreflective surface stared back at her with an air of foreboding. A dented metal bucket sat in a corner, like an unloved memory, and the lingering smell of stale urine pervaded the air.

At twenty-two, Savannah's older brother, Jago, was her senior by six years. An animosity deeper than sibling rivalry existed and there was no love lost between them. He displayed the same headstrong streak as her, but in that laid the only similarity. In complete contrast, he possessed a ruthless ambition to reclaim his ancestor's individual authority over Opulence.

Jago stood over her, dressed in his white and light green robes, looking every bit the image of a Grecian statesman. His ruddy auburn hair rested on his broad shoulders. His dark olive complexion and features matched his hardened and brooding temperament. 'You shame us all,' he spat at her. 'I have watched you disgrace us for far too long. Well, no more. You have no family. We disown you. I have no rebellious sister.' He looked at her with distain, as if she offended him more than the stagnant bucket. His lips curled back in a half sneer, half derisory smile. 'You are Transported.'

Without another word, he turned his back on her, and two light blue uniformed guards parted to let him exit. A subtle nod passed between himself and one of the guards as he strode out of the door.

She felt the blood drain from her face like the fall of a curtain. Even though she was seated, her legs shook nervously. Fear gripped her stomach in a knot, and she leaned forward to throw up what little there was left of the food, which she had consumed earlier on that day.

How could they? How could they? The question repeated itself in her head, scratching on her nerves like a needle stuck on an old gramophone record.

She ran the back of her hand across her mouth; the taste of vomit burnt her lips and throat. The smell of the regurgitated food on the floor threatened more nausea. One of the guards threw her a pair of thick-soled boots and some jet-black overalls: the uniform of the Transported.

'Strip!' he ordered. 'You take nothing with you, *and* you can use what you're wearing to clean up the mess you've made.'

'I want my father!' she screamed back at him; blood flushed her cheeks in anger.

'You have no father. You are Transported,' he barked back.

She stood up and faced them in adolescent defiance. That was when both guards stepped forward. One grabbed her, taking her in a bear hug from behind, and squeezing the breath from her. The other produced a medi-gun, its steel cylinder the host to a variety of debilitating concoctions.

'You are Transported,' he growled through gritted teeth as he jabbed the weapon against her neck.

With a whispering hiss, darkness folded in on her like the closing of a cellar door, and her senses were dragged down into a drug-fuelled unconsciousness.

The next thing she was aware of was the screaming of the gulls.

4

EARTHLAND

Savannah and her escorts weaved their way through the small passageway for maybe twenty minutes before they emerged into a larger, brick-lined tunnel. This was of a more solid construction and gave the impression that it was part of an old drainage or maintenance network. A cold, damp atmosphere surrounded them like an unhealthy disease, and the odour of mould and fungus hung in the stagnant air.

Their crossbows slung across their backs, the two men walked slightly ahead. The smoky flames from their torches picked up the reflection of water as it glistened and trickled down the dark green and black-slimed walls.

Now that she had room, she walked alongside Tanis, and their footsteps sent out splashes of wet echoes.

'Where are you taking me?' she asked.

'We're heading for the old city. To Base One.'

'What's going to happen to me there? Will I be safe?'

'You'll be as safe as you need to be. There are a few people waiting to meet you. Interested in what you know. They have a few questions for you.'

She looked at him sideways. 'It sounds like an interrogation to me.'

'Just questions. You'll be given some fresh clothes and a hot meal, and the opportunity to clean yourself up.' There was a pause. 'We only interrogate our enemies,' he added rather pointedly.

'So, I'm not the enemy?'

'You tell me,' he answered flatly.

Ahead, the two men had just eased themselves around the edge of a large, rough-hewn hole in the floor of the tunnel. They chose to ignore a wide plank that had been lain directly across it. Tanis guided her to the side.

'What's wrong with the plank?' she asked.

'Booby trap,' he replied. 'For any unwelcome visitors; it'll snap like a twig once you get to the middle. There's a five metre drop onto a pile of twisted metal spikes.'

The hole reached across to the opposite wall of the tunnel, leaving just a narrow ledge for them to negotiate on their side. The structure of the tunnel was arched, which meant that the curvature pushed the top half of her body precariously forward. She had no option but to lean and stare into the black, empty space below as she eased herself along, arms spread out, fingers feeling for purchase against the wet and slippery brickwork.

'It's okay, just take it easy,' encouraged Tanis. 'I've done this loads of times. We've rescued hundreds of Transported, and got them past this without losing anyone.'

She steeled herself, and with slightly trembling breath, focused on the shuffling of her feet, until the edge of the hole curved away, and she moved out onto wider ground.

'See, I knew you could do it,' he said, as he stepped out and alongside her.

'You don't sound patronising at all,' she said sarcastically. 'What else do you know about me?'

He continued to look ahead as they walked. When he spoke, the words came out as though he was reading them from a report.

'No one like you has been Transported before. You're part of the Loveday family. You're important. You're valuable. You've spent your whole life amongst the different levels and corridors of Opulence. You've had access to restricted areas, and you have knowledge about its layout that can help us. Most important of all, you don't like the system. We're going to give you the chance to change it, to prove yourself. You've been safe in your privileged position, living in luxury, never having to sacrifice anything. There are those who say you're just a spoilt Fortunata girl, one who likes to *think* that she's a rebel.' He paused, went to say something else and then changed his mind. 'I guess that'll do for now.' He gave her a brief look.

And in that look, she detected animosity, disdain and a suggestion of pity.

The reality of what had happened finally hit her. Emotions assaulted her thoughts. Anger, despair, betrayal, loss. All accompanied by a feeling of wretchedness. It burst inside her like a pressure valve releasing steam. She breathed in with a shudder, held her breath and felt her heartbeat hammer inside her breast. The red mist of her anger rose up like a flood. She reached out and grabbed his shoulder, pulled him around, and stared him straight in the eyes.

'Look at me!' she gestured at herself – her dirt-streaked face and matted hair, the grubby black overalls. 'Do I *look* like Fortunata? Do I?' Warm tears welled up and hung on her eyelids. 'I've been drugged and left on a beach to be torn apart by flying freaks. I've been abandoned. My family have disowned me. The only thing I have left is what I feel. You *don't* know me.' She hammered his chest with her fists. He grabbed her wrists. 'You don't know me. *Nobody* knows me,' she shouted as tears came flooding down in hot tracks across her cheeks. Her anger dissolved into self-pity, and her shoulders heaved as she sobbed uncontrollably.

Tanis released her arms and let her bury her face into his neck. The smell of salty sand, trapped in the tangles of her hair, drifted into his nostrils. He instinctively put an arm around her, just for a moment, until unwanted emotions began to well up in the pit of his stomach, and in a reflex action, he gently pushed her away.

'You're right. I don't know you,' he said softly, 'but I do know *about* you. That's my job, and that's why I'm here.' He reined his sympathy in and changed his tone, almost to that of a chastising parent. 'We haven't got time for this now, so stop feeling sorry for yourself. You can do that later.'

The rejection was like a cold slap across her face. She was furious with herself; she felt exposed. She very rarely let anyone see this side of her, the vulnerable side. So now she bit her lip, enough to draw blood, and as she tasted it, she let the hatred wash over her. Hatred for the Fortunata, hatred for her family, hatred for anyone she had felt love for. An image of Beth flashed through her mind, and she sensed the bitter pain of loss. Protectively, she shrugged it to the back of her mind. She used her sleeves to wipe away the tears from her face. Her palms streaked back the hair from her eyes. Her breath quavered under control.

'Sure,' she said, jutting out her jaw. 'Why the hell should I feel sorry about myself when no one else does?'

Tanis said nothing as she turned and walked away from him. He felt a small pang of guilt for treating her so coldly, but he sensed she was strong; he was sure she could cope with the pain, both emotional and physical. His job was to get her safely to Base One. There, they would find out if she really was serious about overthrowing the Fortunata. If she was, they would train her in the skills that she would need to survive, and to help them fight back. If she wasn't interested, then she became someone else's problem. He couldn't afford to let his feelings or emotions get in the way – that only led to painful memories and disappointment. That way led to trouble and distraction.

She didn't speak for the rest of the journey, save to ask for a drink from one of the water bottles, and as she drank, she noticed her hands trembling slightly from her now subdued rage.

Two hours later, they reached the end of the tunnel. A grill of thick metal latticework, with a steel gated door at its centre, sealed the exit. Tanis produced a key chain and chose the appropriate key from half a dozen others.

He used it to release the securing padlock and chains, and the door swung outwards with a tired and mournful moan.

Savannah followed the two men and emerged from the shadows. They stood on a narrow ridge, maybe ten metres up, and she looked out onto a scene of complete desolation. It almost took her breath away; she had heard stories about the destruction that had been wreaked on a once humanly fertile landscape. They were schooled in the history and triumph of Opulence, but the "old world" was only referred to as a place of chaos and devastation. Hushed stories and tales were the only source of information. No pictures or images were allowed. In fact, owning or being found in possession of any such material was punishable with immediate Transportation. Even so, the descriptions exchanged in hushed conversations, and the visions, which she conjured up in her mind, had not prepared her for this.

Bleak didn't even come close. The air was tinged with an orange haze, which emanated from behind a dirty unwashed, overcast sky. There were no primary colours, just shades of orangey black and grey. Depression oozed out of every crumbling chunk of brick and masonry. Every piece of metal seemed cruelly twisted and shaped into sculptures of despair. As far as the eye could see, it was a landscape of rubble, of indiscernible structures. Columns of filthy smoke rose from scattered places like funeral pyres, only to add to the gloom.

The two men extinguished the torches and loaded their crossbows. Savannah noticed there was a sudden urgency in their manner.

She watched as Tanis relocked the gate, and then he moved to an alcove, where two pigeons perched silently on a white-flecked ledge, encrusted with excreta. Their grey feathers were puffed up, and gave them anonymity against the dark granite recess. He removed a small green slip of paper from his pocket and rolled it tightly up before he inserted it into a tiny brass cylinder. Then, he selected one of the birds, and attached the capsule to one of its legs. He cradled the bird in his hands and whispered quietly to it, before he freed it to flutter urgently upwards. Its shape quickly became diluted and swallowed up by the murky dishwater sky.

'Welcome to Earthland,' he said, almost to himself. He pulled back his sleeve to reveal a steel chronographic, wind-up wristwatch. 'Four hours,' he announced. 'We're cutting it fine.' He turned to Savannah. 'Now comes the easy bit,' he said with obvious irony. He unclipped a leather holster and produced a ball-bearing handgun. 'Here, take this.' He clasped her hand around it; the metal felt warm and almost comforting to her. 'It's air compressed and you've got twenty rounds. Just point, and shoot,' he instructed, mimicking the gun shape with his right hand.

'At what?' she quizzed.

'At anything that moves. Especially if it's coming towards you. You'll be lucky to kill with it, but if you get a head shot in, it'll buy you some time.'

As if on cue, a blood-curdling howl echoed out of the distance. It was a sound of pain and despair, of malice and brutality.

'Damn, they know we're here,' said Tanis.

23

'They won't come out yet, not till dark,' said one of the men. 'Let's get a move on.'

'Okay,' said Tanis. 'Carl, you go up ahead left. Drake, you take the right. Savannah, you stick close behind me. Wherever I go – you go. Don't worry about these guys, they can handle themselves.'

Carl and Drake exchanged edgy smiles, and then moved to take up their positions.

'Let's do it,' said Carl. After a moment's hesitation, they were off, working their way down the rubble-strewn slope, kicking up dust as they slithered towards what looked like the rusty shells of old cars, busses and lorries. Rows of them, nose to tail like the skeletal remains of a giant, broken spine. As they reached the bottom of the gradient, Carl and Drake ran ahead and disappeared amongst the tangled ruins. Tanis and Savannah steadily picked their way over and around the buckled and corroded vehicles.

'Watch out for anything sharp,' warned Tanis. 'We can't afford to have you cutting yourself and bleeding out. Not here. It'd be just like ringing a dinner gong!'

'What's out there?' she asked.

Tanis didn't even turn around to reply. She heard him mutter just one word.

'Death.'

5

JAGO

'I hate you! I hate you!' Beth was grief-stricken. 'I want Savvy. I want my sister,' she demanded, her voice now scratched and hoarse with emotion. Red-faced and puffy eyed, she had been crying, shouting and pleading for nearly an hour since her parents told her Savannah had been Transported for doing "bad" things.

From the moment of her birth, Beth and her sister shared the closest of sibling bonds. It was Savannah's calming voice that stilled Beth's infant cries. Her eyes would light up at the sight of Savannah's smiling face; her small arms would reach out for the comfort of her sister's embrace. As Beth grew, Savannah was the one who chased away her nightmares, built up her confidence and shared sisterly dreams and secrets, much to their mother's admiration and sometimes, maternal jealousy.

Now, in the privacy of their the family apartments Jago stood silently by as his father and mother tried to calm her down, to no avail. Beth ran from them, and took sanctuary in her own room, falling onto her bed to claw at the covers and smother her face in the bedclothes. Her body heaved and shook with inconsolable sobs and tears.

Corda turned and confronted both husband and son. 'Here, I can speak out,' she said. 'This is not right. We should not be made to suffer. I will not lose the love of both of my daughters,' her voice trembled. 'Bring Savannah back, if only for the sake of Beth. *We* are descendants of the Founding Fortunata. They would not dare to Transport one of the most important families on Opulence. The young upstarts of the Élite are in pursuit of absolute power, and they must be stopped. If we tolerate this, then who is next? Beth?' She waved an arm aimlessly in the direction of the girl's bedroom. 'Will not even our children be safe? Tiberius, you must appeal directly to the Masters for their intervention.'

Tiberius knew that she spoke the truth. He knew their influence could not be easily destroyed, nor the power that the family's name carried. Uncertainty had made him panic, and now for the first time in his life, guilt overcame greed. He lifted his head and wearily exhaled. 'You're right. I will request a meeting with the Masters. They *will* overrule the arrogant young rabble.' He turned to leave, only to find Jago blocking his path.

'You dare to consider risking our reputation, our wealth and power, to bring back that uncontrollable brat, that embarrassment to the family name?' Jago spoke venomously. 'I will not stand by while *my* status and *my* inheritance are jeopardised because of *your* guilt.' He moved to a portrait of a younger Savannah, and grabbed the ornate gilt frame with both hands. He wrenched it from the wall, and smashed it to the floor, to viciously kick out at the crumpled canvass, which folded to give the girl's image a distorted and deformed expression.

Now he was shouting, his face red with rage. 'It has always been about Savannah. I have endured the shame of her actions. I have had to fight for respect and credibility while you have spent your energies excusing her, protecting her insolence. Well, no more.' Jago's eyes blazed wide in anger. 'I am but one step from leading the Élite. *You* will not stop me.' With deadly malice, he jabbed a finger at Tiberius' face. 'Do not get in my way, or so help me, if I have to have you both Transported, then it shall be arranged! A change is coming. The old Council, the Masters, they will be replaced by the Élite.'

Both Corda and Tiberius saw the insanity in his expression. His eyes bulged white as the evil, menacing tone of his voice raged on. Instinctively, they held each other for comfort.

Jago always had been ruthless in his ambitions, and Tiberius had encouraged it, enjoying his son's pride in his heritage. However, in this moment of terror, Tiberius reflected on the dark change in his son. He had noticed a distancing between them for some time, a lack of father and son communication. The signs had been there that all was not well: Jago's increasing absence from family meetings and meals, his seething aggression towards Savannah, and the coldness with which he spoke to his mother. Tiberius had been too preoccupied with his daughter's distractions to confront the matter, and now, it was too late. A poison gripped his son for which there was no parental antidote, and that poison was an insatiable greed for power.

Jago paced in front of them, ranting at their faces, and yet his eyes seemed to look right through them, as though he was addressing an unseen audience.

'I will lead the new order, the Masters shall fall!' He punched his chest. 'I will claim my place as Supreme Leader. What was once our sanctuary has now become our prison. We will reclaim Earthland and cleanse it of the filth that masquerades as humanity. None shall stand in our way.' Spittle flew from his mouth and glistened as it dribbled down his chin. 'The Diss shall become our slaves; their sole purpose will be to build our new world, and *anyone* in Opulence who opposes us will be consigned to their ranks, or die!'

He stood there, breathing heavily, trembling. His hands clenching and unclenching, pumping his fury. His hair fell in lank strands across his face, distorting his expression. The image of madness complete, he stared coldly at his parents. 'Heed my words. If not for your sake,' he added, 'then for Beth's.'

Corda pushed herself towards him. 'You wouldn't dare!'

He stared into her eyes and a demented smile spread across his lips.

Enraged, Corda slapped him across the face. The sound of skin on skin cracked through the tension in the room. Jago grabbed her wrist, roughly inflicting pain on her that no son should impose upon his mother. The imprint of her fingers blotched rose-red against his cheek. The smile did not leave his face, and in the corner of his mouth, a crimson stain appeared. His tongue fleetingly licked the blood away from his lip.

'You will shame me no more. You are dead to me.'

His words hung coldly in the air as he twisted her arm, and pushed her to sprawl sobbing on the floor. Tiberius rushed forward to her aid.

'Get out! Get out and do not return,' he shouted.

Jago turned on his heels, and left his family's apartments. As the door closed on his exit, Corda struggled to her feet and ran to Beth's room. Tiberius slumped into a chair; his son's betrayal filled him with bitter despair. A cold sweat crept across his skin, and for the first time in his life, he felt truly vulnerable and afraid.

6

Plan C

Working their way through the butchered terrain for what seemed an age, Savannah had lost all sense of time. She stole a look backwards. There was no past horizon; the orange mist, which seemed to permeate everything, was now fading into a curtain of grey smog.

Sometimes, Tanis would lead them along a well-worn trail, over the tread patterns of unknown footwear previously imprinted in the dust, left like dirty tattoos for them to trample on. Then, he would suddenly veer off for them to climb over awkward heaps of crumpled structures. They stopped only to take a couple of gulps of water. Tanis kept an even pace and Savannah was determined not to fall behind. She had always kept herself fit, but she had never walked such a distance, and twinges of pain jabbed at her calf muscles.

The shadows became darker, and stretched out unevenly across the landscape, like distorted spectres.

She was scrabbling down a large, tilted slab of concrete, into a wide gully below, when the sound of a whistle pierced the silence. It was one sharp warning, loud and clear, followed by a dull echo, which was swallowed up in the stillness. A metallic, shrill noise, which made the hair on the back of her neck stand up.

Tanis was already below her, in the alcove of an overhang. 'Down! Quick!'

She half slid, half rolled the last metre, to land in a crouching position beside him. A cloud of dust trailed down with her and covered them both for her efforts.

He pulled her into the cover of the overhang. 'Thanks for that,' he whispered, spitting, and wiping dirty, grey powder from his face and eyes.

'You need to brush up on your sarcasm,' she grimaced, and licked a dry dust from her lips. 'What was that whistle?'

'It's Carl's signal. One blast for stop, two for all clear. Any more than that means – run like hell!'

Tanis took a glance at his watch. The luminous numbers on its dial were starting to take shape. 'We've cut it fine, too fine. Nightfall is coming early.'

Before she could stop it, a sneeze exploded from her mouth and resonated across the stillness. For some reason to her, it sounded unnaturally loud.

'Oh, great,' muttered Tanis. 'Why don't you just wave a big flag with "Come and get us" written on it?'

'I didn't do it on purpose!' she retorted. She grasped her nose to stifle another outburst. 'It's the dust,' she added defensively.

He turned to her, his eyes staring, the whites standing out against the mixture of camouflage and grime on his face. 'Quiet!' he hissed.

'I am being quiet,' she scowled back at him.

Tanis placed a finger across her lips. He eased the catapult from his belt. She pulled his hand away, and was about to protest, when a tiny waterfall of small rocks and dust clattered down from above them. He jerked a thumb upwards, as he deftly loaded a ball bearing into the catapult's leather sling.

In the heavy silence, there came a sort of throaty snuffling, almost pig-like, but deeper, more menacing. Savannah pressed her back against the hard, broken stonework. Tanis signalled disapprovingly for her to stay still. A gloom descended around them with a sudden finality. If there was a moon in the sky, then it only served to create a ghostly and claustrophobic twilight. She could feel the greyness pressing against her face like a musty, damp cloth.

Another stream of debris rattled down; a few much larger rocks fell amongst them. One viciously hit Savannah's outstretched leg, striking her on her shin. Her stomach turned with nausea and she bit into the material of her sleeve to stifle a cry as the pain ricocheted up through the bone. She prayed that it wasn't broken.

Tanis pulled himself close to her. 'Are you all right?' he mouthed.

She nodded back through the tears. She sucked in air and tried to reassure herself. Nervously, she fumbled with the oversized overalls, and pulled the material up to inspect her leg. Even in the shadow, she could see dark red lines, running in small rivulets down her shin. The blood was already seeping into her boot. Her stomach gave another lurch and she swallowed hard, keeping down the bile. Gingerly, she ran her fingers over the pain, feeling the wet, sticky blood, and a large lump, which had already formed around the torn skin; but thankfully, no bone protruded. She was sure there was no fracture, but nevertheless, it hurt like hell and her foot had already grown numb.

Tanis looked at the wound; she could see the alarm in his eyes.

'It's okay, I'll be fine,' she encouraged meekly.

'Cover it up! Quickly!' he hissed.

More snuffling and grunting came from above. This time it sounded agitated and excited. There was frantic movement, and another landslide of rock and rubble cascaded down.

'Get that gun out, you're going to need it,' said Tanis. 'It knows we're here.'

No sooner had she wrestled the weapon from her waistband, than a low grunt resonated from above; the tone and pitch began to rise into a frenzy of guttural eruptions. Large fragments of stone and masonry, along with filth and debris, fell from above. There was one last, gut-wrenching squeal followed by a thump. The sound of something large and heavy landed in front of them in a cloud of dust.

Savannah tried to swallow, her tongue stuck to the roof of her mouth and the back of her throat felt like corrugated cardboard. Beside her, Tanis pulled the thick bands of elastic back to a full arm's length; tautness quivered nervously along their span. The skin of his knuckles tightened white around the grey steel handle. Muscles strained with tension.

'When I let this go, you fire off three rounds, dead

ahead. Then we run, off to the right. Follow me and don't stop until I tell you to.'

'My leg,' started Savannah. 'I… I'm not sure I can.' She hated to admit defeat, it wasn't in her nature; but realistically, she knew she was in trouble. If she ran, there was the possibility that the pain in her leg would drive into her senses like a cold dagger. She would be crippled within a few strides. Whatever was hidden in the dusty gloom would descend on her like the stuff of nightmares.

'Looks like it's Plan B,' said Tanis, resignedly. 'I'll try to draw it away. The moment you see it following me, you head in the opposite direction. Try and find somewhere else to hide. I'll come and find you later.'

He knew in his mind that Plan B didn't have a hope in hell of working. The creature had come for *her*. It was her blood that it sensed, her life scent, and it wasn't going to be distracted from feeding from it. He had a couple of alternatives; it was probably going to have to be him and his knife, up close and personal with the damn thing.

On the other hand, he could run, leave her to the beast – mission failed. A shrug of the shoulders. He could deal with disappointed superiors. Besides, he'd already got too close to this girl, and allowed her to stir up old feelings. Perhaps it was for the best.

As the dust settled, a hideous shape formed. Then, a slight breeze cleared the air. Savannah finally swallowed. Her mouth filled with nervous saliva, her eyes widened, pupils shrank, whites extended. She had never heard of anything like this; indeed, she didn't even know *what* it was.

The warthog was enormous; it was the size of a young rhinoceros, and this massive bulk of dusty grey malice stood just a few metres in front of them. It shook its head to throw up an unkempt mane and shed a coating of filthy dirt into the air. Gobbets of speckled drool flew from its flared nostrils and mouth, and strands of elasticated spittle caught on the four evil tusks, which protruded from its abomination of a face.

Its black eyes, surrounded by crusted folds of skin, stared at her. Savannah looked into them, and all she saw was emptiness, and her death.

'I… I think that I can run,' she stammered. 'Better than sit here and die.'

Tanis lowered his catapult and shoved it back into his jacket.

'What are you doing?' she asked.

'You won't even get to your feet. It'll pin you to the wall as soon as you move,' he said as he slid the long, serrated blade of a hunting knife from a sheath in his combats. 'Plan C – on my signal, you keep firing at its face until you're out of ammo. Just don't hit *me!*'

He eased himself slowly onto his knees. The warthog shifted itself, sensing that an attack was coming. It stamped a cloven hoof into the ground, and emitted a short, arrogant grunt.

'You're crazy. There must be another way,' she pleaded.

'I could run and leave you here,' he said with honesty, throwing her a grin. Their eyes met, and in that second, in that moment, she felt a connection.

'But you won't,' she said, smiling back.

A familiar emotional twinge hit his stomach. He turned away, keen to deny it, and he focused on the dreadful, four-legged animal in front of him.

The warthog shuffled a step backwards in preparation for its charge.

'Fire!' yelled Tanis.

Savannah jerked the trigger. Every shot seemed to take an age as the clumsy mechanism released and reloaded each ball bearing. Various sounds of impact rang out amidst the animal's grunting and squealing: Metal on bone, metal on flesh. A steel ball embedded itself deep inside one of its flaring nostrils, causing it to raise its head back in a sneezing reflex. At that instant, Tanis took the opportunity to leap forward. He grabbed a tusk with one hand and drove the knife up and into the creature's exposed throat with the other, severing the jugular vein. Blood gushed over his hand as he twisted and pushed the blade up through the roof of its mouth.

The noise was deafening as the warthog expelled its last convulsive, bubbling screams. Its lifeblood splashed crimson across the colourless ground. Its great body gave a shudder and it fell sideways, to collapse on Tanis and trap his legs beneath its bulky corpse.

"Click. Click. Click. Click." A repetitive metallic sound disturbed the following silence.

Tanis craned his head sideways to see Savannah, her arms outstretched, her hands clasped around the ball bearing gun. Her fingers mechanically squeezing the trigger; her reflexes were locked on automatic. Her eyes hypnotically wide open, staring ahead, seeing nothing.

7

Hungry like the Wolf

'Savannah! Savannah!' Tanis shouted. He scrabbled hold of a small rock and lobbed it in her direction. It hit her arm harmlessly, and shook her out of her trance.

It took a few seconds for her to digest the scene, and then she threw the gun to one side and frantically crawled towards him, the pain in her leg numbed by adrenalin.

'I can't believe you did that!' Then, she added with dread, 'Tanis! Hell, Tanis, your arm! Your arm!'

The warthog had come down with its head across Tanis's blood-soaked arm. It looked to all accounts that it was jammed inside the creature's mouth.

'Stay still,' she ordered. 'You need a tourniquet.'

Tanis lay there, gathering his thoughts as he watched her tear a strip of material from the leg of her overalls. She gently reached forward, and tied it around his upper arm, pulling it tight. He grimaced as it pinched his covered skin.

'Sorry,' she apologised. 'But we've got to stop the bleeding. Besides, after saving my life twice in one day, I can't afford to lose my hero now.' She absently stroked a stray dreadlock away from his face.

She cares about me, he thought. *Damn.*

'Savannah, just lift its head for me so I can get my arm out.'

'You're sure that it's not broken?'

'Trust me on this. Just lift it a little.'

Overcoming her revulsion, she grabbed two of the bloody tusks and pulled the head to one side. Tanis withdrew his arm and slowly extracted his hand, the knife still in his grasp. The blade coated with thick, dark liquid.

'That's better. Now if you could just help me push this brute off my legs; I'm starting to lose all sense of feeling in them.'

Savannah positioned herself alongside him. She placed her feet against the huge body and pushed with her good leg as hard as she could, while Tanis shoved with both arms. Determination turned into frustration. It wouldn't budge; its dead weight was far too much for the both of them.

'It's just too big,' she said resignedly.

'Well, I'm getting out of this mess, even if I have to cut myself free.'

She looked at him with growing concern. 'Before you do anything else, let me have a look at your arm. I want to see how bad the cut is, and if I can loosen the tourniquet.'

'No need to,' insisted Tanis. 'It'll be fine.'

'What's the matter, don't you trust me?'

'Of course I do,' he replied. 'But I can take care of myself.'

'Well, pardon me, mister tough guy, but I'm not the one stuck under a dead animal,' she said sarcastically.

'Yeah, well not for long,' he said as he plunged his knife into the warthog's body. Thick, dark blood oozed from the slashed flesh.

'I'm not going to watch this,' she complained, and she turned her back on the scene. A small stone rattled down from above her and bounced away into the shadows. She slowly brought her gaze up to the top of the ridge. For a moment, she thought it was her anxiety playing on her senses. A dark shape silhouetted against the gloom, and four reflective pinpoints of light stared down at her. Then, the shape divided into two of equal size, two separate pairs of eyes.

'Tanis,' she called quietly, without turning around.

'Yeah?' he replied as he hacked away a large chunk of the animal's hide.

'I think we've got more company.' She hobbled a step backwards.

He stopped slicing at the body, and glanced up. 'Oh, shi...'

The word was cut off by a resonating howl.

As opposed to the brute force of the warthog, these new aggressors were agile, deliberate and sure-footed. They crept stealthily forwards on either side of the rubble, coming down in a semicircle, trapping Tanis and Savannah between them.

'Don't run,' advised Tanis.

'Yeah, right,' replied Savannah, gesturing to her crippled leg. 'As if!'

One of the wolves curled its lips in a snarl and bared

its teeth, to expose yellow ivory daggers, perfectly evolved for ripping flesh from bone. Again, these animals were larger than normal. Their long, sinewy legs supported lithe, almost malnourished bodies. Their fur was matted and lank. Savannah glanced from one wolf to the other, which was sweeping its head from side to side in a lazy, mindless movement. A sickly coloured tongue lolled from its open mouth. One of its eyes was half closed, a puss-crusted slit, while the other eye was unnaturally large and stared crazed and unblinking at her.

'I think there's something wrong with that one.'

'You think?' answered Tanis. He picked up a lump of the warthog's bloody flesh and threw it at the wolf behind him. The animal attacked it with relish.

'He's hungry and after the carcass,' he said. He threw another piece at the other wolf; it landed with a soft, bloody thud right between its paws. The animal looked down at it with derision, and then looked back up with its wild, crazy eye. An unnatural sound came from its throat. It let out a series of strangled, rasping noises, almost as if it was trying to speak, trying to curse at them.

'I think it means that he doesn't have a taste for warthog – he'd rather have us!' said Tanis.

He reached inside his jacket and produced the catapult and a ball bearing. 'Here,' he tossed the objects to her. 'Load it up and if he makes a move towards you, try and hit him in his good eye.' He turned his attention back to the carcass. 'One more chunk and I reckon I can shift myself free.' He gritted his teeth.

Tanis peeled the large, bloody mess to one side and heaved himself back on his elbows. His legs finally slid free, wet and covered in gore. He lobbed another, larger chunk of meat to the other wolf, which grabbed it with a snarl and then retreated into the shadows.

'Right,' he said to Savannah. 'I'm coming over to you. Cover me.'

Savannah aimed the catapult at the now pacing wolf. Its head resumed the slow sweeping movements, shifting side-to-side and low to the ground.

Tanis half crawled, half hopped to her, his legs deadened from the weight of the warthog. They both sat back against the wall of rubble, propping each other up, shoulder to shoulder. Tanis frantically rubbed his legs. His hands slithered on his blood-wet combats as he forced life into his numb limbs.

Abruptly, the wolf stopped moving its head. It lowered its haunches, flattened its ears, and bared a set of misshapen fangs.

The instrument of delivering gory carnage was one leap away.

Under the strain of the catapult, the muscles in Savannah's arm twitched with spasms.

Tanis gripped the knife in his bloodied hand.

The wolf leapt, crazed and rabid. Its disfigured eye bulged, almost popping from its head. Crimson foam drooled from its open mouth. They pushed themselves upright and braced for the impact, anticipating the pain.

Before its back legs completely left the ground, two short arrows thudded into its body, one just behind the ear and the other in its ribs. It didn't even cover half the distance, and just dropped like a discarded rag doll, to land on a bed of broken rocks and corroded metal.

Savannah released the tension in the catapult. Her arms slumped to her sides. She closed her eyes with emotional relief and turned her head to sink her face into Tanis' neck. She breathed in the earthy perfume of his musk, and her romantic streak formed pictures in her mind of them together in another place, a safer world. A thought ran madly in her head – she could willingly give herself to Tanis; the attraction was deep inside her. It was as if they were destined to meet.

Her mind wandered back to the one intimate relationship she had so far experienced in her life. On her sixteenth birthday, she had argued venomously with her father. She wanted him to arrange an audience with the Masters for her, so that she could confront them directly with her views and opinions.

'You're still just a girl,' he had jibed, and he had belittled her coming of age. With the flush of anger and adolescence on her cheeks, she had stormed from the apartments.

There was a boy she knew; he was eighteen and she'd quietly developed a crush on him, nothing too serious. They had indulged in a couple of petting sessions, mostly kissing and cuddling. Previously, she'd allowed his hands to wander, but had controlled his touching within her personal boundaries; she liked to think she was sensible in that respect.

This time, she went to where he lived. His parents were working, and so she found herself alone with him. She was still furious. She wanted to hurt her father, to disappoint him in the most personal way. She wanted to take away his "little girl", as he still saw her, to take her innocence and throw it in his face.

I'm sixteen, and when I tell him that I am a woman, he'll have to take me seriously, she thought, and so for that reason alone, she let it happen. The boy had been gentle with her, but afterwards she felt no sense of being, no afterglow, no triumph. She felt ashamed and cheated.

She returned home, and showered in water so hot that it stung her skin. Curled up on the floor of the cubicle, arms wrapped around her knees, she let the steam rise around her until the water ran cold, until finally, standing in front of her mirror, she dropped the bath towel, studied her reflection, and went through phases of self-pity, self-hate and remorse. Then came the fury, not just at her father (who she now resolved never to tell of her reckless sacrifice), but also at the Fortunata and all that Opulence stood for. She vowed to devote herself to bringing about change; she would be bold and fearless. She would *make* them take notice of her.

Now, it all seemed so long ago.

A combination of the pain in her leg and Carl's voice brought her back to the present and out of her musing.

8

TURNPIKE

Silhouettes in the gloom, Carl and Drake looked down into the gully.

'You certainly know how to show a girl a good time,' Carl shouted.

'You took long enough!' complained Tanis. 'There's another wolf,' he added quickly.

'S'okay. It took off as soon as it saw us,' replied Carl.

Tanis and Savannah slid to the floor, exhausted. The two men made their way down the slope, loading their crossbows and furtively scanning the landscape as they moved, until they finally stood side by side, grinning at the couple.

'You look a bloody mess,' commented Drake.

'If you had to dig your way out of a hog, you'd look the same,' retorted Tanis.

'I wasn't talking to you,' said Drake, with a wry smile.

'Thanks,' said Savannah, 'I feel all the better for knowing that.'

'Take a look at her leg,' said Tanis. 'It could be broken.'

'No. No,' she objected. 'It's his arm. He could lose it. I've put a tourniquet on to stop the bleeding, but it's been on too long.' Her fingers scratched and picked at the rag, loosening the knot and pulling it free. 'You'll need to let it bleed for a few seconds, and then we'll have to tie it up again and get it some stitches,' she stressed.

'It's okay,' insisted Tanis. 'You don't have to fuss.' He pulled away.

'But that creature bit right into your arm. The blood…' She looked at Carl, pleadingly.

'Here, let me see,' said Carl. He crouched down, gripped Tanis' arm and rolled up his sleeve. The arm was caked with congealed blood.

Tanis shook his head, and tried to pull away again.

'Hold still.' Carl produced a small canteen of water and washed the arm down, wiping it clean with the rag. He turned it from side to side, inspecting the flesh. 'There's not a scratch, it's all hog's blood.' He shrugged his shoulders.

'You mean, he's all right?' asked Savannah, with confused relief.

'I tried to tell you,' pleaded Tanis. 'But you insisted on helping me and I didn't want to upset you. Besides, you were so concerned.' He was grinning from ear to ear like a cheeky schoolboy.

Savannah looked at the blemish-free arm, and then regarded Tanis' expression. A look of fury crossed her face, the prefix to an emotional storm. 'I was worried about you, damn it!' She struck out sideways, thumping him across his chest. 'I hate you. I hate you. I hate you,' she shouted with every blow.

She continued to lash out in frustration at Tanis as he scrabbled away clutching himself, coughing and laughing.

'Right,' said Drake as he gently restrained her. 'I need to fix you up, and we need to get to safety before any more predators get a sniff of this blood. No doubt our wolf friend will be bringing some of his pals back soon.'

Savannah glared lividly at Tanis, and fumed silently.

Drake turned to Carl and Tanis. 'You two go and do something useful, like watch our backs for any more trouble.'

He tended to Savannah, cleaned the wound, and bandaged a makeshift splint to her leg. 'It's just for a bit of support. You're lucky, no broken bones,' he confirmed, to her relief.

Carl and Tanis kept watch on a ridge. The odd snigger and barely suppressed laughter came from their direction.

Savannah sat there seething, her arms folded tightly across her chest. Anger diverted her senses away from the throbbing pain in her leg.

'Take no notice, missy,' Drake advised, as he rolled down the trouser. 'He's like a big school kid, needs to grow up if you ask me. It's dangerous enough out here without him fooling around. He can take risks with his own life if that helps him to cope with the past, but not while I'm about.'

He gently patted her thigh. 'Right, let's see if you can walk on it.'

With his help, she stood and tentatively put pressure on the leg. A slight wince crossed her face.

'Thanks. That's a lot better,' she complimented. 'I think I can hobble along.'

'Don't mention it,' he replied. 'I'm a field medic and I get plenty of practice. This is a pretty dangerous place, what with the wildlife and the Crazies.'

'The Crazies?' she asked.

He let out a short laugh. 'Compared to them, what you've experienced so far has been a tea party. Come on, we've got to get moving.'

Despite her protests, Drake insisted she put her arm around him for support. 'We need to move a bit faster than hobbling speed,' he explained.

For the rest of the journey, they travelled in a tightly knit group. Tanis, to Savannah's relief, kept up front, while Carl and Drake took it in turns to help her along. She occupied her thoughts with an analysis of Tanis. As far as she was concerned, he was an attention seeker. Vain. Immature. Rude. He'd better not try to make a fool of her again, or so help her, she would bring him to his knees.

There was, however, a strange attraction to him, and it made her feel vulnerable.

For what seemed the hundredth time, she stumbled, nearly tripping up Drake who was supporting her. 'Sorry, I just can't see in this gloom,' she apologised. 'Haven't you got a torch you could light?'

'No, that would just attract unwelcome attention,' he replied. 'Besides, we're nearly there.'

He gripped her waist and hoisted her onto his hip. She could feel his muscles tighten and strain. She caught the faint aroma of his slightly bitter, but not unpleasant sweat. His bicep flexed against her back. The word *fit* popped into her head.

As with Carl, he was much older than her, probably in his late twenties. A long, white scar ran unevenly from just under his right ear and along his jawline to the cleft of his chin, adding an element of romantic danger to his rugged features. His short-cropped red hair complimented the ruddy-coloured stubble on his rough and careworn face. His eyes were dark brown, and it seemed to her that they had witnessed far too many sorrowful scenes, and a lifetime of strife.

The ground flattened out and became level, with a dusty yellow surface. Through shifting veils of vapour, all she could see ahead were the blurred outlines of a fragmented landscape.

'I'm glad that you know where you're going,' she said.

'Have to,' he replied. 'If you get lost out here, the survival odds are less than twenty-four hours. I'll be glad to get home.'

She wiped a wayward wisp of her hair from across her face, and looked up at him. His profile was expressionless.

'Where is home, Drake?'

'Right ahead,' he replied, and a smile broke through the hard contours of his face.

Carl appeared beside her and Tanis fell in line alongside Drake.

'Nearly there,' he confirmed.

A blanket of mist parted and she looked out across a plaza. About forty metres in front of them, there was a large mound of rubble, the height of a single-storey building. A steel-gated entrance was set into a wall of sturdy brickwork, above its centre hung a battered sign: a faded red circle with the word, "Turnpike" was stencilled across it in blistered, black paint.

Drake carried Savannah as they broke into a jog for the final distance. She was further impressed with his fitness, as he was hardly out of breath by the time they assembled in front of the entrance. He released her, and she supported herself against the structure. Both he and Carl loaded up their crossbows and surveyed the area around them as Tanis slid a lose brick out from the wall, and reached into the dark hole to retrieve a small metal funnel, which was attached to a length of corrugated flexible tubing. He pulled a rubber stopper from inside the funnel and blew down into the tube, and then he placed the funnel against his ear. A few seconds passed before he spoke into it.

'Password, Fortunata,' he said. 'Four to come down, and make it quick. We have one injured.' He replaced the stopper and put the whole piece of apparatus back into its hiding place, carefully replacing the brick.

'Here, take this. It's been reloaded.' He held out the ball bearing gun to Savannah without making eye contact with her.

Guilt? Or embarrassment? Savannah thought as she took the weapon.

He pulled out his catapult and loaded it up, tugging at the elastic, testing its strength.

'Can you feel it? If it's gonna happen, it'll happen now,' said Carl. His eyes flashed across the murky horizon.

The four of them stood with their backs to the gates, staring out at the semi circled ridge of crumbling architecture, a grey silhouette against the wavering glow of scattered, methane-fuelled fires.

'What are we waiting for?' she asked.

'A lift to safety, with maybe some Crazies thrown in for good measure. Let's see which arrives first,' replied Drake.

9

CRAZIES

When law and order disintegrated, chaos ensued. The prison system collapsed, and with it, the security structure that used to keep society safe ceased to operate. The murderers, the violent, and the anti-social seized their freedom and wreaked vengeance on anything and anyone who couldn't fight back or showed a weakness.

As the years went by, the consumption of all manner of drugs from raided hospitals and laboratories, along with contaminated water and food sources, removed the last shred of humanity from their minds. They turned on each other until only the most aggressive and strongest of them survived. Their basic animal instincts overpowered all sense of reasoning. The rules became – kill or be killed, take what you want, love nothing; pain is a by-product of survival.

A breed of cannibalistic, cunning, psychotic killers evolved. They were worse than the nightmare of mindless zombies for they retained basic human intelligence.

The name given to them by Earthland's surviving humanity – "Crazies" – was an understatement. One thing they did learn very quickly was that there was safety in numbers, and it was this tactic, as chaotic as it was, that they employed in any attack towards the underground communities.

As the group waited for the arrival of the lift, out of the gloom came a singsong, child-like voice. 'Pretty, pretty.' There was a chilling undercurrent of insanity in its tone.

'Sounds like you've got a secret admirer,' Carl said to Savannah.

'The state that I'm in,' she replied, 'I'm almost flattered!'

The three of them closed in protectively around her, almost pinning her to the steel gate. Frustrated, she pushed them back, away from her.

'I can fight. You don't need to treat me like a child,' she protested.

'You don't know what we're up against,' said Tanis.

'Are you ready to come and play with us, little girl?' sang another deranged, high-pitched voice.

'Whoever they are, they can't be any uglier or more dangerous than what we had to deal with earlier,' said Savannah. 'Besides, I'm still mad at you, Tanis, my leg's hurting like hell, and I'm just about ready to take it out on anyone who gets in my way.'

A maniacal laugh announced the launch of a fiery object that arced out of the darkness, flames trailing orange in its wake, like a miniature, fiery comet. It hit the ground about five metres in front of them. Glass shattered on impact, and liquid ignited to release bright burning balls of brimstone, which sizzled and hissed across the ground like glowing marbles of venom. A dry, chemical taste invaded Savannah's nostrils and clung to the back of her throat. She swallowed hard to summon up saliva, in an effort to spit the taste out.

'Don't get any on you,' warned Drake as he pulled his neckerchief up across his face. 'It'll burn right through your clothes, your boots, literally anything, until it reaches your skin. Then it'll keep on burning through your bones and boil your insides.'

Savannah spotted a fresh glow from behind the ridge, and she anticipated what was to come. She brought the gun up, holding it in both hands, one cupped underneath for support. She closed one eye, and sighted along the short barrel with the other. A flare appeared at ridge level and she squeezed back the trigger. With a metallic "ziiing" the steel ball bearing burst out, and in two short seconds it hit its target.

The glass container exploded in a flare of yellow and red hail. Screams rent through the air. Gut-churning screams of agony. A flaming figure briefly appeared; its arms cartwheeled in a vain attempt to extinguish the flames before it fell backwards and out of sight. In the stillness that followed, a plume of orange-tinted smoke trailed skywards. The odour of burning flesh wafted unpleasantly across the plaza.

Three pairs of eyes stared in wonder and surprise at Savannah.

'Where the hell did you learn to shoot like that?' asked Carl.

'We have airgun ranges back on Opulence. I was junior champion three years running,' she said with a satisfied grin. 'Besides, I told you. I'm pissed off and I don't like people throwing balls of flame at me.'

A loud, thrumming noise filled the air. It growled and reverberated, a throaty roar of mechanical fury.

'Well, you've certainly got their attention,' said Tanis. 'They're not going to mess about now.'

Two white beams of light cut through the air like narrow spotlights searching for prey in the grey night. With another roar, the beams accelerated up and over the ridge to illuminate the plaza. A black mechanical shape rolled down the incline, and connected itself to the four figures with its umbilical shafts of light. It lurched to an uneasy halt.

They shielded their eyes with their hands and arms, blinded by the light's intensity.

'Can't see a damn thing,' said Carl. 'We're sitting targets.'

Above the noise of the rumbling engine, there was a sudden, sharp bang. Carl howled in pain, and collapsed sideways, clutching at his leg. His crossbow clattered away from his grasp.

'They've got ammo! They've got ammo!' shouted Tanis. He dragged Savannah down beside the prostrate body of Carl as Drake crouched forward in a futile attempt to shield them. Savannah saw a dark patch melt across the material of Carl's trouser leg, just above the knee.

'Your belt,' she instructed. 'Give me your belt.'

Dazed, Carl wrestled his belt undone and yanked it free. Savannah quickly looped the leather around his thigh, and pulled it tight to stop the flow of blood.

Carl sucked in air through clenched teeth. 'Hell's bloody bells!' he exclaimed.

Another gunshot sounded out and sparks ricocheted from the metal gate above their heads.

'What the hell is it?' asked Savannah. She ducked low and brought her arm over Carl's head.

Tanis turned his face towards her. 'It sounds like they've got a hand gun, but what's worse is they've also managed to get hold of the right ammunition for it.'

A third shot rang out; the bullet hit the ground about a metre in front of them. It kicked out a streak of dust before it deflected up to narrowly miss Drake's head.

'Whoever's using it is a useless shot,' he shouted. 'I think they hit Carl by luck more than anything.'

'Thanks, buddy,' retorted Carl. 'I feel so much safer!'

The engine revved up to the sound level of a motorised chainsaw. The lights throbbed brighter, like miniature twin suns, and the carcass of a vehicle, now thirty metres away, crawled forward, bringing the smell of fuel and exhaust fumes with it.

Three long blasts of an air horn sounded, which temporarily drowned out the noise of the engine. At the same time, behind them, steel doors glided back with the hiss of hydraulics. Then, accompanied by the complaining squeal of dry metal, the gates slid apart. Savannah turned to see the empty metal box of a lift behind them, the space inside large enough for fifteen or so people. Two dull fluorescent lights valiantly flickered and blinked in the ceiling.

'About bloody time!' shouted Tanis. 'Get in, get in.'

They half crawled, half stumbled in. Savannah

and Tanis unceremoniously dragged Carl between them. Drake retrieved Carl's crossbow, before he too scrabbled in to finally sit on the floor, his back propped against Tanis, his legs splayed out before him. He held a crossbow in each hand, levelled them off, and let loose both bolts into the curtain of light.

One of the beams fractured and extinguished as the vehicle lurched sideways. Its engine screamed to a new sound level of motorised pain. The remaining headlight angled drunkenly away into the surrounding darkness. As the gates locked together in front of them, they could just see the dark shape of a body slouched across the steering wheel. Both of Drake's bolts had found targets. The weight of the dead driver pushed his feet down on both the accelerator and on the brake pedal. Smoke plumed and bellowed from the engine, which continued to scream in motorised fury. A fuel line burst under pressure and the now red-hot engine ignited the spray of flammable liquid into a fireball.

As a billowing red and black cloud of incinerating heat reached out towards the group, the steel doors of the lift closed, and denied the scorching inferno four more victims.

They were sealed in a claustrophobic sanctuary. Savannah studied the violent graffiti around her. Bullet holes of various calibres riddled the steel walls and formed erratic patterns, which were mixed with a jumble of scratched messages such as:

Kev was here – Lisa loves James – Who gives a shit – Death to the Crazies

The lift travelled slowly downwards, accompanied

by squeals, groans and thuds from hidden, ancient machinery. Overhead, the buzzing and popping of the strip lights added to the soundtrack of their journey. They remained sitting, their backs propped up against the rear wall of the lift. Savannah checked Carl's tourniquet for any further bleeding, then let him rest his head on her shoulder. He was obviously in pain, but nevertheless he still managed to display a couple of toothy grins at Tanis and Drake.

'Some people will do anything for attention,' remarked Tanis, sarcastically.

Savannah sensed a little jealousy in his tone. A twinge of satisfaction crossed her mind, but then she thought – *Why the hell should I care?*

10

The Élite

With his father's words still echoing in his ears, Jago decided that the time had come for him to initiate his plans, and he called for an immediate gathering of the Élite. This would be his defining moment, and he would allow no one to stand in his way.

He strode purposely through the elaborately decorated corridors of the Fortunata apartments. His pale blue, cotton cloak billowed out behind him, rippling like a gentle wave. Within, he was mentally controlling the madness that fuelled his ambitions, and with each step, he looked more self-assured, more confident.

By the time he reached his destination, there was no perspiration on his brow, no sign of anxiety. He was calm, focused and resolute. A tinge of anticipation fluttered in the pit of his stomach, like a butterfly caught in a killing jar.

He stood square shouldered, upright and composed as he faced the trailing vine leaves and grapes that adorned a garishly painted door behind which, he knew were gathered the Élite Fortunata – those who held the key to his powerful ambitions. Each of them possessed their own desires. For some it was wealth and luxury, for others it was control and domination, but not one of them was ruthless enough to lead a coup against the old guard of the Fortunata Council, and eventually, the Masters.

As far as Jago was concerned, this was their weakness. They were scared of failure and recrimination. They dithered, discussing strategy, playing personal politics, waiting for someone else to be brave (or foolish) enough to take the lead and oust the present regime.

Over the previous months, he had busied himself buying favours, financing loyalties amongst the Transportation Police, and gathering information and knowledge about certain individuals amongst the Fortunata Council. He discovered their weaknesses, their embarrassing flaws and scandalous secrets. He was ready to use blackmail, threats and violence; after all, this was second nature to him. In Jago's mind, all power was corrupt. He firmly believed that you were only weak if you did not acknowledge and use your immorality.

Now was the time to stand up and declare himself as their leader. Now was the moment to use his power and corruption. He could feel it pulsating through his veins; it coursed through his body like a venomous poison, aching to be released. This was his path to greatness, and those who refused to follow him, for whatever reason, would be cast aside. He would use his unstoppable influence and strength to challenge the Masters. Their arrogance fuelled their ignorance of weakness, and he had already discovered some of their identities.

Eventually, they too would be swept away as if they were pieces on a chessboard.

Jago allowed himself a shiver of dark pleasure as he calmly breathed inward. He studied the engraved, gold wall plate that announced this was the residence of the Fortunata Dan family. They were of founding Fortunata lineage, and like him, they believed a time had come for the wealthy to return to, and reclaim Earthland; that they had the inherent right to free themselves from the boundaries of Opulence, and become the rulers of a new world order.

He smoothed back his hair, licked his lips, and gave two soft knocks on the panelled door.

A few seconds passed before the door slowly opened. The curly ginger hair and chubby, freckled face of Roth Dan appeared. At twenty-three years old, he was an only child, and still lived with his parents. He harboured an unpleasant and cruel nature, and in private, he practised a personal pleasure of inflicting cruelty against others. He had grown up in Jago's companionship, and his allegiance to Jago was unquestionable; indeed, he was the only person to whom Jago entrusted and shared all of his ruthless ideals and plans. There was a bond between them that most interpreted as an unsettling, but true friendship. The real depth of it, however, was a love that knew no boundaries. Needless to say, Roth would protect Jago at all costs, and when needed, he would gladly be an instrument of Jago's wrath. His position as Leader of the Transportation Directive, and whose role it was to oversee the duties of the Transportation Police, allowed him to manipulate and command all manner of corrupt judgements.

Roth widened the door to let Jago in, cautiously glancing up and down the corridor before closing it behind him.

'You're late,' he insisted.

'I had a few final matters to resolve,' snapped Jago.

'Well, at least you're here now.' Roth gave Jago a fleeting kiss on the cheek. They allowed themselves to share a knowing smile. 'They're waiting for you.' Roth nodded for Jago to walk ahead.

They entered the large lounge area of the Fortunata Dan apartments, the walls were resplendently adorned with several oil paintings from the old world, which hung in their lavish gilt frames, displayed like trophies: Rembrandt, Van Gogh and Monet amongst many others. Symbols of wealth traded by desperate refugees from Earthland, in exchange for the chance of a new life in the Servanti community, and what they saw as the relative security and safety of Opulence.

The lounge was filled with Fortunata Élite, adorned in their gaudy robes like psychedelic peacocks in full display. The colours clashed and mirrored the frenetic style of a Picasso; its jagged profile looked down with a distorted eye from one of the walls, as if in disdain. Three of the household's Servanti dutifully circulated, offering drinks and canapés to the thirty or so men and women, gathered in and around a circular seating area, a sunken centrepiece of the room.

The conversation dribbled to a silence as Jago appeared. Heads turned and expressions changed. Some smiled, some showed relief, while others tried to remain indifferent. Jago knew that any challenge to his claim of leadership would be isolated. At a previous gathering, he had demonstrated his influence by having a few prominent scientists, engineers and designers informally attend. Having already conquered most of their hearts and minds, he would crush any remaining opposition without any display of mercy, no matter how small.

Roth's parents ushered the Servanti from the room, as if they were troublesome children, and closed the doors behind them. Then, smiling with pomposity, they joined their son alongside Jago.

'My friends,' a smiling Jago announced. 'The time is upon us to bring about a change. A time for us to breathe purpose and ambition back into the stagnant leadership of Opulence. For too long, we have followed the ways of our short-sighted leaders. What was once a sanctuary has become a prison. We deserve *more* than this!'

He paused to scan the group, allowing his eyes to make contact with as many of them as possible, searching for any indications of doubt. 'Earthland is out there for the taking,' he gestured over their heads to an imaginary horizon. 'It can be ours, to conquer and to rule, to live in unimagined luxury. It will not take long to enslave a workforce, to build an army. We have the technology; our technicians and scientists tell us that we are on the verge of perfecting solar weaponry. The Diss and any other opposition will be no match for us; we shall exterminate them like vermin.' A pause, and his smile hardened. 'Firstly, we must seize power, here on Opulence. *I* can give you that power. Follow me. Let me lead you. Let us take what is rightly ours.' He held out his hand with a grasping fist.

Roth and his parents broke into animated applause, and encouraged it to quickly spread throughout the room.

Jago soaked it up; he could taste the energy, the expectation, and the greed.

As the clapping subsided, a hand was raised from amongst the group. Jago knew the owner's face well: Bertram Fox, a son of one of Opulence's most flamboyant and self-opinionated dynasties. He was always the questioner, always the debater. Jago knew that Bertram opposed the idea of having a figurehead, a single leader. His view was that all power and control should be shared, particularly with himself. Quietly, only a handful of the Élite agreed with him, with uneasy restraint.

'I recognise friend Bertram,' said Jago. He adopted an expression of humbled interest.

All heads turned in Bertram's direction in a wave of nervous curiosity.

'Very stirring, friend Jago, and a sentiment which I am sure is shared by all present.' Bertram smiled and cleared his throat, forcing confidence into his voice. 'But tell me. Why should we agree to place such power into the hands of one single person?'

It was a direct challenge, and many sensed that it was too late for such a statement. Indeed, there was an act of "distancing", a subtle movement of bodies shifting away, creating an empty space around him.

Now, thought Jago. *Now I'll show you that I am not to be underestimated.*

'You are right,' he replied, with a mask of pleasantry. 'We must present absolute unity amongst ourselves. Come,' he gestured. 'Come and stand with me.'

Bertram's arrogance and his belief of self-importance spurred him to walk through the group that eagerly parted to open a corridor and allowed him to step up alongside Jago.

Jago reached out and firmly shook the man's hand, and he placed a friendly arm across Bertram's shoulders. He could smell Bertram's perfume, and mentally noted how it matched the man's ego – sour and overused.

'I'd like you to meet some friends of mine,' Jago announced; a malicious rictus smile spread across his face. 'Roth, would you be so kind as to let them in?'

As Roth turned the ornate handles of the double doors behind them, he and Jago exchanged a slight, but meaningful nod. The head of the Transportation Police entered with two of his commanders. All three were dressed in their cobalt uniforms, embellished with black steel buttons, and trimmed with a silver braided collar and cuffs. The disturbingly multi-eyed, silver and black insignia of the Transportation Police was woven into their breast pockets. Their wraparound, dark-red tinted glasses asserted their presence, adding to their air of authority and menace.

Jago felt Bertram's shoulders stiffen. He tightened his grip on the man's hand; the skin on his own knuckles whitened under the inflicted pressure. A bead of sweat emerged on Bertram's temple and tracked like warm treacle down his suddenly pale complexion. Panic registered in his eyes, the whites enlarged with dread.

All the while, Jago smirked deep into his gaze. In that moment, Bertram saw nothing but his own mortality reflecting back at him.

The two commanders moved forward to flank Bertram and restrain his arms as Jago released his grip.

'This is outrageous,' Bertram protested loudly. 'Release me, damn you!' he shouted, as he struggled with futility.

The dull grey steel of a medi-gun pressed against his neck, and the hiss of compressed gas announced Bertram's silence.

As Bertram's limp body was unceremoniously dragged out of the apartment, the Commander saluted Jago in acknowledgement, and stood by his side in an exhibition of unity.

Jago continued to smile, and all those who were caught in his smile knew they had found their leader, and that they would follow him, with gratitude and with fear.

11

A Mixed Reception

The lift stopped with a jolt, quickly followed by a dull bump. The steel doors rolled noisily back to reveal another set of trellised metal gates, through which a number of figures aimed various weapons at the group. In the light of the flickering fluorescent tubes, Savannah saw the familiar arms of crossbows and catapults, along with a large, multi-barrelled apparatus, which was set on a tripod; a World War Two, M2 Browning machine gun sat poised to deliver death at the rate of five hundred rounds per minute.

'Identify yourselves,' barked a female voice.

'It's Snow White and the seven dwarfs,' shouted Carl. 'Who the hell do you think it is? I'm tired, I'm hungry and I've been shot, so let us the hell out of here.'

There was immediate activity. The gates were pulled back and several people crowded into the lift. A tall, thirty-something, dark haired woman, dressed in green and black combats, pushed her way through and crouched down in front of Carl, her sharp-featured face severe with concern.

'Is it bad?' she asked.

'I think the bullet went straight through,' answered Savannah. 'And he's lost quite a lot of blood.'

'I wasn't talking to you,' replied the woman curtly. She turned her attention back to Carl. 'Let's get you to the medics; we'll need to run some tests, just in case the ammunition was contaminated.' She took him by an arm and helped him to his feet. Savannah hobbled herself upright and continued to support him.

'Thanks for your help,' he grinned at Savannah. 'I owe you.'

'I'll take it from here,' ordered the woman. She hoisted her arm around Carl's waist, and guided him towards a waiting stretcher.

'No problem. Glad to have been of help. I just probably saved his life. You don't have to thank me,' said Savannah sarcastically.

The woman turned her head; 'I'll be seeing *you* later,' she said sternly.

Tanis and Drake got to their feet, and were joined by three others: two girls, roughly the same age as Tanis, and a man. They were all dressed in army fatigues, and wearing tri-colour sashes around their waists. Savannah stood to one side, feeling isolated and ignored. She noticed that the man was a dead ringer for Drake: an identical twin except for the facial scar. He and Drake exchanged a pattern of hand movements, which constituted a handshake, culminating in a hug, and then one of the girls briefly embraced Drake and kissed him on the cheek. Savannah studied the girl, who she thought looked pretty, even with her fair hair tied back in a slick ponytail, and no obvious make-up on her face.

The other, an ebony skinned girl, with patterned, braided black hair, hugged Tanis. When she stood back and inspected him, she noticed his blood-stained clothes, and she panicked.

'You've been hurt!' she exclaimed. 'How bad? Do you need a medic?'

'No. No, I'm fine,' he insisted. 'It's not my blood; I just had to dig myself out of a hog. I'll tell you about it later.'

'Word already is, that you had quite a party up there,' said Drake's twin, with obvious envy. 'Barbequing Crazies from what I've just heard.'

'Not guilty,' said Tanis. 'That was Drake and Savannah.'

The three of them turned their attention to Savannah.

'So, *this* is what all the fuss has been about,' said the dark skinned girl, crossing her arms, and jutting out her chin. Her deep brown eyes looked Savannah up and down, and reflected contempt. '*This* is what they sent you out to risk your lives for?' she added.

'Now, now, Solli,' said Tanis. 'Be nice.'

Drake's twin reached forward and offered a hand. 'Jake. Drake's brother, only more handsome,' he announced with a bright smile. He even sounded like Drake. 'Nice to meet you, Savannah.'

She took hold of his hand, clasped it firmly and gave it a shake. He responded, giving a second shake and freeing his hand with a "snap" of his finger and thumb.

The girl with the ponytail gave Jake an elbow in the

ribs. 'Hi. I'm Penny,' she said with a friendly smile and a fluttering wave of her fingers. 'Jake's partner.'

They stood there in silence for a moment, before Savannah spoke. 'So what happens now, time for another barbeque?'

'I like her style,' said Jake, raising his eyebrows and flashing her a grin.

Penny furrowed her brow at him. Savannah could see quite clearly that her message to him was – '*Stop flirting!*'

Penny turned her attention to Savannah and announced that she was to be her escort and companion, and the first item on the agenda was to get someone to check her leg, and give her something to dull the pain, despite Savannah's insistence that it felt much better.

They said their goodbyes to the others, which included a curt '*Later*' from Solli. Leaving the group at the lift, they crossed to a large open hall where Penny guided Savannah to a medical centre. This time, a man in his fifties, wearing a white coat, which bore a red cross on the sleeve, examined her leg. He washed away the blood and cleaned the wound. Finally satisfied, he sprayed a stinging antiseptic on it for good measure. Savannah cursed and apologised in the same breath.

'I've heard worse,' he said blandly. After putting a light dressing on it, he handed her four plain white tablets. 'Take two now, and the other two later on if you need them. If you don't, then pass them on to someone who does; medicine is precious down here. Keep the wound clean and it should heal in a week or so. It'll hurt for a couple of days, but you'll survive,' he added, matter-of-factly.

'I bet you say that to all the girls,' Savannah remarked with a wink, which was met without even a flicker of humour.

The girls crossed the hall to a row of ticket barriers that no longer demanded proof of passage; the rubber gates had long ago been ripped from their housings. Savannah followed Penny down a steep, dimly lit, metal-stepped stairway; a dormant escalator, which was once used by thousands of commuters. Redundant red signs instructed users to "Stand to the right". Its black handrails like strips of liquorice, polished smooth and shiny from hands that were long dead. The curved ceiling hung with tattered, charcoal-coloured cobwebs that shifted lazily like miniature, ragged spectres in the slight currents of the subway air. The lights, as sparse as they were, didn't so much flicker, but slowly pulsed between dim and bright. All around, shadows eerily ebbed and flowed in a constant rhythm, and the dull thrum of generators ensured there was never complete silence or darkness.

Some old advertising boards had been painted over with green, red and orange stripes, and displayed the slogan – "Together We Are One".

Now and then, they passed numerous people, all steadily going about their business, the familiar tri-colour sashes hung from their waistbands. Some nodded at Penny in recognition; a few glanced at the untidy, mud-and blood-caked girl at her side, but most carried on by, paying no attention. Savannah asked several eager questions about where they were, and what Penny's background was. Penny replied in one-word answers, politely making it clear she did not want to strike up a social conversation.

Eventually, they reached a rail platform; torn and faded posters adorned the far wall of a brick-lined tunnel with images of the old world. Advertisements for lavish theatre productions or celebrity perfumes and aftershaves. Savannah noticed the guards positioned at either end of the platform, and armed with crossbows. Penny approached one and there was a short conversation, during which she showed him her ID. He turned and opened the door of a small yellow box, secured to the wall, and pulled out the same type of tubing and funnel that Savannah had seen Tanis use at the entrance to the lift. The guard removed the stopper from the funnel; he followed the same routine of blowing into the tube, listening for a response, and then speaking into it. Finally, he replaced the funnel and nodded to Penny.

'Transport for two, arriving in a few minutes,' she said on her return.

They heard the rattle of the shuttle well before it emerged from the gloom of the tunnel – a pump trolley, with two large men at the handles. A four-seated trailer was attached, and the whole contraption slowly came to a halt in front of the girls. They climbed down into the steel bucket seats, and without any exchange of words, the men jerked the pump handles into action.

The clattering noise of the ancient transport echoed noisily to announce their entrance into the dark maw of the tunnel, where the gloom wrapped its inky arms around them. A paraffin lamp on the front of the trolley valiantly created a moving halo of light, which held the black shadows constantly at bay just a metre or so ahead of them.

Savannah's eyes became fixated on the semi-circular halo of light, until a short while later it faded as they emerged into a relatively well-illuminated complex. Sidings extended on either side of the platform, where the trolley came to a lurching halt. These were occupied by red and cream carriages, resembling giant inanimate caterpillars joined together in long rows, their destinations blank, the drivers' cabs now dark and empty.

Here, there was a hive of activity of comings and goings. The hubbub of conversation and community echoed around. Groups of people sat at small tables in discussion, drinking from grey metal cups, in an almost café atmosphere.

Penny and Savannah walked along the platform, and as they passed the open doors of the carriages, Savannah could see they were dwellings, simply and comfortably furnished, some with curtains or blinds at the windows. When they reached the last carriage in the row, Penny slid back the semi-curved door. 'Welcome to my home.' She outstretched her arm.

A short while later, feeling self-conscious and exposed, Savannah showered in a white-tiled communal cubicle. Cold water chased away her fatigue, and she purposely stood beneath it until her skin began to grow numb in an effort to wash away her recently acquired emotional demons.

Now, clothed in clean combats (but, she observed, without a tri-colour sash), she sat in Penny's carriage, at a foldout table sharing a simple, but welcome meal.

Again, she tried conversation, which remained sparse as Penny continued to keep her responses to a minimum. As they ate, Savannah's eyes wandered around the compartment. Patchwork-patterned quilts covered two single bunk beds, both with storage cupboards underneath them. A camping stove and a few meagre utensils represented a compact kitchen area. On a small table, two simple wooden picture frames sat on display; one held a pastel coloured snap of a smiling, elderly couple posing beneath the outstretched branches of a pink-blossomed tree. The man had his arm around the woman, and they gently held hands. There was no mistaking that their eyes shone bright and alive with love for each other.

The other picture was a pencil sketch, a head and shoulders portrait of a pretty girl with long pigtails; she was maybe eight or nine years old. Her features were not too dissimilar to Penny's. Except for these, there were no other pictures, no ornaments or decorative objects. The simplicity of Penny's life eased its way into Savannah's awareness, and comfortably appealed to her. An immediate impression struck her that in Earthland, possessions were of greater value when you had fewer of them.

When they finished eating, Penny started to clear the table.

'Here, let me help,' offered Savannah, rising.

'No. It's okay,' asserted Penny. 'I have to take the dishes along the platform to the communal sinks, to wash and store them. Besides, I'm sure you're used to being waited on.'

For a moment, they both froze in a tableau of awkwardness.

Savannah's face flushed. 'You don't like me, do you?'

Penny took in a breath. 'I'm sorry. I shouldn't have said that,' she apologised.

'You didn't answer my question,' insisted Savannah.

Penny sat back down on her stool. 'Please,' she indicated for Savannah to do the same.

'I'm trying not to judge you,' she began. 'It is hard for me, because all I've ever seen are the results of your "Transportation" methods. We take it in turns to go out on the rescue missions. We try and snatch to safety the poor souls who are left on the estuary beaches, before the Screamers inflict their carnage.' She looked down at her feet and a wisp of her hair slid across the bridge of her nose. It didn't distract her. 'The image of a child being torn to shreds never leaves you. *Their* screams are always the loudest.'

In the stillness of the carriage, an image of her long-lost friend, Kelly, desperate and pleading, flashed into Savannah's mind. With her own eyes now moist and her throat dry with emotion, she reached out and clasped Penny's hand.

'Some of them have been my friends,' said Savannah, with a whisper. Two pearled teardrops, two symbols of grief, tracked down her cheek, to fall and splash onto the surface of the table. The tiny droplets ran together and formed a miniature pool of sorrow.

For a short while, they sat there in silence, hands holding hands in mutual comfort, until Savannah slowly lifted her head, her eyelashes moist from crying.

Penny passed her a white handkerchief; a small pink "P" was delicately embroidered in one of the corners. 'I'm sorry. I misjudged you. That was wrong of me,' she said. 'If you'd like to rest, yours is the left-hand bunk. There's a small packet of basic toiletries on the pillow for you. I'll be back in a bit.' She rose and resumed collecting the dishes. 'I'd better get these done,' she smiled.

Later, in the soft light of a large, half-used beeswax candle, Savannah found herself talking quietly to Penny. She told her about her hopes and fears, about her childhood, her family. Intimate and personal things, and all the while, Penny just sat and listened, smiling, nodding and comforting. That night, Savannah dreamt of nothing. Her sleep was a void. The space between falling asleep and opening her eyes in the morning, seemed but the length of a single breath.

12

JEAN FAIRFAX

With Penny beside her, Savannah sat at a metal oblong table, large enough to seat at least a dozen people around it. The room was grey and featureless, its walls devoid of decoration or character. Overhead, two sets of uncovered fluorescent tubes hummed their bare light to enhance the room's stark setting. As a result, the oddity that ticked away in one of the corners, a tall grandfather clock, held an overpowering presence. Its oak cabinet and brass face were a testament to lasting craftsmanship. The minute hand clicked onto the roman numerals, which indicated twelve, the counterweights shifted and a mechanical whirring sound announced the arrival of its chimes. It was eight o'clock in the morning.

On the first chime, the door opened and Tanis entered. Now, he wore a pair of dark navy combat trousers, and a charcoal-grey hoodie; the faded image of a bespectacled man and the word "Imagine" adorned his chest. However, it was only Tanis' dreadlocks that made him recognisable to Savannah. Gone was the camouflage make-up to reveal a brown-skinned face and the features of Afro Caribbean descent. She flashed him a smile, but he remained expressionless, passive to her presence.

A middle-aged man and woman, both wearing brown military tunics, the breast pockets embroidered with tri-colour braids, followed him in and quietly took their seats on the opposite side of the table.

They sat there, listening as the clear musical tones confirmed the passage of time. On the eighth chime, the door opened once again, and Savannah's eyes widened with recognition, as the combat suited woman who had helped Carl from the lift, now entered the room and took her place at the head of the table. She placed two large paper-filled files, one orange, the other red, in front of her. Some of their ivory pages protruded untidily, the corners curled through the rigour of examination. Savannah could just make out her own name, handwritten in black capital letters across the centre of the orange cover.

'Good morning,' said the woman.

'Good morning, Commander,' all but Savannah replied.

'Savannah Loveday,' the woman announced, looking directly at her. 'My name is Jean Fairfax. Commander-in-chief, Jean Fairfax of Base One, Earthland Defence Network.' She placed a hand purposely on the orange file and leaned forward. 'You are now my responsibility, young lady.'

The rebel in Savannah stirred, egged on by a sense of frustration, and fuelled by the dull ache in her leg. Her father used to call her "young lady", particularly when chiding her. The term still stuck in her throat.

'What if I don't want to be your responsibility?' she said sourly. 'What if I just want to be left alone to take care of myself?'

Jean Fairfax stared at Savannah; her steel-grey eyes met Savannah's with unconcern. She produced a slightly dented, metal glasses case from her jacket pocket, removed a pair of delicate, gold-framed spectacles, and perched them gently on her nose. She then focused her attention on the orange file, and turned back the cover.

'Savannah Loveday,' she read. 'Second child of Tiberius and Corda Loveday. Younger sister Bethany, and older brother Jago. Fortunata, and descendants of Franklin Loveday, founding member of Opulence.'

Without looking up, she went on to read Savannah's personal and medical details, right down to the self-inflicted black tattoo of a butterfly on her right thigh, and the small white scars across her stomach; the results of a short period of misguided self-harm, inflicted during her early teens, the memory of which filled her with self-regret, like the bitter taste of reckless surrender.

After running over her education and high levels of achievement as a student, Jean Fairfax conveyed the anecdote of Savannah's first encounter, and close association with a family of Servanti.

When she was an inquisitive nine-year-old, and exploring the lower levels of Opulence, Savannah had a chance meeting with a Servanti girl, Kelly, the same age as her. They became close companions as their secret friendship grew, until two years later and the fateful day when Kelly's whole family were selected for Transportation. Savannah was there when the

Transportation Police arrived; she was restrained and taken to one side, eventually to be escorted home and presented to her distraught parents; little could they imagine the long-term implications of the incident.

The sound of Kelly calling out Savannah's name, pleading for help as she was seized roughly and without compassion by Transportation Police, her cries suddenly stifled by a leather-gloved hand, this was the catalyst for Savannah's rebellion, further fuelled by her father's refusal to use his influence to save the family.

She spent more of her waking hours exploring the lower reaches of Opulence, seeking out and befriending the Servanti. She began crawling through air ducts to access restricted areas, to steal valuable objects from storerooms and trade them for credits, which she passed on to Servanti families who were in danger of falling into poverty and the prospect of being Transported.

Sometimes, she would be apprehended with stolen items, and stubbornly refused to reveal how she had come by them. In due course, her father would be summoned, whereupon he would reprimand her, issue the usual apologies (and complimentary credits to the officials), and as a punishment, place restrictions on her movements, including a curfew. Needless to say, these penalties had no lasting effect on Savannah's attitude or behaviour.

Jean Fairfax continued to read through the pages, citing the details and numerous incidents of Savannah's dissent over the years.

'How do you know all this about me?' Savannah impatiently interrupted.

'Our information is gathered from those who have survived Transportation, from the humble Servanti to the outcast Fortunata, who we have been lucky enough to rescue before they have fallen victim to the Screamers or the Crazies,' said Jean Fairfax. 'Did you think that when people were Transported, they left their memories behind? They bring with them a wealth of knowledge. Over the years, we have compiled such files as these on most of the key figures who live on Opulence. Even some of the Ruling Fortunata, would you believe? A person such as yourself particularly, does not go unnoticed, especially when she befriends Servanti families.'

She removed her glasses and stared quietly into Savannah's eyes for a few moments. 'You need to listen, what you hear may well determine your future.' She settled the rim of her glasses comfortably on the bridge of her nose and continued reading from the file, moving on to the Loveday family's details, along with their connections and influence within Opulence.

Savannah didn't want to hear it. She didn't want to conjure up any thoughts or visions of the life behind her. She refused to regurgitate any sour regret. She wanted to suppress any emotional link. Her eyes wandered to the clock; she focused on the polished wood casing. Her eyes absorbed the detail, how the intricate grain rippled its deep black lines of age in naturally formed patterns. Her attention started to drift; the words became a boring drone to her ears.

'Tiberius. Greed. Luxury. Uncaring. Privilege. Founding family. Blah, blah, blah…'

She wondered about the people who had created the

instrument: the carpenter, and the clockmaker. Where the wood had come from, the tree and its setting, the landscape, the old world.

It was the phrase, 'Jago presents the biggest threat to us all,' that invaded her escapism, and jolted her mind back to attention.

'What? What was that?' she stammered.

Jean Fairfax looked up, and fixed another stare at Savannah over the rim of her glasses. 'I beg your pardon?'

'The last bit, about Jago. What were you saying?'

'We have reason to believe that your brother, Jago, intends to lead a coup d'état. His ambitions are far more ruthless than those of the existing dictatorship that rule Opulence. Combined with reports that their scientists are intent on developing powerful solar weapons, we find the threat alarming, to say the least.'

'What has all this to do with me?'

'It has everything to do with you,' said Jean Fairfax pointedly. 'We need you to go back. To help stop the course of events.'

Savannah crossed her arms, and pushed her shoulders into the back of her seat.

'Go back?' she almost laughed with derision. 'Go back to what? I have no life back there, just betrayal and bad memories.'

'You still have a family,' said Jean Fairfax.

'What family?' Savannah curled her lip. 'My brother had me Transported – probably hoped I would die, and my mother and father allowed it to happen.'

'And your sister?' added Jean Fairfax. 'What about your sister, Bethany?'

A stab of concern invaded Savannah's self-imposed, emotional barrier.

'She'll be okay,' she said unconvincingly. 'My parents wouldn't let anything happen to her. They love her too much.'

Jean Fairfax decisively and purposely leaned forward. 'And Jago? Does he share that love?'

The implication bored into Savannah's chest. Her heart skipped a beat and she straightened her back. 'He wouldn't dare to harm her!' she protested, and as the words tumbled out of her mouth, she heard the chilling doubt in her own voice.

13

JAGO AND ROTH

Jean Fairfax pushed the red file towards Savannah. It slid effortlessly across the polished steel table, turning in a semicircle under its own momentum as it reached her. In the top right-hand corner of the jacket was a name in capital letters – JAGO LOVEDAY. With reluctant curiosity, Savannah pulled the file towards her and folded back the cover. On the first page was a strikingly accurate pencil portrait of Jago's head and shoulders, along with notes outlining his basic personal details. The face pouted out its familiar sneer at her, and she looked away, inwardly embarrassed to be intimidated by the image. The next page contained a medical report in the form of a psychiatric assessment and diagnosis. The words "psychotic", "delusional" and "dangerous" stood out to her eyes.

She glanced up, her lips loosely parted, ready to ask an unformed and worrying question.

'Read the reports on the next few pages,' Jean Fairfax said quietly.

Savannah turned the page. She noticed that her

fingers had begun to tremble, ever so slightly. The report was headed – "Statements of evidence".

Patiently, they sat there, the ticking of the clock a soundtrack to dark revelations as, at first, Savannah read the initial page in detail. Then she began to thumb through and anxiously scan subsequent sheets. During the process, she occasionally looked up into the passive faces around her, her expression varying from shock, to horror and disbelief. After a few minutes, her face regained its pallor, and with her cheeks now flushed red, she slammed the file closed and pushed it away, as though being in contact with it tainted and dirtied her hands.

'This is lies!' She shook her head. 'Lies! He could *never* be such a monster.' The denial in her voice hung in the air.

'Everything in that file has been verified,' said Jean Fairfax. 'From multiple witness statements, from the mouths of survivors.'

'It's a mistake,' Savannah insisted. 'He wouldn't. He couldn't.'

Jean Fairfax gently folded her glasses, and glanced at the middle-aged couple. 'Show her,' she said, her voice almost a whisper.

With a trace of weariness, the man pushed his chair back and stood. He slowly unfastened his tunic, and as he did, his fingers stumbled over a couple of the large, black buttons. Beneath, he wore a grey cotton shirt. This too he unbuttoned, to finally pull the material apart and reveal a scar. The surrounding skin still flared red with the anger of its infliction. The unmistakable letter

"J" had been cut with neat precision into his chest and stomach.

His eyes met Savannah's. He spoke with a faint, trembling voice, and she sensed no trace of anger.

'We survived for ten years as Servanti,' he began. 'Content to live in the lower levels, happy just to be alive and together. Twelve months ago, our elderly employer passed away, and we were reassigned to the service of another Fortunata family, who treated us with contempt from the start. One of the younger children was verbally abusive to us, and I made the mistake of commenting on their lack of manners. That night, Transportation Police broke down our door and arrested us, citing "disrespectful conduct towards a Fortunata child" as our crime. The family used their spiteful influence to have us removed.

'We stood in a corridor, in line with twenty or so others, waiting to be Transported. With no explanation, two Transportation Police pulled us out of the group and escorted us to a separate room, a steel cell with no windows. In the centre of the room, under a single light, there was a chair, similar to a dentist's chair, but with leather restraining straps. There was just one other piece of furniture positioned against a wall: a metal cabinet, similar to a tool chest. The drawers were closed, but I sensed the horrors that were laid out within. They left us there, locked in and alone, holding onto each other. Alone with a smell I will remember until my dying day. The smell of cleaning fluid, excrement and blood.'

He took a deep breath. His Adam's apple shifted in his throat as he swallowed.

'When he and Roth entered the room together, Jago was smiling. It was a smile that made me kiss my wife and tell her how much I loved her, as though those would be the last words I would be allowed to utter. I feared our lives would end in that room. His was a smile of madness, and it froze my body to the core.

'I cannot bear to tell you everything that happened to us, but I can tell you Roth was the willing instrument of Jago's instructions. It was Roth who inflicted the pain, but it was Jago's precise methods he followed and put into practice. It was as though our pain was a drug to them. Every drop of our blood that they spilt, gave them pleasure. I remember that at times, the more we screamed, the louder Jago laughed.

'He told me this mark was to remind me of him, that I would never be free of him. That no matter where I went, I could not escape him.' His jaw quivered. He paused and took a trembling breath, then swallowed again.

Jean Fairfax nodded. 'Thank you,' she said, kindly.

Silently, the man buttoned up his shirt, and before he left the room, he bent over to tenderly kiss his wife on the cheek. As the door shut with a hollow click behind him, she studied Savannah.

'I bear you no ill, but if I could play even the smallest part in ridding this world of those monsters that masquerade as human beings, then it would fulfil any remaining ambition that I have,' she said, with barely controlled emotion.

She brought her arms up and onto the table and she grasped her right hand with her left one. Savannah noticed the woman was wearing black leather gloves.

'When Jago touched me, I slapped his face, and so he had Roth cut off my hand.' She twisted the limb, and a soft, metallic click sounded. She pulled the prosthetic from her sleeve and placed it onto the table; the moulded fingers seemed to point accusingly at Savannah. 'Then, he instructed Roth to carve the same mark into me as he had into my husband.' The fingers on her remaining hand absently stroked the breast of her tunic. There was a brief moment until she exhaled again. 'We were their entertainment, just objects to be used as amusement, nothing more. I suppose we should be grateful in that we have no other family for them to search out and brutalise. In a way, we were lucky that he let us both live. At least we still have each other,' she finished as she reconnected her hand.

She looked at Jean Fairfax, who returned a soft smile and mouthed a gentle 'Thank you.'

The woman rose, and as she opened the door, she turned once more to face Savannah. 'There is one thing I am certain of. An unimagined evil has been walking the halls and corridors of Opulence. Once that evil achieves power and control, it will not stop until it has touched us all.'

After the door closed, an uneasy silence followed. They sat there in their own thoughts until Jean Fairfax spoke.

'I think we should give Savannah some breathing space,' she announced. 'Penny, go and organise a hot drink for us, and Tanis, see if you can use your persuasive powers to get some of those special oat biscuits, which are so hard to come by.' She rose to her feet. 'I'll go and see if there are any fresh messages or updates waiting for me.'

Savannah was so lost in her own thoughts, she hardly noticed them leave; if she did, then she gave no indication or acknowledgement.

She sat there for a few moments staring at the tabletop; its surface began to fill with the recalled images of times spent with her sister. Echoes of past happiness and sisterly conversations wandered into her mind. Memories of two young girls embraced in the innocence of growing up. Without warning, the scene shattered into fragments, to form the grinning, menacing face of Jago. With a catch of her breath, she wiped her hand across the steel surface to disperse the vision. Her fingers left streaks of moist sweat across the metal. She sucked on her cheeks, forcing saliva into her mouth, and she rolled her eyes upwards to the flickering ceiling lights. When she exhaled, it came out as a juddering sob. Her chest jerked, and she lowered her head as hot tears flooded down into her cupped hands.

Five, maybe ten minutes passed before her breathing calmed to a steady pace and her tears came to a halt. She reached up and untied the white bandana that held back her hair. Regaining her composure, she gently wiped her face. The cloth soaked up the precious emotion that had spilled from her eyes. She gently blew her nose, folded the material and put it into her pocket.

With a resolute intake of breath, she reached for the red file, opened it, and controlling her anxiety, she continued to read its contents.

14

Dead or Alive

Under cover of a dark and menacing sky, two inflatable dinghies moved steadily along the estuary; the efforts of the rowers were made easier by the flowing tide. The oars rhythmically dipped in and out of the oil-black surface, leaving disturbed swirls in their wake. The soft splash of black plastic entering and leaving the water was the only sound that could draw attention to their existence. Four men occupied each boat. Dressed in black drysuits and balaclava hoods, the shifting whites of their eyes added a ghost-like quality to their presence. The night was complete in its absence of a moon, which allowed them to travel relatively unseen; their dark silhouettes of spectral floating shapes merged in and out of the shoreline's natural shadows.

A couple of hours earlier, their solar-charged jet skis had brought them across the sea from Opulence to the mouth of the estuary. It was there that they transferred into the dinghies, and the stealth they needed. Theirs was a long and physically demanding journey, many miles upriver to where their targets went about their unsuspecting business.

The mission was unknown to all but a few. Forays into the heart of Earthland were rare, only previously being used for the rescue and extraction of important and useful people many years ago during the construction of Opulence. This, however, was something entirely different.

The dark threads of Jago's design to dominate and rule already reached out through a network of spies, and he had long acquired knowledge of Earthland's primary commanders, whose guidance and providence held the morale and optimism of the Diss together. Now, two of them had been selected as his first targets.

'Bring them to me, dead or alive,' he ordered. 'Alive, they will give me information, and myself and Roth, a little personal amusement. Dead, they will give me no more trouble. Either way, it will show the Diss that we are capable of inflicting harm and disruption into their very midst. It will sow the seeds of uncertainty and help to weaken any resistance in preparation for when we lay our rightful claim to the old world.'

With his established loyalty amongst the Transportation Police, and with Roth's commanding influence, a skilled "kill or capture" team were dispatched. First on their list of targets was the name of Commander-in-chief, Jean Fairfax, Base One, Earthland Defence Network.

Accumulated knowledge from old plans and documents supplied them with details of the underground network. Armed with this and a rehearsed method of breaching security procedures, they now rowed purposely towards their destination. Under the drysuits, they were dressed in Diss style clothing, each one adorned with a tri-colour sash to add to their guise, which in theory, and hopefully with relative ease, would help them to infiltrate Base One.

When global borders had collapsed, and as a consequence of the initial public and political divergence, small wars and conflicts had broken out; but with the loss of technology, weaponry became reduced to basic guns and artillery. As the availability of explosive ammunition became a rarity, those fighting eventually resorted to using blades, spears, bows and arrows, and the odd chemically enhanced petrol bomb. The tools of technological warfare became redundant and useless. Most of them were left to rust and rot, impotent without any electronic power sources.

Unsurprisingly, there were those who gathered what firearms, bullets and conventional explosives they were able, to stockpile and maintain them as a last line of defence. Rumoured locations of underground arms caches remained undiscovered, and what may have been fact drifted into urban myth. Because of their limited availability, the use of all munitions was eventually restricted, and employed only in the direst of situations.

Many of these surviving weapons were now in the hands of the Diss, to be allocated and strategically placed in and around their compounds. However, some inevitably made their way onto Opulence and had been secretly stored for "special" circumstances. The eight occupants of the dinghies were in "special" circumstances, and each one was therefore armed with a loaded pistol and a snub-nosed Kalashnikov machine gun.

In the early hours and against a sky that heralded the first signs of an approaching grey dawn, the dark silhouette of a city bridge loomed ahead of them. Once a marvellous feat of engineering, it now stretched across the black tide, its twisted metal skeleton misshapen and hanging like the flesh-stripped remains of an ancient dinosaur. Its melted roadway the result of an act of anarchy and the explosive ignition of two fuel tankers trapped in a traffic jam of abandoned cars. Further evidence of a society hell-bent on self-destruction.

As they reached the tangle of metal beams and struts, one of the boats turned towards the shore. A brief signal was made between the two craft as the other continued its journey to a location further on upriver, and a second target.

The flow of the tide pushed the first boat towards a charcoal-grey foreshore. Two figures leapt out; one of them uttered an obscenity as they were engulfed up to the knees in thick, stinking, glutinous mud. After further cursing, all four figures half crawled, half slithered to the bottom step of a metal stairway; its treads rose above them, fixed by unseen, oxidized bolts, to a catwalk linking to the bridge itself and a doorway in the side of the bridge support tower. Here, an old service entrance would lead them inside to a long-forgotten maintenance tunnel, a weakness in the defence of Base One.

'One at a time,' a man's brusque voice commanded. 'It's been a while since this was used and we don't know how much weight it'll take. When you're up, tap on the rails for the next man to follow, and then take up your positions inside the tower.'

As agile as the shadows they resembled, the four figures took it in turn to climb the corroded stairway. It groaned and grated in complaint, but stayed firm and allowed them safe passage. Once inside, a flare was lit; its laser red illumination transformed the darkness of a large room into a surreal scene of smoke and distorted shadows. An open stairwell beckoned in the far corner. Down they went, following concrete steps to ground level and a storeroom. Stacks of old crates and fuel drums occupied the far end of the space. In the wall to their left was framed a double doorway; the faded words above it announced its old purpose of "Emergency exit".

'Time to change,' ordered the leader. 'Leave the drysuits and anything else that you don't need.'

Once free of the suits and balaclavas, the group stowed their guns out of sight into a large green holdall, which the leader slung across his back. Then they were off, splashing along the waterlogged tunnel. Rivulets of water seeped down the sides and became glistening, red veins in the flare's light.

It took them just under an hour and a half to reach their destination: a length of metal rungs set into a wall, which reached up into a circular shaft. In the light of a flare and through the rising smoke, they could see a round hatch above them.

Their leader produced a small map. 'Okay, this is it,' he said, confirming the detail and accuracy of its information. 'This hatch should bring us out into an old storage depot. We'll regroup at the top, and then make our way out into the left-hand tunnel. According to our sources, this will lead us to Base One of the Defence

Network, about half a mile away. Our target should be two levels down.' He folded the map up and tucked it into his jacket, and then he checked the face of the steel Rolex on his wrist: 07.35. He inspected the faces of the three men around him; their eyes reflected the hell-red flare light; their stern faces stared back, impassionate and alert with adrenalin.

'Follow me, keep together, and do not engage anyone. Leave the talking to me.'

15

COFFEE AND KALASHNIKOVS

The door opened and Penny entered. She carried a wooden tray on which were seated four steaming china mugs. Jean Fairfax and Tanis followed closely behind and returned to their seats while Penny placed the tray onto the table.

'Use the handles, the mugs are hot,' she warned.

'Black coffee,' announced Jean Fairfax in Savannah's direction, as she blew across the rim of her own mug. 'Milk and sugar are rare and kept for special occasions. However, I'm sure Tanis has managed to get a little treat for us?' She raised an eyebrow in his direction.

Tanis' white teeth gleamed into a broad smile as he produced a green cloth bundle. He placed it onto the table, and unwrapped it with nimble fingers to reveal four golden brown oatcakes. He held out the cakes, for each of them to take one.

'Mmmm. Still warm,' announced Penny as she took a delicate bite of the honeyed texture.

Tanis and Jean Fairfax followed suit.

'Tanis, I hope you haven't been raiding the bakery,' remarked Jean Fairfax as she protectively caught a few falling crumbs in the palm of her hand. 'You know what the penalty is for stealing.'

'No! I have a friend who works there and he owed me a favour,' replied Tanis, somewhat nervously.

'Good. I wouldn't want to be helping you to destroy the evidence,' she said with a smile.

Penny noticed that Savannah had touched neither her drink nor her oatcake. 'What's wrong?' she asked.

'My stomach still has the cramps from reading some of the things in Jago's file.'

'All the more reason for you to get some food into you,' said Jean Fairfax. 'I'll spare you the added trauma of reading Roth Dan's file,' she added. 'I need to know your thoughts. Besides, we don't waste anything here, especially food.'

Savannah brought the mug of coffee to her mouth and tentatively sipped at it. A strong, bitter aroma invaded her senses, and a hot, chicory taste washed over her lips and across her tongue. She swallowed the raw, unrefined liquid, and found a welcome relief in its effect. When she bit into it, the taste of the oatcake was in complete contrast and it caught her by surprise. She could not disguise her pleasure as the delicious flavours burst in her mouth.

'This is wonderful,' she said as she licked an errant crumb from the corner of her lip.

'Honey. From our hives in the countryside compounds,' explained Tanis. 'One of the few regular luxuries we can get here at Base One.'

'The countryside is not like it is here?' quizzed Savannah.

'No, not where we have our compounds. They were set up in remote places far away from any ruined areas,' explained Jean Fairfax. She took a last mouthful of coffee and placed the mug in front of her; her hands cradled it protectively. For a few seconds, she studied the now empty vessel before looking up at Savannah. 'Now we come to your thoughts. We need your help. I need to know – Are you with us?'

Savannah opened her mouth. She wanted to say how much she hated her brother. How she despised the Fortunata's regime on Opulence, but in that instance, the only sound they heard was of gunfire. Against a background of screams and shouts, the staccato clatter of machine guns and the thud of bullets invaded the room's momentary silence.

All of them stood, their chairs screeching in protest across the tiled floor as they urgently pushed them back. Tanis was first to the door. From a sheath, hidden beneath his jacket, he drew a long-bladed hunting knife. Penny produced a similar weapon from the leg of her combats, and placed herself in front of Jean Fairfax.

'You know the protocol,' said Penny. 'In this situation, we give the orders and you follow them. Understand?'

Jean Fairfax nodded.

There was a break in the gunfire.

'What about me?' asked Savannah.

'Under the table,' ordered Tanis. 'Get under the table.'

She held her ground. 'I've not gone through everything only to hide under a bloody table,' she replied.

Tanis could see from the look on her face that there would be no arguing with her. 'Okay. Join Penny and Commander Fairfax. And-stay-with-them.' He emphasised the last four words.

Another burst of gunfire prompted Savannah to pull herself across the table to join them, scattering the files and mugs to the floor as she did so. She put herself alongside Penny, and looked jealously at the knife.

'One of those would be handy right now,' she mused.

Penny unzipped a pocket in the side of her combats and unsheathed a smaller, but just as deadly-looking blade.

'Here you go; just make sure you can use it if you have to.'

The staccato sound of gunfire returned, closer this time.

'If it's you that they're after, Commander, then we're sitting ducks in here,' said Tanis. 'I'm taking a look.' He pulled the door open a fraction at a time, as if any sound from the hinges would betray them. He edged himself closer and peered through the gap. There was another salvo, followed by the muffled explosions of bullets as they thudded into the other side of the wall. Tanis dropped to the floor, shouting, 'Down! Down!'

All three quickly followed suit and crawled towards him.

There came a man's voice, rough and full of frustration.

'Find Fairfax. Find her now!'

There was more gunfire, but this was faster, a rattling and urgent sound of hot-headed fury.

'That sounds like one of our machine guns,' said Tanis. 'Hopefully, it'll put us on even terms with whoever's managed to get into the Base.' He pulled the door open wider and glanced out, anxiously.

The meeting room was at an intersection of three corridors: one to the right, one to the left, and a wider one opposite. It was from this one that all of the firing had come, and he could see, in a doorway about fifteen metres away, the crouched figure of a man frantically trying to unjam a machine gun.

Grasping the opportunity, which he felt could mean the difference between life and death, Tanis pulled back the door. 'Move! Move now!' he yelled.

All four of them spilled out into the corridor. Tanis crouched against the wall on the left, and Penny followed. She signalled for Savannah and Jean Fairfax to wait; it was then that the man in the doorway looked up in their direction.

There was another burst of Kalashnikovs from around the far end of the corridor, followed by a longer burst of the Browning.

The man in the doorway shouted. 'Jonesy? Barnes? Liam?'

Another voice, less confident, came from further on down the passage. 'It's Liam, sir. I'm okay, but the other two are hit, sir. They're dead.'

The man reacted with seething temper and rage. 'I'm not going back to Jago empty-handed!' he roared. 'Cover me. I'm going to finish this now!' He launched himself forward in a running crouch.

At the end of the passage, Liam's Kalashnikov spat

metallic death overhead, most of which hit the ceiling above Tanis and Penny. Before they could move, fluorescent tubes exploded and sent shards of splintering, opaque glass into the air. The large, heavy light fittings, along with chunks of fractured plaster, dropped onto their heads, knocking them to the ground, unconscious and bleeding.

In a chain reaction, the weight of the metal frame tore the power cables from the ceiling, which ripped out the next light fitting. It dropped from one end and swung precariously just above Savannah and Jean Fairfax. Electricity sparked and fizzed from the exposed wires like an errant roman candle. Unable to stand, they eased themselves along the wall in an attempt to reach the other corridor.

The man strode towards them; his hands jerked and pulled in frustration at his gun's mechanism as he tried to release it. Frustration overcame patience, and like a petulant child, he finally threw the weapon to one side, to send it clattering and skidding across the floor. He produced a snub-nosed pistol from the inside of his jacket and pointed its muzzle at Savannah and Jean Fairfax. His tall, bulky figure towered over them.

Now he was closer, Savannah recognised the man. His name was Brent, a member of the Transportation Police, and she already had a hatred for him. She'd witnessed him several times in the past, roughly and sometimes brutally manhandling those unfortunates chosen for Transportation.

'Well, well,' he sneered at Savannah in recognition. 'I'll let your brother know that you're alive and you've made some new friends.'

'You can tell him when you both meet in hell,' spat Savannah. A red mist of anger and misjudgement clouded her fear, and she launched herself at him.

Brent brought his fist down hard across her face. She felt the cartilage in his knuckles pop on contact, and pain exploded across her cheekbone. White lights streaked across the inside of her eyelids, and the world folded into blackness, as she sprawled on the floor in a crumpled heap.

Brent directed the gun at Jean Fairfax. 'You! Get up! You're my ticket home.'

She pushed herself up, her back pressed into the wall. 'You won't get out of here. It doesn't matter what you threaten to do to me; they won't let you out,' she said defiantly.

A fresh barrage of shots preceded Liam's voice from the passage. 'Sir, we have to leave. Now!'

Brent reached out and grabbed the back of Jean Fairfax's head, clamping a fistful of her hair in his vice-like fingers. She screamed in pain as he spun her around in front of him.

'Secure the end of the corridor!' he ordered Liam. 'Now then,' he said through stretched white lips. 'We're going to leave here together, and I don't care if I walk you out alive, or I have to drag you out dead. It's your choice.' He brought the barrel of the gun up to her temple.

Jean Fairfax knew what would happen if she let herself be taken alive. In desperation, she brought her elbow back and into Brent's ribs, but to no effect. His fitness and muscular physique proved a more than adequate protection to her blow.

'You bitch!' He swung her around, almost lifting her from the floor. A gasp of agony escaped her lips as a clump of hair tore loose between his fingers; her scalp burst with pain akin to a thousand sharp needles. She landed heavily on her bottom, facing up at him. There was murder in his eyes and she began scrabbling frantically backwards like a drunken crab, as he pursued her.

'Dragged out dead, it is then,' he shrugged with cold resignation. Her eyes focused on the gun as he pointed it at her head. She waited for the barrel to blaze the announcement of her death.

In that moment, an expression of bewilderment spread across Brent's face. His brow furrowed, the muscles in his cheeks sagged, and he let out an involuntary noise. 'Uhh?' His legs crumpled, and he collapsed onto his knees, arms limp by his sides.

Savannah stood there, her face a mask of fury, a swollen and purple bruise already formed across one cheek.

Brent's body toppled forward, and he folded up with a last exhale of living breath. His face hit the smooth concrete floor with a soft "smack", and his head came to rest between Jean Fairfax's outstretched legs. That was when she could see the handle of Savannah's knife. The blood-soaked hilt protruded from between Brent's shoulder blades.

There was another burst of machine gun fire further around the corridor, followed by shouts of pursuit.

Savannah stepped around Brent's body and held out a hand for Jean Fairfax. 'In answer to your question, I guess that I'm with you,' she said, with a smile of grim resolution.

16

SOLLI

The other attack by Jago's assassins had fared no better. Their information had been less accurate, and they found themselves exiting a tunnel in darkness, right into the centre of a Crazies' encampment. All hell had broken loose, and before they knew it, they'd been overwhelmed and torn apart – literally.

In the days that followed, the whole mood in the Defence Network changed dramatically. Consequently, Diss patrols were doubled, and plans of the old underground drainage and rail system were re-examined and explored for any other unknown breaches or weaknesses which, when discovered, were well and truly sealed off.

Tanis and Penny spent two days in the medical centre. Both escaped with a few stitches and twenty-four-hour headaches. Jean Fairfax took the opportunity to have her hair cropped; she would, however, retain a small, bald patch on the crown of her head for the rest of her life.

Shock finally hit her, and Savannah suffered an episode of the shakes for a couple of hours after the event. Not so much down to the physical trauma of the attack, but as a reaction to killing someone. No matter how much she hated the man, it wasn't really in her nature to purposely end a life. However, after a great deal of soul – searching, she admitted that given similar circumstances, she wouldn't hesitate to do it again.

When she awoke in the medical centre the following morning, there were two oatcakes on a cabinet beside her bed, along with a note that simply said – "From Tanis, Enjoy". The internal grapevine spread news of her heroics, and her circle of new-found friends widened overnight. In fact, a few days later, she had an unexpected visit from Solli.

Savannah lay on her bunk in Penny's cabin, reading one of the many files that Jean Fairfax had given her. 'Get well, but get reading,' were her orders.

Some of the documents contained a general history of events since the old world had degenerated into chaos and re-emerged as Earthland. Other files were specific to certain people who were important in the Diss hierarchy, along with information on how the Earthland Defence Network came to be formed, and its general operational structure. These files were labelled "Confidential", and Savannah noticed that in each case, the contents did not match up with the indexes – some pages had been removed. It appeared that even saving Jean Fairfax's life did not give Savannah the privilege to see everything!

She was rubbing her tired eyes for the tenth time when there was a knock on the doorframe. She closed the file and sat up, massaging her neck with one hand.

'Come in,' she managed, stifling a yawn.

Solli stepped into the cabin. A friendly smile adorned her face, and in her hands, she carried a white-cloth bundle, tied with a colourful green, red and orange ribbon.

'Hi,' she said coyly.

There were a few seconds of silence between the girls as the memory of their first meeting ran through their minds. In those seconds, Savannah took in Solli's appearance. Her face in particular seemed less careworn and tense; she looked calmer, more at ease with herself. Savannah also noticed she wore a double tri-colour sash around her waist.

'Hi,' she returned with a smile.

Solli held out the package. 'Peace offering, you didn't exactly catch me at my best the other day.'

'Likewise,' acknowledged Savannah with a smile. She held out a hand. 'Take a seat.'

They both sat at the table, and Solli placed the bundle between them.

'Go on, open it,' she said with all the excitement of a ten-year-old at a birthday party. 'I hear you've developed a taste for them.'

Savannah pulled the ends of the daintily tied bow, and the cloth fell back to reveal half a dozen golden oatcakes.

'How… how did you get these?' asked Savannah.

'I pulled in a few favours,' said Solli. 'Go on, taste one.'

Savannah picked up one of the biscuits as though it were a fragile work of art. She gently cupped her hand beneath it so as not to let even a crumb escape, and she bit into the sweet, honeyed texture. She rolled her eyes skywards.

'Oh my. Absolute heaven. Go on, you have one.'

'They're a present for you,' insisted Solli.

'Part of the present would be to share them with you,' said Savannah. She paused and reached out a hand, placing it over Solli's. In that instant, they both knew they shared an unseen bond, one of life's mysteries, which connects people together.

For the next hour or so, they sat there talking, like old friends. Girl stuff. Life stuff. Hopes, dreams, fears. Sometimes giggling, sometimes sharing bittersweet moments in silent pauses, completely at ease with one another, and all the while savouring the oatcakes as if it were their last meal.

Savannah learnt that Solli was Tanis' younger sister, and in her sixteenth year, the tie between them so great that Solli pined for him, worried for him whenever he went out into the dangerous terrain of Earthland. She also became very jealous when he got any attention from other girls. Savannah bore the brunt of both tensions when they had first met.

Steadying her emotions, she told Savannah what had happened: their parents had been killed two years ago as they were bringing a family of Transported back across the wasteland. They'd got caught in the open after dusk, and an attack by a band of Crazies had taken six lives. The next day, a search party came across the aftermath: torn clothes, pools of blood and the chilling absence of bodies.

Jean Fairfax took Solli and Tanis under her wing,

and moved them both into her quarters. She assigned a counselling team to their welfare, and monitored their progress. It took time. Tanis healed quickly, at least on the outside. He began to help Solli deal with the pain and the loss. He spoke to her of survival and of revenge. He gave her a purpose, toughened her resolve. He was her rock, her anchor, but he also became her weakness, her Kryptonite, when he was not with her. Her self-confidence diminished when she felt that he was in danger.

'I am getting better,' she admitted to Savannah. 'The tears stopped ages ago. I guess I'm all cried out, ready to move on. In eighteen months, I'll be trained and allowed to go out on rescue missions, with or without him. Then he can worry about *me*,' she added, with a wry smile.

Savannah suddenly found herself struggling with her own thoughts, particularly about her brother, Jago. There was a moment's silence before Solli spoke again.

'Sorry. All we seem to have talked about is me and my problems.' She studied Savannah's face. The left cheek was still puffed. The pomegranate-coloured bruising was fading, but there still remained a yellow tinge to her skin, and bloodshot veins streaked across the white of her eye like threads of red lightning.

'Is it still painful?' she asked.

For a moment, Savannah thought Solli had read her thoughts. 'No. I've decided he's not going to hurt me any more,' she replied.

'Sorry?' Solli answered, now a little confused, as she knew that the man who had inflicted the injuries on Savannah was dead.

'Oh! My face,' said Savannah, reassembling her thoughts. 'It aches, but I've been given plenty of painkillers. Apparently, my cheekbone's chipped and it'll take a while to settle down. Anyhow,' she said cheerily, 'oatcakes seem to have a *much* better effect. I don't suppose we could get a regular supply as a medicinal need?'

'Dream on,' replied Solli. 'You'd need to be in a medical centre bed for any remote chance of that happening.'

'Oh! I feel as if I need medical attention,' said Savannah, bringing her hand across her forehead and faking a swoon.

Both girls laughed, and enjoyed the warmth of shared humour.

Solli stood. 'I'd better go. I'm on catering duty tonight.' She paused. 'Before I do go, there's something I need to give you. Stand up.'

Savannah got to her feet, expecting a warm embrace of friendship.

Solli untied one of the tri-colour sashes from around her middle, reached forward and tied it around Savannah's waist.

'It's from Jean Fairfax,' she explained. 'She wanted to present it to you herself, but I persuaded her to let me have the pleasure.'

She hugged Savannah. 'I'll catch you later, maybe in the canteen.' She turned to leave and just as she stepped out of the cabin, her head reappeared, and she gave Savannah some parting words.

'By the way, I think Tanis is developing a crush on you!' she smiled.

17

FAILURE IS NOT AN OPTION

How Liam had made it back to the dinghy was more by luck than by judgement. Once he found his way to the storage depot and the open manhole, he managed to retrace the route back to the bridge. Without even attempting to put on the drysuit, he slithered across the mud like a half-exhausted seal pup, almost panicking at one point as he felt the mire sucking at the material of his trouser leg, its soft gelatinous tentacles threatening to pull him down. The tide was running as he struggled into the water, splashing and kicking his way towards the dinghy. He blindly gripped out at the lashing ropes for purchase, and gasping with exertion, he hauled himself up into the boat, rolled over onto his back, and gratefully laid back to regain his breath.

His total focus was on survival and getting back, but now a new sense of alarm hit him – daylight! He was totally exposed! No doubt, Diss would be searching for him. He scrabbled to the bow end and untied the mooring rope to watch it slip lazily away into the water. Grabbing both oars, he swung the dinghy around and out into the current, thankful for the speed with which it carried him towards the mouth of the estuary. Even so, he pulled hard on the oars, straining his arms, willing the boat to travel at an impossible pace.

The return journey to the reed beds, and the concealed jet skis, had indeed been much quicker, and he wearily steered himself into their sanctuary, not noticing that their tall, brown stalks surrounded him like the bars of a surreal prison cage. He tied up the dinghy to one of the jet skis and climbed aboard another. The energy cells built into the vehicle's body were so sensitive that they had continued to charge as soon as the grey light of dawn touched their solar panels. He pulled on the starter chord and smiled at the welcome bubbling-gurgle of the motor blades. Easing his way through the reeds, he twisted back the throttle and the jet ski surged out into open water. A wake spread out and across the bay, which followed behind him like an arrow, pointing towards the grey, crested waves and the horizon beyond.

As Liam headed for Opulence, his mood turned sombre. The prospect of how to deliver the bad news to Jago was daunting. He knew from Jago's reputation, that he did not react kindly to failure.

Liam had no idea how much of an understatement that was.

On arrival, with no regard for his cold, wet and bedraggled demeanour, he had been ushered down to a small room in the Transportation Centre.

Now, here he was, having just run through the details of the operation with Jago. Roth hovered around in the background, fidgeting like a junkie waiting for his next fix.

'Savannah killed him?' said Jago, with stunned disbelief. 'You watched her kill Brent?'

'Yes, sir,' affirmed Liam.

Jago rung his hands and leaned forward, so close that Liam could smell the stale alcohol on his breath. 'How come you're the only survivor?' he said with narrow-eyed suspicion.

'I guess because I kept calm and focused. Sir,' replied Liam, not allowing his expression to change, or his eyes to even flicker.

Jago turned to Roth and let out a sideways laugh. 'He guesses because he kept calm and focused!' he mockingly repeated.

Roth joined in with juvenile laughter, his shoulders hunched in spasms of near-hysteria.

Jago swivelled on his heels; his arm came up and pointed accusingly at Liam.

'You survived because you ran!' he shouted. He bared his teeth in red-faced anger. His expression froze, a vein pulsed in his neck and he stared, wide-eyed, at Liam. A few seconds passed, and then a schizophrenic change came over Jago. His shoulders dropped and tension fell away from his face, which melted into a calm, kindly countenance. His voice became almost child-like and matter-of-fact. He placed a finger on his chin and raised his eyebrows; his eyes looked towards the ceiling, his bottom lip pronounced in a pout.

'Perhaps, it's a good thing. If you hadn't taken the initiative, then you wouldn't have made it back here, and

I might not have found out what happened to Brent. I might never have learnt that Savannah is still alive.'

He started to pace slowly backwards and forwards in front of Liam, like a lion, sizing up its prey.

Liam was mentally struggling to focus on a safe end to his debrief. Beads of cold sweat escaped from the pores on his forehead, and leaked their salty moisture into his eyes. He didn't notice as Roth casually circled behind him.

'You see, Liam,' continued Jago, in the manner of an advising parent. 'It's very important that people are aware of who does the killing. It keeps you on your guard so that you can protect yourself and strike first.' He turned and faced Liam. 'For instance, Roth likes killing,' he smiled. 'Don't you, Roth?'

In that millisecond, Liam thought that the wink from Jago was meant for him, a sort of mocking gesture; then in the same thought, he knew his time had come.

The needle from the medi-gun pierced his cortex, just below the atlas vertebrae in his neck. The last thing Liam Donohue was aware of before his brain ceased to function, was a "snick!" in both of his ears. His body dropped like a marionette whose handler had become bored of supporting it.

As Roth replaced the medi-gun into its holster beneath his robes, Jago stepped over Liam's lifeless body and walked towards the door.

'Anything else that I can do?' said Roth; a smile of smug satisfaction creased across his face.

'Yes,' Jago replied, so calmly that it gave Roth a tinge of excitement. 'My parents – kill them.' Then, almost as an afterthought, he added, 'But make it quick.'

'And Bethany?' asked Roth. His cheek gave an involuntary twitch of anticipation.

'Leave her to me,' replied Jago. 'I'll take care of her. After all, I'll be the only family she has left.'

Later that day, two bodies were secretly and unceremoniously jettisoned from a desalination plant's waste tubes.

Eventually, their lifeless forms would float to the surface, arms spread-eagled as in a watery crucifixion. Death masks of empty, soulless eyes and mouths open in exclamation, as if to announce Bethany Loveday's transition to that of a cruelly orphaned child.

18

A CHANGE OF SCENERY

Two weeks after the attack, Jean Fairfax called another meeting. This time it was held at one of the lowest levels of the old tube network, in a carriage that had been converted into a small office and briefing room. All of the windows were blacked out, and Savannah noticed the sliding doors had steel brackets and padlocks attached to them. Inside, metal shelves, filled with cardboard box files, ran the whole length along one side of the carriage. An old, heavy oak desk, its surface busy with cluttered paperwork, took up the space at one end of the cabin. It was behind this that Jean Fairfax sat, straight-backed on an equally antique brown, leather-bound chair.

Tanis, Penny, Drake and Savannah stood facing the desk.

Jean Fairfax held out a buff-coloured paper file towards Drake.

'These are your orders, you're going to the countryside for a while,' she announced.

'Any particular reason?' asked Tanis.

'Yes. You all need a break, but don't get too excited,'

114

she explained. 'You three are tasked with getting Savannah skilled and mission-ready, so you're off to one of the training retreats.'

'Why me?' enquired Drake.

'Because I need someone with, let's say, a little more maturity, discipline and experience behind them, and tough enough to handle three teenagers.'

'I'm flattered,' replied Drake.

'I'm glad,' said Jean Fairfax. 'Because you're team leader, and responsible not only for Savannah's training, but also for ensuring *you all* gel and work together as an outstanding squad.

'Each of you bring a particular requirement to the group: Tanis, as young as you are, you're an outstanding field operative. Penny, you're a natural in psychology skills; you can prepare these guys to deal with any mind games and stress situations that may be thrown at them. Savannah, you have more knowledge with regards to the layout and structure of Opulence than any other person that we've been fortunate enough to have with us.'

'And what about me?' asked Drake.

'Well, someone's bound to get hurt, so they'll need a medic with them,' she answered.

'Thanks for that,' he replied, his offense obvious.

'Also,' she continued, 'if I was asked to choose the best person to cover my back in a hostile situation, without any question, it would be you.' She glanced at Savannah. 'No offence, but you do come a close second.

'You've got to trust each other with your lives. You've got to know what each other's thinking before they've thought it themselves. You're going to teach Savannah every technique and trick in the book, and in return, she's going to teach you everything she knows about Opulence, so you'll feel as if you were born there.'

'When do we leave for the retreat?' asked Tanis.

'It's all in the file,' she nodded.

Drake folded back the cover, glanced down at the front sheet and closed it shut again.

'One hour,' he said to the others.

After packing a change of clothes and a few personal requirements into small holdalls, Savannah and Penny met Tanis and Drake back at the ticket barriers. Tanis threw a shy smile in Savannah's direction, and then avoided further eye contact.

At Drake's feet were four large backpacks.

'These are your field packs,' he said. 'Sleeping bags. Camo-jackets. Ponchos. Your basic survival gear. They also contain your field rations and a water bottle, which will have to last you for the next twenty-four hours. You can pack anything you've brought with you as long as it'll fit in,' he instructed. 'If it doesn't, it stays here.'

He passed Penny and Tanis a wooden crossbow and a quiver of feathered bolts each, and then from his backpack he pulled out a large hunting knife sheathed and attached to a brown leather belt.

'This is for you,' he said, handing it to Savannah. 'We already know that you can use one.'

She weighed it in her hands, and then withdrew the highly polished and serrated blade. The flawless steel reflected her eyes back at her, and she momentarily studied herself before she slid the weapon back into its sheath. She buckled it around her waist and tied the leg chord so that it hung securely down the outside of her thigh. The pressure of the weapon on her leg filled her with mixed feelings. She hoped she would not need to use it, but also knew that if she needed to, she would.

When they finished reorganising their gear, Drake looked at his watch and swung his own pack over his shoulder. 'Right. Time to go,' he announced. He strode towards the lift, which only a couple of weeks ago had brought them down from the surface. His finger jabbed the black call button and within a minute, the lift arrived. The mesh gates and steel doors slid back noisily, and along with the others, Savannah stepped into the familiar graffiti-strewn interior. The overhead fluorescent tubes seemed to flicker a nervous welcome to her. Drake took a key chain from his pocket and thumbed through a selection of small keys. Finally, finding the correct one, he inserted it into the control panel and gave it a quarter turn. A red button marked "service" lit up and he punched it with his thumb. The gate and doors closed with a metallic squeal, and with a slight lurch, the lift descended.

Sixty seconds later the doors slid back with their now familiar, noisy complaint, to reveal a dimly lit platform, much shorter than any Savannah had so far seen. Waiting on the track in front of them was a pump trolley; this time, four heavily built men dressed in fatigues, and with the muscular physique of body builders, stood waiting patiently at the handles. Attached was a four-seat trailer. The seats faced each other, two on two with enough room between them for their packs.

'Four to Broadway,' announced Drake, as they took their seats.

'Four to Broadway, it is,' replied one of the men.

'Sit back and enjoy the ride, ladies and gentlemen; we've got a couple of hours ahead of us,' said Drake.

Savannah turned to Penny. 'Have you made this trip before?'

'A few times,' she replied. 'My most enduring memory is as soon as you lose all sense of feeling in your arse, thankfully we get a crew change, and a chance to stretch our legs.'

'I can't believe that you haven't figured out a mechanical way to power these things,' said Savannah.

'I think that they had a go, but it ended up choking everyone on fumes. There's not enough ventilation in the tunnels. On top of that, the noise was deafening, so they gave it up as a bad job,' replied Penny.

As the trolley journeyed, the curved brickwork of the tunnel just ahead of them was illuminated by two hurricane lamps, which hung on short poles at the front, creating a constant halo effect. Savannah, however, sat facing the rear of the cart, and she recoiled as dark shapes skittered across the tracks and melted into the darkness.

'Rats,' explained Penny. 'We don't get any trouble from them. They've spent so much time living in the dark that their eyes have become over-sensitive to light. Mostly, they're a food source for our other "friends". She jerked her thumb towards the roof.

Savannah glanced up at the black, pod-like forms that hung in clusters above them. Some stretched their membrane wings in annoyance at the sound of the rattling trolley, which dared to disturb their slumber. She caught glimpses of glinting, beady eyes and sharp white fangs as the colony emerged into the lamplight, and melted back into the darkness.

She shivered in revulsion and pushed herself closer to Penny for comfort.

'They're just bats,' said Penny.

'I've never seen a real one before, let alone so many, and I hate them already,' Savannah confirmed with another shudder.

The monotonous chatter of the wheels on the tracks was only broken when they stopped at a small sub-station, by which time, as Penny had predicted, Savannah had lost all sense of feeling between her thighs and her hips. To her relief, they were allowed to stretch their legs by walking around on a small wooden platform for a few minutes while a fresh crew, with fresh arms, prepared to take over the pump trolley.

About an hour after the crew change, Penny nudged Savannah, and signalled ahead. A silver-grey light began to spread along the tunnel. As they continued, the greyness shifted into a bluish hue, which heralded an end to the underground. Light reflected along the steel rails, and revealed the ruddy brickwork of an oval opening. A sudden, bright sunlit sky caused them all to shield their eyes, as they rolled out into the open. Warm sunlight caressed their heads and faces. Fresh air washed into their lungs, and their senses shook off the stale gloom that had shrouded them during their journey.

The trolley slowed to a halt, and Savannah's eyes blinked themselves into accepting a clear vision. New voices approached from either side of the tracks. Diss Commandos, three men and a woman, all in combats and armed with crossbows, exchanged greetings with the trolley crew. Sullen and straight-faced, one of them wandered up to Drake. His thick-soled black boots crunched on the grey and black-flecked gravel.

'Documentation,' he said. It sounded more of an order than a request.

Drake pulled the file from his pack, opened it, took out a heavily typed sheet, and passed it to the man, who proceeded to read through it, occasionally glancing up to scrutinise each of their features in turn. Satisfied, and without a change of expression or a single word, he passed the sheet back to Drake and returned to his companions.

'Well, they're happy in their work,' said Savannah sarcastically.

'You can't blame them,' said Tanis. 'They're from City Command, on a three month tour of duty out here in the countryside. They're bored to tears and itching to get back into action, out on rescue patrols, tackling Crazies and the like.'

After a short, muted conversation, the four Commandos stood back and sternly waved the trolley on.

The rest of the journey continued at a steady pace until they turned a bend, and Broadway came into sight. It was a restored rail depot, straight out of the twentieth century, with four platforms and a large locomotive shed, along with a couple of single-storey warehouses. There was also a high presence of Diss Commandos.

This was the beginning and end of two rail points that were now used to access several countryside community compounds. Mostly, they functioned to transport produce and essentials into the city bases via the underground network.

There was no longer an overground mainline into the city. Too much of it was blocked by the tangled remains of crashed and wrecked commuter trains. Even if it were possible to restore the link, it would still be too dangerous, and be liable to debilitating attacks by gangs of Crazies.

The most impressive achievement was the fully restored steam locomotive, with a row of five goods wagons and one passenger carriage connected behind it, which stood majestically at one of the platforms. This was a testament to a long-dead national rail network.

The trolley slowed into a siding, and was brought smoothly to a halt alongside a small hut. As they climbed down onto the gravel track, Drake raised a hand to the crew. 'Thanks, guys,' he shouted. 'The next time you're in Base One, I'll buy you a brew.'

'We'll keep you to that, for sure,' one of them answered with a soft Irish accent and a smile.

Drake led the way up a short flight of wooden steps and onto one of the platforms. A large black and white sign above the platform announced, "Broadway Junction". What was once a busy commuter station had, over the years been reclaimed and transformed into a military-style transport centre. Brown and green paint was the order of the day; signs simply and plainly declared the function of the buildings. There were no advertisements, no encouraging banners, and no timetable. If you didn't know where you were going, then you had to ask. Either that, or you shouldn't be here in the first place.

The locomotive idly hissed and belched steam; its dormant power suppressed by brass valves and the skills of an engineer, who stood in his blue overalls at the footplate looking every bit like a working class refugee from a past era. The smell of engine grease and coal smoke drifted over the group as they followed Drake along the platform, until he stopped at the only passenger carriage. The cream and maroon livery still sported the words, "South Coast Railways".

Once on board, they chose to sit together, not that they didn't have the pick of sixty-odd seats, as no one else appeared to be travelling with them. After retrieving their water bottles and rations, they stacked their packs across the aisle and settled into their places.

'How long is this part of the journey?' asked Savannah.

'About an hour and a half,' replied Drake. 'It's down to how much steam the engineer gets up and whether or not he has a deadline to make.'

'And then we reach our destination?' she pressed.

'No. We'll have at least an hour's trek,' answered Drake.

'Or, we could grab some bicycles at Little Halt,' announced Tanis.

'Or, we could trek, enjoy the scenery and get some exercise,' emphasised Drake. 'You heard Commander Fairfax; this is a training operation, not a holiday. Besides, I'm team leader, so we do it my way.' Tanis and Penny groaned, rolled their eyes heavenward and patted their mouths in a display of boredom.

'So, Little Halt is the name of this mysterious place that we're going too?' asked Savannah.

'No,' answered Tanis. 'That's just a stop-off point. Our final destination is Greentrees; don't let the nice name fool you. In the old world, it used to be an operations centre for special army forces. Now it's one of our countryside training camps. Beautiful setting and stunning scenery, miles from anywhere, and lots of unusual wildlife for company: a bit like heaven and hell all rolled into one.'

The shriek of the train's whistle rent through the air to announce the power of the iron beast was about to be released. The carriage reverberated, juddered and rocked slowly forward. The platform rolled past, to give way to a panorama of open fields and distant hills. From behind flat clouds, an afternoon sun streaked out narrow rays of light, which flickered across the carriage windows.

'Greentrees,' mused Savannah. 'Anywhere is better than Opulence.'

19

WILD LAVENDER

Just one small platform dominated the aptly named Little Halt, and in the long shadows of a late afternoon, the expert and practiced judgement of the train driver ensured that their carriage came to a halt along its short length, so as to allow them to alight safely.

They watched the train as it chuffed into the distance, leaving a smoke-plumed trail of farewell, which drifted lazily up into an otherwise clear sky.

'Where's it going now?' Savannah asked.

'To drop off and pick up supplies at a couple of coastal Bases,' replied Penny. 'I've never been that far down the line, so I can't tell you much about it. Have you ever been, Tanis?'

'No. Never really been bothered,' he replied. 'What about you, Drake?'

'Went there on a tour of duty a few years ago. Grey sea. Grey sky; and they spend most of their time trying to catch fish that taste like crap! That's about it as far as I can remember.' He hoisted up his backpack and led the way along the grey, foot worn flagstones of the platform.

A wooden, single-storey building served as a storage area-come-waiting room, and Tanis paused at its open door.

'Look, I told you. Bikes!' he indicated to Penny and Savannah.

With their front wheels slotted into a metal rack along the length of the far wall, half a dozen assorted old bicycles stood in a row, handle bar to handle bar.

'That's as close as you're going to get to them,' shouted Drake over his shoulder. 'Now move it!'

Tanis shrugged in disappointment and resignation, and followed along as they trailed behind Drake across the single rail track.

'This is more like it,' announced Drake. He led the way up a zigzag flight of steep, wooden steps, which were cut into a twenty-metre or so high embankment.

It was late spring and the grassy banks bustled with all shades of colour; wild flowers the like of which Savannah had never seen. Her wonderment grew at the natural beauty unfolding around her. She relished at the unspoilt surroundings, breathing in the splendour of the remote landscape. A flock of swifts silhouetted against the sky; they wheeled above her with their scythe-like wings and short forked tails. The air echoed with their shrill cries of freedom and delight, as they chased down and fed on swarms of small airborne insects.

Tanis craned his neck in pursuit. 'At least there are some beautiful things left in this world,' he mused.

After about half an hour of walking, as pretty as the vista was, Savannah began to fall behind; the muscles in her legs stiffened and threatened cramp. Each foot became heavier to lift.

Penny looked back over her shoulder. 'Come on, slowcoach, we've got another hour's walk yet.'

They started to climb another ridge and Savannah gritted her teeth as she mentally steeled herself to fight off the pain. When she reached the top, she noticed with slight embarrassment that she was the only one out of breath. To her relief, none of the others were looking in her direction. They were distracted by the view.

They stood on the edge of a chalk ridge. Spread out ahead of them was a low plain. At its centre, the desolate remains of what was once a small market town formed a grey, sullen scar on the landscape. The pinnacle of a church spire rose up and pointed somewhat accusingly at the sky. Here and there, islands of green, yellow and purple flourished amongst the ruins. Nature asserted its right to reclaim the land.

Now, a hundred and fifty miles from Base One, the sky was a patchwork of slow-moving, white cloudbanks. For short moments, the sun broke through ragged holes to bathe the earth with warmth. Then, like a mischievous child, it would retreat behind a veil of altostratus.

'Beautiful, isn't it?' said Penny. 'Just smell that air,' she elated, and blissfully breathed in.

'It's almost paradise,' said Savannah.

Penny turned to her. 'Don't get fooled,' she warned. 'When night-time comes, it has its fair share of creatures out there just waiting to kill you.'

'Never mind the air,' Drake interrupted. 'Just think of the food at the compound: eggs straight from the chickens, fresh meat, and milk in the coffee!' He shrugged his backpack, and strode purposely off along the path.

Penny trotted after him. 'Is that all you think about? Food?'

'I'm a growing man, Penny. I need my nourishment, and it's a good incentive to get me through the wilderness training,' he answered, with a hungry conviction.

Tanis stood quietly, seemingly feeling awkward to find himself left alone with Savannah. He chewed his lip and gave her a coy, sideways glance.

'I guess we'd better catch them up,' she smiled warmly.

As she turned, cramp bit into her calf muscles and she hobbled forward like a toddler exploring its first steps.

'You're not going to get far like that,' he said.

"It's okay. I'll walk it off,' she insisted, only to limp another two paces.

He stepped in front of her and swung his pack to the ground. 'Sit down. I can fix it.'

Pain and dignity triumphed over her stubbornness. It was one of those rare occasions when she gave in.

'Roll up your trouser legs; I'll be back in a minute,' he said. He disappeared over the side of the ridge and into the long, green grass.

'I've heard of some chat up lines in my time, but that one beats them all,' she shouted after him.

No sooner had she done as he'd asked, than his smiling face appeared from the ditch, rising up through the slender grass stalks. He was carrying a bunch of purple-flowered stems.

He knelt before her, and stripped a handful of the small delicate buds off the stalks before he rolled them between his palms. The scent hit her almost immediately, as he started to massage the pulp into her leg muscles.

She threw her head back as the aroma filled her senses, and she groaned with relief as the tension began to dissolve beneath his hands.

'What *is* that?' she sighed.

'Wild lavender. It grows around here; it's great for aches and pains.'

He started to knead her other leg, working his thumbs along the tendons and into the muscles behind her knee.

She looked down at him. 'It doesn't hurt that far up.'

Tanis pulled his hands away and went several shades of red. 'Sorry, I was just...'

She leaned forward and put a hand on his arm. 'I'm teasing,' she said. 'Carry on; do your magic.'

He continued, tentatively, slower, but no less effectively, until after a short while, he leaned back on his haunches. 'There, that should keep you going until we reach Greentrees,' he announced, as he rubbed the residue from his hands.

Savannah jolted back from her daydream – a fairy tale world, featuring herself, Tanis, and a field of lavender. The images that she conjured up caused her neck and cheeks to flush and she hastily rolled down her trouser legs.

'Are you okay?' he enquired.

'Sure. Sure. Just enjoying the moment,' she flustered. She got to her feet and dropped her pack twice in a clumsy attempt to get her arms through the straps. 'I mean, enjoying the relief... from the pain,' she quickly added.

They hurried along in silence, both of them running thoughts over in their heads, but not able to translate them into comfortable words.

Penny and Drake had slowed down their pace as soon as Tanis and Savannah dropped out of sight. Although Drake felt they were relatively safe this far from the city, he didn't want to take any unnecessary chances, and he finally stopped. 'We'll give them ten minutes,' he told Penny, 'before I go back and kick their slow arses.'

Penny was a little more sympathetic. 'Don't be so hard on them. You were a teenager once,' she reminded him.

'Just because you're a couple of months shy of your twentieth birthday doesn't make you worldly-wise. Oh, great Penny,' he joked.

Shortly, Tanis and Savannah came into view. Drake shouted his customary 'Get a move on' to them, and eventually ushered them past to take the lead.

Penny couldn't help but smile to herself as she caught the scent of wild lavender, which drifted from Savannah in an unseen cloud.

20

The Cabin

The training camp consisted of a dozen wood cabins spread out amongst a hundred and fifty square miles of forest and rugged valleys, beyond which lay a vast open plain scattered with the burial mounds and stone monuments of a prehistoric society.

Just as dusk threw its grey, foggy blanket over the surrounding fields, the temperature dropped and brought an evening chill. The group approached a tree line at the eastern edge of the forest and entered to follow a well-worn pathway into the sentinel shadows of the woods. After a short walk, they grouped together in a small clearing where tendrils of mist began to shift and curl around their ankles like the transparent ghosts of restless snakes.

Above, a full moon bathed the landscape in a silver sheen, and streaks of broken clouds allowed clusters of distant diamond stars to flicker their mystery across the cosmos.

'Okay,' said Drake. 'I'll take the lead, Penny follow up, and then Savannah and Tanis can cover the rear. Load up, safety catches on and keep in single file.'

Savannah watched as they loaded up their crossbows. 'Are you expecting trouble?'

'Thankfully, for whatever reason, the Crazies don't like it out here,' explained Tanis. 'They seem to prefer living in the squalor of the city ruins, but we still have a variety of animals to contend with. Most of them escaped or were let loose from zoos and wildlife parks, and then there were others that found freedom from genetic research laboratories with the help of animal rights activists. Unfortunately, there's been a lot of crossbreeding over the years, and that has resulted in some pretty vicious and nasty hybrids.'

'You mean, like our friend with the crazy eye, and the giant hog?' asked Savannah.

'Oh, they're pussy cats compared with what you could find yourself facing out here,' chimed in Drake. 'In the main, the freaky ones tend to hunt and feed on the weaker, more natural animals, but there are some real mean ones that have developed a taste for human flesh: we're a speciality to them, like prime steak or caviar.'

'If this is a training zone, why don't you clear the area of them?' asked Savannah.

'Because they serve a purpose,' said Drake. 'If you're going to survive in the wastelands, you're not going to learn how to do it with the safety of role-play. Out here, you get the real deal. Just something for you to think about before your training,' he smiled. 'Now, let's get to it and move on.'

Savannah's hand fell onto the moulded grip of her knife; she felt comforted by its presence, but inwardly she wished for something more substantial.

The track from the clearing led them through an avenue of pine trees; a soft carpet of past-life needles layered the floor, and the woody, herbal smell of resin permeated the crisp evening air. As they moved deeper into the forest, it opened up its sounds to them. Rustling and scuttling from nearby undergrowth, small mammalian feet pattering on dried leaves, foraging for food, or running from danger. Boughs sighed and creaked in the dark canopy of shadows above them. The sudden, annoyed shrill of a small bird as it fluttered away, disturbed from its nocturnal resting by their approach.

To Savannah, the sounds were a nervous cacophony to her ears. She shifted her head from side to side with each noise, her body tense and alert. More than once she tripped or stumbled, until Drake raised his hand to a halt. He turned and addressed Savannah.

'There are animals all around us. They live here. Most of them are scared of us and will keep out of sight. It's the really big ones that can hurt us, and believe me, you'll know when they're around! So, until one of us tells you otherwise, chill out and enjoy the walk.' He turned and resumed leading them along the track.

For a while, they continued in their own thoughts until Savannah whispered urgently to Penny, 'Sorry, but I need to pee.'

'S'okay, I was just thinking the same,' Penny replied. 'Guys,' she announced, 'us girls need to use the bushes.'

Drake and Tanis raised their eyes at each other.

'Okay,' breathed Drake. 'Knock yourselves out, but don't go too far.'

Penny led Savannah into a leafy screen of shrubbery.

After a few minutes, and much rustling and giggling, they reappeared, relieved and smiling.

As they set off in procession again, Tanis quietly withdrew his knife and used the tip of it to flick a large red and black spider into the undergrowth. Its slow but determined crawl across Savannah's backpack towards the soft skin of her neck was brought to an abrupt and silent end.

'Just a word of advice,' he whispered into her unknowing ear. 'If you see any large red and black spiders, steer clear of them; they can give you a very nasty bite!'

The rest of the journey was uneventful, and Savannah settled into the group's steady walking pace along the forest track, which sometimes seemed to close in around them almost oppressively, or at other times it would widen out enough for them to walk in pairs.

'About half a mile to go,' Drake announced. 'Come on, let's pick up the pace and jog it!' Without looking back, he accelerated away from them.

'We'd better keep up with him,' encouraged Penny. 'Otherwise, we'll never hear the last of it.'

Six minutes later, when they broke out of the woods and into a large clearing, Savannah realised once again how out of condition she was. She couldn't conceal the fatigue in her legs or her shortness of breath as she came to a halt in front of Drake. She put her hands on her knees to support her exhausted and shaking body.

'Looks like I've got my work cut out,' he grumbled.

Penny patted Savannah on the shoulder and almost sent her to the floor.

'Well, here's home sweet home for a while,' she announced as she helped Savannah to straighten up.

A large log building dominated the glade, and even in the moonlight, Savannah could tell that it was pretty basic. The cabin was built in a Scandinavian style, with round logs interlocking at each corner, and a decked porch along one side. Time and nature had well and truly covered whatever material had been used for the sloping roof, with a layer of moss and foliage. At one end of the structure, a grey stone chimney broke through the roofline. The absence of smoke escaping from its stack warned Savannah that it would be no warmer inside than in the chilly night air where they stood.

They gathered around Drake on the porch, and he took down a hurricane lamp, which hung on a bracket by the door. He gave it a gentle shake, and satisfied there was fuel in the reservoir, lit it with a small spark lighter from his pocket.

'Let's see how tidy the place is,' he said, as he lifted the metal latch and pushed the heavy logwood door. Without any complaint from its hinges, it glided easily and silently inwards.

Savannah was pleasantly surprised by the interior. With boarded and panelled walls, it seemed less rustic, and more homely than she had anticipated. All of the furniture looked as though it had been crafted from natural timber. A stout wooden breakfast table and four chairs sat at the centre of the room, with two bunks on either side, set against the walls. At the far end, the kitchen area consisted of a small iron cooking range, and an open fireplace. Two large wooden storage chests sat just inside the door.

'Okay,' announced Drake, setting the lamp down on the table. 'It's just gone nine and we have an early start in the morning. I hate to be the chauvinist, but Tanis and myself will do the man thing, and go and rustle up something to eat. You two light the rest of the lamps, haul in some firewood and get the stove and fire going. If you've still got time before we get back, fill up the barrel with fresh water from the hand pump.'

Before either of the girls could object, he and Tanis disappeared through the door and back outside.

Savannah looked at Penny. 'What a cheek! What did his last servant die of?'

'I've been asking myself the same question for years,' she replied. 'Come on, at least they're doing something useful.'

After fires and lamps were lit, it didn't take long before Drake and Tanis returned with an assortment of wild vegetables and two freshly killed rabbits, which they all set about preparing and cooking up a large pot of stew. Savannah's initial introduction to two bloody rabbit carcasses took her on an emotional journey of sadness and curiosity. It was only when she realised how hungry she was that she decided the animals had died for a good cause. (At least, that's what her conscience told her.)

In a now warm cabin, they lounged in their chairs around the table, the cooking pot empty, their plates clean, and their stomachs full. The aroma of fresh cooking hung in the air.

'That was delicious,' sighed Penny.

Drake let out a loud, satisfied belch. 'Ditto,' he announced.

'Pig!' scolded Penny.

'I'll see if I can catch you one for tomorrow evening's meal,' said Drake. He pushed himself to his feet and collected the dishes and cutlery. 'Tanis, bring the pots and pans, we'll wash it all at the water pump.'

'Do we have to? I'm really comfortable,' he complained as he cradled his stomach.

'You know the rules,' said Drake. He gave Tanis' dreadlocks a playful tug. 'Women cook. Men wash up. Besides, we have to do our duty.'

Tanis and Drake left the cabin, leaving a draught of chill air as the door momentarily opened and closed. Savannah raised her eyebrows with irritated astonishment, and looked at Penny.

'I hope he's joking,' she remarked.

'Take no notice. It's one of Drake's wind-ups. He's just testing you,' Penny advised.

'Well, I might just get some fresh air myself,' said Savannah, rising from her chair.

'I'd leave it until they're back,' suggested Penny.

'Why?'

'It could be embarrassing if you go out now. They're probably scenting.'

'Scenting?'

'Scenting,' repeated Penny. 'Peeing around the perimeter. To keep unwanted animals away.'

Savannah's eyes widened. 'Oh!' she exclaimed, as she put her hand to her mouth and sat back down. A moment passed and she impishly looked at Penny. 'Now I really am tempted!'

Outside the cabin, Drake and Tanis caught the sound of girlish laughter escaping from within.

'How are you doing, big boy?' Drake called across the clearing. 'Do you want me to give you a hand?' he said, mocking.

'I can manage quite well on my own, thank you,' Tanis called back.

About a metre in front of him, there was a rustling from the dark undergrowth. His bladder froze and he zipped up his combats, cautiously taking a step backwards. He slowly drew his knife from its sheath, and screwed his eyes up as he tried to make out any movement in the shadows. The foliage just in front of him shifted slightly, and then, to his relief, a small, wet hedgehog waddled out. Its black, beady eyes looked accusingly up at Tanis, before it gave an indignant little snort and shimmied out across the clearing.

Tanis realised that he had been holding his breath. He exhaled slowly through his lips. 'I won't tell anyone if you won't,' he whispered after it.

21

LIES

With the fresh stain of false tears on his cheeks, Jago sat on the edge of Beth's bed. He wore the solemn expression of someone who was giving confession to a priest, but it was just a mask of deceit. Beth was curled up in a foetal position, bedclothes tangled around her grief-racked frame. She had ceased to cry out loud for more than half an hour now, and her red-framed eyes stared out, tired and puffed with emotion. She clutched at a white bed sheet, and absently chewed on a spittle-soaked corner of the cloth.

'Tell me one more time what happened. I want to hear it again,' she said, with a fragile voice.

Jago played the grieving son. He took in a deep breath and recounted his story of lies.

'A Transportation guard spotted their bodies floating in the sea, just below one of the eastern observation decks. He raised the alarm, and a rescue party was alerted. By the time I got there, all efforts to revive them had ceased. Their necks had been broken; they were dead before they were thrown into the sea.' He paused and rubbed the ball of his hand against his forehead, purposely adding a stifled choke for effect. 'I will never forgive myself. The last time that we spoke, we argued, and now I'll never be able to tell them how much I love them.' He forced out another false sob. 'Now, the only family I have is you.'

'And Savannah,' whispered Beth.

The hairs on the back of Jago's head bristled. He clenched his jaw. *Now*, he thought, *now is the time to drive home the knife.*

'There's something I haven't told you,' he continued. 'You must be brave.' He turned and placed a hand softly on Beth's leg. He bit his cheek, hard. Blood ran in his mouth. He savoured the taste and the pain. He welcomed the tears.

Beth raised herself up on one elbow; she searched his expression with a new horror.

'What is it?'

'I found some wooden beads in our father's hand,' he lied. 'He was holding them tightly in his fist. I recognised them. I knew where I'd seen them before – Davis, one of our household's Servanti, used to wear them around his wrist; they were given to him by Savannah. I've never really trusted Davis, so I asked the Transportation Police to question him. I can't remember all of the details, but eventually he confessed that he led our parents to their deaths.'

'Why would he do that?' asked Beth.

Jago chose his words carefully and spoke them slowly. 'Because, Savannah sent word for him to do so.'

'No!' she choked.

'It's true,' Jago pressed.

'Why would she do such a thing?' Beth sobbed.

Jago closed his hands around Beth's. He fixed his eyes upon hers. 'Savannah has joined the Diss in Earthland. She blames our parents for her Transportation. So bitter was her anger, that she arranged for assassins to kill them out of revenge and jealousy. She wanted to punish you and I. She sent us a message, Beth. It said, "*I have no family*".'

With unnatural ease, and without conscience, Jago continued to spread his web of deception.

'Davis enticed them to the lower levels. He promised them news of Savannah, but he abandoned them to their killers. You know she has always been too friendly with the Servanti. She used to spend more time amongst them than with us, her own family and at times, she chose their company over ours,' he plied. He stood and paced across the room, and turned his emotions into a rehearsed fury. 'I will find those who are guilty, even if I have to Transport every Servanti on Opulence in the process. I will see to it that Earthland is torn apart in the search for our parent's killers.' He threw himself to the floor, to Beth's knees. 'I will protect you. I will not let your sister harm you.' He forced one more false teardrop to fall down his reddened cheek.

Beth's eyes narrowed, her face became flushed with anger. A dark veil poisoned her memories and a cold fist wrapped itself around her heart. The words slipped easily from her lips. 'I have no sister.'

Jago buried his face in her lap; he concealed the satisfied and evil grin that spread like a vicious scar across his face.

★

In the following days and months, Beth became a constant presence at his side. He fed her with his cruel hatred. He poisoned her thoughts with distrust against all Servanti, and he cultivated a loathing in her towards the Diss.

He enrolled her into the rank of Transportation Cadet, and entrusted Roth with her training in all matters concerning the defence of Opulence and her allegiance to the Elite Fortunata. She became brainwashed into what he wanted her to be – and everything that Savannah was not. He removed her compassion, destroyed her generosity of thought. He infected her with lies and propaganda; the adolescent fourteen-year-old became cynical and egoistic, not caring for or interested in anything, except for Jago and his teachings of self-preservation, control and revenge.

While Savannah was going through her own journey of mental and physical challenges, Beth was indoctrinated into Jago's world of dominance and aberration. If thoughts of Savannah ever infiltrated her resolve, they were accompanied by feelings of hatred and ambitions of vengeance.

Jago also used the demise of their parents to fuel his ambitions. He organised rallies around the squares of Opulence and preached his damning philosophy to drive a wedge of mistrust amongst the communities. He inflamed suspicion, and with prejudice and disrespect, he further reduced the social standing of the Servanti. He accused the Masters of failing to protect its citizens, and he demanded a full review of the Fortunata's safety be conducted, starting with increased security measures across Opulence.

Everywhere he went, a posse of loyal Transportation Police surrounded him. The Elite Fortunata campaigned for him; they celebrated his false wisdom and spread his words throughout the population. Popular opinion grew into a baying voice of greed and selfishness, until, without ceremony or formality, the Fortunata Council were ousted in a coup, and the Elite Fortunata, with Jago at their head, stepped seamlessly into place.

Recognising their impending demise, the Masters retreated to their inner chambers, seeking the protection of their loyal guards. In a desperate act to hold onto power, they prohibited all public gatherings and decreed an immediate curfew. They demanded that Jago present himself to them, to face their judgement and punishment.

When he received word of the command, Jago relished the news. 'We have them like rats in a trap,' he told Roth. 'This is almost too easy,' he regaled. 'Let us end it this day. Send word that I will meet with them in an hour. In the meantime, there is work for your busy hands, my friend.'

Jago gave his instructions and Roth smiled his smile of death's ambassador. 'I'll be there to welcome you,' he said in gleeful anticipation.

By the time Jago and his entourage reached the chamber steps, a large mob had broken down the doors. On seeing him, they parted to let him through. Roth appeared from inside, his face a mask of false distress. He stepped over the prostrate body of a purple-faced guard.

'There has been another attack on our sanctity,' he announced. 'The Diss have found their way onto

Opulence and poisoned some of the ventilation shafts. All inside are dead.'

He reached within his robes and retrieved the object of his false evidence, and brandished it above his head: a torn piece of cloth that bore the tri-colours of the Diss. 'I found this where they entered the basement to release the gas,' he lied.

Jago looked into the chamber at the crumpled figures. He studied the ghastly faces, distorted and agonised in the last moments of life. Eyes fixed and staring, bulging in their sockets like oversized marbles. Some had their mouths open, still searching in death for a last gasp of unpolluted air. Black lips pushed apart by blue protruding tongues.

Jago grasped the coloured rag and held it out to the crowd. 'This,' he announced, 'this must strengthen our resolve. It is time to act. It is time to go to war, to claim back that which is rightly ours – Earthland! I will lead you. I will take on that responsibility. Death to our enemies! Death to the Diss!' He threw the cloth to the floor and ground his heel into it.

He spread his arms out in submissive acknowledgement, his head turning and nodding at the baying crowd. As one, the mob cheered, frenzied by the event.

'Jago! Jago! Jago!' the chant began.

He leaned his head sideways towards Roth, and beneath the chanting clamour, he whispered, 'My dear friend, the deception is complete. You have excelled yourself. A body count of at least thirty; it must be a personal record.'

22

FEAR IS GOOD

After a loud awakening by Drake, the first dawn saw Savannah set with the task of chopping and stacking logs. Penny stripped down to a tee shirt and combat shorts, and demonstrated the technique of using a long handled axe. Savannah could not contain her surprise and admiration for Penny's lithe and muscular frame, and when Penny swung the axe with ease, and split a sizeable log with minimum effort and maximum efficiency, Savannah exclaimed – 'That's damn near half a tree!'

With a mixture of determination and a stubborn resolve not to show any weakness, Savannah laid into the task, pushing herself mentally and physically. Each log became an image of Jago. Each slice of the axe dispensed his retribution.

That evening, a quietly impressed Drake gently wrapped her blistered hands in a soothing salve. She ate her supper slowly, then she collapsed onto her bunk; fatigue numbed her aching muscles and allowed her to drift into a dreamless sleep.

On the second day, with slightly tender, but

nevertheless remarkably blister-less hands, she was up, outside the cabin by six thirty, kitted, and in line with the others for a twenty-five mile hike and orienteering exercise. Drake raised an eyebrow at her, gave her a quick up and down inspection, nodded in approval and gave her three words of encouragement: 'Don't fall behind.'

Again, in the evening, she ate her supper on autopilot before stumbling into her bunk, and slipping into an uneventful sleep. Her routine became early to bed and early to rise. Her body clock adjusted until eventually, rising at 6 a.m. developed into a natural habit for her.

The days merged into a seamless blur of physical tasks, treks, field craft and survival exercises. Tanis helped Savannah with her crossbow and catapult skills, to discover that she proved to be just as proficient a markswoman with those weapons as she was with the ball-bearing gun. It wasn't long before a smiling Tanis finally and unceremoniously presented her with her own crossbow and quiver of bolts.

Drake demonstrated his impressive ability and knowledge of various martial arts skills and disciplines. He passed on techniques in his favourite expertise of Krav Maga, a particularly lethal form of hand-to-hand combat, which had been developed in the old world by Israeli special forces. Savannah channelled her anger and resentment into the lessons with such ferocity that Drake was inwardly both alarmed and in awe at her ability to handle the punishing physical regime that he put her through. No matter how hard he pushed her, she absorbed the pain and in some instances, gave him back as good as she got. At one point, he quietly confided in

Tanis that she had the ability to be a "bloody awesome" opponent.

In complete contrast, both as a group and with each of them individually, Penny held meditation and counselling sessions. Savannah found the self-hypnosis techniques particularly helpful in de-stressing and conditioning herself to cope with her worries, both real and imagined. Penny's mantra of *"If you change the way you look at things – the things you look at change"* helped Savannah to overcome most of her anxieties, although it slightly contradicted Drake's philosophy of *"Fear is good; it helps you to survive"*.

Now, a month into the retreat, the everyday muscular aches and pains that assaulted her body weeks earlier had dissipated. She could feel the change in her physique. A more toned, muscular and conditioned Savannah emerged, fuelled by the intense exercise and tasks set by Drake, along with eating healthy, fresh, natural foods. Her mind was more alert and focused. Sometimes, as sleep closed its end-of-day curtain across her mind, she wondered what her parents would think of her now, and if Beth would still greet her with the same sisterly love.

When the next opportunity arose, she was determined to confront them, for good or for bad. She needed closure and resolution. She missed them.

★

The group were relaxing around an open fire, after having fed themselves on a particularly substantial supper of wild root vegetables and venison steaks, the latter acquired earlier in the morning, courtesy of a spectacular crossbow shot by Tanis. Once she had tasted the culinary results, Savannah overcame her dewy-eyed remorse for the young deer.

'What's on the agenda for tomorrow?' Tanis asked.

'A little session of Krav to start the day off,' replied Drake. 'Followed by some long-overdue field medical training. After lunch we need to get the cabin domestics up to date, and then you can get in some R and R.'

'Hang on,' said Tanis. 'Did you mean rest and relaxation? You haven't let us have any free time at all since we arrived here. What's the catch?' he added suspiciously.

'Oh, ye of little faith,' smiled Drake. 'I just thought it's about time we had a game of Night Tag.'

'That's great,' said Penny unenthusiastically. 'Except that you *always* win.'

'I can't help it that I'm so good,' he replied with a knowing smile.

'Okay, what am I letting myself in for now?' asked Savannah.

Between them, they explained to her that Night Tag involved a three-hour hike after dark. On top of that, they'd be blindfolded, with their hands tied, and Drake would lead them to a remote location and leave them there. Their objective was to free themselves while he made his way back to the cabin. Once there, he would pin a small red flag to the door. His role was to stop any of them from reaching the cabin and capturing the flag. They'd have until sunrise to complete the task.

'Sounds good fun to me,' said an excited Savannah, her competitive nature rising.

'You're forgetting one small issue,' said Penny. 'You haven't been out in the training area at night. That's when we get company.'

'What sort of company?' asked Savannah.

'Mutants,' interjected Tanis. 'Big. Bad. Bloody mutants. The upside is they sleep between sunrise and sunset; they can't see in daylight because ultraviolet and infrared light blinds them. When it gets dark, well, that's a different matter. They're nocturnal and they have perfect night vision.'

'Give me a clue as to what I might be dealing with,' encouraged Savannah.

'Well, there's your tree Mutes; these live up in the canopy. They're crafty buggers,' explained Drake with a wry smile. 'They'll hear you coming from a mile off, even if you're on tiptoe and wearing feathers on your feet. Their trick is to hang upside down from the branches, perfectly still, just waiting for you to pass underneath them, and when you're close enough – bam! They drop head-first on top of you. Before you know it, you've got a row of fangs clamped around your jugular; they can drain a human body of blood in about sixty seconds flat. When they've finished, they crawl right back up their tree, and leave the dry husk that's left of you to be chewed on by the other hungry nasties.'

'Surely you can spot them, if you're ultra careful?' said Savannah.

'They're Mutes,' emphasised Tanis. 'A cross between a chameleon and a massive snake with vampire tendencies. Their camouflage is incredible; they just blend into their surroundings.'

'Okay,' she tapped a finger thoughtfully on her lips, 'and what's at ground level?'

'Ah! They're interesting,' said Drake, a touch of irony in his voice. 'Firstly, the biggest of them are the bears. Somebody thought it would be fun to genetically replace a Grizzly's hair with the body armour of a Rhino. These bears are over two and a half metres tall on their hind legs. They're not all that fast, but what they do lack in speed, they make up for with brute force and tenacity. I've seen one bring down a substantial tree to get at a wild cat that had climbed up it for refuge. Ordinary weapons can't stop them; you need something like a bazooka! Best thing to do is avoid them at all costs.'

'The worst in my mind are the Jackals; they hunt in small packs,' joined in Penny. 'What makes them stand out from the normal forest dogs are their legs – they've got six of them. It's the front ones that they'll try and scratch you with; the claws can rip your chest open, *and* they contain a toxin. Just one nick from these sods and you'll get the walking death, a type of rabies. If you manage to get away, it'll take up to a week for you to die, during which time you'll slowly go mad, until you haemorrhage to death. There's no known cure,' she added solemnly.

Savannah was going to ask if they knew anyone who had fallen victim to the horrific death. Then she changed her mind. The three of them had become precious friends to her, and she would be mortified if she were insensitive enough to bring up painful memories for them. Instead, she tried to lighten the conversation.

'Hey, Drake. What are the odds that I can snatch your precious flag from right under your nose?'

'In your dreams, missy,' he replied.

Penny straightened herself up in her chair. 'Too scared to take on the challenge?' she goaded Drake.

'Okay. What are you prepared to bet? Don't give me crap like you'll clean my kit for a week,' he taunted.

Savannah thought for a few seconds. 'I'll work off enough kitchen duties when we get back, to supply you with a half a dozen oatcakes.'

'This is going to be so easy,' he said with a smile. 'You've got yourself a bet.' He spat in his palm and held out his hand. 'Shake on it!'

'There's a payback,' Savannah announced. 'If I win. No, *when* I win. You have to do the same for me.' There was a twinkle in her eye as she spat in her own palm and held it out.

Drake hesitated for just a second and then clasped her hand. 'Done!' he announced.

Tanis looked on, smiling, drinking in Savannah's confidence. Against his better nature, he had allowed his feelings for Savannah to continue to grow. So far, he'd managed to keep his emotions tempered, outwardly treating her as a friend and companion, steering clear of being alone with her, and focusing on the task of passing on skills and knowledge. He'd kept their conversations impersonal and suppressed the words that he wanted to say. With a mental jolt, he brought himself back into the moment, and tactically threw a camouflage over his thoughts.

'I'm sorry, Savannah,' he chimed in. 'If there's oatcakes up for grabs, then you've got me to reckon with as well. Besides, I've been after that flag for a *long* time.'

'Me too,' added Penny. 'Let's make this interesting. Whoever gets the flag is supplied with three oatcakes a week for a month from each of the others.'

'That's a lot of kitchen duties,' mused Drake.

'What's wrong? Frightened of getting dishcloth hands?' teased Penny.

'Okay. It's a four way bet. Agreed?' He slammed his hand down onto the table.

'Agreed,' they echoed, and brought their own hands down upon his.

'Right,' said Drake. 'Let's get started.' He got up, opened one of the wooden chests, took four items from it, and placed them onto the table. 'We'll need these.' They were yellow canisters, about the same size as a deodorant aerosol.

'What are they for?' asked Savannah. She weighed one deftly in her hand.

'Pepper spray. The Mutes hate it,' explained Penny. 'If you can get it in their face, it really screws them up. You can also spray it to cover up your scent, but use it sparingly,' she added.

'Hold on. I've just thought. You guys have me at a disadvantage,' objected Savannah. 'You've done this before; you'll know the quickest and safest ways back.'

'Trust me,' said Drake. 'I never take anyone in the same direction or to the same location twice, and there is no such thing as a safe way back!'

'I can vouch for that,' said Tanis. 'There was one time when he even left me sitting blindfolded, on a rock overlooking a Mute lair.'

'Yeah. I remember that,' remarked Drake. 'I thought you needed a bit of a challenge. Anyway, you escaped, didn't you?' he laughed.

'Sometimes,' said Tanis, 'you take your duty of team leader too seriously.'

'By the way, talking of duties,' announced Penny with a grin, 'it's the macho boys turn to clear up and wash the supper things!'

'Since when was washing-up a macho thing?' challenged Drake.

'Since us girls provided all of the chopped wood for the fire to cook the meals on.' She stared at Drake. 'If you don't like it, you can light your own fires and cook your own food!'

'You should never have been given the vote!' he growled as he collected the plates. 'What are you grinning at, Tanis? Get those dishes out to the pump and start scrubbing.'

23

AMBUSH

There was no moon, just a canopy of starlight in a clear sky. Constellations flickered and signalled their diamond bright presence. The temperature was dropping quickly and the night already carried a late summer chill as Drake led Savannah, Tanis and Penny, now blindfolded and tethered to each other with a length of rope, into the woods.

During the trek, Savannah used the opportunity to practise some of her newfound observational skills. Her awareness became heightened, and she focused on her sense of hearing to pick up clues about the trail they were being led on. She could feel a gradual uphill slope and the ground beneath her feet became firmer, grittier. At one point, she could hear running water in the distance. A slight vibration in the ground indicated that there was a fairly substantial waterfall in the vicinity. Smells also gave her landmark clues. Aromas of wild garlic and mint blended into a heady mix, and then gave way to the heavy scent of pine resin.

Even though they had taken a couple of short rest breaks, three hours seemed to pass in no time at all. Drake brought them to a halt in an open area. He guided them to sit back-to-back on a carpet of thick moss. Then, after hiding the backpacks in the surrounding undergrowth, he placed their weapons in the centre of the clearing.

'I should keep very quiet if I were you,' whispered Drake, his breath a white cloud. 'You don't want to disturb the local residents,' he warned. 'Tanis and Penny know the rules, but I'll just repeat them for Savannah's sake. It's simple. This is all about trust. You don't start to free yourselves until you hear my air horn. You'll never know when I'll be watching you. Any cheating and you forfeit our agreement, *and* you'll be on latrine duty for a week! Got it?'

They all nodded blindly in agreement.

'Good,' he said as he checked their bonds. 'Because I can taste those oatcakes already!'

They heard him retreat into the bushes, and it seemed like an age passed until the distant blast from an air horn reached their ears.

Through her sensory skills, Savannah obtained a great deal of information about the terrain. A mental map of the route she would need to seek out had already formed in her head.

She arched her fingers up and into her sleeve, and the tips of her nails eased down a fold in the lining. The small penknife she'd secreted there earlier, slid down into her palm, and she mentally welcomed its smooth shape like an old friend. It took her only a matter of seconds to flip it open and cut through her ties. When she pulled off her blindfold, she noticed that Tanis and Penny, themselves still blindfolded, were busy picking at their bonds, their own fingers working to untie the awkward and seemingly temperamental knots in the thick twine Drake had used to bind them.

She quietly got to her feet and scanned the area, looking for clues. Her eyes noticed a patch of disturbed foliage, where she retrieved a backpack – It was Tanis'. A further search revealed her own, which she immediately slung over her shoulders. Next, she picked up her hunting knife and sheathed it, then her crossbow and quiver. In her haste, she carelessly knocked over Penny's crossbow, which clattered noisily against some quivered bolts. Tanis and Penny froze their frantic efforts to untie their bonds.

'Who's free?' whispered Tanis.

Without answering, Savannah made her way into the undergrowth, and just as she disappeared into the tree line, she tauntingly sang back, 'Catch me if you can!'

'I don't believe it!' complained Tanis. 'How did she get free so quickly?'

'It must be a girl thing,' answered Penny as she gave one last tug at her bonds and wriggled her hands loose to remove her blindfold. Soon, she had also found her pack, claimed her weapons and headed into the woods. 'Don't get lonely,' she shouted back to Tanis.

As the two girls headed down the wooded slopes in different directions, Tanis freed himself. He frantically searched the perimeter for his backpack, but to no avail. 'Now what?' he asked himself with growing frustration as he retrieved his weapons. 'If you've set me up again, Drake, so help me, there'll be trouble,' he yelled into the trees.

As he scoured the tree line, he noticed the dark

shape of his backpack lodged in the branches of a black-trunked pine. Where, with a certain amount of mischief, Savannah had swung it up earlier.

'Oh. Very funny,' he said sarcastically.

It took him a good ten minutes to shimmy up the trunk and untangle the straps to recover it. He traced the girls' tracks and quickly decided which of them to follow. *You want to play dirty?* he thought. *I'll show you a trick or two.*

An hour passed and Savannah's plan to follow Drake's route back to the cabin failed. Everything was fine until she reached a point in the track where it looked as though a couple of elephants seemed to have performed a waltz. There were broken branches and torn up foliage everywhere that made it impossible to tell in which direction he had gone. *Clever boy*, she thought. *You think that this will stop me from getting your precious flag? No chance.*

By her reckoning, it was about six hours until sunrise. The main thing, she told herself, was not to panic. She stood there, breathing in slowly, calming her thoughts. It was then she heard the click. Her mind registered the sound of a crossbow being fired, and a bolt brushed past her shoulder and embedded itself into a tree trunk behind her. Her instincts kicked in and she dropped to the ground, quickly belly crawling into as much cover as she could find. Confusion, more than panic, set in. *Who would try to kill her? Was there a secret agenda? Could there be a traitor amongst her new friends?*

She lay there trying to make sense of things, weighing up her next move. Her hand fumbled into one of her jacket pockets. In the soundtrack of her heartbeats, she heard the crush of pine needles from behind her and she froze, willing herself to become invisible.

'Get up,' ordered a deep, throaty voice. 'Slowly.'

Savannah reluctantly obeyed.

'Turn around.'

In the thick gloom of the trees, a dark figure stood a couple of metres opposite; she couldn't believe how close he had got to her. A loaded crossbow bolt was aimed at her head. She squinted in an effort to make out the face. Only two white, sharp eyes stood out; the other features were disguised by a black balaclava, which covered the mouth and nose.

Drake's words echoed in her mind – *The main technique of Krav Maga is to finish a fight as quickly as possible. If you can't escape, get as close as you can to your attacker and bring them to the ground. Then you can either neutralise them or kill them.*

Instinctively, she stepped forward and brushed the crossbow to one side with her forearm. The bolt discharged harmlessly and thudded into the ground without purpose. She sent out a clenched fist, which connected perfectly with her assailant's cheekbone and eye socket, and then her other hand brought up the canister from her pocket. She fired a two-second burst of pepper spray into her assailant's face, and quickly stepped to one side as the figure collapsed, eyes streaming, hands tearing at the mask, mouth gasping for precious oxygen.

'Shit!' hissed a muffled voice.

She looked down at the doubled-up, retching figure, and quickly pulled her neckerchief up across her face as the bitter smell of the spray tainted the air and invaded her own nostrils.

'I don't know who you are, or if this is part of the training, but if you come after me again – I'll kill you.' To accentuate the sincerity of her threat, she gave the crouched body a well-aimed kick to the ribs.

As a further bout of coughing and wheezing racked the now foetal-shaped figure, she slipped quietly into the undergrowth, her senses and determination further fuelled by confidence and satisfaction.

Fifteen minutes later, and in her haste to put as much distance as possible between herself and her attacker, she lost her bearings, and she found herself wading waist high, through a sea of broad-leafed ferns. Pine trees closed in around her. The air was heady with the clinical scent of sap and resin. A high thicket of brambles blocked her way.

'Damn!' she cursed out loud. 'Think, Savannah. Think,' she chastised herself.

She remembered Tanis' first rule of surveillance – a three hundred and sixty degree visual assessment, followed by an overhead scan.

Everything was in the dark, shadowed in a monochrome of night. The tangle of brambles in front of her spread out in a natural deep, wide, thorny barrier, which faded into gloom in both directions. Tall sentinels of pine towered over her; their minions receded into the dense forest on either side. Shifting clouds of mist crept around their bases and across the woodland floor. The ground beneath her feet was a firm carpet of natural mulch and scattered pinecones, a soft cushion in a harsh environment.

She titled her head back and stared into the canopy, and she caught a glimpse of a midnight-blue sky. One solitary star shone through the tangle of branches and bristly foliage; a silver jewel trapped in a cage, its distant light flashed like a beacon of distress.

A piercing, mournful cry echoed around her, seemingly to emanate from the trees themselves, from their very bark. Behind her came the sound of undergrowth being savagely trampled by a hunting pack. Instinctively, she launched herself into the pine forest; her feet pounded on the ground to leave damp footprints in her wake.

Expertly avoiding tree roots and unseen hazards, she ran into a grey curtain of mist where tree trunks spread out before her in every direction like oversized prison bars.

Another high-pitched howl came from her left, answered by a second, more urgent yelp from her right; they were trying to cut her off, to encircle her. In that instant she resigned herself to the fact that they were too fast and she would not be able to outrun them. She glanced back and two dark shapes tore out of the undergrowth, about fifty metres behind her. Menacing eyes reflected a luminescent red, and homed in on her like needlepoint laser beams.

She sprinted to the nearest tree, its first full branches spread out about five metres above her. The lower stumps of long-gone limbs jutted out from the trunk, and provided a natural climbing resource. Savannah gripped the resin-caked bark and hauled her body upwards; her feet dug in as she gained purchase and pushed herself up to safety.

Out of reach, she rested on a bough and swung her legs over, as the pack arrived and encircled the base of the tree below, their frenzied excitement accentuated by howls and guttural barks. She studied the grotesque, squirming bodies: four mutated Jackals; two deformed legs protruded grotesquely from their chests. One large, venomous claw extended from each crooked paw.

'Unless you're going to grow wings, you're not getting to me tonight,' she taunted, somewhat recklessly.

Provoked, one of the Jackals leapt at the tree; it gripped the gnarled bark with its front claws, and scrabbled frantically upwards with its hind legs, stubbornly intent on reaching its quarry.

'The hell you do!' she exclaimed in surprise.

She swung her crossbow from over her shoulder, loaded it up, and fired a bolt into the creature's open, slavering mouth. The bolt pierced its brain, and it crashed down into the rest of the pack, who immediately displayed their cannibalistic nature, and tore into its body. Blood and gore splashed out like a scene from an abattoir. Without a second glance, Savannah turned to climb further up into the higher reaches of the tree.

24

GET A GRIP, SAVANNAH!

Climbing as high as she dared amongst the now thinning and feebler branches of the tree, Savannah positioned herself as comfortably as she could. Below, the Jackals sniffed and clawed around the base, their appetite for her not satisfied by the butchery and bloody consumption of their fallen cohort.

She looked down as another of the creatures leapt at the trunk and started to heave its lean bulk upwards. Quickly, she loaded another bolt, but this time her aim through the branches would give her no clear shot at the animal.

It hauled itself up to the first of the branches, and its companions started to howl and yelp in frenzied excitement and encouragement. With measured care, she shuffled her body sideways, out along a precariously thin limb. Nervously, she felt it start to sag under her weight. Frustratingly, the thickening foliage obstructed her sightline even further.

'Okay,' she breathed out resignedly. 'I'll just have to come to you.'

As she shifted herself to manoeuvre down to the next branch, a yelp of pain expelled from the climbing Jackal. In its eagerness to pursue her, it had managed to slip and trap its head and front paws between the fork of two branches, twisting itself in the process, and leaving its hindermost legs to kick aimlessly in mid-air, as if running on an invisible treadmill.

She dropped as nimbly as she could to land on the branch above the animal's head, which looked horribly comical, wedged between its own front legs and the branches. Its eyes blazed with fury and panic. A guttural growl escaped from the restricted airways of its mangy neck, and frothy saliva drooled from its curled-back lips, like a savage, weeping wound.

'What's the matter?' she taunted. 'Cat got your tongue?'

She positioned her body and grasped an overhead branch for security.

'Why waste a crossbow bolt, when I have a trusty boot?' She brought the full weight of her foot down onto the creature's skull.

With a sickening crunch, its head snapped free of the branches, and the body, limp and lifeless, dropped like a sack of dead meat. Savannah looked down, mesmerised by the carnage inflicted on the animal by the remainder of the pack.

'And then there were two,' she mused.

If she were going to make a break for it, it would have to be now. A snap decision spurred her into action; she dropped down and used her momentum to swing from the branch like a dismounting gymnast to land feet first on one of the Jackals. Its vertebrae shattered under the impact of her weight. To avoid breaking her ankles, she somersaulted forwards, and smoothly regained a standing stance. The remaining Jackal stared at her; a bloody, torn hunk of its previous companion protruded from its jaws. She brought the small canister forward and delivered a well-aimed blast of pepper spray into the animal's face – it went physically ballistic, with seemingly no control of its movements, as though someone had jabbed it with electrified prongs or a Taser. The sounds that it emitted, a mixture of distress and fury, truly belonged to a creature from hell.

Savannah turned and ran into the unwelcoming gloom of the forest. This time she scanned the terrain as she went, looking for breaks in the trees, for any suggestion of a clearing.

Twenty minutes later, and she was rewarded when she spotted a trail: an earthy path, which wound between the trees and through an otherwise pine-needled carpet. Stepping onto it, she noticed numerous track marks, some identifiable as natural woodland inhabitants, and others that belonged to a more vicious and alien creature.

She crouched there on her haunches, swigged some much-needed water, and considered which way to go. Back could take her into the company of more Jackals. Forward could lead to new dangers – bears, vampire snakes and the like. Instinctively, she scanned the tree line above her. In the shallow light, she narrowed her eyes, seeking any sign of movement, any unusual shape.

A bird broke for cover; its shrill cry scattered out amongst the trees, piercing the stillness with alarm and panic. Savannah's heart missed a beat; she turned and loaded her crossbow in one fluid movement, only to watch a black-feathered shape flutter into the gloom. Her heart continued to race under her breast.

'Get a grip, girl,' she told herself. Her voice sounded dull and muted to her ears. Warily, she conducted a 360-degree sweep of her surroundings. Her ears picked up a faint sound in the distance, and she tilted her head to one side. She'd heard it on her blindfolded journey – it was running water. The waterfall. Sure that it was somewhere ahead, and her mind made up, she resumed her way forward along the track. With confidence rising, she broke into a jog.

When the twig snapped, it was a gunshot to her ears. She turned with the bow, but too late.

Afterwards, she chastised herself for carelessly forgetting a golden rule that Tanis had repeated to her many times during her training – 'Your brain may be thinking ahead, but your eyes should be constantly scanning all around you.'

The matted, grey body hit her sideways with a force that knocked the crossbow from her hand. As she rolled to a recovery position, she smelt the pepper spray. With her knife drawn, she turned to face her attacker.

'Sonofabitch!' she gasped.

She was lucky. The Jackal had leapt using mainly its sense of hearing for guidance; she could see that it had not fully recovered its sight. Its face and muzzle were crusted with puss and caked with dirt, and its eyes were still streaming with chemical tears. She shifted her knife from hand to hand in anticipation of an attack. That slight movement was enough for the Jackal to lock on to her position, and it lined itself up. Haunches tensed like coiled springs, it extended its deadly front legs, readying the two dirty, lethal claws to rip into her.

There was a slight, involuntary quiver along its body as it prepared to launch itself forward. In a desperate thought, Savannah swung her backpack in front of her, with the hope of creating a barrier against the venomous talons.

The snake dropped out of nowhere, its body undulating and pulsating in a myriad of colours, a reflex action brought on by the prospect of a kill. It was a good three metres in length and twice as thick as her arm. She stood transfixed as it clamped its unnaturally wide jaws around the Jackal's neck. With incredible speed and dexterity, its slender form coiled around the animal. She heard the breaking of bones as it crushed the animal's ribcage with the power of a steel vice. The Jackal's life breath rattled from its throat, and the snake gorged on its blood.

One, two and then three more slender bodies, dropped from invisibility to form frenzied colours on the ground before her. She sheathed her knife and grabbed at the fallen crossbow, and in a clumsy panic, she stepped backwards. Her heels hit against the rotting trunk of a tree, which rolled away, and she tumbled down an unseen slope.

Savannah closed her eyes and prayed she would not collide with any boulders or trees, which were anonymously waiting to greet her falling body. The impact would crush her senses and smash her skull like a ripe watermelon.

Above her, the silent threat of half a dozen bloodthirsty reptiles slithered their serpentine bodies towards the ridge, and in pursuit.

While gravity pulled her flailing body, she somehow managed to manoeuvre herself onto her back and wrap her arms across the backpack. She pulled it close into her chest, refusing to lose her grip on the crossbow. The world spun past as she descended feet first through a blur of green vegetation. It was like a nightmarish flume ride. The only consolation was that the thick undergrowth cushioned the pounding that her back and shoulders were subjected to. Even so, she knew that *if* she survived, a myriad of painful bruises would be the very least to show for the experience.

Her head juddered up and down, and through a blurred and distorted vision, she craned her neck, desperately trying to catch a glimpse of what was ahead. She slalomed her body left and right, in an effort to avoid a collision with curtains of slender stems and saplings.

The trailing edge of a serrated fern whipped across her cheek, and she let out a startled and angry cry. Furiously, she bent her knees slightly and dug the heels of her boots into the ground, hoping somehow to slow her descent. This did have some small effect, although the spasms of razor-sharp pain in her Achilles heels and calf muscles seemed a high price to pay.

Through her knees, a new terror reached out to greet her and with inevitable speed, she blindly and helplessly plunged into a grey sea of mist. At the same time, she soared out into an unseen destiny as the ground beneath her fell away with the suddenness of a gallows trapdoor.

25

NIGHT MOVES

The landing, as cushioned by moss and a thick carpet of dead leaves as it was, knocked the breath from her lungs. Her body almost bounced on impact. A haze of vapour and leaves swirled around her as she lay there gasping through the layers of pain, mentally checking for any immediate signs of serious injury.

With an effort, she pushed her backpack and crossbow to one side, and rolled over, only to come face to face with the wide, stupefied eyes of a young deer, frozen to the spot as if caught in the headlamps of an approaching car. A sudden rustle from above her announced the immediate arrival of a snake. It emerged from the ceiling of mist like a spear, and sunk its reptilian jaws into the deer's neck. With a shock of adrenaline and a childlike scream, the poor animal ran off through an eerie grey curtain of vapour, dragging its killer with it.

Her own survival instinct spurred Savannah into action. She retrieved her pack and crossbow and ran in the opposite direction, as somewhere behind her, other elongated bodies arrived with dull thuds. She was in a gully; the shifting mist gave her glimpses of roots, and fern-covered walls. Her hand felt for guidance, and as she stumbled forward, the musty smell of disturbed mulch and damp earth reached her senses. A faint noise came from her right, then another from behind her. Small beads of perspiration formed on her forehead to cool instantly, causing her skin to turn clammy and wax-like. A rustling, this time to her left and closer, forced panic into her chest – her attackers were closing in on her.

An arm outstretched, her hand felt the large, slimy trunk of a tree, which rose up to her right, and she instinctively tucked herself in behind it, and silently prayed it would give her sanctuary.

She slid her knife from its sheath, and gripping the hilt with white-skinned knuckles, held it out point first, ready to cut and thrust at anything that appeared towards her out of the gloom. Her senses went into overdrive; she could feel her heart thudding against her breastbone. Blood rushed and pounded in her ears like an internal raging torrent. The smell of something acrid mixed with the strong aroma of pepper spray, washed over her face, and her eyes stung and watered up; she must have somehow punctured or damaged her canister.

With blurred vision, she held her breath, and waited, anticipating the arrival of a violent and blood-sucking death. In that moment, her mind unlocked a promise.

Although she still harboured anger towards her parents for deserting her and allowing her to be Transported, she did not want to die without the opportunity to reconcile with them. If given the chance, she would seek them out, but not for vengeance. Not now. Unexpectedly, she couldn't remember the last time she had told them that she loved them. An image of Bethany formed in her mind and her heart ached for the companionship of her sister.

Choices began to form in her mind. *I'm not going to die like a rat caught in a trap,* she thought. She remembered what Drake had told her. 'Take the fight to the enemy. Attack is the best form of defence. When all else fails – run like hell!'

She steeled herself, and prepared to leap out into the murky grey unknown. To cut and run, and hopefully to survive.

The next few moments unfolded like a dream – an episode of confusion.

A palm clamped over her mouth and another gripped her wrist, immobilising her knife hand.

'Trust me,' a voice, barely audible, whispered into her ear.

She was pulled backwards, through soft ferns, which closed together in front of her, like dark green curtains, to envelope her in total darkness. The pungent aroma of pinesap mixed with the bitterness of pepper spray stung her eyes again.

The voice spoke as soft and as quiet as a thought. 'If you want to live, don't make a sound. Don't even move, or you'll get us both killed. Kiss my hand if you trust me.'

She reasoned with herself. She'd had an unknown attacker, and now, it would appear, she had a mysterious rescuer. If there were a price to pay for her deliverance, she would deal with it later – as long as she survived.

She puckered her lips, then realised how dry they were, so she brought out her tongue and moistened them to softly kiss the skin of the stranger's palm. The hand dropped away from her mouth, but the grip on her knife remained tightened.

How long they stood there, she could only guess. Her thoughts were diverted by the complaining hisses and agitated rustling sounds, which filtered through from the other side of the fern barrier. She felt more than trapped, almost claustrophobic. A survival plan formed in her head. At the first sign of a gaping, fanged mouth, she would swing the individual around into its path and hope that the resulting chaos would create a diversion for her to escape.

In the dark, she waited for an uncertain future to unfold.

Eventually, her fears were unfulfilled and the noises faded. Her wrist was released, and she stepped back into the darkness, ready to strike out at any assault. There was a "snap!" and a glow stick ignited with its eerie green light to reveal what was a small cave, and the identity of her redeemer.

'I see you've made some new friends,' he smiled.

'Tanis!' she exclaimed. The light-headedness of physical and mental relief unsteadied her and she sunk to her knees.

He crouched down in front of her. 'You look as though you've been through the wars. Have you pissed off *every* creature in the forest?'

She smiled back at him. 'No. But I'm working on it.'

He gently ran a finger along her cheekbone, his eyes searching hers. 'Come on. Let's get you cleaned up.'

He led her towards the back of the cave, to where his pack and kit was. The steady trickle of water attracted her gaze to a small spring, which bubbled up in a little stone grotto. Moist stalactites hung like ghostly icicles from parts of the ceiling, and the floor was covered in dry fern leaves. Tanis led her to a flat stone area where a pile of kindling rested untidily near the ashen residue of a small fire.

'Looks like you've got yourself a nice little place here,' she observed.

'It's just a bolthole, somewhere to hide up in an emergency. I've got a few others like this, scattered around the area. Nobody knows about them – not even Drake.' he added with a grin. 'And don't worry. Nothing will come through that barrier; it's soaked with pepper spray, and my own urine!'

'Thanks,' she sniffed at her jacket, 'and now it's on me!'

'It does the trick. We're alive, aren't we?' he grinned. 'Now, sit down and let me clean you up.'

She did as she was told. He produced a strip of clean cloth, soaked it in cold spring water and proceeded to gently wipe away the blood and the grime from her face.

'Are you hurt anywhere else?' he asked.

'Apart from a few bruises, only my pride,' she replied.

He stroked her hair back from her face and gently dabbed at the raised red weal across her cheek. He cupped her chin with his other hand, and turned it slightly towards the glowing light.

For a moment, their eyes met and they stared at each other, soul connecting to soul, thoughts running wildly in their own heads. His hand caressed her face, and she kissed it once again, but this time with tenderness. She reached up and wrapped her arms around his neck, and pulled him to her.

'So, I never did thank you properly for those oatcakes,' she whispered.

26

NOW, IT'S PERSONAL

Savannah awoke with a start, not of panic, just from an unconscious awareness of the passing of time. Disorientated, she blinked into the ruddy half-light of the cave. She had no idea how long she'd been asleep, but the glowing embers of the small campfire, and the tiny flickering flames, which danced like golden fireflies, signalled that it could have been for a period of minutes, rather than hours.

Tanis' sleeping bag slid down and exposed her arms; her bare skin rippled with goose bumps as the damp air of the cave caressed it. She looked down at his sleeping form; his head turned in profile and shadow, a stray dreadlock lay across his face. She had a longing to lie back down and lose herself again in his warm body, but this was a new Savannah: a Savannah who knew how to channel her energy and play to her strengths. At this moment, she intended to win.

Quietly and carefully, she dressed and collected her things. As she reached the fern doorway, she paused momentarily to check for any sound outside. Satisfied that she sensed no danger waiting there, she eased herself through, turning once more to look at Tanis.

'All's fair in love and war,' she whispered, and she blew him a kiss. Then, she melted through the camouflaged entrance and out into the hour before dawn.

Tanis opened his eyes to her exit. He sat up stretching and flexing his arms. His exposed torso muscles rippled slightly, his fitness a testament to his youth, and to regular exercise.

'You cunning little vixen,' he said with a smile. 'And I thought I was competitive!'

He dressed within minutes, and carrying his pack and weapons, silently left the hideout, not only in pursuit of Savannah, but also of the prized flag.

Climbing out of the gully, he surveyed the view from the top of the ridge and then checked his watch. It was 04.38, just under an hour until sunrise. He smiled confidently, knowing his advantages over Savannah – he knew where he was, and he was familiar with the terrain. There were two ways back to the cabin; one was a downhill trek along a rocky path, and the other was relatively short, but very dangerous. Tanis being Tanis, he chose the latter.

When he reached the top of the falls, dawn's twilight brought a silver-grey aura to the landscape. The white noise of cascading water as it rushed over the edge filled his ears, and he removed his backpack, retrieved a length of cord, which he used to tie the crossbow to his pack, and then tethered it to his ankle. Carefully, he stepped out across the wet rocks, to balance on the brink of the waterfall. He'd done this before, and knew the safest spot, where there would not be any bone-breaking boulders submerged and hidden by the white spray waiting with deathly intent below him. For a moment, he studied the gushing force of nature as it fell into the deep pool, some twenty-five metres below.

In one fluid action, he filled his lungs, threw the pack before him, and jumped out feet first, to allow the white, foaming curtain to swallow him up. He fell, arms outstretched in a crucifix shape as he plunged towards the deep water below, all the while concentrating on the fall, praying his breath would hold, and hoping he would not become disorientated beneath the surface.

Engulfed in the rush of water and air, his senses flooded with adrenalin and euphoria. Time seemed to pause. In his mind's eye he imagined himself suspended, defying gravity, then the world came whooshing back and he was submerged. The swirling current tugged at his legs, intent on claiming his waterlogged soul. He swam for his life.

Savannah, meanwhile, had made good progress and was halfway down the boulder and rock-strewn track that ran adjacent to the waterfall. She turned to take a look at the resplendent cascade of water. It was then she saw the figure leap from its rim and merge into the white, molten fury of the torrent. She cried out his name, but it caught in her throat, trapped in the sudden dryness of her anxiety.

The breath in her lungs paused as she scoured the turbulent waters. Finally, he surfaced and swam lazily to the bank below her; a sodden figure pulled itself ashore and rolled over onto its back, chest heaving, gulping in air like a beached fish. It was only then that she breathed out herself, her head dizzy with oxygen. She leaned far enough over a ledge for him to see her and he gave her a half salute, half wave.

'Bloody fool!' she shouted at him, but her voice was lost in the resounding rush of the falls.

Tanis untethered his gear to sling it casually across his back. Without another glance, he pushed his way through a mass of tall ferns, and disappeared into the trees.

A scowl of frustration remained on her face as she turned, and with reckless intent urging her on, she increased the speed of her descent down the path, her progress fuelled by a mixture of grim determination and stubbornness.

Forty minutes later, the ground flattened out and she re-entered the familiar wood, which surrounded the cabin. It was then she heard a sound to her left. A quick glance through the tree trunks revealed Tanis, running parallel to her in the early morning light. Now, it had come down to a race, a sprint through the trees. She dug her heels in and pushed her legs to the limit; thigh muscles burnt as she dodged boughs, leapt over fallen trunks and avoided hidden potholes.

Simultaneously, they broke through the tree line and into the clearing. If Tanis had the breath to spare, he would have laughed, as his eyes fell upon a beaming Penny already standing in front of the cabin; her arms aloft in jubilation, the red flag gripped triumphantly in one of her hands.

A morning mist, tinged pink by dawn's arrival, swirled in ribbons across the ground and gave the scene a dreamlike feature. Tanis sank to his knees, panting, drawing in gulps of air. Savannah bent over double. Her arms and legs trembled as she supported herself with her hands on her thighs; lactic acid burning her muscles. Short rasps escaped from her throat as she also gasped for oxygen.

'You snooze, you lose!' crowed an elated Penny, as she shuffled around in a victory dance.

'I don't get it,' panted Tanis. 'Where's Drake?'

As if on cue, Drake appeared through the trees on the other side of the clearing. Another figure, a tall, slim man in combat fatigues, walked beside him.

'You sneak!' Savannah accused Tanis as she regained control of her breathing.

'Me?' He responded with mock offense. 'You're the one who slunk out without saying goodbye. Without even waking me!'

'I didn't want to disturb you. You looked so peaceful,' she answered defensively.

'You set me up, just so that you could win,' argued Tanis.

'Not true,' she said, forcing a wounded expression on her face. 'Anyway, I'm not the idiot who could've drowned himself.'

Penny raised an eyebrow and stepped forward. 'What's this? A lover's tiff?'

Savannah's reddened cheeks were further crimsoned by sudden embarrassment. 'Who said anything about love?' She narrowed her eyes at Tanis. 'Don't you even go there!' She turned to walk towards the cabin, when Drake called her name.

'Savannah. We need to speak to you.'

Glad of the diversion, she made her way over to them.

'This is Jameson,' introduced Drake. 'He's the head of communications at our Greentrees compound.' He paused. 'He has some news of your parents. Unfortunately, it's not good.'

Savannah stared at Drake's swollen cheek and black eye. A realisation formed in her mind as she re-ran her encounter with the assailant in the woods.

Jameson's voice brought her attention back. '…and sadly, they were pronounced dead at the scene. We have it on good intelligence that Jago ordered their deaths.'

She turned her gaze to Jameson.

'Sorry? What did you say?'

'It's your parents,' answered Drake. He gently placed a hand on her shoulder. 'Savannah, I'm afraid that they're dead.'

She looked back and forth several times between Jameson and Drake. She searched their eyes, their expressions; all the while her mind tried to find some other meaning for the words that she had just heard.

'I… I don't understand. How? Why?'

'Let's go and sit in the cabin while Jameson gives you a few more details,' said Drake, and he guided her towards the door.

While Jameson was inside with her, Drake took the opportunity to brief Tanis and Penny on the situation. Much later, after Jameson had gone, Savannah's disbelief turned to anger and then to grief. Penny sat with her, talking quietly, counselling, listening, sympathising, but mostly being a friend.

★

The rest of the day passed slowly as if every second hung onto itself. Savannah had lain on her bunk and drifted in and out of a restless sleep, while the others had catnapped between chores. Finally, the evening came and they sat around the table; each of them absently picked at their supper, which had become unappetising, and soured by the sadness that they felt for Savannah.

Later, while Penny and Savannah spoke quietly once more, Drake and Tanis walked the perimeter; a windless, moonlit night created frozen shadows around them. Tanis harboured his own thoughts; he wanted to be with her, to hold her, to comfort her grief. He wanted to share the emotional embrace that only those who have experienced loss can share. Then, negative thoughts started to run through his mind – it seemed to him that in his life, the people he loved either ended up being hurt, or he lost them. He felt so helpless.

Drake picked up on Tanis' brooding mood.

'She'll be all right. She's a fighter.'

'How can you be so sure?' Tanis asked.

'They hurt her. She felt betrayal and abandonment, and in her mind she thought that she had already lost them,' reflected Drake. 'What's happened now, in its own cruel way, is closure. A finality. She'll grieve; she'll regret the things she said, and the things she didn't say. Then, like the rest of us, revenge will be her medicine. Jago's actions have brought us closer together with our hatred for what Opulence stands for. More importantly, she still has something left to fight for – her sister. I wouldn't want to be on the end of Savannah's anger when she finally comes face to face with Jago.' He gingerly rubbed his face, and touched the swollen tissue under his fingers. 'I put her to the test earlier on, and found out that she already has her own dark fury.'

Tanis studied the bruised, misshapen cheek with curiosity.

'*She* did that to you?'

'*And* I think that I've got a cracked rib as a bonus,' added Drake, with an uncomfortable wince.

27

GREENTREES

Next morning, in a sombre atmosphere, they cleaned the cabin and prepped it for the next occupants, whoever they may eventually be. Under an overcast sky, as grey as their own moods and thoughts, the four of them gathered in front of the small wooden porch.

'Okay,' announced Drake. 'An hour's gentle trek and we'll be at the village for a well-deserved break.'

'How long are we going to be there?' asked Tanis.

'Long enough to recharge our batteries, and at least until we get orders that we're needed back at Base One. I'm sure we'll be kept up to date with any developments on Opulence,' replied Drake.

'That's the last place I want to think of at the moment,' said Savannah.

'I can totally understand,' said Drake. 'That's why we're going to take things slowly and give you some breathing space. However, we still have a way to go, and if you'll pardon the pun, we're not out of the woods yet. Keep alert and watch each other's backs.'

Penny moved off with Drake, and Savannah walked side by side with Tanis.

'I feel your pain,' he said quietly, as he slipped his hand into hers.

'Thank you,' she replied, without looking at him. 'For now, let's just walk.'

'Sure,' he said, and he gave her hand a gentle squeeze.

★

After about four miles, they emerged from the woodland onto a grey tarmac road, wide enough for two cars to pass. The absence of overgrown weeds and vegetation across its surface was evidence of its continued use by some form of transport. However, shallow potholes, along with the scars and gouges of something metallic having been dragged along it, confirmed that even basic maintenance was long overdue. Tall trees lined either side and created a green avenue for the man-made thoroughfare. Ahead, in the middle of the road, a black-feathered carrion crow tugged angrily at the bloody remains of a careless rabbit. A bright black eye turned to examine the group, and it cawed in complaint at being disturbed, before it spread its wings and flapped noisily up into the shelter of the trees.

Twenty minutes later, they rounded a sharp bend to see a sudden change in the landscape. The trees fell back on either side of them to give way to a flat, brown and green patchwork of open fields and farmland. Ahead of them, the road headed up to a pair of substantial steel gates, which were flanked on either side by concrete lookout towers where, beneath corrugated canopies, silhouetted figures silently observed the group. Double rows of five-metre high chain-mesh fencing, topped with razor wire, spread away in opposite directions. This encompassed the entire square mile of the compound. At first sight, Greentrees village looked like a forbidding prison camp, not the countryside haven that Savannah had imagined in her mind's eye.

About fifty metres from the gates, a thick red line had been sprayed in paint across the tarmac, and as they reached it, Drake brought them to a halt. He opened up his pack, brought out a flare gun, loaded it with a shell and fired it into the air. A star-burst of emerald green smoke trails vividly splashed across the pale blue sky, as if painted urgently by an artist's aging brush.

The two-tone blast of an air horn broke the relative silence, and the gates swung back with a soundtrack and guttural roar of primitive engines, which announced the emergence of five modified, off-road buggies. The driver and passenger of each one were accompanied by a third person that stood on a small platform affixed at the rear of the buggy. Each of them was harnessed to the roll bars, and their hands gripped the trigger handles of large machine guns, which were mounted onto the top of each vehicle.

Two of the buggies roared with throaty menace around each side of Drake's group, and corralled them in a semicircle, while the fifth slewed to a last-second halt in front of them. Black steel gun barrels pointed threateningly at the group, and Savannah instinctively reached for her hunting knife, but Tanis stayed her hand and shook his head.

'It's all for a show of strength, and to give them a

chance to flex their muscles,' he said, his voice just breaking through the cacophony of stuttering engines.

All of the occupants wore camouflage uniforms, goggles and masks. Sashes of tri-colour broke up the monotony of green and brown. The sound of the engines quietened as they stopped their revving, and the passenger of the lead buggy stepped out and removed his goggles and facemask to reveal a beaming, Afro-Caribbean smile. He stood nearly two metres tall and greeted them with a voice as big as his stature.

'Drake! You son of a gun! It's good to see you. It's been far too long,' he boomed, and took Drake in a bear hug.

Drake gasped as his tender ribs took the pressure. He quickly patted the man's shoulders in a signal to be released.

'Looks like you've been in the wars, as usual,' he said, as he let go and inspected Drake's face. 'Anyone that I know?'

Drake instinctively turned to Savannah. 'Miss Savannah Loveday, meet Commander Danny Hench.'

Danny Hench extended his hand and Savannah shook it.

'My condolences, Miss Loveday,' he said apologetically. 'It may come as small comfort, but you've got some good people around you, and while you're here at Greentrees, there's a whole community that will welcome and support you.'

Savannah managed a dry-throated, 'Thank you.'

Without any intent of disrespect, Danny Hench gave just a moment's pause, before a grin of perfect white teeth flashed across his face again. His attention turned to Penny and Tanis.

'You look lovelier every time I see you, my dear.'

'Flattery will get you everywhere, sir,' replied Penny, almost blushing.

'And you, young man,' he said to Tanis, 'you need to get a haircut. You look too much like me when I was your age! Ha!'

'I'll take that as a complement, sir,' Tanis replied with a smile.

'Okay, that's enough of the pleasantries. I think we've put on a sufficient show for anyone who could be watching us,' said Danny Hench.

Drake quickly scanned their surroundings. 'Are you expecting trouble then?'

'There was an attempt to breach our perimeter, around about the same time as the attacks on the city bases,' explained Danny Hench. 'Futile when you consider our defences. Five unwelcome visitors from Opulence didn't even make it to the second fence. We spotlighted them. They fired at us. We fired back. They're all dead. End of story,' he said, as a matter of fact.

'First attack since I don't know how long, so now we're not taking any chances, hence the show of hardware.' He nodded at the guns. 'Intel suggests that there may be a few more unwelcome guests hiding out in our region, waiting for an opportunity to strike. With that in mind, let's get moving. Right, each of you pick a buggy and we'll get you into the village and accommodated.'

Once the team were seated, the convoy moved with

military precision back through the gates, which were closed solidly and firmly behind them by armed guards.

They passed through a concrete corridor of blast blocks and then out onto a large quadrangle. On one side ran a long, two-storey wooden barrack hut; beside this, a huge water tower stood imposingly over two large fuel tanks. On the other side, an array of vehicles that consisted of modified motorbikes, quad bikes, and numerous machine-gun equipped buggies, was parked. A white flag pole dominated the centre of the quadrangle, and in the slight mid-morning breeze, a tri-colour flag of green, red and orange rippled in defiance. At the far end of the square, a small hut and a red and white striped barrier signalled a checkpoint. Beyond this was a row of tall poplar trees, which screened off the village in the distance.

Pluming up a cloud of dust, the buggies pulled in front of one of the huts, and Drake's team alighted.

'Jameson will sort out your accommodation,' shouted Danny Hench. 'I'll catch up with you, tonight at 20.00 hours in the Tavern. Remember to wear mufti in the village – no combats or uniforms are allowed. It's a community and we keep our military presence to a low profile there, except in an emergency. By the way, Drake…'

'Yes, sir?'

'You'd better have a drink waiting for me on the bar when I arrive!' he smiled.

The procession of buggies moved noisily away towards the static vehicles on the other side of the square, and the tall figure of Jameson appeared at the hut's open door.

'Come inside and I'll give you the details of your accommodation, and your security passes. I also have an update for you from Commander-in-Chief Fairfax, regarding your duties while you're here at Greentrees.'

Fifteen minutes later, Jameson escorted them to the checkpoint, and their passes were scrutinised by a straight-faced guard.

'But he just issued these to us no more than five minutes ago!' a tired and agitated Savannah indicated to Jameson.

'I know, miss,' replied the guard, glancing at her. 'And later, when *he* wants access, *he'll* have to provide me with a pass also.' Finally satisfied, he handed their passes back to them and indicated for the barrier to be raised.

'I'll see you tonight at the Tavern,' said Jameson.

They walked towards a gap in the line of trees, and a twin terrace of red, brick built houses came into view.

'I know you probably don't feel like socialising at the moment,' Penny said to Savannah. 'But believe me, you need people around you.' She put a friendly arm around Savannah's shoulders. 'Don't worry; I'll stay by your side. Everyone here is very friendly and welcoming, and the Tavern is really just a community centre.'

'A community centre with home brew!' said Drake. 'Come on; I can smell it already.'

Savannah smiled weakly at Drake's enthusiasm. She knew he meant no disrespect, and she also knew that Penny was right. She really didn't want to find herself alone. Not just yet.

28

JAGO'S RULE

Within the first three weeks of Jago's rule, he began to enforce his authority. Firstly, he had Roth enlist the most ruthless, heartless and loyal individuals that could be found amongst the ranks of the Transportation Police. They were intensely trained to become groups of hit squads; their sole objective was to infiltrate Earthland and the Diss network to cause chaos, death and destruction. A specific order was to track down Savannah's location.

'Drag the scrawny bitch back here. If she gets a little damaged in the process, so be it, but I want her alive,' he ordered. 'Don't even think about returning without her.'

Jago focused all of his attention and energy towards a campaign of absolute rule. Leaflets were sent out, posters displayed, and announcements broadcast across Opulence. All Servanti – men, women and children – were ordered to report within a seven day deadline to new registration centres, which had been set up on every community plaza. Once there, amidst a menacing atmosphere governed over by Transportation Police, they were subjected to an intense process. Their old identification papers were scrapped, and if they could not provide any means of official ID, then they were taken to "holding cells", pending verification or Transportation.

Photographs and blood samples were taken and personal details cross-matched with existing records. All Servanti now became the direct property of the State of Opulence. Women and girls were to be consigned as domestic labourers, allocated and assigned by directives of the State, and all children would be educated in a manner solely designed for them to respect and serve for the betterment of Opulence.

Able-bodied men, and boys sixteen years old and over, were to be conscripted into the New Opulan Army. Any refusal would be perceived as an act of treason, resulting in execution by hanging, and any immediate family members would be Transported.

Jago issued a decree that while the Servanti menfolk pledged their allegiance, and fought for Opulence, their loved ones would be unharmed. Likewise, as long as the women were loyal and worked for the good of Opulence, then their children would be safe. The Servanti were now, without doubt, slaves by any other name.

'Loyalty and obedience through fear,' he said to Roth. 'We might not win their hearts and minds, but we will control their actions. They will fight for us. They will bleed for us and they *will* die for us.'

*

The months washed by, blurred by activity and change, and the Elite Fortunata watched as Jago's regime took on an almost hypnotic hold. He entranced all with his visionary speeches. They believed his passionate, sometimes manic rants and revelled in his ideals extolling the Fortunata as being a superior people.

'We must distance ourselves from all others in any relationships,' he declared. 'Ours will become a pureblood kindred – a master race worthy of conquering and ruling all others.'

His image appeared on banners, which hung above the many plazas and public meeting places. His "Mona Lisa" smile looked down, appeasing the Fortunata and discomforting the Servanti. Many of the Fortunata, particularly the younger men and women, were inspired enough to enlist as officers in the new army, to join the ranks that were needed to discipline and command the Servanti conscripts.

As yet, and despite Jago's encouragement (which included threats of physical punishment), the scientists were unable to perfect the solar weaponry that he craved. While they toiled night and day in their laboratories, Jago continued to build his war machine. Manufacturing plants were constructed to produce all manner of weaponry, including the spears, swords, knives, and bows needed to arm his militia. From the cache of firearms available, these were issued only to the high-ranking. Military training centres became established to instruct and prepare the enlisted minions for the planned and developing assault on Earthland.

And so, a new age was born. The regime that was inspired and built by Franklin Loveday, which existed in relative peace, now came to a rapid end. The rich and the privileged ruled without compassion, and

Opulence became an aggressive oppressor of the weak and the poor. Ironically, the Fortunata were oblivious to the fact that they too had fallen under the rule of those with much darker and crueller ambitions.

There was a complete segregation of culture, lifestyle and opportunity – the Fortunata lived to excess, the Servanti lived to survive.

Similarities to long-dead despotisms and apartheid echoed and breathed through Opulence. As with history, once again the evil ideals of one man disguised fascism as patriotism. Like a virus, it infected and brutally segregated a population.

In the midst, a young girl walks upright, outwardly emotionless and with one ambition on her mind: the opportunity to kill the person who she once regarded as her sister. Indoctrinated into his madness, Jago's mantra whispers like a viper in her head.

'Death to the Diss. Death to Savannah Loveday.'

29

ACHING HEARTS

Greentrees village was another world filled with the remnants and echoes from a way of life that existed well before the earth hit its social self-destruct button.

What had originally been constructed to house and accommodate the families of armed forces personnel during the 1960s had now been restored and fortified by the Earthland Defence Network. Its infrastructure functioned around agriculture and self-sufficiency. Power and lighting came from small generators and hurricane lamps, and heating from wood burning stoves and log fires.

Now, it was home to some two thousand men, women and children. Everyone from the age of sixteen worked to support the community, farming food and livestock from the surrounding land or providing maintenance and service expertise. Enlistment into the Earthland Defence Network was not mandatory; however, at least one member of each family was expected to dedicate eight hours a week to defensive duties. There were two schools, a hospital and a church. The whole village ran as a cooperative – everyone contributed, everyone was provided for.

To Savannah, it became a haven, a distraction from a path she knew she would eventually have to follow. A path on which she would have to confront the anger and the grief of her past, where pain and deliverance lingered for her like a festering wound, waiting to be lanced and cleansed with revenge and retribution.

To her surprise, the group were allocated housing in the village itself. They each had their own small rooms in a hostel. She relished having her own private space for the first time in a long while. A sparsely furnished room provided her with a private sanctuary, one where she could eagerly close her door for precious moments of privacy and contemplation, and occasional bouts of tearful melancholy.

A semblance of normal life developed into days, and then weeks. The hub of her activities became one of the barrack rooms, mostly studying disjointed, hand drawn maps of Opulence, filling in gaps and adding intelligence where she could. She focused her energies on describing the environment and answering questions from the small group around her. On other days, either Penny or Tanis would take her to village gatherings, and introduce her to members of the community.

Penny's birthday came and went, but not without the appropriate celebration, amongst which there was a tearful moment when Penny was presented with a personal message from her partner, Jake, who she now missed with an aching heart.

Within the routine, Savannah and Tanis joined patrols to accompany and escort working parties to and from the fields, watching over them as they gathered produce, and helping to secure precious livestock in fortified barns each night.

Their relationship blossomed and deepened, enhanced by frequent escapes to the solitude and privacy of his or her room. Amongst the passion of a gentle intimacy, they would shut out the world and talk of a future for themselves, and to share mutual dreams of living in a trouble-free world.

Her love for Tanis lightened the weight on her heart of her parents' death, however, the disjointed intelligence reports of Beth's constant appearance at Jago's side, filled her with concern and apprehension, and she yearned for news of the mission that would take her back to Opulence, to rescue her sister and allow her the brooding need to dispense angry punishment upon Jago and Roth.

Eventually, a morning dawned when they were called together for a meeting with Danny Hench. Assembled in the plain surroundings of his barrack office, they listened earnestly as he delivered the news they had been waiting for.

'Information came in by courier pigeon this morning that Commander-in-Chief Jean Fairfax requests your return to operational duties at Base One. You are to leave here at 14.00 hours this afternoon. You'll get a buggy escort to Little Halt in time for a train link to Broadway Junction, and your journey back to the city. That gives you two hours to pack and say any goodbyes. I'll see you here at 13.45. That will be all.'

He dismissed them without any pleasantries.

'Something's happening. Danny only gets that

intense when there's something serious going down,' Drake commented.

'Like what?' asked Savannah.

'Could be a threat to Greentrees and the community, or something bigger,' he guessed aloud. 'Whatever it is, we'll soon see an increase in activity, you mark my words.'

As if to confirm Drake's suspicions, the doors on one of the barrack buildings opened and a stream of combat-dressed, military trained individuals emerged in an orderly, unrushed fashion, to form up in lines on the quadrangle. Savannah noticed with some satisfaction that a good number of female faces made up the ranks.

Drake smiled, shrugged his shoulders and raised his eyebrows at them.

'I hate it when you're right,' glared Penny.

30

I NEVER LEAVE HOME
WITHOUT ONE

14.01. An overcast August day. Four buggies roared down the tarmac road and away from Greentrees compound. Drake, Tanis, Penny and Savannah held on, firmly harnessed into their seats next to their drivers, as the caged vehicles bumped and bounced along with bone-shaking momentum. Tanis elected not to wear a crash helmet, complaining it would crush his dreadlocks, and his style!

To Savannah's distorted vision, the tree line on the left was a blur of greens and browns; it was the best she could do to focus her eyes on the road ahead. Her hands gripped the front and side roll bars with a painful determination, particularly when the buggy slewed around a bend, which the driver navigated sideways and at speed. She had the feeling that behind his mask there was a smile of quiet enjoyment at the expense of her near terror. Now, she appreciated why the gunner behind her needed to be harnessed to the frame, and she could only admire his nerve and tenacity. No matter how quickly they reached their destination, she vowed she would never complain at the prospect of a long foot march again.

They were halfway through their journey when, with unavoidable consequences, a large tree toppled across the road in front of them. The noise of the buggy engines covered up the complaint of splintering bark, and the flaying of leaf-laden branches. Savannah's driver proved his skill. If it had not been for his quick actions and ability to cut the engine and perform a handbrake turn, they would have careered headlong through the thrashing foliage and into the thick, knurled trunk. Unfortunately, Tanis and his driver were not so lucky; in an effort to avoid crashing into Savannah's buggy, Tanis' driver had only one other direction to go – and the tree was in the way!

She watched in horror as his buggy slewed onto a large branch, which acted like a ramp and lifted the front of the vehicle up, sending it flying into the air. It somersaulted sideways through the fringes of the tree's still violently heaving limbs, shredding leaves and scattering them like emerald confetti in its wake.

Drake and Penny's buggies passed in the shadow of the tree before it fulfilled its strategically planned purpose to break the group up, and they swerved to a halt in time to see Tanis' vehicle emerge upside-down from the branches, and crash grindingly along the road, with sparks flying out from its metal carcass. It came to a juddering halt, petrol spewing out across the tarmac from a ruptured fuel line. In the background, the tree settled across the road, branches flaying in its final death throes.

Tanis' body hung limp from his harness. The blood-soaked shape of the now dead driver hung next to him, a shard of thick, splintered branch skewered through the man's chest. The gunner's body was a distorted human form, his limbs twisted and deformed amongst the steelwork of the crash-cage. Spikes of broken bone jutted through his crimson-saturated combats.

In the noisy chaos, two shots rang out, and both of Drake and Penny's gunners died before they could gather their senses enough to bring about their guns and seek out the attackers.

'Get to the ditch,' ordered Penny's driver, as they loosened their own harness and rolled onto the road. Penny punched the release button in the centre of her chest, and her straps fell away in a loose tangle. Another shot ricocheted and sparked off the metal bar above her head. The "ph-zinng!" of a red-hot bullet encouraged her to body-roll across the hard road and into the comparative safety of a waterlogged gulley. Her driver unholstered a pistol and returned fire before scrabbling to the ditch and tumbling down next to her.

Penny watched nervously as Drake and his driver zigzagged across the road towards the same wet sanctuary. A hail of bullets bounced dangerously and erratically around their legs. Drake dove the last metre and landed headfirst in a ditch full of stagnant mulch, mud and leaves. His driver followed closely behind until a bullet thudded into his own back. He arched in agony; one hand reached behind him to claw with futility at the fatal wound, as the bullet exited from his chest, and he collapsed to his knees. For a moment, his lifeless, unseeing eyes stared at Drake before he toppled forward onto the verge, finding death as his only sanctuary.

Staccato bursts of gunfire continued, most of it aimed at Savannah and her driver who, having already kick-started their buggy and spun it around were now driving at full speed away from the incident. From the ditch, the others heard the frantic roar of the receding vehicle as bullets spat at the road like angry fireworks in pursuit.

'With a bit of luck that'll be Savannah and her escort getting away,' guessed Drake. 'It'll take them at least half an hour to get back to the compound and raise the alarm, and then another half hour for help to arrive. Whichever way you look at it, we're pinned down.' He cautiously removed his crash helmet. 'I should get rid of yours too,' he suggested to Penny. 'It's going to make you more of a target in this ditch. Did you manage to grab your backpack?' he asked hopefully.

She eased off her helmet. 'No time,' she replied.

'Me neither,' he added. 'How much ammo have you got, fella?'

The driver removed their facemask and goggles, to reveal the firm facial features of a woman with boyish, short-cropped brown hair, and hazel eyes.

'The name's Tess, and any cracks from you about women drivers and you'll find that I'm lacking a sense of humour at the moment.' She glared at Drake, and then checked the breach of her Glock semi-automatic pistol. 'Four in the gun and a spare magazine of seventeen rounds,' she confirmed.

Drake reached up and hauled the body of the dead

EARTHLAND

driver into the ditch, which prompted a further response of gunfire, this time to splatter into the bank and bushes behind them. He patted at the man's pockets and retrieved a clip of bullets, along with another Glock, and he handed both items to Penny.

'Your crossbow's on the buggy,' said Penny. 'What are *you* going to use?'

Drake unzipped his jacket and reached inside to withdraw a gunmetal-black Beretta.

'I never leave home without one,' he grinned. 'Ten rounds in the gun, and I've got two spare magazines. All in all, that should give us about eighty rounds between us. Trouble is, we don't know how many of them there are, or what firepower they've got.'

'It's all semi-automatic up until now,' said Tess. 'They must have a couple of snipers with scopes to have taken out our buggy-gunners so accurately.'

'One thing's at least for certain,' said Penny. 'They knew we were coming. It can't be Crazies; they can't cope with daylight, and it burns their skin. Anyway, whoever it is, they're organised, so I'm assuming that it's a hit squad from Opulence.'

'That makes sense,' said Tess. 'We were put on high alert this morning. According to Danny Hench, Intel advised him to expect further attacks on our compounds and bases.'

'That probably explains why Jean Fairfax wants us back at Base One,' said Penny. 'But I don't think even she would have reckoned on this.'

Penny warily raised her head above the level of the ditch, only for a loud barrage of gunfire to be let loose.

The air echoed with the cracks and retorts of gunshots as bullets smattered around them. All three crouched as low as they could, their knees brought up to their chests, and their arms crossed protectively around their heads. Each one of them silently prayed that they would not fall victim to a fateful ricochet.

The gunfire finally stopped, accompanied by a surreal calm.

Drake grabbed one of the dead driver's arms. 'Sorry if he was a friend of yours, Tess,' he apologised. 'But he may still be able to help us.'

'His name was Mike and he was a damn good man,' she replied.' I guess he knew the risks; we all do,' she added sombrely.

'Give me a hand to get him upright,' continued Drake as he struggled with the limp and uncooperative corpse. 'Penny, when we raise him up, you take a good look at where the shots are coming from, at least we'll get some idea of how many we're dealing with.'

Drake and Tess hoisted Mike's body into view, and the distraction worked. Penny stole precious seconds to scan the scene as a hail of bullets peppered the juddering torso of the dead driver.

At that same moment, in the centre of the road, Tanis opened his eyes to an upside-down world of nausea, pain and noise. He gazed wide-eyed and confused at Penny, who frantically signalled for him to stay still. A bullet embedded itself in the verge, just centimetres from her head, grass and earth splattered up across her face, and forced her to slide, spitting and cursing, back down into cover. Drake and Tess let the driver's bullet-riddled body slump sideways, as they too sunk back into the ditch.

Penny splashed cloudy ditchwater across her face and into her eye, which stung and smarted. Stagnant water worked its way into her mouth and the foul taste resulted in another bout of spitting and cursing.

'Well?' asked Drake impatiently.

'Tanis is alive,' she finally announced as she dabbed the complaining eye with the fold of her cuff. 'If they see him move they'll use him as target practice!'

'What's Tanis' condition?' he asked.

'I couldn't tell, apart from a bloodied head wound. He could have concussion, maybe worse.'

She wiped a sleeve across her face and unknowingly left a smeared residue of sludge on her cheek. 'I counted at least eight discharge points, all opposite us, and from ditch level. Two more shots came from tree height, one at ten o'clock and one at two o'clock. I'm guessing that's where the snipers are positioned. Gun-happy arseholes, they must have a bloody good supply of ammo,' she mused.

'If we fire a salvo in the general direction, and spread the shots low, mid and high, we're bound to hit a couple of them,' suggested Tess. 'That'll help improve the odds. Apart from that, *I* need to exercise some payback!'

'Okay,' said Drake. 'Let's see what sort of response we get. A five-second burst should do it. Tess, aim at the verge. Penny, you take the tree line, and I'll keep the snipers busy. After three.'

They checked their pistols, released the safety catches and drew in nervous breaths.

'One. Two. Three!' counted Drake.

In Penny's mind, the five seconds seemed to last an eternity, at the end of which, one sniper hung lifeless from a branch; a trapped ankle suspended him upside-down in a frozen death dive towards the ground. One other figure lay dead and crumpled against the base of a tree – a victim of Tess' steady aim. Two others suffered wounds to their arms and shoulders, courtesy of Penny's spread of fire.

An eerie silence followed, and the three of them crouched, their backs against the damp earth. They felt the heady effect of adrenalin course though their veins as they reloaded their weapons.

'Damn! I hate this killing,' breathed Tess.

'Then why volunteer?' asked Drake, bemused.

'Because I'll do anything to protect my kids. Anything to get them a better future so they don't have to live with shit like this,' she replied.

They hunkered there, as if in limbo, and let her words merge with their own thoughts.

The silence was broken by a man's voice. 'You've got five minutes to give yourselves up. Then we're coming to get you!'

'There's no giving up now. Let them come,' snarled Tess. 'I'd rather go down fighting. At least my death will be meaningful.'

'Hang on,' said Drake. 'It's got to be a bluff.'

'How do you figure that?' asked Penny.

'There's about eight of them now, and they know that if they rush us, we'll get at least half of them as they cross the road. I'm willing to bet that they don't *all* want to die today. I've got an idea. Let me try something.'

'Parley!' he shouted, and he handed his gun to Penny.

'What are you doing?' hissed Tess.

'I'm buying us some time. Trust me.'

He pushed both of his open hands above the road level. 'Will you grant me parley?' he shouted.

After a few seconds of silence, the voice responded, 'Okay. Amuse me.'

Drake hesitantly raised his head. A menacing figure dressed in a black combat suit, and wearing a full-face balaclava, stood on the edge of the road opposite. A gloved hand gripped a semi-automatic handgun, which at the moment pointed to the ground. Drake took the opportunity to scan the road.

'Tanis is gone!' he whispered down to Penny. Then, he raised himself a little further, to stand at full height in the ditch. He spread out his arms, and stood completely vulnerable. 'I haven't got a gun,' he emphasised.

'Well, I have,' the man replied flatly.

'What is it you want from us?' asked Drake.

'Give me the girl. Savannah Loveday,' came the reply, 'and I'll let you live. I know you've got her in the ditch. You're the one charged to protect her. Drake, isn't it?'

Thoughts of informers and a mistaken identity rattled through Drake's head. 'And you are?' he asked.

'It doesn't matter who I am. We can either do this the easy way, or the hard way. Give me Savannah Loveday. Now!'

31

NICE OF YOU TO JOIN THE PARTY

Savannah's whitened knuckles continued to grip the buggy's roll bar. She braced her legs and arms against the inevitable crash, and clenched her jaw so tightly she thought that it would shatter. The buggy careered left, and then lurched right across the road like a drunken dodgem car on rocket fuel.

Her driver struggled to control the steering wheel with one hand, while with the other he tried to stem the profuse bleeding from his neck. Above them, in response to the vehicle's erratic momentum, the rag-doll body of the gunner jiggled like a crazed puppet. A sniper's bullet had claimed him before they could speed the buggy out of range.

Finally, weakened through loss of blood, the driver lost his grip on the steering wheel, and it spun violently out of control. The wheels twisted sideways and the buggy jerked, to reverse around in a semicircle. Thankfully, because of the gyrating path of the vehicle, its speed was somewhat lessened as it careered backwards into a ditch, and embedded its rear into the soft earth of the bank, coming to rest at an almost vertical angle.

Savannah sat there and stared up at a pale blue sky, which was framed by the buggy's roll bars and spinning front wheels. Clouds of steam rose up from the now silent engine, as ditchwater made contact with the scorching hot exhaust pipes beneath her.

She inhaled a gasp, as if waking from a fitful nightmare, and then her senses kicked in with renewed clarity. She reached across to pull away the driver's mask. As her eyes met his, he opened his mouth, uttered the word 'sorry,' and exhaled a last pink, bubbling breath.

After briefly fumbling with the harness lock, she clambered out, only to stand ankle deep in sludge and mud. Without a second glance at the two bloodied corpses, she retrieved her backpack and crossbow, discarded her crash helmet and scrambled up the bank to the sanctuary of the forest.

She heard a burst of gunfire echo through the trees, and wondered if it heralded life or death for Tanis and her friends. Refusing to fear the worst, she crept cautiously around in an arc, back towards the source of the firing.

She was about fifty metres from the road when she heard another barrage of gunshots from ahead, which prompted her to take cover behind the stout trunk of a tree. She could only imagine that the group were pinned down, and she resolved to help them at all costs. She pulled her water bottle from her pack and poured a small amount onto a handful of the brown and black mulch from the forest floor. After kneading it with her fingers to make a deep coloured paste, she applied it to her face in streaks and blotches, careful not to get it into her eyes. The earthy smell of natural camouflage infiltrated her nose and awakened the primeval senses of the hunter within her.

'Nice of you to join the party,' said an as yet unseen figure that reclined against a tree a few metres from her.

Her head shot sideways and a smile crossed her face, which then faded to concern as she took in the full appearance of Tanis, who sported a bloodstained strip of material around his head.

'You're hurt!' She scrabbled across to squat next to him.

'Don't worry, it's nothing that a couple of stitches won't fix,' he grinned.

She fussed over him and tentatively lifted the sticky, coagulated makeshift bandage. 'Perhaps, next time you'll wear a crash helmet,' she gently scolded.

'It's okay,' he insisted, as he took her hand away and kissed it. 'What about you; are you hurt anywhere?'

'A few bruises, but what's new?' she breathed. 'How did you get away?'

'I waited for a lot of shooting to start, grabbed my pack and took advantage of the chaos to slip into a gully. I managed to slither far enough away to sneak into the trees. I take it your buggy crew didn't make it?'

She shook her head. 'It looks as though it's just us for the moment,' she confirmed. 'I'm not sure about Drake and Penny.'

'The last I saw, they were pinned down in a ditch with one of their drivers,' said Tanis. 'They're being shot at by a bunch of black suited mercenaries.'

'Then let's go and even out the odds,' she replied. She placed two crossbow bolts between her teeth, and one in the breech of her crossbow.

Back at the road, the gruff voice issued an ultimatum to Drake. 'Last chance. Give me Savannah Loveday.'

Drake noticed the man's hand tense around the grip of his gun. At the same time, he felt his own pistol, as Penny pressed it against the back of his thigh.

The sniper's body dropped with a crackle of broken branches, which momentarily distracted Drake's antagonist. Drake grabbed his pistol from Penny's hand, but the man brought his own gun up and levelled it at him. Drake knew that he didn't have time to dive for cover. It was close range and inevitable that he would be hit, probably fatally.

Before the man could squeeze the trigger, a crossbow bolt punctured his neck and split open his jugular. He dropped his gun and staggered into the road, zombie-like, one arm outstretched, the other clutching his neck. His eyes bulged with rage, or maybe with surprise; only the man himself could have said which, if he only had a larynx left to use!

Shouts came from the treeline, and then gunfire erupted into the woodland.

The noise jolted Drake into action. 'Come on,' he shouted. 'The cavalry are here!'

Penny and Tess hauled themselves from the ditch, and all three of them ran across the road, firing at anything dressed in black.

In a matter of twenty seconds, eight fresh corpses lay strewn around the forest floor; four of them the victims of various crossbow bolts, which protruded from fatal wounds.

Savannah and Tanis shouted out to Drake. 'Don't shoot, it's us.'

'Anybody else back there?' asked Drake.

'No,' replied Tanis as they emerged from the trees. 'This is all our own work.'

'Does this mean you two are going to do *everything* together?' joked Drake. This earned him a jab in the side from Penny.

Under her camouflage, Savannah blushed slightly, and then countered with – 'You can talk, Drake; looks like *you* needed the help of *two* girls!'

'No. Ours was a team effort,' replied Drake defensively. 'This is Tess,' he announced.

Tanis nodded and Savannah raised her hand. 'Hi, Tess. I'm Savan—'

Tess cut her off. 'I know who you are. I was briefed about you this morning. I just hope that you were worth the loss. Now, if you don't mind, I'm going to tend to my dead colleagues.' She turned and made her way to the tangled and bloodied occupants in one of the buggies.

'Well, I think that was a bit harsh,' said Savannah.

'Best to leave her be,' suggested Penny. 'She's the only one of her group that's survived. Let her deal with it in her own way.'

After a short discussion, it was agreed that Drake would apply some of his medical expertise to Tanis, while Savannah and Penny made their way back to the buggy left in the ditch. They carefully removed the bodies and laid them out by the roadside. The plan was to retrieve the buggy and get it started; they could then drive back to Greentrees for help. It took them both all of their strength to manoeuvre the vehicle out of the ditch and back onto the road. After several cranks of the engine, it reluctantly coughed back to life. It stuttered and spluttered noisily as Penny drove up the road until, after a couple of miles, they saw a convoy of vehicles and motorbikes heading towards them. She brought the buggy to a halt as a two-seater quad bike reached them. Behind the driver sat the familiar figure of Danny Hench.

'What's the damage?' he asked with concern.

'How did you know we were in trouble?' asked Penny.

'I arranged for an outrider to follow you from a mile behind; as soon as she heard the gunfire, she returned to base and alerted us. Now. I'll ask you again – what's the damage?'

Penny listed the casualties as far as she knew, both from their group and the attackers.

'Right,' he announced, 'let's go and clean up the mess, then we'll finish delivering you guys to your destination. Fall in behind and follow.' He tapped the driver on the shoulder, who opened the throttle and accelerated away.

'Oh, by the way, we're all right. Thanks for asking,' muttered Savannah sarcastically, as the convoy roared past.

32

A WORD OF ADVICE

At the scene of the attack, Danny Hench took control of the cleanup operation, but not without firstly ensuring Tanis, Drake, Penny and Savannah were securely harnessed into four buggies, complete with new drivers and gun crews. Sternly and officiously, he told them to, 'Get the hell out of here!'

The four drivers took the buggies along a varied route, sometimes off road skirting the hedgerows of fields, and at other times on tarmac, keeping to the middle of the highway. All the while, they kept a measurable distance between each of the vehicles. It was a tense and at times uncomfortable journey, until with relief, the group rolled up at Little Halt station. Here, the gargantuan of steam and steel waited for them. It seemed to hiss impatiently like a petulant child.

They said their grateful goodbyes to the drivers and gunners, and clambered the thick, splintered wooden steps to the platform. To their mild surprise, they found it occupied by half a dozen Diss commandos. They were in full combat gear and equipped with Heckler and Koch machine guns, along with personal side arms.

'Papers!' snapped a burly figure as he stepped forward to block their progress to the carriages.

'I should have thought it was obvious who we are,' complained Drake.

'Papers. Now!' he repeated, thumbing open the clip on his sidearm.

Two of the other commandos moved grim-faced towards them, their gun barrels raised in warning.

'Show him our papers, Drake,' encouraged Penny. 'They're in no mood to mess around. This is level one behaviour if ever I saw it.'

Drake muttered under his breath and swung his backpack to the ground in front of him.

'Slowly,' warned the man as the other two figures took up positions either side, their weapons aimed at the group within point blank range.

Drake purposely took his time to unzip a side pocket and extract the documents before he begrudgingly handed them over. The man scrutinised them suspiciously. He glanced at the four of them in turn, until, with his authority sufficiently satisfied, he handed them back to Drake. Without a further word, he and the other commandos stepped back, to allow the group access to an open carriage door.

'You're lucky; I've been shot at enough for one day,' Drake growled as he eyeballed the stony-faced man. 'Else you and I might have had a little dance. Fella.'

Penny gave Drake a push of encouragement. 'Leave it, Drake. He's just doing his job.'

'Yeah, but he looks as though he's enjoying it *too* much!' grumbled Drake as he boarded the train.

In an otherwise empty carriage, they stowed their packs and clambered gratefully into well-worn but comfortable seats, and just as the train lurched into motion, six Diss commandos boarded and spaced themselves evenly down the length of the train, to stand as watchmen, anticipating the unknown.

The train shrieked its whistle in a steamy farewell to Little Halt and the group settled down for the journey. The tension of the previous hours, along with the soporific momentum of the train, gradually tugged on their senses, until they were drowsy and dozing, and their eyelids fluttered gently into sleep.

In the passage of time, something in his survival senses brought Drake awake and open-eyed with a start. He sat up, alert. His hand gripped the butt of his concealed pistol as he craned his neck around his seatback and scanned the carriage. The nearest figure he could see was at the end of the compartment, and busy in conversation with another commando.

Drake looked at Penny, Tanis and Savannah, who were all lost in their slumbers; it was then that he noticed the buff oblong envelope on the table before him.

Written in bold capitals across it, were the words – DRAKE. FOR YOUR EYES ONLY

For a moment, he studied his sleeping colleagues, and then he surreptitiously folded the envelope inside his tunic. He slowly eased himself out of his seat and looked in the direction of the commandos; one of them glanced back at him for a second, then uninterested, continued his conversation. Drake made his way into a toilet compartment and locked the door. He sat on the toilet seat and studied the envelope for a moment before he tore it open and read the message.

Tanis' eyelids completed their tentative journey open. He had watched Drake through the filtered eyelashes of one eye, and now he mused why he had acted with such secrecy. What was Drake hiding? He had always trusted Drake, but why had he concealed the envelope, and more importantly, who had put it there? Tanis turned the situation over in his mind like a challenging puzzle, finally deciding to keep the incident to himself, for now.

A sudden metallic clattering and vibration announced the crossing of multiple points as the train approached Broadway, and this acted as a wake-up call for Penny and Savannah. Both stretched their arms and arched their backs in an effort to chase the remnants of sleep away. Meanwhile, Drake returned and took his seat opposite Penny.

'Where've you been?' she asked.

'Taking a leak, if you must know,' he said irritably.

Penny almost reprimanded him for being rude, but then thought better of it. They were all tired, aching and stressed.

Savannah absently folded her fingers around Tanis' hand and sunk her head contentedly onto his shoulder.

'A word of advice,' said a stony-faced Drake, as he leaned towards them, 'I should refrain from any public show of affection for each other from now on.'

The red-rag of being told what not to do, egged on by short-tempered fatigue, stirred in Savannah. 'What's the problem?' she snapped. 'Since when was having a relationship banned?'

'I'm just saying,' continued Drake, 'that if Jean Fairfax got wind of your – what shall we call it? – romance, then I'm sure she'd pull the plug on any exercise or mission involving Tanis and yourself.'

'That's ridiculous,' said Tanis defensively.

'Actually, he has a point,' interrupted Penny. 'She's split partners up before, to minimise any conflict of interest.'

'What do you mean?' protested Savannah. 'That I can't be trusted?'

'This mission is far too important to allow the needs of one person to get in the way and put others in jeopardy,' continued Drake. 'I'm telling you now – she'll remove Tanis from the team.'

'Why not me? Why Tanis?' asked Savannah.

'Because, sweetie,' said Drake, as he pointed an index finger straight at her, '*you* are the mission!'

Savannah pushed herself back into her seat and crossed her arms; she pouted like a spoilt child. She knew Drake was probably right, but she hated the thought of concealing her and Tanis' love for each other. Most of all, she hated it when Drake called her *sweetie*!

'Look, we have to keep together,' encouraged Penny. 'Besides, you need to realise you're not the only one who has to make sacrifices.' She looked directly at Savannah. 'I've missed Jake terribly, and goodness knows how little time I'll have with him when I get back before I have to say another goodbye, not knowing when, or if, we'll see each other again.'

'You don't have to go!' retorted Savannah.

An uncomfortable silence followed, until Penny

lifted up the edge of her sash and presented it to Savannah.

'Do you know what these colours stand for?' Without waiting for Savannah to reply, she continued. 'The green is for freedom, the land, our home. The orange is for the courage that we need and the sacrifices we have to make, and the red is to remind us of the blood that has been spilt, and of our lost loved ones, our family and friends. These colours unite us and bind us together. So don't tell me that I don't *have* to go.' In a rare moment of displayed anger, her face reddened and she threw the last words at Savannah. 'I would suggest it's time for you to prove that you're actually wearing it for the right reason. Either that, or take it off!'

As the train pulled up alongside the platform, Tanis was grateful for the sudden jolt that brought the conversation to a halt.

Drake stood up impatiently, grabbed his backpack and barked at them.

'Enough! You can make your decisions when we meet with Jean Fairfax. Meanwhile, keep any further opinions to yourselves. This is not the time. Now, get up and move out.'

33

BATTERED AND BRUISED

It was a long haul back to Base One. Apart from Drake snapping the occasional instructions at them, in the main, they were all left to their own silences and thoughts.

While they exercised their legs during a trolley crew change, Tanis purposely guided Savannah to one side.

'Look, I know it's been tough on you,' he consoled, 'but don't forget that we're your friends.'

'I thought you were more than that. I expected you to take my side,' she spoke reproachfully.

'This isn't about sides,' he argued. 'It's about doing the right thing for the right reason.'

'And what about us, Tanis? Are we the right thing for the right reason?'

'*You* tell me, Savannah.' He took her gently by the shoulders, and she tried to push him away.

'Look at me. Look at my face,' he pleaded. 'What you're feeling now is what we *all* feel. Everyday. This is how we live. This is why we know loss more than any other thing. This is why we fear love, because it can be ripped out of us any day, at any time. Destroyed by the actions of a bunch of Crazies, or a mutant animal, and now by other human beings who want to turn us into their slaves or kill us in the process. Penny wasn't trying to be unkind; she was trying to get you to see that you're one of us. You have to learn to live with the pain; it's a cost we all have to endure.

'Get it into your head, we've *all* lost loved ones, you're not alone. Grief unites us all in the end. That's why it's so important to me that we spend as much time as we can together, even if it has to be in secret – I don't mind. Because I love you.'

She looked into his eyes and the last of her emotional barriers crumbled, totally. It was then that her stomach churned and the final, deep darkness of loss came crashing over her, drowning her like a black, oily wave. She shook uncontrollably and the pain racked from her chest in big, heaving sobs. The words came spewing out.

'I didn't get to say goodbye to my parents. I didn't get to tell them that I loved them.'

She felt arms cradle her, embrace her in kindness and pity, and through the tears she saw those arms belonged not just to Tanis, but also to Penny and Drake. They stood there entwined, united in her grief and in her sorrow, while she exorcised the bitter selfishness of her loss.

*

They returned to Base One, physically and mentally bruised and battered.

When she arrived at the debriefing session, Jean Fairfax took one look at them and exclaimed her disbelief.

'Hell, Drake! I know you ran into a spot of bother on the way back, but what the bloody hell else have you been putting them through?'

'We *are* mission-ready,' he insisted. 'Give us twenty-four hours to rest and re-kit, and we'll be ready for the off.'

She looked at them; Tanis sported four fresh, angry red field stitches in his forehead. Penny had a weeping, crusted eye infection from the ditchwater. Savannah had tear-bruised, sunken eyes, and even Drake with his fading black eye and yellowed cheek, looked pale and haggard, as though he was carrying a huge weight on his shoulders.

'Twenty-four hours?' she mocked. 'You'll be lucky to find what's left of your arses in twenty-four hours! I'm standing you down for at least seven days. When I recall you I want you refreshed, and nothing but one hundred and ten per cent fit and ready.'

She lowered her voice and turned to Savannah, 'I'm sorry for your loss, Savannah. Please, let me arrange for some counselling for you.'

'No, thanks,' she replied. 'I have enough help; I have my friends.' She exchanged a smile with Penny. 'There is one thing I need to do though.'

'What's that?' asked Jean Fairfax.

'When we go to Opulence, I want the opportunity to rescue my sister.'

'I saw this coming,' admitted Jean Fairfax. 'That's why I've had some additional Intel collected. Your sister is constantly in the shadow of Jago, except at night when she insists on sleeping in your family's old apartments.

Luckily, for whatever reason in his twisted mind, Jago refuses to go there. You'll have a fifteen-minute window to get her out. The details are all in this briefing folder.' She slid it across the table to Drake.

'Now. Penny, go and get a medic to sort that eye out, and after he's finished with you, go and see Jake. You both need some time together, so I've arranged for him to be given a break in duties; he seems to have been working anywhere and everywhere lately. Tanis, you go off to the medic also, or you'll end up with an infection like Penny's. That field stitching needs tidying up and treating – one of your sloppier jobs, I think, Drake. Savannah, anything, any help you need, tell me. Do not hide away, make sure you spend time with people.' She cast a stern eye over them. 'That's it, off you go.'

As they filtered through the door, she added as an afterthought, 'Drake, I need a word.'

The others left and he closed the door.

'Can she do it? Has she got the nerve?'

'I have no doubt that we have her loyalties.'

'I didn't ask you that. Has she got the focus and the resolve to get through this?'

'Yes.'

'You know we could lose her.'

'That would be a shame.'

'Things have changed. There's an informer in the Network, maybe two.'

'Any ideas?'

'I have my suspicions.'

'Are you going to stop them?'

'Not at the moment; they may be useful.'

'That's a dangerous game, playing on both sides.'

'It's a risk that I'm willing to take.'

'Is there something else you're not telling me?'

'I could ask you the same question.'

'That's not the answer I was expecting.'

'I'm just being cautious.'

'There's a difference between being cautious and not trusting someone.'

'I'm trusting you to do the right thing when the time comes.'

'I always do the right thing.'

'Good. Then this conversation never happened.'

'As you wish.'

Outside in the corridor, another conversation was in progress.

'There's something that Drake's not sharing with us,' said Tanis.

'Why? Because he's being debriefed separately?' asked Penny. 'It's usual for team leaders to make an individual report.'

'No. There's something else.'

'Like what?' asked Savannah.

Tanis looked at the expressions on the girls' faces, and then he thought better of sharing his thoughts, for the time being at least.

'I'm not sure.' He shrugged his shoulders. 'Perhaps it's just me. Forget it.'

'If you say so,' Penny replied, and gave him a sideways look. 'Anyway, I'm a lucky girl. I've got two dates. One with a medic, and the second with my Jake. You two can use my cabin, but remember not to get caught! I'll see you in twenty-four hours,' she said with a wink and a smile.

'I'm going to throw myself into a shower; I need to feel clean again!' said Savannah. 'You'd better go and get those stitches sorted out and I'll see you later,' she encouraged Tanis. To his delight, as she walked away from him, she blew him a kiss.

★

Over the next three days, Drake was not to be seen.

Penny spent most of her time with Jake. She returned just once to pick up some clean clothes. Savannah and Tanis hid out in Penny's cabin, sleeping, eating and talking. Tanis surprised her by sharing his love of reading. He produced some "old world" books that he had managed to acquire over the years. This was a new experience for her, and she found another affinity with him, lying in a warm embrace, listening to him read in his soft, descriptive tones as candlelight flickered around them. He read her the story of *Romeo and Juliet* by William Shakespeare. A tale of love, violence and tragedy, which filled her mind with such emotions and imaginings, that she made Tanis repeat passages over and over again, as she relished every word.

'Do you think it's a true story?' she asked.

'I don't see why not,' he replied. 'There will always be warring families and there will always be a Romeo and a Juliet stuck in the middle. I like to think that sometimes their story does have a happy ending.'

'Do you think we'll have a happy ending?' she asked quietly.

Her eyes searched his. He put the book down and took her face gently in his hands. 'I don't want to think about the future, about the end of things. I only want to think about the here and now, with you.'

In the fairy tale glow of candles, he kissed her, and they surrendered to each other, to become softly lost in the intimacy of tenderness.

34

THE MISSION

It took two full weeks before Jean Fairfax deemed them all fit and mission-ready. This was not without them being subjected to medical examinations, physical and psychological, with the results being reported to her for scrutiny and clearance. Only then did she give them two days to pore over the newly compiled blueprints of Opulence, read the level one mission brief and present to her, in every detail, how they would expedite and complete their assignment.

The full objective of their task had not been revealed until Drake read through the contents of the file to the group. Theirs was a mission of terrorism by any other name. Explosives set with timers were to be deployed in strategic locations on Opulence, below and above the waterline. Maximum structural damage, along with minimum Servanti casualties, was a high priority. It was Savannah's role to lead the four of them through the service corridors and rat runs of Opulence, to keep them undetected, while they positioned and set the destructive packages. Most importantly, she was responsible for ensuring that she finally rendezvoused with the rest of them in time to leave safely – with or without Beth.

The time came when, just after midnight, with a chill autumn breeze scattering ragged grey clouds across a moonless sky, the rare sound of a gurgling outboard motor could be heard as it steadily powered an inflatable dinghy out of the estuary. It bounced like a yo-yo over small whitecaps of surf and out towards the open sea.

Cold fans of spray thrown up by its momentum escaped from under the craft to drizzle down the black waterproof clothing of its four occupants.

As the dinghy sped along, a dark shadow appeared and took shape on the horizon. A blot amongst the starry skyline of constellations. The towers of Opulence reached up like the grasping fingers of greedy sentinels.

Two miles from the city, Tanis pulled back on the throttle, and brought them to a slow crawl towards their goal. The engine purred and bubbled, and yet it seemed to their ears that it announced their coming with a deafening noise.

'Kill the engine,' ordered Drake. 'I don't want to take any chances; we'll row the rest of the way.'

Since they had begun the mission, Tanis noticed that Drake had a certain quiet nervousness about him; it was as though his focus was unusually distracted by some hidden inner thoughts.

On Opulence, such was the complacency and arrogance of the Jago regime, that security was now confined to the official landing and transportation platforms, where a few jetty lights illuminated the flat, steel pontoons, which bumped and jostled against the gargantuan hull sections.

The party steered their boat into the shadows of an overhanging observation deck, silent and deserted apart from a few seabirds, which peered down accusingly with disturbed agitation from their white-stained ledges. Drake reached out and grabbed a salt-crusted mooring ring; he quickly tied off a rope to secure the dinghy from drifting. Tanis pulled himself up and into the ink black opening of a rain gully – their entrance into a rarely used service hold.

He clambered through the opening, taking with him a pair of bolt cutters to remove a security grill, which barred their way into the hold, and which in turn (according to the blueprints), would allow them access to the first of the maintenance tunnels. A few moments after his disappearance, he gave a low whistle for them to follow. One by one, with their backpacks and weapons, they crawled into the darkness.

Savannah felt the angle of the floor suddenly fall away before her, and unsure of the descent that waited, she hissed out to Tanis.

'Tanis! Where the hell are you?'

'There's a bit of a drop,' his voice echoed. 'I'd suggest you come down feet first,' he advised.

'Are you kidding? There's only just enough room to kneel, let alone turn around,' she complained.

'What's the problem?' Drake's voice came from behind her.

'There's a drop,' she answered.

'Where's Tanis?' he asked.

'Down below.'

'Then you'd better join him, 'cause we're not going back. Now get a move on,' he urged.

She inched forward; her hands lost their grip and she tumbled out and down. The narrow passage slanted like a chute and the greasy metal surface gave no resistance. It was only a short drop, but in the uncertainty of darkness, she thought that she would fall forever. Her arms and face hit cold, rank water. A hand grabbed her, and pulled her up to stand in what was less than a metre of oily liquid. She spluttered and gagged as the claustrophobic stench filled her nostrils and throat.

The steel compartment was abruptly illuminated with the green light of a flare, and Drake's body barrel rolled past her, to land with a splash and sit upright, the flare dry in his hand, as if he had practised the movement a hundred times before.

'Okay, Penny,' he shouted. 'Come on in, but watch the fall.'

Penny's arrival was as unglamorous as Savannah's, except that she at least managed to keep her head above the water.

Drake held the flare aloft, to reveal the metal rungs of a ladder that reached up on one side of the shaft, to a hatch in the ceiling.

'This should take us up to the storeroom,' he announced. He grasped the first rung.

Five minutes later and they were all crouched in semi-darkness amongst stacks of large, wooden crates, most of which were stencilled with the word, CONFISCATION. The contents contained the possessions and belongings of those that had been Transported. The intention was that the crates would eventually be opened up, and anything of value be auctioned off amongst the Fortunata, with no thought given to the fate of the previous owners.

Savannah ran her hand along the rough edge of a crate.

'I used to come here sometimes and steal things to pass on to some of my Servanti friends,' she said wistfully. 'I thought I could help them, but in the end, I guess all that I did was to delay the inevitable.'

'Well, now's the chance for you to make up for it,' said Drake. 'There's been a change of plan.'

In the ghostly light of the flare, all three of their faces met his with perplexity.

'This is not open for discussion; and I will not repeat myself, so listen up,' he said forcefully.

He explained that instead of completing a circuit of the locations as a group, the plan was now for them to split into two teams.

Savannah and Tanis were to take the south side of the city where, on large platforms that jutted out high above sea level was a sizeable solar panel farm. This enormous solar complex accounted for eighty per cent of Opulence's generated energy. Destroying it would put the regime's activity back months, if not years. The second target for Savannah and Tanis would be a desalination plant. Although there were several of these utilities, even destroying one with a couple of well-placed charges, would have a serious impact on supplies. Finally, Savannah was to make her own way to find Beth.

Tanis knew that Savannah was nervous, not just about facing Beth, but also about visiting what used to be her family home. Without question, and with or without Drake's approval, he had already decided he would go with her, not only to guard her back, but also to give her moral support. Personally, he had no intention of leaving without Savannah, no matter what transpired between the two sisters.

Next, Drake announced that he and Penny were to target the greenhouse facilities. These resembled hanging gardens; long terraces, which rose up on the western side, and were protected by glass domes of transparent honeycomb bubbles.

'You want to slow something down or kill it,' Drake said. 'Hit it in the stomach. Cut off its food supply, make it hungry and weak.'

Their secondary target was the Research Centre; ideally, enough damage would be done here to slow down or even prevent the development of solar weapons.

During their time planning the mission, one of the critical issues discussed was their all important exit strategy. Everyone recognised the consequences of being captured, particularly if they fell into Jago and Roth's hands. As a result, they decided that each one of them would retain a single charge of explosive; if they found themselves stranded, with no chance of escape, they at least had the option of dying swiftly by their own hand.

Now, to their bewilderment, Drake placed a bag of explosives against the side of a crate, and lifted a cover to expose a small metal alarm clock. Wires trailed from its circular case and into the bag. He moved the hands on the clock face to correspond with the time on his watch, and then he slid a small lever across the top of the clock to the ON position. The second hand clicked into movement.

'What the hell are you doing?' asked Tanis.

'This is your incentive to get the job done and get back here in time,' Drake announced. 'We've got ninety minutes to set the rest of the charges and leave in the dinghy. Once that time's up, this blows, and like the rest of the charges, if anyone tries to defuse it, it'll explode instantly. There is no override.' He pulled back his sleeve. 'Time to synchronise watches; I make it coming up to 02.38.'

None of them responded. There was a silence, which was only flawed by the low hum of machinery, which resonated from deep within the structure of Opulence.

'I'll make this simple for you,' he said. 'Either confirm that you are taking part in this mission, or I'll relieve you of your explosives and weapons, and you can remain in the dinghy. You'll have plenty of time to think of what you'll say to Commander Fairfax and the court martial that will await you – it's your choice!' He stared at them, stony-faced. 'I repeat. Time to synchronise watches.'

'When this is over,' said Tanis, 'you're going to have to answer to us. Big time.'

'I don't owe you any explanations for doing my job,' answered Drake. 'Now, are any of you going to jeopardise this mission?'

With mixed emotions tumbling in their heads, and in resignation they checked their watches.

'If anyone's late, we go without them as agreed,' he

said. 'Agreed,' he emphasised, more as a confirmation than a question.

'Agreed,' the others nodded in unison, each one taken aback by Drake's aggressive stance.

Drake unfolded a blueprint, and in the flare's light, he pointed with a gloved finger and traced along to a black-circled intersection. 'This is where we split up,' he said.

He made them run through a weapon check, confirm how many rounds each of them had been issued for their pistols, and how many crossbow bolts they were carrying. He also seemed obsessed on them repeating the precise locations where they would place the explosives. Finally satisfied, he insisted that they check their watches one more time.

Tentatively, they moved out into a dim corridor. Condensation dripped from a tangle of metal pipes overhead, and black, greasy puddles populated the floor.

'I'll take the map – just in case,' said Drake. 'And if all goes well, I'll see you back at the dinghy. Don't be late,' he added, and with that, he and an anxious-looking Penny stole away into the shadows.

35

Best Laid Plans

Thirty minutes into their task, and without any exchange of words, Savannah and Tanis worked their way along puddle-strewn corridors, setting three periphery charges and hiding them securely behind pipework or in shadowed recesses, to eventually make their way up a narrow set of metal stairs, which allowed them access into the centre of the solar complex.

As they reached the top stair, Tanis stopped. 'Wait. I need to think this through,' he said.

'What's the problem?'

'I've been on plenty of operations with Drake and this is totally out of character. Something's not right, he's hiding something.'

'And you have an idea what it is?' she prompted suspiciously.

Tanis told her about the incident with the envelope on the train.

'I can't believe that you chose not to tell us,' she complained. 'That you didn't even confide in *me*.'

'In the end, I thought it may have been from Jean Fairfax,' responded Tanis.

For a few moments, Savannah ran the events though her mind.

'You could be right,' she finally considered. 'In fact, the more I think about it; maybe this whole change of plan *is* down to her. Drake's told her about you and me.'

'No. There's something else. Drake's involved with something, and I've got a bad feeling about it. There's a voice in my head telling me to get the hell out of here, now.'

'I can't just leave, not now that I have a chance to save Beth. Besides, we also need to think about Penny,' she replied.

'Apart from being even more cautious, the best I can suggest is that we change the way we do things,' he said. 'Firstly, let's put all of these charges together, and set them to go off earlier.'

'Okay, but still leave me enough time.' She checked her watch. 'We'd better get on with it.'

Savannah cautiously pushed back the steel doorway, and the monotonous drone of solar power hummed through the gap. As they stepped inside, there was no breeze, no draught, and an invisible curtain of heat hit them with the intensity of an oven. The skin on their faces tightened, and the backs of their throats became parched by the arid air. She gasped and hastily retrieved a water bottle from her backpack, quickly unscrewing the cap to gulp greedily at it before splashing a good amount of the liquid onto her face. Tanis needed no prompting and he hastily followed suit. For a moment, they crouched there, panting, trying to acclimatise as best they could in the oppressive atmosphere.

Stretched out in front of them, in fifty-metre rows, the enormous panels, each one at least ten metres square and angled skyward at forty degrees, were supported by a network of thick, steel tubes, allowing enough room for Tanis and Savannah to crawl beneath them.

'Head for the centre,' she indicated. 'But don't touch anything with your bare hands; the metal will blister your skin off!'

Slowly and laboriously, they moved crab-like amongst the web of metal struts, pausing several times to draw in a precious breath, and summon up what moisture they could in their mouths.

'It helps if you breathe through your nose,' suggested Tanis.

'It would help if I could just breathe!' grumbled Savannah.

Finally, they crouched, panting like two over-exercised greyhounds, and together with gloved hands, they managed to pull up a maintenance grill from the floor. Tanis dropped down into the dark channel and secured the deadly packages. He checked his watch and set the timers ten minutes early, before he struggled back out to help Savannah replace the cover. The heat sapped at their strength as they crawled on hands and knees back to the doorway, where they closed it behind them.

Slumped in the damp gloom with their mouths open, they sucked in the reviving cool air like gasping fish. Perspiration chilled on their brows, and they pulled open their jackets to allow the cold, damp air of the stairway to caress their sweat-soaked bodies. Slowly, their breathing regained its natural rhythm.

Tanis checked his watch. 'We've gained seven minutes,' he announced.

'Good,' said Savannah. 'Let's get to the desalination plant and set the second batch of charges.'

At that very moment, Drake and Penny were setting their deadly packages along the garden terraces. Drake had dropped over a ledge to secure an explosive charge amongst some tall trellises of well-cropped tomatoes.

'There, that should do some damage,' he said with satisfaction, and he reached up to re-join Penny. As his head cleared the ledge, he stopped himself and dropped back down.

'What's the matter?' she asked.

He looked up at her and placed a finger across his lips. 'I'm sorry, Penny,' he whispered. 'I can't tell you what's going on; you're going to have to trust me.' He fumbled with his pack. 'Take this and make sure you tell them everything we've planned tonight; do that and you won't be hurt.'

He passed the blueprint to her, and then he ducked back down to quickly disappear amongst the shadowed vegetation.

Penny caught a movement from the corner of her eye. She turned to face two figures as they emerged from a darkened alcove – Transportation Police.

Meanwhile, Tanis and Savannah furtively made their way past a row of closed doors. As they reached the end of the corridor, they crouched in a small recess and scanned the scene for any movement. In front of them, a vast, cathedral-sized space opened out, and in a maze of organised engineering, a myriad of shining steel pipes filled the area, to connect with half a dozen enormous tanks that formed part of the desalination process.

'It's too quiet,' said Savannah. 'As far as I can remember, there have always been at least a couple of technicians working here, day and night.'

'Do you think we're expected?' asked Tanis.

She didn't need to answer.

'Don't move, or the last thing your eyes will see, is your insipid little brains splattered across the floor,' came a chilling voice from behind them.

Savannah's stomach turned cartwheels. Even the thought of the man's name made her want to retch.

Rough hands pulled them to their feet, and they were dragged out into the open area of the plant.

'Search them, and remove everything and anything that could cause harm to others, and to themselves,' commanded Roth. 'That pleasurable pastime is mine.'

Restrained by four burly Transportation Police (the term *thugs* immediately entered Savannah's mind), they were searched and relieved of any weapons and explosives. She noticed that along with their usual nightstick-style batons, each of the men also carried a short, flat bladed sword, sheathed at the waist.

Roth sauntered back and forth in front of them. His jet-black robes billowed around him with an air of malevolence. He had let his hair grow and it now cascaded past his shoulders in locks of ginger-red venom. His eyes stared wide with crazed excitement, and a tombstone smile creased his face.

Savannah launched herself at him, but her captors merely brought her arms up behind her and forced her to her knees. With a screech of muscle-torn pain, she vented her anger at him.

'I'm going to kill you! I'm going to make you suffer for what you did to my parents!'

He bent forward, gripped her jaw with his rough, gloved fingers and pulled her face towards his. His sickly perfumed scent reached out with invisible tendrils to invade and pollute her senses.

The smell brought back unwelcome memories, of a time when she was much younger and inadvertently stumbled through a service door into one of Opulence's funeral parlours. It was not the lidless coffin which contained a recently departed resident that had caused her the most anxiety at the time, but the pervading aroma of cloying incense from the parlour's burning oil lamps. She fled home and spent an hour showering, convinced that the smell had become impregnated into her skin.

This summed up the vileness of Roth. He chose to use the same perfumed oil in his hair – the scent of death.

'Savannah Loveday,' he hissed. 'Welcome home.' His sickly grey tongue slid from between his lips and licked a trace of wet saliva across her cheek.

Tanis struggled, enraged and helpless.

'Leave her alone, you sick monster!' he shouted.

Roth stood back. He glanced from Savannah to Tanis and back again.

'What have we here?' he mused. 'Do I sense love? A romance?'

'You don't know the meaning of love,' she shouted.

He waved a finger at her. 'You would be surprised, my dear. Love comes in many forms.'

From amongst the huge desalination tanks, another half a dozen Transportation Police emerged. Sandwiched between two of them was a pale and visibly shaken Penny.

Roth turned in acknowledgement. 'Nice of you to join us, my dear. Now, which one of you will tell me where the explosives have been placed?'

'We'd rather die than tell you!' spat Savannah.

'That may well be necessary,' smiled Roth. 'But, as time is of the essence, let us find the weakest link, shall we?' He indicated to Penny. 'Bring her here.'

Two Transportation Police frogmarched her over to Roth. She wore an expression of dazed bewilderment, and offered no resistance at all.

'These two,' he announced, flourishing an arm at Savannah and Tanis, 'I'm sure, will be a challenge to me. However; you, my dear, I sense will be an easier conquest. He stroked her cheek with the back of his gloved hand. 'Such a pretty face. Such unblemished skin.' He pressed his thumb and index finger together and the glint of a thin, five-centimetre metal spike slid out from the leather fingertip. He drew a figure of eight with it in the air, tantalisingly close to her face. With a suppressed whimper, she flinched and closed her eyes.

'Leave her alone!' a voice shouted from above. 'The deal was that she would be safe. You've got what you wanted, now let her go!'

'It's Drake!' exclaimed Tanis.

Heads turned upwards to an overhead walkway,

where three figures stood in silhouette against the overhead lighting, their features indiscernible.

'Now, now, Roth,' said another voice. 'He's right; I must honour my agreements – sometimes. She's given us a map, and the information we need to retrieve the explosives. Our people are in the process of removing them as we speak. You can let her go; she has a dinghy to catch with her friend here.' Jago walked forward to the railing; the lights created a theatrical spotlight on him. 'You can have your fun with my dear sister and her little friend later, in that special room you have in your new Transportation Centre. In the meantime, hold them there. I'm coming down.'

Roth turned back to Penny. 'Shame,' he cooed. 'Until we meet again, my dear.' He clicked his finger and thumb and the spike retracted into the glove.

As she was escorted through the storage tanks, Penny shouted over her shoulder and back to Tanis and Savannah. 'Drake told me to tell them everything.'

Tanis glanced up and noticed only two figures remained on the walkway. 'I'm going to get you, you double-crossing traitor. Do you hear me, Drake?' he shouted.

Savannah stared venomously up at Jago. 'I hate you!' she hissed.

36

THE REUNION

On their knees, with their heads forced forwards, Savannah and Tanis heard Roth's footsteps recede with cold, dull echoes across the floor.

'I can't believe Drake sold us out,' rasped Savannah.

'Maybe it wasn't just Drake,' answered Tanis.

'You don't think Penny had a hand in it, do you?' She furrowed her brow.

'Well, I don't see her helping us out of this,' he replied.

'Why would Drake do all of this to save Penny?'

'It's not about Penny,' guessed Tanis. 'We've been used as a bargaining tool for something much bigger than that. I've come to agree with you; this has Jean Fairfax written all over it.'

'Quiet!' shouted one of the guards.

'Quiet yourself,' retorted Tanis.

A steel baton came down swiftly across his arm, and he grimaced as the impact made his nerve endings scream in agony.

'Go to hell!' he shouted, struggling. The uniformed thug kicked Tanis sideways and towered over him, his baton raised for another strike. Enraged, Savannah twisted around, and freed herself enough to kick out at the man's legs and throw him off balance. It was then that all hell broke loose, and batons rained mercilessly down on their bodies as they curled up like helpless foetuses. When Roth returned, they both lay concussed and unconscious, like discarded rag dolls.

It was only a matter of minutes before cold water was thrown with brutish force into their faces.

Savannah's vision cleared, and as her eyes focused, her senses were shocked into clarity.

'Beth!' she gasped.

In front of her, flanked on either side by Jago and Roth, stood her sister. She seemed taller and leaner now, with a harsh, stony-faced expression, no longer the girl with the pleasant, bright face that Savannah remembered.

Beth moved forward to crouch down in front of her sister and stare unnervingly into her eyes. Savannah heard the sound of flesh on flesh a fraction of a second before she felt the sting of Beth's palm across her cheek. Her face drained of blood, and she gasped as an ice-cold stab of shock ran through her stomach.

'You killed our parents,' said Beth, her voice flat and detached.

'That's not true,' interrupted Tanis.

'Shut up, you filthy Diss!' sneered Beth, and she spat at him. Her saliva splattered against his face. She turned her attention back to Savannah. 'Jago told me what you did. You deserted me and had our parents killed out of your own selfish jealousy and spite.'

'No! It's all lies. I loved our parents. I love you.

You're my sister,' pleaded Savannah.

'Save your breath,' said Beth. 'I know you've come to kill me.'

Savannah could see Roth in the background; a nauseating smile dominated his face. He was enjoying the situation. 'I just love a family reunion,' he chuckled.

Jago stood next to him, displaying a smug grin of satisfaction.

'I didn't arrange to have Mum and Dad killed, and I haven't come here to kill you either,' Savannah continued. 'I'm here to try and stop those two monsters that are standing behind you, and who have poisoned your mind, from destroying us all.'

Beth stood and turned to Jago.

'Can I kill her now?' she asked, without a hint of emotion.

Jago placed a protective arm around her, and the blood in Savannah's veins turned cold at the sight. 'Patience, little sister,' he cooed. 'There's a time and a place for everything. Now, just in case our search parties have not retrieved and disarmed all of the explosives, I would suggest we retire to the security of the interrogation centre. Bring them,' he signalled to the guards as he, Beth and Roth turned towards an exit. 'Oh.' He paused, and added, almost as a casual afterthought, 'If they resist, you have my permission to beat them senseless again. However, don't dare to kill them. We still have to have *our* sport.'

Tanis and Savannah were pulled to their feet; two batons jabbed them in their backs and encouraged them to move forward. 'You heard the man. Move!' growled one of the men as he hoisted the seized backpacks and weapons over his shoulder.

The procession worked its way out of the desalination plant, down a long corridor and then out into the night air, and onto a small plaza. As Jago, Roth and Beth disappeared through a doorway into a main building opposite, Savannah heard the hushed swish of a crossbow bolt.

The man gripping Savannah's arm fell like a stone; blood gushed from his head. Instinctively, she dropped to the floor beside him and grabbed his baton just as Tanis' captor suffered the same fate from a second well-aimed bolt. She swung the baton around with such force that the impact shattered one of the remaining men's ankles. He dropped the backpacks and weapons, and howled as he clutched at the broken limb. She brought the baton across his other leg and he crumpled to the ground, to roll around in agony. Her hunting knife lie next to her backpack, and she grabbed it. She pulled it from its sheath and quickly brought it up to the man's throat.

'How do you like a taste of your own medicine?' she hissed. 'Now keep still and I might let you live.'

Tanis reached for one of the fallen crossbows. The last guard hesitated, and then, a mixture of self-preservation and cowardice motivated him to turn and run. Tanis didn't even have time to load his crossbow before another bolt shot through the air and implanted itself between the fleeing man's shoulder blades. The tip of the bolt penetrated his right ventricle, and his heart exploded before his body hit the ground.

Tanis swung his crossbow around, a bolt now in place.

'Who's there?' he shouted. 'Show yourself.'

He slid across to Savannah as she restrained the remaining guard.

'Are you okay?' he asked her.

'I've got bruises in places where I didn't even know I had places, but apart from that, I'll survive,' she replied, and then she added, 'Who the hell is it?'

'I haven't a clue, but whoever it is may just have saved our lives.'

'Come on out,' shouted Savannah.

There was no movement, no answer.

'What happens now?' she asked.

As if in response to her question, the ground shuddered. An enormous explosion boomed and resonated from somewhere behind them.

Tanis checked his watch. 'That'll be the solar panels,' he confirmed. 'At least they didn't get to *them*.'

The guard moved nervously and Savannah pressed the blade of her knife closer to his Adam's apple. A thin line of blood streaked across his throat.

'What'll we do with him?' she asked.

Tanis raised an eyebrow. 'Your call.'

Five minutes later, they'd dragged the guard to the side of the plaza and left him there, gagged and bound. Savannah gave him a warning that if she ever came across him again, she would break both his arms and legs.

Their mystery rescuer had disappeared without a word, and they decided that Drake and Penny had probably taken flight in the dinghy. The only option for them was to find an alternative means of escape. Savannah reluctantly conceded that any attempt to rescue, or even kidnap Beth, was impractical – for now.

She suggested they head for the docking bays at the Transportation Centre, in the hope that some solar charged jet skis may be moored there. However, this meant heading in the same direction in which Jago, Roth and Beth had gone.

'It's not the best idea you've come up with lately,' Tanis pointed out. 'But what the hell; let's live dangerously!' he grinned,

After cautiously entering the main building, they made their way down a series of corridors, until Savannah had to admit that she had lost her bearings. As they retraced their steps, they heard shouts and the sound of running feet coming towards them. Savannah desperately tried the handles of several doors until one thankfully opened. They slid inside the room, and closed the door behind them; it was then that the acrid, chemical smell of an interrogation cell hit their nostrils. In the subdued lighting, they turned to see a pair of figures gagged and strapped to two metal chairs.

Tanis shook his head in disbelief. 'Penny? Drake? What the hell is going on?'

Savannah released Penny's gag.

'I'm so sorry,' Penny sobbed. 'I didn't know.'

'What the hell's the matter with you, Drake?' asked Tanis as he pulled at the cloth muzzle.

'No!' cried Penny. 'You're wrong. It's not Drake. It's Jake!'

37

BROTHERS AND
SISTERS IN ARMS

It was Jake who had arranged for his brother to be delivered the letter on the train –

I KNOW THAT I WON'T BE ABLE TO STOP PENNY FROM GOING TO OPULENCE. I COULDN'T BEAR TO LET THEM TAKE HER OR HARM HER, SO I'VE MADE A DEAL WITH THEM. PENNY DOESN'T KNOW ABOUT THIS, SO DON'T BLAME HER. I LOVE HER AND I'LL PROTECT HER AT ANY COST, AT ANY PRICE.

I COULD TELL YOU NOT TO GO ON THE MISSION, BUT I KNOW YOU WILL, NO MATTER WHAT I SAY, SO I CAN ONLY TELL YOU TO STAY AWAY FROM THE GIRL, SAVANNAH. LET THEM HAVE HER AND GET YOURSELF AWAY AS SOON AS YOU CAN. WHEN PENNY AND I GET BACK HERE, WE'LL DISAPPEAR INTO THE COUNTRY.

WHATEVER THEY SAY, I'M NOT A TRAITOR; I JUST THINK THAT WE'VE ALREADY SUFFERED ENOUGH LOSS, AND I'M NOT LOSING ANOTHER PERSON THAT I LOVE.

DON'T BETRAY ME, BROTHER; YOU AT LEAST OWE
ME THAT.

FORGIVE ME.

ALWAYS, YOUR BROTHER, JAKE.

★

'He lied to me!' said Jake. 'Jago said we would be safe
and set free, that all he wanted was Savannah.'

'Why would you trust a man who arranged the death
of his own parents?' mocked Savannah, as she released
Penny's restraints.

Jake looked at her, suddenly ashamed. 'I'm sorry. I…
I didn't know.'

'He fooled me, and I'm his sister,' she said consolingly.
She couldn't be angry with him. She knew that love
could drive you to do desperate things and she knew
how much he loved Penny. As Tanis finally released him,
Jake stood up, and Savannah reflected on how easy it
had been to mistake him for Drake. Firstly, they hadn't
expected him to be there; secondly, he was dressed in
the same style of black combat suit as the rest of them;
and thirdly, Drake's recent behaviour had skewed their
judgement.

Tanis, however, was less forgiving. 'You sold us out!
You sold out your friends and even your own brother.
You betrayed us.'

'I wrote to him. I warned him to stay out of it,' Jake
replied defensively.

At that moment, another explosion reverberated through the walls and rocked them on their feet. Then another followed, this time closer and louder.

'Luck appears to be on our side,' said Tanis. 'They haven't found all of the packages in time.'

'That can't be the others we planted,' said Savannah, as she checked her watch. 'Those should have gone off five minutes ago.'

Tanis turned to Penny. 'I thought that I heard Jago say you'd given them a map with the locations on.'

'I did. Before he disappeared, Drake gave me the blueprint and told me to tell them everything.'

'He must have given you a fake copy. He's still out there planting explosives. He's buying us time,' encouraged Tanis. 'We need to get out of here, now.'

They left the room and made their way unchallenged to the end of the corridor, where they pushed their way through double doors that opened onto the large steel platform of a covered marina. Across a wide expanse of deck, and illuminated by floodlights, half a dozen jet skis bobbed up and down against a padded jetty. To one side, two large transportation barges were moored, their grey container bulks like sleeping monoliths.

'Get to the jet skis,' shouted Tanis.

Ahead of them, to their right, half a dozen Transportation Police, led by Roth, burst through a door. The expression on his face was one of retribution and murder. He strode forward purposely; the material of his garments flapped around him like a black sail caught in a storm. Along a causeway to their left, another group of

Transportation Police ran forward to cut off any escape route.

'We're screwed!' said Savannah. 'We'll never get to the jetty.'

'Then we'll just have to make them move,' said Tanis as he pulled an explosive charge from his backpack.

'I can play that game,' said Savannah, as she removed two more from her own pack. 'Just make sure that Roth is within range when we set them off.'

Penny, Jake, Tanis and Savannah pulled themselves defensively into a tight circle, back to back.

Roth's group suddenly came to a halt, ten or twelve metres away, while the Transportation Police formed a line along the causeway as a barrier.

'Give yourselves up,' shouted Roth. 'There's nowhere for you to run.'

'Come anywhere near us and we'll blow you to hell,' shouted Tanis. He raised a primed charge in his hand.

Everyone froze. No one dared move. The scene became a tableau of human beings, both good and bad, quietly calculating their personal survival odds.

Into this moment of inactivity came Jago; he walked casually along the causeway with his arm around Beth.

'This is growing quite tiresome,' he said. 'So I'll tell you what I'll do. Here's the deal. I'll trade Beth's life for yours.'

Beth's head jerked up at Jago. Confusion spread across her face.

'Come on, Savannah. This is a once-in-a-lifetime offer.' He smiled at his own joke. 'Beth and all of your playmates can go free, if you'll just come over here and give yourself up to me.'

'Jago! What are you doing?' asked Beth. The wide-eyed look of a lost child crossed her face.

'The time has come for us to say goodbye, little sister,' he said in a patronising tone.

'I don't understand,' she said.

'If I let your sister go, she will become ever more troublesome. Revenge can drive people like that. So here's a chance for you to do something useful. Change places with her.'

She turned to face him. 'I don't want to go. I want to be with you.' She studied his face and a question formed. 'What do you mean; revenge?'

He grabbed her roughly by her arm, and brought up a pistol. He pressed the hard, cold barrel to her head.

'You are as irritating, stubborn and rebellious as Savannah. Now, shut up!' he snarled through clenched teeth.

She felt the muzzle of the gun push painfully into her temple.

A dialogue unfolded in her head. *How could he do this to her? Hadn't she believed in him, shown him brotherly adoration, followed his teachings and nurtured their mutual hatred for the sister who had killed their parents?* Then, through this mental confusion, deeper questions tumbled from her subconscious. *Had he told her the truth? Did Savannah really have their parents killed, and if she didn't, who did?*

Savannah's voice broke through Beth's thoughts.

'No! Don't hurt her. You can have me if you let her go.' She passed the explosive to Penny and stepped forward.

Tanis grabbed her arm. 'Savannah. Don't,' he pleaded.

'I have to, Tanis; she's my sister.' She turned, gently caressed his face and kissed him. She stared into his eyes. 'Take care of her. Be her strength and her spirit. Don't worry. He won't make me suffer. I'll take him with me.' She pulled back her jacket to show Tanis the second charge that she had hidden there. 'Thank you for loving me.' She kissed him again and turned away before her emotions fractured her willpower. With steely resolve, she walked towards Jago.

'I want to meet her halfway,' she shouted.

'Lose the crossbow and dump the backpack,' he ordered.

Savannah did as she was told, and Jago shoved Beth forward. 'Get moving.'

In those moments, the truth hit Beth. *Her sister was willing to give her life for her, without question. How could she have ever doubted her? How could she have been so blind?*

They met in the middle of the platform. Two sisters reunited in truth and love. Tears tumbled down Beth's cheeks; her chest heaved in short sobs as guilt and loss twisted in the pit of her stomach like an agitated serpent.

'I'm so sorry,' she wept. 'He told me so many awful things about you.'

Savannah reached out and embraced her sister. 'It's not your fault,' she whispered, and she gently stroked Beth's hair.

'Yes, yes, yes,' shouted Jago impatiently. 'Get on with it.'

'I love you, Beth. Be a good girl. My friend Tanis will take care of you.'

She pulled her hand from Beth's clinging fingers and guided her on her way. She watched her nervously, gauging her sister's distance to safety, patiently picking the moment when she would turn towards Jago and take him to oblivion. Beth was a couple of paces from Tanis and his group when Jago fired a shot into the air; the report echoed across the marina and startled them all.

'Come on! Come on! I'm tired of waiting,' he yelled.

Savannah turned and strode purposely towards him. She slipped her hand inside her jacket to find the warm metal pull cord that would deliver bloody vengeance on Jago, and in her mind, send her to meet her parents in whatever afterlife there may be.

'Put your hands in the air,' shouted Jago as he levelled the pistol at Savannah.

She needed a couple more steps to be sure, and she mentally steeled herself to absorb any bullets. She was determined that nothing would halt her momentum towards him.

The next explosion was by far louder than the sound of any gunshot that either she or Jago had anticipated would pass between them. The ground rocked so violently that everyone was thrown off balance to the floor. Part of an overhanging observation deck twisted with a grinding, metallic screech as it collapsed into the sea. The metal crumpled and folded like a grey cardboard structure; flames and smoke proclaimed the destruction.

Savannah was already on her knees as she saw Jago thrown forward. His gun fell from his grasp and it skittered across the metal decking and towards her, far from his reach. He turned, and his eyes met hers as she withdrew the explosives from her jacket.

Fear and adrenalin gave him almost impossible speed to get onto his feet and run away towards the causeway. Savannah scrabbled after him. As she reached the gun, she picked it up and pointed it in his direction, only to see him slip down onto one of the jetties.

An idea formed in her head in an instant and she acted without hesitation. She threw the explosive, and as it reached its arc above the edge of the causeway, she fired the gun into the air, round after round after round, until a red-hot bullet hit the package and ignited the charge. An angry ball of fire exploded above a still running Jago. Through a crimson flare of smoke, she saw his robes in flames: orange and yellow, like dragon's breath. His arms cartwheeled frantically in the air as he was lifted up, and thrown out into the dark sea.

On the other side of the causeway, a dinghy came into view. Its black rubber bow bounced over the waves, as if nodding in approval. Drake steered it along the row of Transportation Police, who were still recovering from the shock of the explosions.

'Catch!' he shouted as he threw a ticking package at a surprised figure. The man cradled it like a rugby ball, before he realised, too late, what he now possessed. With a final "tick", he and several of his colleagues were blown into unrecognisable human debris.

Savannah spun around as more explosions filled the air, and with them came a new danger. Shrapnel and debris rained down. Burning material and jagged metal fragments crashed indiscriminately around her, and amongst the noise and chaos, bodies were either falling or running in all directions. She tried to focus. She saw Tanis standing with the others, and as their eyes met, he slid her crossbow across the metal floor so that it came spinning towards her.

'It's Drake!' he shouted. 'He's brought the dinghy. It's time for us to get out of here.'

'Get Beth to the jetty,' she yelled back.

'I'm not going without you,' shouted Beth.

'Don't worry; I'm coming,' encouraged Savannah. 'Now go!'

Tanis ushered Beth away through a veil of grey smoke.

Savannah was trying to extract an obstinate bolt from her quiver, when Roth appeared and grabbed her shoulders from behind. He slid an arm around her neck and held her in a headlock.

'Not so quick, my dear, I've a vacant interrogation chair waiting for you,' he threatened.

He lifted her off the ground, and the crook of his arm tightened around her windpipe. Black dots exploded across her vision and she dropped her crossbow. Her hand clawed desperately at the air behind her and she managed to grasp a fistful of Roth's hair. She tugged and twisted at it. She felt the skin of his scalp curl in tiny ribbons beneath her fingernails.

'Pull all you want,' he said through clenched teeth; his spittle sprayed at her neck. 'The pain gives me pleasure. I feed on it.'

She moved her fingers across his scalp to grasp his

ear and pull his head forward, onto her shoulder.

'Then feed on this!' she yelled. She brought up her other hand that still gripped the crossbow bolt.

His high-pitched scream nearly burst her eardrum. Instantly, he let her go and she pushed herself away. As she ran, she glanced back to see him on his knees, his hands clutched at the bolt that protruded from his eye socket. Blood, as black as his cloak, ran through his fingers.

Another explosion rocked the platform and she heard Tanis shouting for her. All around, several Transportation Police were regrouping as Roth screamed manically, 'Kill them! Kill them all!'

She stumbled through drifting smoke and towards the jetty, to find Drake standing in the dinghy, his hand on the tiller of the motor. His face was ashen; his eyes looked right through her as Tanis and Beth reached out to help her into the craft.

'Get into the boat. There's nothing we can do for them now,' he encouraged.

She suddenly realised that Penny and Jake were missing. In a panic, she turned around to see them in the middle of the debris-strewn plaza, huddled together on the floor. Penny had one arm cradled around Jake's body; a shard of jagged metal jutted from his bloody neck, his eyes were dull and lifeless. In her other hand, she held an explosive charge to her chest, as half a dozen Transportation Police closed in on her with their swords raised to exact a final and bloody end. Penny smiled a goodbye at Savannah. Then, she was engulfed in the self-administered ice blue and crimson maelstrom of the explosives. Tanis and Beth dragged Savannah into the dinghy, as all she could do was cry out Penny's name.

Drake pulled back the throttle and turned the craft towards the open sea. With the cold tears of sorrow on his cheeks, and grief burning a hole in his heart, he willed himself not to look back.

38

I CAN SEE CLEARLY NOW
THE RAIN HAS GONE

On their return, Jean Fairfax had them all escorted to an isolation facility, where they were treated for their injuries, and a debriefing process was conducted. Needless to say, emotions ran high, particularly with Drake, who in the main was comforted by the rest of the group.

Fairfax disclosed to them that Drake had shown her the letter he received from Jake, and as a result of its content, and of other Intel in her possession, she and Drake had drawn up the new mission schedule. The aim was to fulfil the original objectives, and to neutralise Jake's actions without compromising the safety of the group. She agreed at the time that any decisions regarding Jake and Penny's futures would be dealt with afterwards under level one, secrecy protocols. They had not, however, expected Jake to make an appearance during the operation of the mission.

Drake had chosen to bear the burden of conflict himself. He insisted that he and he alone was responsible for the team, the mission and for Jake's actions.

In the aftermath, Jean Fairfax arranged for all information involving Jake's personal activities to be suppressed and filed as classified. The official report stated that he had been a covert member of the mission, and that he and Penny had died securing the rescue of Savannah's sister.

*

A few weeks later, in a countryside meadow, many miles from the city and Base One, a group of people stood in a circle, hands joining hands. A pale blue sky, streaked with white clouds, allowed an autumn sun to reflect on the scattered gold of wind-strewn leaves.

Various tributes of remembrance for lost loved ones were spread around them amongst the grass. A stone plinth. A wooden cross. A small carved totem pole. A Buddhist figurine. These were just a few of the symbols that inhabited this secluded homage to the dead.

There was no single religious faith, creed or belief represented here. This was a home for the spirit. In whatever sense it was perceived. This was no cemetery. No bodies or remains had been interred here. This was a place for the living to honour those whose physical forms had been irretrievable and lost.

At the centre of the circle, two new symbols stood side by side. A black metal guitar stand, and a small sandstone carving of the sun. In front of these knelt Drake and Savannah, their heads bowed, their eyes wet with grief and loss. Around them, joined in sadness and sorrow were Jean Fairfax, Tanis, Solli, Carl, Beth, Drake's older brother Joe, and a dozen others who were particularly close to Jake or Penny.

The sound of a softly played guitar broke through a background of early morning birdsong. A gentle melody emerged from the player's deft fingers, and the words of an old song escaped from her lips, which spilt into the hearts and minds of all who were there. It was one of Jake and Penny's favourite songs that he'd picked up from an old musician he had come across when visiting one of the countryside communities. Jake had learnt to play and sing it with a passion. He used to say that the song gave him hope of a better world.

At the end of the song, the singer handed Drake the instrument, which had been Jake's, and he placed it in the metal frame. One by one, the mourners blew a gentle kiss at the newly placed tokens, and turned, to take their memories and thoughts with them.

39

BICYCLES

At Base One, Savannah asked if she could stay in Penny's cabin, because it gave her comfort to feel that Penny's presence still lingered there. Jean Fairfax not only gave consent, but also suggested that Beth move in with Savannah, which both sisters eagerly accepted.

Tanis brought Solli along with him one evening and introduced her to Beth, and both he and Savannah were delighted that the girls found empathy and comfort in each other from the start.

Drake was given compassionate leave to return with his brother Joe, to one of the northern compounds.

Tired of the subterfuge, Tanis and Savannah declared their relationship to Jean Fairfax, who admitted her knowledge of it. 'You've proved that you work well together under pressure, and that you're prepared to make sacrifices for the greater good,' she said. 'However, Savannah, you have a sister who you're responsible for. Her welfare and security must be your priority,' she advised. 'With that in mind, I have decided that this is no place for her at the moment. She needs to acclimatise herself fully into her new life on Earthland.' She paused, and studied Savannah's face. 'I'm sending her to Greentrees compound.'

'You can't!' appealed Savannah.

'I can, because Tanis and yourself are going with her. I've arranged for you both to serve with the community protection unit under Danny Hench's command until further notice. Accommodation has been organised for you all, as has a suitable role model who shall be Beth's companion.'

Savannah let the idea run through her mind for a few moments until finally, she spoke.

'Who is this companion?'

'Why, Solli, of course,' replied Jean Fairfax.

'She knows about this?' asked Tanis.

'Knows about it and has willingly agreed.'

Savannah turned to Tanis. 'What do you think?'

'You know I would go anywhere to be with you. This is even better. We're all going to be together. We're...' he paused, running the word through his mind before saying it... 'family,' he smiled.

Three days later, the four of them stepped down from the train and onto the platform at Little Halt.

'This time, we're going in style!' said a grinning Tanis, as he headed for the bicycles.

40

WOUNDED ANIMALS

In the devastation and aftermath on Opulence, half of the solar farm, forty per cent of the food terraces, and most of the research and development facilities along with the whole of the south side marina had been destroyed. This also included a large section of a newly constructed invasion fleet. Human casualties amounted to over a hundred Transportation Police, and numerous research staff.

Jago survived with burns to his arms, neck and back. He was saved from a painful death by his quick submersion into the icy seawater. Unseen, he had surfaced, coughing and spluttering, to swim his way back to one of the jetties, where he was rescued and rushed to the medical treatment centre.

Roth, however, had endured a level of intense agony and pain that even his anger could not suppress. Shrieking obscenities, he'd plucked the bolt from the bloody socket, along with the glutinous remains of his eye, and cast it to one side as he stumbled, half blind, into the arms of two Transportation Police.

'Get me to a surgeon,' he had screamed.

Now, he sported a crimson leather eyepatch, which made him even more menacing to behold. Sometimes, he would study himself in a mirror, and in his own disturbed mind, he would thank Savannah Loveday for enhancing his hatred of her. He would examine the stitched, puckered eyelid and scarred skin tissue. He would touch it with trembling fingers as he fantasised about the awful reprisal he planned to inflict on her body and her mind, when he next laid his hands upon her.

The back of Jago's head was scarred with pale and wrinkled skin, and as a result, he had chosen to shave the rest of his hair off and cover his baldness with a white skullcap, which he wore for most of his waking hours. In private, he too would sometimes run unsteady fingers over the deformed tissue. However, his hatred festered beyond Savannah. He ached for revenge on the whole of Earthland. He pledged to raze the Diss communes to the ground. There would be no mercy. He would have them all hunted down. He would eradicate their existence.

There were some, however, who expressed concern about the magnitude of the attack and the destruction. The balance and relatively safe way of life for the Fortunata had been disturbed in a manner that had never been experienced before. In social circles, individuals began raising questions. *Did they really need to pursue conquest for the sake of conquest? Was it wise to antagonise the renegades of Earthland? Should they not revert to the ways of the old regime of the Masters?*

Needless to say, as soon as these ripples of dissent reached Jago's ears, action was swiftly taken. A series of disappearances and "accidents" followed, whereby certain outspoken individuals ceased to have any living presence to voice their opinions.

The old process of Transportation ceased. Instead, with an unsettling frequency, only the white, bloated corpses of victims were now washed up onto the shores of the estuary.

'Why waste time and energy Transporting those who are of no use to us?' asked Roth. 'If they survive, they will only join the Diss and multiply their ranks against us.'

'Let it be so,' agreed Jago.

Now, in whispered circles, the term Transportation no longer held any chance of survival, but was the course to certain death. In the soundproof interrogation rooms beneath Opulence, Roth continued to practise the act of killing as an art form.

Following several more unsuccessful attempts to infiltrate and disrupt the Earthland community, Jago's temperament cooled, and he decided to bide his time, giving the order to withdraw all actions against the Diss. 'Let them think that we have been weakened,' he counselled with Roth. 'Over time, they will become complacent, and then, when we are ready, we shall strike!'

The laboratories and research centres were rebuilt and work progressed with a frenetic urgency, until one late summer evening, just before sunset, a group of technicians and scientists presented Jago and a small selection of his guests, with the result he had been craving for. They gathered on one of the observation decks amidst an atmosphere of excited and nervous fervour. There, a white-coated scientist cradled a cumbersome-looking gun in his hands.

'Solar-powered laser technology,' he smiled to Jago, who responded with an icy-cold stare. 'Of course, you must take into account that this is the first fully functional prototype,' he added uneasily.

He slotted a black battery pack, about the size of a normal handgun magazine, into the underside of the weapon.

'This is a rechargeable unit capable of delivering up to one hundred energy bursts,' he explained. 'All you do is press the power button like so,' he demonstrated, and there was a high-pitched whistle from the gun as a row of lime green lights lit up along its barrel. 'Then, you squeeze the trigger, thus.'

He aimed the weapon at a human-shaped target fixed to a floating buoy about fifty metres away, which bobbed up and down as waves restlessly splashed around it. An infrared beam lit up and formed a pencil-thin line that connected with the centre of the target. The scientist applied the slightest pressure to the trigger and the beam turned white. The target and the buoy exploded in a fireball of flame.

Jago took the weapon and weighed it in his hands. 'How long before production can begin?' he asked, his face expressionless.

'A month, maybe two,' answered a technician. 'It is a complicated process.'

'I'll give you a month to produce the first hundred weapons for me,' snapped Jago.

'A hundred? In a month?' said the technician in disbelief. 'Impossible.'

'Wrong answer,' said Jago. 'I suggest that you start swimming.'

'I… I don't understand,' stammered the technician.

Jago turned to two Transportation Police. 'Help him to understand,' he smiled.

The two uniformed men moved forward and seized the technician by each of his arms; they dragged him to the edge of the observation deck and threw him head first over the handrail.

Jago and the rest of the group congregated at the rail to look down at the man floundering some fifteen metres below in the choppy, oil-black water.

'Help! I can't swim,' the man's words spluttered out, with salt water and fear.

'It's just not your day, is it?' said Jago as he pressed the power button and pointed the weapon at the flailing technician. The infrared beam lit up and formed a pencil-thin line at the man's body. Jago pressed the trigger and the man disappeared in a bubbling, boiling pool of crimson seawater.

'Very impressive,' said Jago dryly.

He handed the gun to another technician. 'A hundred, in a month,' he repeated.

Sixteen scientists and technicians, their faces as white as their lab coats, stared back at him, dumb with shock.

'Perhaps you need an incentive,' he added, as he inspected his recently manicured fingernails. 'Very well. For each week that there is a delay, one of you will be used as target practice.' With that, he turned on his heels and exited with his entourage, who followed in his wake like nervous schoolchildren.

★

Later that evening, after dark, he walked out onto the balcony of his apartment and leaned on the polished steel handrail. The restless sea air buffeted his dark blue robes around him; the gold braiding rippled like bursts of static electricity in the moonlight. He glared, narrow-eyed, out across the shifting blend of ocean and sky, and towards the unseen coast of Earthland.

'I'm coming to get you,' he whispered into the night. 'And I'm going to kill you all.'

41

JUST BEFORE DAWN

Roth stood before her, his face as white as a corpse and in stark contrast to his jet-black robes, which fell like a shroud from his shoulders. Where his left eye should be was a dark hole, as though someone had taken a thick, black ink marker and filled in the eye socket. In his right hand, he held out a bloodstained crossbow bolt.

'I want my eye!' he screamed.

Savannah's breath caught in her throat.

'I want my eye, now!' he screamed again, like a spoilt child; his voice reached an ear-piercing pitch.

She was frozen to the spot, unable to move. Invisible hands held her head in a vice. An unseen force refused to allow her eyes even the slightest blink.

'Very well,' he said, parting his bloodless lips to reveal a rictus smile of yellow teeth. '*You* took my eye,' he spoke accusingly. 'So I took this.' With a dramatic pause, he slowly and purposely brought his other hand from behind his back, to reveal the decapitated head of her sister, Beth. His fingers gripped the locks of tangled and blood-matted hair and he thrust it out, straight-armed in front of him. The sinews and bloody, ragged

268

skin of her neck hung down in red, dripping ribbons, suggesting that it had been viciously twisted and torn, rather than cut from her body. The eyes were without pupils, just white, almond slits, and as the horror filled Savannah's vision, Beth's mouth opened and wailed her sister's name.

'Saaavaaanaaaaah!'

She awoke with a start, her white vest stuck like a second skin to her sweat-drenched body.

'Beth!' she gasped, hyperventilating.

With an effort, she pushed back the heavy blankets, her body shaking and trembling; she swung her feet onto the cold wooden floor, unaware of the winter chill in the room as it hit her skin, raising her hair follicles and causing tiny pimples to cascade across her arms.

'Beth!' This time she managed to shout in trembling terror.

She staggered as if in a drunken stupor, grasping against a wall for support; her hands eventually clutched at the cold brass door handle, while her senses fought to drive away the nightmare images.

'Beth!'

Desperate to reach her sister, she pulled the door towards her and a deeper panic hit her when it would only open a few centimetres, in her confusion, oblivious that she was the obstacle.

'Beth!' she cried as tears streamed down her already sweat-soaked face. She wrestled frantically with the door, her cold panic blinding her awareness to the fact that she needed to step backwards to allow the door to open inwards.

She heard her sister's concerned voice coming from the other side of the wooden barrier.

'Savannah. I'm here. What's wrong?'

Wakening reality and the dark imaginings of a troubled sleep suddenly merged together in Savannah's mind, and fear swept across her senses to smother them with the darkness of a cold faint.

When she came round, a pale light merged into blurred images as her eyes focused the world back into normality. The troubled faces of Tanis and Beth looked down on her as she lay on the floor; her head was cradled in Beth's lap while Tanis tenderly dabbed a damp cloth across her brow and cheeks. She tried to raise herself up, but was gently restrained by her sister.

'Stay there a while,' she insisted. 'You gave yourself a nasty knock when you fell.'

Tanis softly pressed the cloth to her forehead and she felt the pain of a swelling bruise.

'What happened?' asked Beth, concern etched across her face.

'Nightmare,' slurred Savannah as another bout of dizziness swirled her thoughts. She rolled her eyes, forcing them to clear away the small grey dots that invaded her vision.

'Here, drink this,' said Tanis, as he brought the edge of a glass beaker to her lips.

She allowed the cool, earthy liquid to roll onto her tongue and wash across her palate and down her throat. The distinct mineral taste of naturally filtered well water slid from her mouth and into her stomach, its reviving properties gently clearing her head. She sipped eagerly at the revitalising elixir.

'Not too much,' said Tanis as he pulled the beaker away.

She breathed in deeply, taking control of her senses. A large oil lamp burned on a side table, its light keeping the shadows captive in the corners and recesses of the room.

'How long was I out?' she asked.

'A couple of minutes. No more,' replied Beth.

'I couldn't get to you before you hit the floor,' admitted Tanis.

'I need to sit up.'

'Leave it a little longer,' said Tanis. 'You could be concussed.'

'Don't fuss so,' she insisted as she raised herself on one elbow. She ran her fingers through her fine, closely cropped blonde hair. 'What's the time?'

Tanis checked his watch. 'A quarter to seven. It'll soon be dawn.'

Savannah still clung on to Beth's hand as though to release it would mean the total and permanent loss of her sister.

'It's okay,' Beth reassured her. 'Who was it in your nightmare? Was it Jago?'

'Worse,' replied Savannah with a shake of her head. 'It was Roth.'

'Well, he can't get to us here,' assured Tanis, and he kissed her head in protective affection.

A dishevelled Solli appeared, half awake in the doorway. 'What's going on?'

'Just a nightmare,' Savannah explained apologetically.

'Anything that I can do to help?' she asked.

'Well, I guess that now we're all awake, you could make us a cup of tea,' suggested Tanis.

'But it's still dark outside and I need my beauty sleep,' complained Solli, still not fully alert.

'You're right there,' announced Tanis, not unkindly.

She pointed her finger at him. '*You* can make your own tea!'

42

A MESSAGE FROM JAGO

After executing several scientists, Jago had to finally accept that the manufacturing of solar weapons was going to be a longer process than he wanted. Roth pointed out to him that if he carried on, he would soon be running out of the very people he needed to develop and manufacture the weapons!

'Unfortunately, technology knows no pain,' advised Roth. 'They're scared enough to cut corners and produce something less efficient. I would suggest that if it's worth waiting for, then so much the better. After all, those bitches and the rest of the Earthland vermin aren't going anywhere. It's going to be such fun hunting them down.' He stroked Jago's hair and deftly slipped a grape between his own pencil-thin lips. 'Now, where were we?'

*

Over the coming weeks, intelligence information concerning the development and production of solar weapons was smuggled out to Base One. Then, abruptly, the periodic message carriers – homing pigeons – ceased to arrive, and on a cold, windswept February morning, a patrol retrieved two human bodies from the banks of the estuary. The following day Jean Fairfax was called to the morgue to view the remains of a man and a woman, two of a handful of Servanti who had dutifully smuggled information out of Opulence and back to Earthland. Branded across their torsos in burnt black lettering were two identical messages – **THIS FILTH BELONGS TO YOU. WATCH THE HORIZON. WE ARE COMING TO KILL YOU ALL.**

'From my initial examinations, the autopsy shows that they were force-fed raw pigeon, including the feathers, with such violence that they choked to death,' announced the mortuary technician. 'What sort of sick and twisted mind would commit such an act?'

For a moment, Fairfax studied the bloodless, deathly faces. 'Roth Dan,' she whispered, and the lighting in the room seemed to dim at the mention of his name.

Within days, patrols began to report that mutilated corpses were now the only arrivals to be washed up onto the shores of the estuary. Pale, bloated bodies, their purple lips in a final pleading scream, and their eyes plucked out by scavenging fish, began to float in on the morning tides. Systematically, Jago was searching out anyone suspected of being an informant or message sender, and Roth's hands were wickedly busy in the hellish interrogation rooms of the Transportation Centre. With grizzly realisation, it became obvious that the act of Transporting tortured and dead victims had become a new barbaric practice.

Jean Fairfax knew that the warning was no idle threat. The last information she had received confirmed her worst fears; solar weapons were a reality, and the process of wholesale manufacturing was imminent. Now that all contact with Opulence was lost, she had no idea how much time was left before Jago launched his assault on Earthland. The time to mobilise the Diss had come, for the sake of Earthland and for the sake of humanity.

She sat at her desk, maps and documents spread out before her in a sea of scattered and disjointed information. Papers spilled onto the floor and open files yawned their contents submissively.

Her usual calculating and level-headed resolve seemed to desert her as the enormity of the threat facing the Earthland community became a reality. The mad dogs that were Jago and Roth had been roused, and she wondered if she had made the right decision to send Savannah Loveday back to Opulence as part of the last mission. This morning, the surprise arrival of a homing pigeon, and the message that it carried, made her question her own morals.

IF YOU CARE ABOUT YOUR PEOPLE, GIVE ME SAVANNAH AND BETH LOVEDAY AND I'LL SHOW YOU SOME MERCY. JAGO.

A flicker of foolish hope that sacrificing the two girls would save the people that she loved, and help her to negotiate a way out of a bloody and horrific new war, clouded her judgement.

She reflected on the past, and her own personal loss and sacrifice. Two photographs rested on a shelf. Simple wooden frames embraced the images of long-dead loved ones, the colours fading like memories in the mind of a forgetful old relative. She stared at the smiling faces, looked into their eyes and heard the echoes of their voices. Parents and grandparents, and an older brother. Sickness and violence had taken four of their lives, to leave Jean Fairfax with a brother who, at the age of eighteen, said his own goodbye to pursue life as a mercenary; the taste of bitterness and the hunger for revenge stole him away from her.

Thirty-five years ago, in an underground maternity ward, her own cries of birth announced that another life had arrived into a world of conflict and desperate survival. Jean Fairfax's father was a member of the Earthland Defence Network, and her mother, a trained nurse. Both of them very active in the evolving subterranean community that was Base One. Back then, although the victims of Transportation were periodically found and mostly rescued from the banks of the estuary, Opulence was not seen as a direct threat, and viewed very much the same as a hornet's nest – better left alone. At that time, the surviving pockets of humanity were solely focused on strengthening a link between themselves and an evolving network of established communes, along with defending themselves against Crazies and mutant creatures.

At one point, the inner city above Base One became increasingly violent, with large groups of Crazies threatening to breach the defences of the tunnel systems. A decision was made to evacuate all children, and at five years old, Jean and her brother, Alan, who was her senior by some four years, were relocated to a recently fortified haven in the countryside.

A week after their arrival, the first major disaster of its kind befell Base One. Dozens of Crazies found their way in through an unmapped drainage duct and swarmed with a frenzy of barbaric and cannibalistic horror into a medical centre. The desperate fight to stop the onslaught lasted three days, by the end of which more than fifty of the community had died at the hands of the evil that masqueraded in human form. Amongst the dead were Jean's parents. She was told many years later that they were part of a group cornered and trapped in a storeroom. Her father, rather than see the woman he loved die a slow and painful death, had taken her life with a single bullet, and only after exhausting his ammunition, did he throw himself at the psychotic and inhuman mob, to perish at their hands. He was found terribly mutilated and laying across his wife's body in a last act of protection.

A knock on the door of her carriage chased the grey and emotionally toxic cloud of memories from her mind and she snatched her thoughts back to the present.

She felt the wetness of tears on her cheeks, and fished a small white handkerchief from her sleeve to quickly wipe away the ghosts of her sadness.

'Ma'am? Are you all right, Ma'am?'

Jean Fairfax blinked away the shroud, and a steely resolve filtered back into her thoughts. She turned to face the figure standing there.

'Yes. What is it?'

'You need to come, Ma'am. To the hospital. They've brought in a survivor – she's barely alive.'

★

The estuary patrols had become burial teams, and amongst the dunes, a graveyard was established where the remains of the Transported dead could be laid to rest rather than become food for the scavenging gulls. It was by chance, as the bloody and bruised body of a middle-aged woman was being gently wrapped in a burial cloth, that her whispered, 'Help me,' was heard above the sound of the restless waves.

With only a glimmer of hope, she was stretchered along the perilous journey to Base One, to the safety of a hospital bed, where Jean Fairfax now stood over her. A white-coated doctor hovered compassionately like a latter-day angel of mercy.

'I've made her as comfortable and pain-free as possible, but I'm afraid that's all we can do. She's lost too much blood. Too many broken bones. It's a miracle she survived the journey from the estuary.' The tone of his voice changed as his eyes met Jean Fairfax's. 'If I could lay my hands on whoever's responsible for this, I'd forget my medical oath and give them a taste of their own treatment.'

Fairfax stared back into the man's slate blue eyes. 'Be careful what you wish for, doctor.'

'Please.' The word slipped from the woman's mouth with the cracked dryness of autumn leaves.

Jean Fairfax took a beaker of water and gently placed it against the woman's lips and allowed a trickle of relief to soothe her throat.

'Solar guns. Nearly ready.' Her chest heaved with

the effort. 'A month. Maybe more,' she managed. 'Jago's army. Thousands.' Her eyes widened, and Fairfax saw the terror in them. 'Roth! He's coming.' Her breath rattled and her eyelids folded down like small curtains. The muscles of her face relaxed to silently announce the passing of her life.

Fairfax held the woman's hand, and stroked a pale lock of hair away from her already cold forehead. 'Shush,' she whispered as softly as she could. 'You're safe now. He can't reach you. He can't hurt you any more.'

43

CALL TO ARMS

At Greentrees, the months skittered by, and compared to what they'd been through, Tanis, Savannah, Soli and Beth's lives now resembled a routine of stable normality. The two younger girls were almost inseparable, electing to share a large bedroom at the back of the house. They worked the same shifts on the community's farmstead, and attended the same militia training. Soli, more than Savannah, had been the one to guide Beth out of the traumatic dark memories of her time under Jago's influence, and Savannah had welcomed this in jealous admiration.

Savannah's relationship with Tanis was a healthy and loving partnership, particularly buoyed up by the fact that the experience of surviving together against the odds had matured them both beyond their years. They were permanent members of Danny Hench's field protection team, and spent their working days, and some nights, patrolling and guarding the field workers, live stock and storage barns. However, on more than one occasion of late, Tanis confessed to Savannah of a small yearning for "a bit of action".

'Tanis! Tanis! Wake up!' Savannah's voice invaded his half dream of clouded visions.

Too comfortable, he thought. *Staying here.*

The bed lurched like a drunken life raft as Savannah's weight descended on Tanis' bed-clothed shape.

'Go away – Tanis not here today,' he responded from beneath the blankets, and he curled himself into a tight ball of rebellion.

Savannah gripped the covers in an attempt to wrestle them away.

'It's Sunday,' declared Tanis. 'Nothing that you can say or do is going to make me get up.'

'How about... Danny Hench is going to kick our arses if we're not at a meeting with him in fifteen minutes?'

The bundle that was Tanis Kane became still, and then his mop of dreadlocks and his bright green eyes slid into view. 'For real?'

'For real,' she confirmed. 'And it's not just us. Something's up. From what I've seen, Jameson's running around, banging on doors and issuing orders to most of the senior ranks.'

Tanis pushed the covers back; morning light flashed across his bare chest and Savannah had to suppress the urge to damn Danny Hench, and climb back into bed.

'What's the time?' He stretched.

'0700.'

'What?' he complained.

'Thought that you'd be impressed. Come on,' she urged. 'Thirteen minutes and counting.'

When they pushed themselves through the doors of the community hall, it was crowded with Earthland Defence Network personnel, and standing room only. On the stage at the far end, with Jameson beside him, Danny Hench had just got to his feet. He looked accusingly over the gathered heads.

'Kane and Loveday,' he announced. 'Nice of you to join us.'

No one turned or glanced in their direction, knowing full well that any movement would provoke a personal reprimand.

'Right,' he spoke with all of the authority of a gunshot. 'We are, from this moment, at level one – Red Flag.'

A murmur of surprise and anticipation rippled across the gathering.

'Quiet!' he boomed. 'I will talk, and you will listen. Following this briefing, all of my senior staff are to remain.' He consulted two pages of notes that he held in his hand. 'As you should be aware, Red Flag is the highest level, and in a nutshell, it means an imminent threat of hostile invasion – a call to arms.' He paused and scanned the sea of faces, all of which wore a variety of expressions. 'The source of the threat in this case is Opulence. That is all I am at liberty to tell you at this time and there will be no opportunity for you to ask questions at the end of this session.

'The process of recruiting and training every able-bodied man and woman will be announced at a public meeting later on today. Your part in the main is to ensure that there is no panic and no disruption. Your group leaders will give you orders that are more specific when you assemble in the barrack buildings at 09.30.' Again, he slowly cast his eyes across the gathering. 'One more thing. Tanis Kane and Savannah Loveday, make your way to the front; I need to speak to you. For the rest of you, that is all. Dismissed.'

Tanis and Savannah stood to one side to let the hall empty, rather than push themselves against the exiting crowd.

'Keep an eye out for Beth and Soli,' she said as she craned her neck and scanned the passing faces.

'Already on it,' replied Tanis. 'There, on the other side of the hall,' he pointed. The two girls waved back in acknowledgement and began to weave their way amongst the exiting tide of bodies. As the last few people filtered through the doors, the four of them met in the vacant space.

'Why have you got to stay behind?' Beth furrowed her brow with concern.

'Yeah. Why have you two been singled out?' Soli demanded.

'We don't know, honest,' said Tanis. 'We're just going to…'

He was interrupted by Danny Hench's demanding statement. 'Did I say that you could have your own private meeting? I don't expect to have to repeat myself, so you two,' he pointed to Beth and Soli, 'best leave the building. Now!'

'Go,' Savannah mouthed with widened eyes. She

grabbed Tanis' arm and wheeled them both away from the two girls, thankful to hear their departing footsteps.

Assembled in front of the stage were Hench's senior officers, to whom he was handing sheets of typed-up paper. 'Jameson has been up half the night copying this out for you, so don't lose it,' he warned. 'These are your orders. We have one week to implement them – no ifs and no buts. Any ongoing queries are to be addressed through Jameson, and there will be daily briefings with myself. Understood?'

'Yes, sir,' was the resounding, and unanimous reply.

'This is what we are here for, to defend our right for a better world. And hopefully to get it right second time around. Let's get on with it. Dismissed.'

There was a group salute and the officers made their way to the exit, their faces poring over their sheets of paper. Danny Hench waited until the last of them had left and the doors were closed.

'Right,' he exhaled. 'That was the easy bit. Let's grab some chairs.' He and Jameson jumped the short distance down from the stage and made their way to a stack of folding seats at the side of the hall. Tanis and Savannah followed. They seated themselves in a semicircle, and Danny Hench held silent eye contact with Savannah and Tanis in turn, until he finally spoke.

'Some of what I am about to say will make sense, and some of it won't, at least not to your ears, but I'm going to ask you to digest it and think carefully before you react. Okay?'

'Sir,' Savannah and Tanis responded in unison.

'There are no written orders for you, it's this simple

– you are both to return to Base One under the direct command of Jean Fairfax. You leave with a small escort in one hour. Soli and Beth are to remain here under my protection and in relative safety. I do not know what plans Fairfax has for you both, but I can only assume that you are going to play a far more important role in determining our futures than I can imagine.'

Savannah's mouth dried like a peach in a desert sun. A moment of panic swept over her as she mentally digested the prospect of leaving Beth behind. Not knowing when, or if she would see her again. She felt Tanis' hand grip hers.

'Will we have the chance to say our farewells?' he asked.

'Of course,' replied Danny Hench. 'But sooner, rather than later. I want you both kitted up and in my office in forty-five minutes. Understood?'

'Yes, sir,' said Tanis.

Danny Hench turned his gaze to Savannah. 'Understood?'

She chewed at the side of her cheek; saliva moistened her mouth and self-control forced its way into her senses. Refusing to let a single tear escape, she raised her wet rimmed eyes to meet Danny Hench's. 'Understood. Sir.'

44

BEEN THERE, DONE THAT

The farewell went as expected, with tears and sobs, with fears and sadness, and in Soli and Beth's minds, a secret pang of envy.

Crisp morning air stung a sense of clarity into Savannah's thoughts, and as the buggies rumbled along, her mind turned towards the source of her concerns – Jago. The frustrations of her adolescence crept up in a daydream, and filled her head with whispered thoughts.

Will you never leave us in peace? Why is it that it takes just one person, one man with distorted, hateful and evil ambitions to spread his ideals like an infection amongst a population, until, like a cancer, it kills everything that is good? Evil men encourage evil men to do evil things. All through history, we keep allowing it to happen. What the hell is wrong with the human race?

The yellow orb of a semi-risen sun flashed through tall, bare tree trunks and patterns flitted across her face like a hypnotic strobe; her mind wandered and she closed her eyes to images of her parent's faces, and imaginings of a perfect life with them.

Ahead, Tanis was busy quizzing his driver. He

shouted over the growling engine in an effort to create a conversation.

'So, where are we headed to, buddy? Little Halt? Broadway Junction?'

The driver continued to concentrate on the road, and without turning his head spoke loudly enough for Tanis to hear the reply. 'My orders are to get you safely to your destination, not engage in conversation or discussion, and with respect, I'm not your "buddy".'

Tanis was about to respond when there was a sharp tap on the top of his crash helmet. He craned his head upwards to see the harnessed gunner point a finger at him, then turn two fingers at his own eyes, before gesturing at the road ahead, finally placing a finger across his lips.

'You know that you two are off my Christmas card list!' Tanis announced, before resigning himself to a journey devoid of dialogue.

It wasn't long before they passed the spot of the ambush, many months before. Unbeknown to each other, both Tanis and Savannah exhaled in nervous relief as the buggies skittered around the next bend and away from the scene of past violence.

The embankment of Little Halt came predictably into view; this time, however, the area was a hive of activity. Armed commandos oversaw the unloading of supplies onto a convoy of small trailers attached to heavy-duty quad bikes, while a variety of boxes and crates were manhandled from the platform and into the goods wagons. The buggies pulled up side by side, and Tanis' driver removed his helmet to reveal the craggy-faced, ginger-haired features of a man in his forties.

'Wait here and don't move,' he ordered in no uncertain terms.

Savannah and Tanis eased their helmets off and digested the scene.

'It's a good job that Drake's not with us,' mused Tanis. 'Else we'd have to hold him down!'

Savannah managed a wry smile at her memory of Drake, and not for the first time, briefly pondered his situation and whereabouts.

'Look,' Tanis pointed in the direction of two commandos furtively checking their driver's paperwork. 'They're authorised to shoot first and ask questions afterwards – directive of Jean Fairfax.'

'How can you tell?' asked Savannah.

'They've all got red armbands with CCA stencilled onto them – Commander in Chief's Authority. I've never seen anyone actually wearing them before.'

At that moment, the driver beckoned them over, and grabbing their kit bags, Savannah and Tanis strode to join him. They were just over a metre away, when one of the stocky commandos brought up a large fingerless-gloved palm.

'Stop right there!' He didn't even look at them, just continued to examine the papers.

'Tanis Kane?'

'Yes.'

'ID.'

'What?'

'ID. Now.' He clicked his fingers impatiently.

Tanis fumbled with his jacket pocket to extract the security stamped pen and ink picture, which had seen better days, and he handed it over. The commando squinted at the somewhat faded image, and then passed it to his colleague, who continued to examine it.

'Savannah Loveday?'

She had anticipated that she would be next and with a satisfied, if somewhat sarcastic smile, she held her more recently issued ID out to him. 'Is there a problem?' asked the driver.

Tanis noticed that a small bead of perspiration had appeared on the man's now reddened forehead.

'There'll be a problem if you don't keep quiet,' answered the commando. He passed Savannah's ID to the other man.

'Oh! Hang on a minute. I think there's another piece of paper,' said the driver, as he reached into the folds of his jacket. Before he could remove his hand, the barrel of a Kalashnikov was jammed under his chin.

'Don't you move an inch,' growled the commando.

The whites of the driver's eyes bulged with sudden dread as his hand was removed to reveal a sheet of folded paper in its grip.

With a practised flip of his wrist, the commando opened the folded paper. His brow tightened as he mentally digested the information.

'Right. You best be on your way,' he said, lowering his gun. 'In future, make sure that your paperwork is in order; it could save you from being shot!'

With precariously loosened bowels, the driver scuttled gratefully back to his buggy, and the commando shared the contents of the sheet with his partner, who exchanged a raised eyebrow and a wry smile.

'Tanis Kane. Savannah Loveday,' he confirmed with a nod as he handed them back their ID. 'It would appear you have Red Level clearance and protection. Pity the chap didn't hand this over first. I'm sure you understand that in the current circumstances, we have to treat everything with suspicion.' He folded the papers and handed them to Tanis.

'For the record, my name's Claymore, and this is my partner, Burns. I'm to assign a protective escort to you for the remainder of your journey. If you'll just follow us, we'll get you settled on the train.'

★

It was an hour later that the locomotive, grunting like a bad-tempered dragon, belched out smoke and steam, and hauled its tail of carriages and wagons away from Little Halt. Savannah and Tanis sat opposite each other, with two stern-faced commandos seated across the aisle acting out their appointed positions as silent, protective sentinels.

'I wish I knew where we're headed,' complained Savannah.

'It's got to be Base One,' supposed Tanis. 'If Jean Fairfax is behind this, then who else are we going to see?'

'You mean, we've got a bloody uncomfortable ride on a trolley cart to look forward to? Oh, joy!'

In the moment's pause, Savannah sensed Tanis' mood change, and he slumped forward to rest his elbows on his knees to stare down at his clasped hands.

'She can't even be considering sending us back to Opulence.' It came out of his mouth as a statement.

Savannah turned her head to take in the countryside. The scraggy bushes and leafless trees of late February rolled by under a grey-blue sky.

'If she asked you to, would you go back?' It was almost as if she was asking the question to her own thin reflection in the window glass, but Tanis knew that it was directed at him.

His response was an emphatic, 'No!'

She shifted in her seat to face him. 'Why not?'

'Been there. Done that. Didn't enjoy it.' He shook his head. 'Let them come. I want to face those two ass-wipes on my turf. In my territory.'

'And what if *I* wanted to go back?'

For a few moments, he studied her eyes, then chewed on his lip and turned his gaze to the shifting panorama. 'I wouldn't understand why you'd want to do such a thing. There's nothing there but bad memories. But, if there's still a ghost or two that you have to exorcise, then I would have to be there with you.' He took her hands in his and raised his eyes to look once more, deeply into hers. 'We live together, we die together. That's the way that I see the rest of my life with you.'

45

BROADWAY JUNCTION

Savannah shifted herself across beside Tanis to rest her head against his chest, and he held her to him. They closed their eyes to reflect on the unfolding events, however, a warm and comfortable sleep crept over their thoughts and wrapped them both in its dreamless arms.

The clatter of the carriage's wheels negotiating their way across forged steel points awoke them from a slumber that had enveloped them for most of the journey, and as they stretched to wakefulness, she stole a kiss from him, and he smiled a boyish smile.

Their carriage levelled with a platform, and through the window, they viewed the full extent of a new urgency, which was mirrored in the many figures that milled around and busied themselves in a swarm of activity. The great behemoth that had laboured to bring them to Broadway Junction propelled jets of steam across the platform and lurched to a halt against the buffers, to send a shuddering shockwave along its trucks and compartments.

Savannah stood in the aisle, and taken by surprise by a sudden lurch, she was thrown against one of the commandos. Her hands came up to rest on his chest in an effort to steady herself.

'Careful, miss; any more of that and I'll have to buy you a drink.' A slight upturn of the man's lips resembled a measured smile.

She allowed herself a blush before Tanis took her arm and jealously eased her back to him.

'Stay here,' ordered the other commando, and with a look that could crack a rock in half, he directed to his partner, 'and keep your wits about you.'

Silent minutes passed until a restless Tanis suggested that they at least disembark from the train to get some fresh air.

'You heard the man. We stay here,' ordered the now stony-faced commando.

He had flirted with Savannah, and that was enough for the temperamental youth in Tanis to challenge the man's authority.

'Well, I'm getting off,' he said as he hoisted up his kit bag.

The commando put a gloved hand on Tanis' shoulder. 'You. Stay. Here,' he growled.

Tanis brought his own hand up, which could barely grip around the ham-sized fist. He cocked his head to look up into the towering figure's eyes. Savannah had seen that look before, and it meant trouble. She was about to intervene when the other commando appeared at the door. His eyes shifted in turn to each of them.

'Problem?'

'Tell this gorilla to take his hand off me, and there won't be,' said Tanis.

'I think that you're punching above your weight, son,' he replied. 'Now, now, Grant, be a good chap and let him be. Apparently, these two are important to people well above our pay-grade, so stop messing about and follow me.'

With Tanis and Savannah sandwiched between the commandos, the little procession weaved its way towards a building at the end of the platform. The brown and white sign above it simply announced that it was the stationmaster's office.

Tanis turned to Savannah and gave a nod of his head. 'Look.'

On the far side of the station, a column of white smoke plumed up to wash under the platform roof, and between the stacks of cargo and milling people, there were glimpses of a steel-grey, armoured locomotive.

They reached the office door, and its brown, flaked surface cried out for a new coat of paint. The commando rapped on the wooden panel, which was answered by a man's voice. 'Enter.'

Grant turned the dark brass handle and allowed the door to swing inwards. 'Good luck, Romeo,' he grinned at Tanis. 'In you go,' he indicated with a movement of his chin.

Savannah followed Tanis into the room and the door was immediately closed behind them. In a far corner, a hot water urn dominated the centre of a trestle table; its lid pouted puffs of steam at the accompanying white china cups and metal canisters. To their left, four combat-suited people were leaning over a small desk, in mumbled conversation, examining an array of paperwork. There was no immediate acknowledgement, no greeting.

Fifteen seconds ticked by until Tanis swung his kit bag to the floor with a thump. 'Any chance of a cup of tea then?'

The hushed discussion stopped, and one of the figures straightened and turned.

'Still as impatient as ever, Tanis.' Jean Fairfax looked over the rim of her glasses, at two surprised faces.

'Sorry. I didn't realise that it was you, Ma'am,' he stammered. He fumbled to release the chord of his kit bag, and gave a panicky salute. Savannah reacted calmly as she brought her hand to her forehead.

'You can relax a little,' smiled Jean Fairfax. 'But not too much; you have a great deal to digest before you leave here tomorrow evening.'

'Back to Base One, I take it?' quizzed Tanis.

'No. I'm sending you both on a little jaunt. Well, not so little really. More like long and dangerous. How does that sound?'

'Opulence.' Savannah's voice made the word sound like the toll of a funeral bell.

'Far from it,' corrected Jean Fairfax. 'In fact, you'll be going inland and in the opposite direction.'

Savannah and Tanis exchanged glances. Their eyes flashed with relief and excitement.

'I hope that we're not going to have those wonderful commandos for company.' Tanis rolled his eyes. 'I mean, I know that they've got a job to do, but they're so, you know. Up their own backsides.'

'There'll be a few of them coming with you, but

their role will be solely to protect and support you. They and yourselves will be answerable to your team leader.'

'Whoever it is,' complained Tanis, 'they're bound to be another stroppy commando.'

Fairfax smiled. 'No. I've arranged for you to be accompanied by someone who makes them look like pussycats.'

Tanis groaned outwardly. Savannah gave him a sharp look and a quick nudge. She didn't relish going on a mission, and that's exactly how she already saw it, with somebody who Tanis had made an enemy of at the outset.

'Now, now, Tanis. I'm sure that you'll not have any problems with your team leader. Will they, Drake?'

The figure next to Fairfax turned around. His face couldn't disguise the pleasure of seeing Tanis and Savannah again.

'You didn't think that you were going to get all of the fun, did you?' he beamed.

He stepped forward and embraced Savannah in a bear hug, and she gripped her arms around his broad shoulders, barely able to contain her emotions.

'Drake. It's so wonderful to see you again,' and she kissed his cheek.

Tanis looked on at the prolonged embrace. He couldn't be jealous – not of Drake. This was the man that he'd risked his life with, fought alongside. Mistrusted. Agonised over. Cursed. Acclaimed. Consoled and grieved with. When it came to his turn, he clasped his arms around the man like a son would his absent father.

'Hey! You're getting soft in your old age,' said

Drake. He patted Tanis on the shoulders, and stood back to examine him. 'You're looking a bit podgy in the middle, and those dreadlocks seem a bit tidy to me. I'm just going to have to knock you back into shape with a couple of days wilderness trekking.' He flicked a wink at Savannah.

'I'll out-walk you any time, old man,' smiled Tanis.

'Right. That's enough of the pleasantries,' interrupted Jean Fairfax. 'We need to get on with the briefing.' She signalled for them to join her at the table. 'Squad leaders Batten and Gillespie.' She introduced the two men.

Although Batten and Gillespie were dressed in the same field uniform, including Fairfax's red armbands, they did not mirror the bulked-up and thickset physique of the commandos that Tanis and Savannah had encountered. These two men were of a tactical breed. Quick-thinking decision makers, to balance out the brute force of their direct reports.

Tanis and Savannah exchanged nods with the men. 'They'll be in charge of your commando support teams, and under the direction of Drake,' she added. 'He and he alone will have total responsibility for the mission.'

'No pressure then, Drake,' grinned Tanis.

Fairfax glared sternly over the rim of her glasses, and his smile melted. 'Sorry,' he mumbled.

Strewn across the table top was a collection of sepia-coloured Ordnance Survey maps. Stencilled in red across the corner of each one, were the letters – MOD TOP SECRET. The map at the centre of attention was of the northern territory, and a pattern of intersecting lines and circles had been recently added, drawn in green and red ink across its landscape of Tumuli and Tumulus. Three locations were marked with red interlocking circles – Wyndham Barracks, Sinfield Quarry, and a nearby airfield called Billingdon.

'This,' Fairfax jabbed a finger at the three circles, 'is where you're going. Two hundred miles north.' She paused. Her finger turned white under the pressure, as though the map needed securing to the table. 'And you'll need to get back. The whole mission should take four days. You'll be joined by a dozen hand-picked operatives from my team at Base One to complete Drake's squad.'

'Anyone that we know?' asked Tanis.

'I think that you'll be pleased to meet a few familiar faces,' she smiled. 'You will be the advance party. Your job is to locate and secure access to our target before Gillespie's extraction team move in. Drake, tell them what they need to know.' She stepped away from the table. 'Gentlemen. Time for coffee.' Batten and Gillespie moved to join her at the urn.

'You probably know that after our last little outing, I went up north to spend some time with my brother, Joe,' said Drake. 'I'm not going to bang on about how losing Jake affected me because I know that you two have also felt that hopeless emptiness, that personal loss. Needless to say, I soon realised that Joe and I needed to help each other through the worst of it. His commander gave him some time off, and we just packed up a load of gear and went trekking and camping. The wildlife up there is just as dangerous and surprising as I've seen anywhere down here, and on a couple of occasions, Joe and I had to fight off some pretty weird crossbreeds! Anyhow, to cut a long story short, as brothers, we've come through the trauma of losing Jake. Don't get me wrong. I'm not over his death by a long way, probably never will be, and my life's ambition is to kill as many of those murdering shit-heads from Opulence as I can. Naturally, when Jean Fairfax contacted me, I jumped at the chance to get back to work, and I joined the special operations team near to where I was stationed. I wasn't going to sit back and do sod all about the situation that faces us.'

'What situation faces us, Drake?' asked Tanis.

'We're running out of ammunition,' he replied. 'And there aren't anywhere near enough weapons to go around for us to face what's heading our way from Opulence.'

Tanis and Savannah exchanged a concerned glance.

Drake leant back over the map. 'Here,' he indicated to the three circles on the map, 'is probably the answer to our needs.' After the Second World War, right up to the year 2000, and despite strong denials from successive governments, several secret underground facilities, some the size of small towns, continued to be maintained, including their large stores of arms and ammunition. This may be one of them.

'Two other locations further afield are being investigated, but this seems to be the most promising from what intelligence we've been able to gather. Our mission is to gain entry and bring back as much ammunition and as many arms as we can. I'm sure that your vigilant eyes spotted the armour-plated train that's standing on the far platform. It's capable of hauling over a dozen container wagons and flatbed trailers.'

'Do you mean to say that there's a rail link to the north?' asked Tanis.

'We've been re-establishing it for some time. Very closely guarded secret,' said Drake. 'It doesn't run all of the way, yet. However, just by chance it'll get us to within a couple miles of where we need to be.'

Jean Fairfax appeared at Drake's shoulder. 'We've already made contact with two previously unknown communities in the northern territory that have managed to thrive and protect themselves over the years. It's been through them that evidence regarding the existence and locations of the underground facilities have been confirmed.'

'However,' said Drake, 'it's not been without considerable cost. Lives have been lost during the rebuilding and repair of the tracks. That train hasn't been armoured just for decoration. There are a couple of stretches where the rail lines pass through some pretty unpleasant terrain, including the remains of old industrial and factory estates, just the sort of places where Crazies thrive. We've laid mine fields on both sides of the tracks as a deterrent, and any expeditions are timed for daylight runs only. Trouble is, there are quite a few tall buildings where the crazy scum can hide in the shadows and bombard us with incendiary bottle bombs, which means that things can get quite hairy. I can tell you that from experience.'

'The journey isn't for the faint-hearted,' added Jean Fairfax. 'However, at the moment we have no alternative.'

'Why involve us? Why not just send a task force of commandos?' asked Savannah.

'This operation needs to be completed quickly and efficiently. I don't want to send in an army of all guts and glory, shoot first ask questions later hell-heads. No offence meant, Gillespie.'

'None taken, Ma'am,' he responded dryly.

'I want the spearhead operated by Diss personnel, by people that I know.' She looked at Drake, Tanis and Savannah. 'Together, you have been through more than any of them and survived to tell the tale. You have a rare and fearless bond. In addition, you're adaptable. We know what we *expect* to find there, but what is actually waiting for us could be a different matter!'

46

The Gauntlet

The following morning, as the shimmering rim of a dawn red sun pushed itself above the horizon of a new day, an armoured train noisily announced its departure. With clouds of dirty smoke erupting from its chimney, a raw harnessed power surged into its great pistons. Wheels turned, at first spinning and squealing on steel rails, until the great behemoth rolled forward, hauling a convoy of cargo wagons and containers obediently behind.

'What happened to first class?' complained Tanis. 'You didn't say that we'd be slumming it in a cattle truck.'

'You can always sit up top. There's plenty of room on the roof,' said Drake, jerking his thumb upwards.

Tanis wasn't far off in his description. It was a bare metal container with ventilation grills running along its topmost sides, wide enough to let daylight slant in through flickering rays and allow dust motes to perform their chaotic and seemingly never-ending ballet. The wagon was originally designed for transporting livestock, and although it had been hosed clean, there was still an underlying smell of animal musk.

Even with fifteen of them seated on the floor, there was still ample room. The initial excitement and banter of reunion with Tanis and Savannah had run its conversational course, and while some of the group continued with their social chatter, others chose to sit in silence, lost in their own private thoughts.

Savannah took a moment to study the faces. All of them knew Tanis and Drake from years of living and working in Base One, and yet even though they had befriended her for only a relatively short amount of time, she felt a bond with them that went deeper than the tri-coloured sashes that everyone wore. This was exclusive company: the brotherhood and sisterhood of the Diss.

It seemed fitting to her that Batten and Gillespie were with the fifty or so commandos, travelling in the other trucks.

Her mind wandered to the journey ahead. 'You still haven't explained how we're going to cover the distance from the train to our destination,' said Savannah.

Drake grinned. 'Motorbikes! Scramblers, to be precise.'

'This is going to be so much fun!' smiled Savannah.

'Anything's better than buggies,' said Tanis, absently rubbing the small scar on his hairline.

During their time at Greentrees, as part of their escort preparation, Savannah and Tanis had received firearms training and learnt to ride off-road bikes, and much to Tanis' annoyance, Savannah showed a natural skill for handling one. In fact, whenever she had the opportunity, she would volunteer to ride out on perimeter checks. She found that it gave her a sense of freedom and allowed her to clear her mind of any troubled thoughts. It was inevitable that now and again, the spectres of Jago and her parents' death would reach out like a black dog into her mind.

'Do we pick them up when we get there?' she asked eagerly.

'They're already on board,' said Drake. 'Along with all of the other gear that we'll need.'

'Like what?' asked Tanis.

'Quad bikes, buggies and trailers. How do you think we're going to get the supplies back to the train? Those commandos are tough, but you didn't expect them to carry everything, did you?'

'Hadn't really thought about it,' said Tanis. 'Anyway, since when were you a commando's best friend?'

'Since I was given ranking above them!' Drake smiled and raised his eyebrows.

Savannah stood and pulled herself up to peer out of the ventilation grill. 'Thought so,' she announced. 'We're slowing down.'

Tanis scrabbled up beside her and took in a view of open marshland. Tall reed beds spread out across the landscape, interspersed with narrow waterways and small lakes. At that moment, the train's whistle hooted out with a prolonged gush of rasping steam. Its suddenness shocked flocks of screeching birds from their sanctuary amongst the rushes. They swarmed in fright; black and grey-feathered clouds scattered briefly into the air from one hiding place to another, until the final panic-stricken stragglers disappeared, to leave the vista seemingly devoid of life, once again.

The "Whuff! Whuff!" of the steel-clad engine, its snake trail of white smoke and the clattering of wheels on rails, caused no further disturbance to the unseen wildlife.

'We'll be stopping in a minute to prepare for the first of the gauntlet runs through Crazy territory,' explained Drake. 'We just need to sit tight and leave it all to the commandos. Believe me when I say that you don't need to be out there getting in their way. This is a well-rehearsed and practised routine.'

The wagon lurched; couplings and buffers clashed and screeched in complaint as the train came to a halt, then the voices of Batten and Gillespie could be heard clearly, shouting orders and instructions. Savannah and Tanis continued to crane their necks, faces pressed up against the metal grills, and a few of the others rose to their feet and followed suit.

'You'll hear more than you see,' said Drake. 'Best to sit back down and I'll explain what's going on.'

'Can't we just stretch our legs and get some fresh air?' pleaded Savannah.

'No can do. Now sit down.' He glared at them. 'All of you.' Reluctantly, they did as they were told.

The sound of movement on the roof above prompted Drake to begin his explanation.

'That's snipers taking up their positions with high-powered guns and scopes. There'll be two on each roof facing either side. Their job will be to pick off as many Crazies as possible before they can launch their chemical-filled bombs at us.'

'Sounds like fun,' remarked Tanis.

'Sure. If you like being dressed in a full chemo suit, including the helmet, and lying on the roof of a fast moving train as you try to keep a steady aim, while a load of Crazies bombard you with flaming bombs,' said Drake. 'That's why the train has been heavily armoured and the rolling stock is made of metal. Way back, on the first run, we made the mistake of including a passenger carriage mostly made of wood. One flaming bottle hit its side and it was burnt down to the chassis in less than five minutes!'

'So, what happens if our truck gets hit?' asked Savannah.

'We're basically in a metal box. As long as none of the toxic stuff gets inside, we should be okay,' shrugged Drake. 'Mind you, it could get a bit warm in here before the boys outside manage to put the flames out.'

The truck gave a double lurch and began to move again.

'Right,' Drake continued, 'lift up and secure the metal flaps over the ventilation grills. We'll be entering a tunnel for a couple of minutes and then we emerge into the old industrial area where our friends will be waiting to greet us in their customary psychopathic way. The first gauntlet lasts about five minutes, and believe me, it's a long five minutes!'

In the semi-darkness, they sat in rows; legs outstretched and their backs pressed firmly against either end of the truck. The passage through the tunnel became accompanied by the boom and clatter of the wheels against the rails, which reverberated and echoed with deafening noise to permeate the wagon. Savannah clamped her hands over her ears, her teeth set on edge by the screeching of steel couplings.

As suddenly as it had begun, the cacophony of noise stopped when the truck emerged from the tunnel; the train had picked up an urgent pace. The momentum of speed and a slight banking of the tracks caused the wagon to rock and sway from side to side. Savannah and Tanis' equipment slid across the metal floor, and she instinctively gripped Tanis' arm as her legs slipped out from her sitting position.

'It'll settle down in a minute, once we get back onto straight tracks,' shouted Drake. 'Just spare a thought for the guys on the roof.'

As Drake predicted, it wasn't long before the truck developed a gentler, rhythmic motion.

'Tanis, get the kit; everyone else, hang on to your equipment just in case we have to make a speedy exit,' ordered Drake, who had kept his own bag securely by his side.

Tanis moved forward. It was then that the loud volley of two gunshots rang out overhead. He hesitated and turned to face Drake.

'Did I tell you to take a tea break?' he shouted. 'Get the kit and yourself back here!'

Tanis scrambled to the centre of the truck only to be knocked sideways by the effect of a muffled explosion from outside, which momentarily lifted two of the wagon's wheels from the rails.

'Okay, people,' said Drake. 'Hang on to whatever you can.'

Further explosions and gunshots continued to paint a mental picture of the unfolding skirmish outside.

'What's that smell?' asked Savannah.

'Smoke,' said Drake. 'From the chemical fires started by their bottle bombs. Cover your mouths and try not to breathe it in. It shouldn't be long before we're through this.' He pulled his neck scarf up over his mouth, and the others followed suit.

The minutes did indeed seem to pass as if they were heavy weights being dragged through mud. The interior of the wagon began to fill with wisps of acrid smoke that wormed itself into the backs of their throats, and they began to cough with the effects of the bitter and dry cocktail.

'Get as low as you can, beneath the fumes,' instructed Drake. The seconds dragged by until, as if through answered prayers, the train and its convoy lurched to a halt.

Drake's fist pounded on the metal wall of the wagon, but it was the door on the opposite side that slid noisily back. Several figures in yellow head-to-toe chemical suits waved frantically for them to get out, and without any panic, they jumped down onto the gravel side of the tracks, to be led, eyes now watering, along the row of wagons to where Gillespie and Batten stood offering out water canteens.

'Rinse your mouths before you actually take a drink,' suggested Gillespie. 'And spit out as much as you can.'

'It's vile,' retched Savannah. 'What the hell is it?'

'Mostly petrol, but from what we've been able to analyse they add acidic chemicals to it,' said Batten. 'You should be okay after a good drink of water and some fresh air back in your lungs.'

'Lucky bounce sent one of the bottles under your truck before it smashed open,' explained Batten. 'I'll just go and see if the chaps have managed to put the fire out yet.'

47

MINEFIELD

Unable to grasp a handhold, Tanis had been pitched around the truck and now felt that he had been on the rollercoaster ride from hell. Now, as he jumped down from the truck, a sensation that heralded the inevitable return of his early breakfast crept through his stomach. He turned away to relieve his embarrassment, and walked towards the embankment, staggering forward into the grass. There, he vomited and the sounds of his discomfort alerted the others.

'Stop him!' shouted Gillespie.

Drake turned, half swallowed a mouth full of water, and managed to cough out, 'Shit! Tanis! Minefield!'

With the word, "minefield" firmly ringing in his ears, Tanis froze, hands on knees, half crouched, amongst the lumps of patchy grass.

'Nobody else move,' Drake bellowed.

'I don't believe this,' mumbled Tanis. The acidic burn of bile on his lips.

'He's only gone a couple of metres,' said Savannah, as Drake and Gillespie joined her on the edge of the track and a short distance from Tanis.

'That would be enough,' said Gillespie. 'There's a last line of defensive mines buried along here just in case any of the mad sods get lucky enough to make it this far.'

The lack of oxygen coupled with the expulsion of food was starting to have its effect on Tanis. 'I hate to bother you guys, but I'm feeling a little dizzy.'

'Tanis. Stand up straight, and take a couple of deep breaths,' said Savannah. 'If you look carefully, you should see the slight mounds where the mines are buried. Just step between the lumps.'

'Easier said than done,' said Tanis. 'I've got a job to see straight at the moment. My head's still swimming.'

'Don't even try it,' said Drake. 'Those mounds could be anthills, or spoil from where the mines are laid. There again, they may well be the mines.'

Savannah shot a look at Drake. 'Doesn't *anyone* know where the mines are buried?'

'There's a map for whenever we eventually decide to clear them,' he replied. 'But we've never had the need to carry it with us. On account that no one usually has the desire to wander in there, unless it's a Crazy, that is.'

'Guys. A little help here?'

'Did you walk in a straight line to get where you are?' asked Savannah.

'I… I really can't remember.'

'What do you mean, you can't remember? It was only a couple of minutes ago!' argued Drake.

'I'm sorry,' replied Tanis. 'But I was a bit preoccupied being sick!'

'I think I might be able to help,' said a voice from overhead.

They all turned to see a commando on the roof of the wagon.

'In what way?' asked Drake.

'Well. From here, I think that I can see some of his track marks.'

Tanis' eyes looked up into the face of the last person that he expected to see. It was Grant. Lover boy, Grant, who had hit on Savannah.

'Hi, Romeo,' he smiled down at Tanis.

Gillespie, who had remained in the shadow of the wagon, stepped out.

'Commando. Do you two know each other?' he asked.

Grant straightened. 'Only in passing, sir.'

'Then I suggest that you dispense with the pleasantries, and help the chap out.'

'Sir!' came the reply. 'Okay, Rom...' He corrected himself.

'Tanis. The name's Tanis Kane,' said Tanis.

'Okay, Tanis. Let's see if we can get you out of there in one piece,' said Grant. 'First thing is for everyone else to get at least fifteen metres away from Tanis.'

Gillespie and Drake ushered the rest of the group backwards, but Savannah stood her ground.

'Come on, Savannah,' encouraged Drake.

She shook her head. 'No.'

Tanis looked over his shoulder at her. 'Do as he says. Don't worry; I'll be okay.'

'Then so will I. I'm staying right here.'

Tanis knew by the tone in her voice that it was a waste of time arguing with her. Besides, he still felt nauseous, and now he needed a pee!

'Grant. Let's do this,' he shouted.

'Do exactly as I tell you. First of all, turn around on the spot – slowly.'

Tanis shuffled a hundred and eighty degrees, and his eyes met Savannah's.

'I love you,' she mouthed.

Tanis returned a nervous smile, and then looked up at the silhouette of Grant's figure on the wagon's roof.

'Okay, Tanis. There's good news and there's bad news. The bad news is that I'm not sure what types of mines were laid in this area. They're either standard Blast mines or Bouncing Bettys. Blast mines are set off when you stand on them. Bouncing Bettys have a trip wire to trigger them.'

'And the good news is?'

'If they're Bouncing Bettys, you must have got lucky on the way in and stepped over the wires, so I suggest that's what you're going to be looking for. From what I can see up here, you have about ten steps to retrace. Are you ready?'

Beads of sweat seeped from Tanis' brow and ran into his eyes. He wiped the sleeve of his jacket across his face, and spat the residue of bile from his mouth. 'Let's get on with it.' He lifted his foot and began the short journey – a journey to safety, or to death.

Savannah's thoughts latched onto painful memories of loss. Clouded images of her mother and father appeared in her mind's eye. She knew that to lose Tanis would be more than she could bear. Something, that until this moment she had not dared to even contemplate. Hardened physically and mentally, she retained her principles but at the end of the day, she could not deny her transition from a young, disobedient, and somewhat naive rebel, to a complex young woman whose love and loyalty gave her fragility, and the moral detachment to take life in order to protect the people that she loved. She had become a formidable and determined adversary, but she knew well that Tanis and her sister Beth were her Achilles' heel.

'Nearly there, Tanis.' Grant's voice jolted her from her distractions. 'There's a slight boot print just at the edge of the grass line, but I can't quite make out the next one that's closest to you.'

Adrenalin had chased away Tanis' nausea and dizziness but he now found himself balancing with uncertainty in mid-stride.

'Need to make a decision, Grant. I can't hold this position much longer.'

'Take a look for yourself, Tanis. I've got you as far as I can. This one's your call, I'm afraid,' replied Grant. 'Besides, if I got it wrong, I have a feeling that your girlfriend would kill me.' He gave Savannah a sombre glance.

As word quickly spread about Tanis' predicament, an audience of commandos looked on from a relatively safe distance. Each of them harboured helpful suggestions, but in the knife-edged silence, none dared to utter a word.

Tanis looked into Savannah's eyes, and he smiled.

She recognised that smile. It said, '*I love you.*' It said, '*My name's Tanis Kane, and I have a zest for life.*' It also said, '*Sod it. Let's take a chance!*'

'Oooooooh! Shiiiiiit!' he shouted, and then he bounded, one foot after the other, across the remaining ground, to throw himself protectively on top of Savannah.

Luckily, her backpack broke her fall, but his impact knocked the breath out of her. For a moment or two, they lay there, silence ringing in their ears, until a pair of brown combat boots crunched onto the gravel next to their heads.

'Hell. Boy. That took some guts. You must have a pair on you,' commented Grant. 'Let me help you guys.' He reached down with two ham hocks of hands, and pulled them to their feet.

Savannah regained her breath. 'What the hell's wrong with you, Tanis? Have you got a death wish?'

'No. I'm bursting for a pee!' He pushed past Drake and Gillespie to disappear between two of the wagons.

'I guess that when you gotta go, you gotta go,' smiled Grant.

*

An hour later, they endured the second gauntlet. No less intense and hazardous than the first. This time, however, behind the windowless floors of derelict high-rise flats, the sub-human culture found no sanctuary in the shadows, as the skilled commandos expertly sighted and eliminated any Crazies before they managed to launch their deadly and toxic Molotov cocktails.

Again, when the urban sprawl of desolation gave way to open countryside, the train rolled to a halt on a raised embankment. This was the opportunity for everyone to take what was, in the eyes of Tanis, laughingly referred to as a "comfort break".

As Grant peeled himself out of his chemo-suit, Tanis took the opportunity to thank him for his help. *After all,* he thought, *the guy can't be all that bad. He could have kept his mouth shut and watched me struggle, maybe get killed!* As it turned out, Tanis found that he and Grant shared the same sense of humour, and like many others, the pain of personal loss; Grant carried the emotional ghost of a younger brother lost to the violence of the Crazies.

'We've always been on the defensive,' said Grant. 'Until we take the fight to them, and start eradicating their kind, we'll never start to build a better and safer world.' There was logic and bitterness in his voice, and Tanis could see in Grant's eyes a brooding for insatiable revenge.

'What about Opulence?' asked Tanis.

'From what I hear, their kind are just as bad. It's been decades since everything went to rat-crap, and all they've done is live in their comfortable little empire without lifting a finger to help us. Now, from what I can gather, they're coming to take away everything we've managed to salvage and build. I joined up as a commando to try and make this world a better place,' Grant continued. 'So did my brother, and as far as I'm concerned, it's not a better place without him. But I'm damned if I'll let what he gave his life for, his belief in a better future, be ruined.' He paused as he checked the breach in his gun. 'Revenge is a dish best served cold, so they say, Tanis. Well, I'm as hungry as hell, and I don't see myself losing my appetite anytime soon.'

'Just as long as you don't let it cloud your judgement,' said Tanis. 'I know that I owe you – big time. You never know, we might find ourselves covering each other's backs, and I just want you to know that you can rely on me.'

Grant faced Tanis. He towered over him, his broad shoulders square and straight. 'You're quite a tough little cookie, Tanis. So, what brings you to the fight?'

'You'd be surprised, Grant. You'd be surprised. Believe me when I say it's for all the right reasons.'

'Tanis!' Drake's voice interrupted the moment.

'We'll talk again,' said Grant. He put his hand out.

'Look forward to it,' smiled Tanis, taking the man's firm hand and giving it a shake.

48

Confrontation

Much to Drake's amusement, Savannah refused to speak to Tanis following the minefield incident, and she continued to give him the silent treatment as they stood on the side of the tracks, taking in some fresh air.

'Look. I've said I'm sorry for scaring you,' he pleaded. 'What did you expect me to do, stand there and wet my pants?'

'What?' she glared at him. 'You mean, as an alternative to you being blown up?'

'Ha!' he exclaimed triumphantly. 'You're talking to me.'

'You're impossible.' She turned to Drake. 'How much further to our destination?'

'It's a straight run from here. Usually about an hour.'

'And then what?'

'We reach what is currently the end of the line – Ridgeway. With an exceptional amount of hard labour, our brilliant engineers and a first-class work force have constructed a new junction, large enough to allow an engine to be turned around for its journey back. Even though it's in the middle of nowhere, the place is well fortified and supported, and one of the most recently discovered community compounds is about twenty-five miles east of its location.'

A piercing blast of steam placed a full stop on Drake's voice, and within minutes, the train, with its human cargo accounted for, continued onwards.

★

Just after 4 o'clock in the afternoon, Drake slid back the complaining metal door of the wagon, and before she jumped down, Savannah studied the platform-less setting laid out before her. There was little resemblance between Ridgeway and Broadway Junction. For a start, Ridgeway's buildings were characterless. There was no history in these structures, except maybe what lay behind the recycled grey block walls and corrugated rooftops.

A flurry of human activity surrounded the train and its rolling stock. Commandos mixed with workers attired in brown overalls, eager to unload the wooden crates and equipment.

Drake gathered his team around him. 'Follow me, and I'll show you where we'll be putting our heads down for the night. Pretty basic, I'm afraid. But the upside is that there's a canteen with decent hot food, so at least we'll get fed this evening and again before we leave in the morning.'

Tanis and Savannah followed, and behind them, fifteen pairs of boots crunched along the coarse gravel as the smell of sooty steam drifted aimlessly around them and dispersed in the damp afternoon air.

Rows of simply constructed, wooden huts dominated an area beyond the station. Shingle paths connected the buildings, and a large signpost, with its five arrowhead fingers, directed the uninitiated to a choice of destinations: Shower Block. Toilets. Canteen. Station. Operations Unit.

A central corridor ran the length of each hut, with rooms leading off, and it was halfway down one of these that Drake pushed down the handle of a plain brown plywood door, swung it inwards, and stepped inside.

'Welcome to the Hilton,' he said.

The narrow room consisted of four bunk beds with just enough space for them to stow their gear. Drake flopped himself down on one of the lower bunks.

'Don't say that I never take you guys to the best places,' he smiled, and he crossed his arms behind his head.

'I can't wait to see the bathroom,' Savannah replied with sarcasm.

'Top bunk or bottom?' asked Tanis.

'Bottom, thanks. Looks like we're in for a boring evening and an early night,' she remarked.

'Don't worry,' said Drake. 'We've got a meeting with Gillespie and Batten later on. We need to run over the maps and finalise tomorrow's plans.'

'I don't know if I can contain my excitement,' she replied.

★

After eating a simple but satisfying meal in the communal canteen, Savannah, Tanis and Drake made their way to the Operations Unit: a section of meeting rooms and offices used by those responsible for the day-to-day running of Ridgeway and its facilities.

In one such room, Ordnance Survey maps were already pinned to the walls, and when Drake, Tanis and Savannah arrived, Gillespie and Batten were studying three smaller, hand-drawn maps laid out on a table.

'Latest information from the survey patrols,' announced Gillespie. 'They've not approached any of the locations, just had a damn good look at them from a distance, in daytime and at night. These are rough maps of the terrain.'

He slid one of the A4 sheets to the centre of the table. 'This is a layout of the area around Billingdon Military Airfield. Most of it has been reclaimed by nature; the runways are overgrown, and the buildings are just empty shells, but the control tower's still standing. However, the most interesting detail that's been spotted is the definite remains of a single track railway cutting. We know a link used to run from the edge of the airfield, down into a deep gully for about two miles. We're ninety-nine per cent sure that this is it.' He positioned the second A4 map against the side of the first, and drew his finger along a hand-drawn red line from one sheet to the other. 'This is Sinfield Quarry. It would appear that the rail line runs right up to a cliff face at the rear of the quarry workings. It's too overgrown to see much detail, but there's a hidden entrance, and it has nothing to do with what used to be the industrial section of the mine.'

'They certainly wouldn't have been transporting rock salt out of there by rail and air,' suggested Batten.

'And,' added Gillespie, almost triumphantly as he slid the third map against the others, 'there are the definite remains of a purpose-built roadway from Wyndham Barracks to where the rail line ends at the quarry cliff.'

'Everything points to it being the entrance to a large military underground facility,' said Batten. 'Possibly for use as a high level Doomsday retreat. In fact, we think that this may well be an old pre-construction blueprint.' He shuffled the various papers around until he slid a metre square, blue-grey document on top of the others. 'A couple of our Intel team have had a go at restoring some of the detail, but I'm afraid that water damage has left sections of the blueprint open to guesswork.'

A variety of bold and faint three-dimensional architectural lines and technical patterns crisscrossed its surface.

'Do you mind if we have a closer look?' asked Drake as he eased Gillespie and Batten to one side to allow Savannah and Tanis access to the drawings.

The three of them pored over the detail, some of which was, indeed, indistinct and unreadable.

'Does that say "Munitions"?' squinted Tanis. His finger traced a water-stained patch near the edge of the blueprint.

'Looks like it,' said Savannah as she tilted her head in an effort to read the detail. 'It's located at the far end of the complex on what looks like level two.'

'Are these scale markings correct?' asked Drake.

'As far as we can determine. Yes,' replied Gillespie.

'A mile deep?' Drake quizzed.

'At least. Comprising five levels, with three square miles of passageways linking up everything; including a hospital, a school, laboratories and a command centre.

We estimate that it was designed to house up to five thousand individuals – men, women and children, in the event of a nuclear attack.'

'Assuming that we enter at level one,' said Drake, 'that means we have to negotiate at least a mile of passageways and stairwells, some of which we have no idea how they link up.'

'We'll need to take this with us,' said Tanis.

'We already have a hand-drawn copy made up for you,' said Batten.

'We'll be taking the original,' said Drake. 'I'm taking no chance that important details have been overlooked.'

Gillespie remained silent and stony-faced.

'How close can we get to this place?' asked Tanis.

'We'll supervise a clearance party to work ahead, with flamethrowers and cutting gear to open the railway track right up to the cliff face. We should be able to drive the convoy straight to the concealed entrance,' said Batten.

'Any sign of life?' It was Savannah.

'There have been sightings of a small group of Crazies around the Barracks complex at night. We don't think that they'll present much of a problem once we've sent in a clean-up team of commandos,' said Batten.

Savannah noticed there was a slight hesitation in his voice. *He's hiding something*, she thought.

'And?' she challenged.

'Nothing you need to be concerned about. Miss.' His tone of voice was dismissive.

To Savannah, this was like a red rag to a bull. 'I'll tell you what you should be concerned about. Mister!' She glared at him. 'That I don't trust you one inch.'

Caught off guard, Batten looked towards Gillespie, as if for guidance.

'Don't look at him,' interjected Drake. 'I'm the team leader of this mission, and if either of you are withholding information, I'll have you relieved of your duties and sent back under escort to face Jean Fairfax. Now, what aren't you telling us?'

Batten swallowed nervously. His Adam's apple bobbed up and down like a cat's toy on the end of a piece of string. 'What you need to understand...' he began.

'Wrong answer!' growled Drake.

'All right, Batten. I'll take over,' said Gillespie. 'There is no subterfuge, Drake, just a matter of priorities. Our priority, that is, of the commando support unit, is to protect your group. I remember that Jean Fairfax's words to Batten and myself were, "At all costs," and forgive me if I sound melodramatic, but I believe if you were to be swamped with every little detail, your focus on the prime objective would be distracted.' He kept a steady and unwavering gaze on Drake. 'If you have any complaints, I would suggest that you take them up with Commander-in-Chief Fairfax on our return and not threaten to jeopardise the whole mission because of your ego. So, if you'll just let us get on with our job, we'll let you get on with yours.'

Drake ran his hand along a day's stubble on his jawline. He thumbed his nose and gave a sniff. 'What do you two know about us?' He indicated to himself, Tanis and Savannah.

'Only that you've been hand-picked by Fairfax from her Dissident squad at Base One, and that you have her authority and clearance.'

'And that your files are classified,' added Batten.

'Savannah. Show him your brand,' Drake said, without releasing his eyes from Gillespie's.

She unbuttoned her tunic and pulled back the collar to reveal the ingrained black letter "T".

'Enlighten the gentlemen on how you came to get that; and of our little adventure over the waves,' he said.

Over the next fifteen minutes, with added dialogue from Tanis; Gillespie and Batten listened, without interruption.

'That,' concluded Drake, 'is why we need complete transparency. Without trust, there is no mission, and believe you me, gentlemen, ego or no ego – *we* are the mission!'

Batten and Gillespie looked at each other to confirm agreement.

'What I'm about to tell you is to go no further than this room. You're to tell no one else. This is on a high priority, need-to-know basis,' said Gillespie.

'You tell us everything, and I mean everything. Then I'll decide who needs to know,' said Drake. 'As I said, complete trust or we call the whole thing off. We do not want any surprises, because if we find out that you've been holding something back and it costs lives, we will come looking for you, and it will not be with the intention of having a conversation.'

'Are you threatening us?' Gillespie's face reddened.

'Damn right!' said Savannah.

'I'll second that,' said Tanis.

The room's atmosphere fizzed with tension. Batten and Gillespie had spent most of their military careers giving orders and having them carried out without question. They themselves could put fear into the most hardened commando, but as they looked into the faces and the eyes of Drake, Savannah and Tanis, they saw something dark and primal. Something that said, *I have seen death, and it fears me.*

'Let the record show that we have not shared this information on a voluntary basis,' said Gillespie.

'Whatever,' said Drake.

Hesitantly, at first, Batten and Gillespie revealed the true horrors of what they suspected may be harboured in the target area.

'The scouting teams have reported back that Wyndham Barracks may shelter what is thought to be a small army of Crazies, probably in their hundreds. Furthermore, the cave complex of Sinfield Quarry is a nesting place for some of the most dangerous nocturnal, airborne creatures ever discovered,' Gillespie disclosed.

'These two pieces of information mean that the infiltration of the underground complex and the extraction of arms and munitions only has a window of ten daylight hours, from start to finish. As soon as dusk falls, all hell would descend on anyone moving within a two-mile radius of the barracks or the quarry,' advised Batten.

'You considered this information to be "little details"?' asked Drake.

'In the greater scheme of things, yes,' replied Gillespie defensively. 'Besides,' he continued, 'as long as we get the job done in daylight hours, it won't make any difference.'

'I'll be the judge of that,' said Drake.

49

MISSING

'What the hell do you mean, "They're missing"?' Danny Hench's voice boomed at Jameson, who stood unflinching. Having had the experience of delivering unwanted news to Hench on previous occasions, he knew that it was best just to stand still and weather Hench's wrath.

'They appear to have gone AWOL, sir. Along with one of the scrambler bikes.'

The skin on Hench's face reached a new level of crimson. 'How the hell did two young girls not only leave the compound unseen, but also manage to leave with a bloody scrambler bike?'

In contrast, Jameson's pallor was now a whitish-grey. 'It's being investigated, sir.'

'Being investigated? I'll bloody well investigate someone with my boot if I don't get answers.' Jameson remained rooted to the spot. 'Move it!' bellowed Hench. 'I want those girls found – now!'

★

The evening of Savannah and Tanis' departure, Beth and Solli lounged on the mattress of their iron-framed bed, which dominated the room. A conversation that had begun in mutual comfort and support drifted into a tearful and brooding silence, until Beth sniffed at the residue of her tears.

'I don't know about you, but I'm not sitting around any more while everyone else treats us like a couple of little kids. We're just as involved in all of this as anyone else. I want to do something. I *need* to do something. I want to hit back.' She thumped a clenched fist into the bed covers, and shuffled herself off the bed to face Soli. 'You know that that vile animal of a brother of mine is at the bottom of this. He won't stop until he's defiled and destroyed everything that we love. Unless…'

Soli's expression hardened. Her eyes met Beth's. 'Unless?'

'Unless we end it,' said Beth.

'Or die trying,' replied Soli.

'Better that, than spend the rest of our lives running and hiding,' said Beth. Echoes of Savannah hung in the air.

'What've you got in mind?' asked Soli.

'They say that the best way to kill something is to cut off its head. Someone needs to go to Opulence and kill Jago.' The words seemed to slip out of Beth's mouth, effortlessly and without emotion.

Soli looked at Beth and wrinkled her brow. 'You'd do that? You'd kill your own brother?'

Beth sat down next to Soli, and gently took both her

hands in her own. She looked into Soli's deep brown eyes. 'He made me witness terrible things. He took away my compassion and my innocence, he filled me with lies and hatred for my sister, and worst of all, he arranged the deaths of our own parents – my parents. It's hard to justify taking anyone else's life, but I'd make an exception in his case and willingly carry that sin. He's a monster who has no value over human life. All I need to do is get close to him, just for a second. That will be enough.'

'How are you going to do that?'

Beth smiled and gently stroked Soli's hair. 'By giving him you.'

★

Now, twenty miles away, the grumblings of a motorbike echoed through the forest fringes. With Soli on pillion, Beth expertly guided the scrambler into the maze of trees. In their minds, a grim and determined plan festered and hungered. They would find a way to Opulence, Beth would feign renewed love and admiration for Jago. To gain his trust, she would present Soli to him, bound and gagged, and when the opportunity presented itself, Beth would kill him. She would cut the head off the snake from whose poisonous veins spilled the venom that infected their lives, and threatened any hope of peace in Earthland.

50

OPEN SESAME

The terrain from Ridgeway was mostly flat heath, covered in a carpet of dull purple scrub, scarred only by a churned-up avenue created by the quad bikes and buggies of Gillespie and Batten's commandos, who had spent the previous day clearing the railway cutting up to its destination at the rear of the quarry. In less than eight hours, they had hacked and incinerated the thick undergrowth away to reveal the ruined and rusted remains of railway lines, which eventually led them to a long concrete platform at the end of which stood sturdy metal buffers and the end of the track. A wide area behind the platform continued on to a concrete roadway, which ran a short distance to a tall, wide curtain of thick creepers and ivy. This was eagerly stripped away to expose great steel doors, which seemed to stand with an air of arrogance and defiance against time and the elements.

This morning, the convoy returned, headed by Drake and his team. Their approach was again loudly announced with the throaty roars of converted kick-start engines, which filled the air like a swarm of angry buzzing giant bees. Savannah and Tanis revelled in their roles as outriders, enjoying the freedom to put the scramblers through their paces, even though they weren't as powerful as those they had ridden at Greentrees.

As the predawn gloom was chased away by a hazy sunrise, the succession of vehicles eventually assembled at the base of the old airfield control tower, and the noisy machines stuttered and coughed until a relative silence was imposed on the gathering. While Batten mustered the small group of commandos who were going to be stationed at the airfield in their role as a rear guard, Gillespie issued instructions to his own squad. These were the drivers of the buggies and their flatbed trailers, who were to wait outside the bunker entrance until Drake and his team located the arms and ammunition, and had determined the best way to extract the cargo for loading onto the vehicles.

'Time to move!' shouted Drake. 'We're using up valuable daylight.'

Within minutes, the air reverberated once again with the coarse rumble of four-stroke engines. Their progress to the bunker doors was much slower than the first part of the journey due to the narrow cutting. Speed had to be kept to a reasonable pace as the buggies with their trailers had to negotiate the uneven track with two wheels inside the rails and two on the gravel pathway. Driving fast or recklessly would risk structural damage to the vehicles and their trailers.

It was with great relief that they finally reached the sealed entrance, but not without Drake venting his frustration.

'Dammit! That's at least an hour we've lost,' he cursed.

The team dismounted and assembled a distance away from the great steel barrier embedded into the rock face.

'Blast doors,' announced Gillespie. 'Their presence confirms that this is indeed no ordinary installation. Beyond them is a major Doomsday facility. It's a good indication that the blueprints in our possession do, in fact, relate to this particular site.'

'Now that we're here, how do we get in?' asked Savannah.

'Hydraulics!' Gillespie sounded smug, as though he was the only person to understand the word. 'Yesterday, we uncovered a control box. Of course, without a pass code and power source there's no way that the door will operate, but then one of my men suggested we locate the pipes that feed compressed liquid or air into the operating system. When we cut those pipes, the pressure will be released and with a bit of brute force, we should be able to open the doors.'

'Please tell me that you've found the pipes,' said Drake, who was tiring of what he felt was Gillespie's long-winded approach to sharing information.

'Oh, yes,' beamed Gillespie, obviously pleased with himself. 'We had to hack out half a ton of quarry rock to get to them, but when you're ready I'll give the order to start cutting.'

'Well, let's get on with it then,' said Drake.

The moment the pipes were cut, there was the sound of metal grinding on metal, and a slight movement from the doors. A narrow gap, just centimetres wide, opened up.

Taking the initiative, Gillespie arranged for two buggies to be backed up to the entrance and ropes were tethered to the steelwork. Revving the engines to screaming point, the buggies, slowly at first, pulled the great doors open until, under their own heavy momentum, they swung out and back to shudder against the rock face and expose a great dark corridor, melting into the hillside.

Stale air gushed out as if eager to be free of the darkness, which retreated almost reluctantly from the light of day to reveal a smooth single roadway. The concrete curvature of the tunnel allowed enough room for a small truck to traverse its corridor.

'Right!' said Drake. 'Gillespie, you know your orders. I'll expect your team to be ready when you get the word.' He turned to address his own group. 'Rows of three, steady pace at least five metres between each row. You two, either side of me,' he said to Tanis and Savannah. He jumped onto his bike and kicked the starting lever, and the rest of the group followed suit. The staccato sound of motorbike engines echoed down into the maw of the tunnel, and Drake fired a bright red flare into the darkness.

The white-hot core of the flare tumbled to a halt far ahead of them and the tunnel turned infrared. Several of the motorbike's headlamp beams crisscrossed like white scars through the crimson smoke, and shadows danced erratically along the wet reflective walls. To Savannah's eyes, the scene resembled an entrance to hell.

After travelling at a slow pace down a slight incline for almost half an hour, they congregated in front of another set of blast doors. To one side, there was a large sliding door with SECTOR 1 EMERGENCY POWER & COMMUNICATIONS spray stencilled across it. Drake signalled for the engines to be silenced, and more flares brought the temporary darkness to an end.

'Tanis. Check it out,' ordered Drake.

Tanis' shadow loomed large as he approached the door, and he grabbed its metal handle with both hands and pulled sideways. It slid effortlessly away on well-lubricated runners.

'It's a generator!' announced Tanis. A large compressor sat bolted to the floor, accompanied by a tall, corrugated drum with its own labelled announcement of FLAMMABLE FUEL. In a small recess, the black plastic receiver of a telephone hung in its cradle like a sleeping bat. Tanis lifted the handset and placed it to his ear. 'Hello?' He waited a moment before he offered it to Drake. 'It's for you,' he grinned.

'Stop messing about, Tanis,' said Savannah.

Tanis shrugged and replaced the phone in its cradle.

'Two of you help Tanis and see if you can get that generator working,' ordered Drake.

In no time, the fuel tap and pulley wheel were located, and with one seemingly effortless yank, the generator roared into life. The ceiling along the tunnel fizzed and popped as rows of fluorescent strips surged into life, illuminating the group with what was, at first, an eye-blinding light.

Eager hands spun the two circular wheels on each blast

door and the generator's power relieved the hydraulic pressure, allowing the thick doors to swing silently back and anchor against the sidewalls with muffled "thuds". The tunnel continued, now lit by twin rows of lights some giving off a steady radiance while others flickered restlessly as if in protest of their interrupted dormancy.

'Leave the genny running,' said Drake. 'I don't want to have to mess about restarting it if we have to shut the doors in a hurry.'

They continued steadily for another hundred or so metres to an intersection where two tunnels branched off right and left. A signpost painted onto the wall announced their options.

To the left, it indicated lifts to levels 3, 4 and 5. To the right, it read, "Armoury and Munitions. Authorised personnel only". A further fifty metres ahead, the road surface descended into a curving bend.

'This is going to be easier than we thought,' said Tanis.

Drake unfolded the blueprint and studied it for a moment. 'Unfortunately, what's beyond the bend ahead is unclear on this plan.' He noticed that Savannah stood in a pensive mood. 'What is it?' he asked.

'Just wondering if anyone made it down here, all those years ago.'

'You mean, to the lower levels?' asked Drake.

She nodded.

'Who knows,' he mused. 'They could've been and gone long ago, but if what's left of them is still down there, in the lower levels, we'll just leave that for someone with more time on their hands to find out.' He checked his watch. 'Let's keep going and hope that the rest of the journey is as straightforward.'

With the entrance well behind them and out of view, the convoy of bikes followed a long curving bend as the tunnel continued to take them deeper into the facility. Much to the frustration of Savannah, Drake restricted their speed to a steady fifteen miles an hour. What he expected them to encounter, she could only guess, but she kept reminding herself to trust Drake's judgement. After all, it had saved her life on at least one previous occasion.

The monotony of the strip lights was broken by an overhead sign that announced – YOU ARE NOW LEAVING SECTOR 1. AUTHORISED PERSONNEL ONLY BEYOND THIS POINT. As if to accentuate the message, a wide expanse of the floor was painted with large yellow and black chevrons.

Ahead, two grey sentry boxes, looking forlornly empty, were recessed either side into the tunnel walls, and the barrier of a red and white striped pole rested across the roadway.

Drake signalled for two of the riders to go ahead and raise the barrier, while the rest of them waited, idling their engines.

'Can we pick the pace up a bit, Drake?' shouted Tanis. 'Only I'd like to get back in time for lunch!'

Needless to say, Drake stubbornly enforced his cautious speed limit, which a short time later, when they rounded another bend, was prophetically justified. Scattered across the tunnel floor were chunks of brick and concrete debris from a sidewall, where a great yawning hole reached into shadows and darkness.

They dismounted, and Drake, Tanis and Savannah clambered over a pile of rubble to survey an exposed, dark cavity. A flow of damp air caressed their faces and a rancid ammonia stench assaulted their senses, which caused them to cough and gag.

'Phew! What's that stink?' asked Tanis.

'I'm not going in there to find out,' said Savannah.

'Probably coming from fractured waste or sewage pipes,' suggested Drake, covering his mouth and nose as he peered into the gloom. Satisfied with his assumption, he turned to the group. 'Right. It's just a wall collapse. So much for military engineering. Let's get this lot cleared,' he ordered. 'We'll need enough room to get the buggies and trailers through.'

Apart from a couple of large slabs of concrete, most of the rubble was in manageable chunks, and working in two organised teams, they proceeded to pitch the debris into the gaping hollow.

Drake wandered further up the now sparsely lit tunnel where several ceiling lights were smashed or destroyed. The thick steel bars of what was once floor-to-ceiling gates were now pushed back against the walls in twisted tangles of metal spaghetti. His mind tried to rationalise the damage; then, in the flickering fluorescent light, he spotted deep scratches and dark patches in the floor. He crouched down for closer inspection. His fingers lazily traced across the concrete's gritty surface.

'Bloodstains,' he reasoned out loud.

Looking up, his eyes momentarily probed the tunnel ahead where shadows danced under an erratic pattern of surviving strobe-like strip lights. Finally, satisfied that he had separated imagination from fact, he turned back to the busy group who were making rapid progress and he gave a cursory glance into the dark emptiness of the hole. 'We need to get a move on,' he announced. 'And keep your wits about you.'

Tanis and Savannah heaved a large piece of rubble through the hole; the sound of its landing was lost amongst the dull clattering of similarly thrown debris from other hands. Tanis arched his back. 'What's up, Drake?'

'I'm not sure. But something's not... right.'

51

EXPENDABLE

It wasn't long before the corridor was sufficiently cleared, and Drake addressed his team.

'Listen up. This is where the map is of no use and we're going in blind. Check your weapons, safety catches off. Single file from now on, and keep alert.'

With throttles gently eased open, and headlamps compensating for the diminished light ahead, the procession of bikes edged forward, and one by one they passed between the mangled steel gates. Tanis fleetingly turned a nodding glance at Savannah and at the twisted bars.

Fifteen minutes later, the tunnel opened dramatically into a high-ceilinged cavern, and the bikes fanned out in a semicircle across a large floor area where Drake signalled for them to kill their engines. It was a warehouse, with high racks of steel shelving that held numerous crates and containers. Six sections of metal framework stretched away in shadow and gloom, their wide aisles barely illuminated by the remains of globe-shaped lights, which hung down on cables in twisted clusters.

'What the hell happened here?' said Tanis.

Two end units of crumpled racking leaned drunkenly over a toppled forklift truck surrounded by fallen crates, which were smashed and splintered open. Their contents of guns and armoury lay strewn across the ground, metal shapes bent and twisted. A few battered and upturned filing cabinets and desks, along with their disembowelled paperwork, lay scattered across the scene before the group. Dried bloodstains and long scratch marks disturbed the floor.

Drake picked up a grey sheet of paper and a coating of fine powder slid from its surface. With a cursory glance, he absently let it fall from his fingers as he turned to the group.

'Dexter and Cass, get back to the extraction party and escort them down here pretty damn quick. Tell them to be on high alert,' he ordered.

Two bikes roared into life; their receding echoes thundered into the tunnel.

'Right,' he continued, 'I want four of you, in two pairs, to check the aisles; use a couple of flares if need be. The rest of you clear this area and make room for the convoy. Tanis and Savannah, you're with me.'

He wandered over to one of the smashed crates, picked up a mangled Sten gun and turned it over in his hands.

'Okay, Drake. What's on your mind?' asked Tanis. 'You've been on edge since we came across the cave-in.'

'I'm always on edge,' mused Drake.

'We're not blind. Mangled steel gates, half the lighting destroyed, bloodstains and scratch marks in the concrete, and now this.' Savannah indicated to the twisted weapon. 'Come on. There's something missing – remains. There'd at least be bones. Skeletons. This has all the hallmarks of a bunch of marauding Crazies.'

Drake handed the gun to Tanis. 'What do you think?'

'I think that we should just get on with what we came here to do. Everything's covered in dust, and whatever happened down here, happened a long time ago.'

'When there were people down here,' said Savannah as she scuffed a thin film of powder away from another dark stain. 'And now…' She looked at Drake.

'…people are back.' Drake finished the sentence for her.

Tanis looked back and forth between Savannah and Drake. 'Oh yeah! The big bad bogeyman's gonna come and get us.' He grinned and wiggled his fingers at them.

'Drake!' All three of them turned their heads at the shout. 'Over here.'

They wandered over to where two of the team stood looking behind a row of tall shelving.

'What's up?' Drake queried.

'This.'

Their eyes followed the pointing finger of a gloved hand. There was an alcove, and in the wall the entrance to a large lift shaft gaped open. The doors had been ripped open from top to bottom and bent aside, as if by a giant can opener. Embedded in the metal frame was what appeared to be a large, hooked blade.

Drake crouched down and wrestled to remove it with his hands until he finally gave up and resorted to kicking at the twisted metal. He reached forward, and with a satisfied grunt, brought the object up for all to see.

'What the hell is that?' breathed one of the team.

Drake turned it around for a closer inspection. It was about fifteen centimetres long, curved like a scimitar and ended in a sharp, pointed tip. Rust-red staining coloured its otherwise grey surface.

In the grimy light of the warehouse, Savannah's mind drifted back to the day she awoke to find herself on the estuary beach with the sound of screaming gulls in her ears. She remembered looking up and seeing the creatures for the first time, their vicious talons clawing at the air, ready to rip her heart out.

'Savannah?' Tanis' voice brought her back to the present.

'It's a claw,' she said. 'A bloody great claw.'

'Mutes,' nodded Drake. He moved to the edge of the shaft and peered down into a pit of darkness. The trace of a familiar stench reached his senses. 'The cables are gone. Whatever's left of the lift and anyone who was in it is lying at the bottom. Tanis. Light one of those flares and drop it down here, will you?'

Tanis dropped the hell-red flare, and the group crowded around to watch it fall and illuminate its passage, steadily fading away until it became nothing more than a pinprick of light before it blinked out of sight.

'That's a hell of a drop,' said Tanis.

'It's probably still falling,' said Drake. 'Remember, that's more than a mile deep.'

Savannah stepped back and surveyed the damaged doors. 'What the hell did this?'

'Something determined to get in by the looks of it,' said Tanis.

'Or out,' added Savannah.

'Let's just hope that whatever it was has long gone,' said Drake.

By the time they heard the sound of the extraction team's vehicles echoing into the warehouse, the area had been cleared enough to allow the convoy of quads, buggies and trailers to assemble in front of the racks. Without so much as a word to Drake or his group, Gillespie immediately assumed command and made his presence felt by roaming around the aisles, barking out instructions and indicating what crates and items were to be loaded onto the trailers.

Drake called his team to assemble around him.

'Absolute arsehole,' he grumbled. 'If he wants any help from us, he'll have to beg me for it!'

'Well, at least he's efficient,' commented Savannah.

Those words were still ringing in her ears nearly two hours later as she sat with the group, their backs resting against a wall in the alcove.

'How much longer, Drake?' she asked. 'I've lost all sense of feeling in my arse. I could do this somewhere more comfortable.'

Drake huffed, and resignedly pulled himself to his feet. He walked over to Gillespie, who was still circulating amongst his team, shouting orders and checking items against a clipboard of sheets.

Savannah watched as an animated conversation developed between Drake and Gillespie, and their voices rose to echo above the busy workforce. Drake's comments of "getting bored of babysitting" and Gillespie's suggestions that Drake's team could always "get off their backsides and help" further fuelled the dislike that each had for the other.

'I don't know why they don't just get married!' laughed Tanis.

Savannah gave a chuckled response, and then, 'Ssh! He's coming back.'

'I've given him thirty minutes to get the last of the stuff loaded,' said a stony-faced Drake.

'What's been the problem?' asked Tanis.

'No forklift,' said Drake. 'They've had to unpack and manhandle a lot of the stuff down from the racks and repack it onto the trailers.'

'The forklift wouldn't have worked anyway,' said Tanis. 'The batteries would've been de-polarised. He should have guessed that everything needed to be done by hand.'

'If he'd just let his team get on and load the stuff instead of holding them up every five minutes by checking every item twice and ticking it off his checklist, they wouldn't be taking so long,' said Savannah.

'Just something else to confirm that the man's a control freak,' said Drake.

'And a knob,' added Tanis.

'And a knob,' agreed Drake.

The group stood around in quiet conversation, stretching their legs, until Savannah noticed one of their team was peering down the lift shaft. She wandered over in idle curiosity.

'Hi. Jenna, isn't it?'

With shoulder length brown hair and eyes to match, at thirty-two, Jenna was a veteran of Diss patrols and estuary rescue missions. Her loyalty to Jean Fairfax was unquestionable and her admiration of Savannah fuelled her own determination to be resilient in the face of conflict.

'Hi.' She pushed a stray lock of hair behind her ear.

'That's a long way down,' said Savannah, nodding into the darkness.

'Yeah. It's just that I thought I heard something.'

'Like what?'

'A sort of clattering, like something metal falling over.'

Savannah leant in as far as she dared and strained her ears.

'There!' said Jenna.

The noise was just audible over the activity and shouting behind them, but there was no mistake; there was a distant sound, a sort of metallic echo.

'Drake!' Savannah called. 'There's something down here. There's definitely movement.'

Drake didn't even approach the lift shaft. 'You sure?'

'Positive.'

Drake's experience, along with a gut feeling for trouble, swung him into action.

'Cliff.' He pointed to another of the team. 'Join Jenna and guard that lift shaft. Either of you see anything, shoot first. The rest of you follow me. We've got company and it isn't my Aunt Annie.'

Gillespie was once more consulting his clipboard when Drake interrupted him.

'That's it. Ready or not, you're moving out,' he ordered.

'May I remind you —?' began Gillespie.

'You can remind me all you want when we're clear of this place, but right now you need to fire this convoy up and get the hell out of here.'

Gillespie chose to push his luck and opened his mouth to remonstrate. No one heard the first syllable; it was interrupted by a long, high-pitched screech, which reverberated from the direction of the lift shaft and echoed around the warehouse.

'Now!' shouted Drake.

Without further hesitation, Gillespie shouted orders and instructions, and as engines roared into life, he mounted the lead buggy. Drake gestured for his team to mount their bikes as he ran back and signalled for Jenna and Cliff to join them.

Gillespie's convoy thundered out of the warehouse and into the tunnel. The Diss team sat astride their bikes, revving the throttles as Drake, Jenna and Cliff appeared from behind the shelving, their haste further encouraged by another ear-splitting screech, closer this time.

'Go! Go! Go!' shouted Drake, thrusting his arm ahead of him. 'We'll meet you at the blast doors.'

A line of scramblers wheeled throatily into the tunnel, except for Tanis and Savannah who remained astride their bikes, unmoved.

Drake and the two others were halfway across the floor. He was still shouting at Savannah and Tanis to leave, when behind him the racks of shelving crumpled with a resounding crash. Tanis stared open-mouthed at the creature, which clawed its way over the wreckage it had just created.

'What the?' was all that he could utter.

Savannah responded with a blast of covering fire that ricocheted and sparked from the ceiling above Drake, Jenna and Cliff, showering shards of concrete and dust on their heads. As they reached the bikes and gunned them into life, all eyes momentarily fell on the monster.

The word, "mutation" didn't do justice to the creature's description. Twice the height of a human, this abomination began as an animal of design rather than evolutionary crossbreeding. Deep within the facility, long before the decision was made for a pocket of humanity to take refuge there, military scientists had excelled their pompous ignorance. Genes had been spliced, experiments conducted, and in the name of scientific progress, petri dishes and test tubes became the artificial wombs for manipulated poultry, bat and primate DNA – a recipe for life forms of unforgivable justification.

At the time, the resulting creature was a small, ape-shaped lizard with leathery wings. Preciously nurtured and monitored, it quickly matured to develop a hostile nature against its creators, which meant that isolation and restraint became necessary. A decision was made to create a partner, a male. The pair, in their own hideous way, courted each other, and to the delight of the scientists, mated. The self-congratulatory applause was, however, short-lived and silenced as the female turned on her partner and slaughtered him, consummating the ritual of procreation by devouring his carcass.

Within three months, a litter of four were born. These developed into stronger, larger offspring, so much so that reinforced confinement facilities were hastily built for them, until, a few months after the underground facility was repopulated and the blast doors closed against a hostile society, the underestimated strength and cunning of the creatures were revealed. Cages were ripped open, and in a frenzy of blood lust, they attacked their creators and escaped to the surface via the lift shaft.

Emerging into a world of chaos, they found refuge within the natural tunnels and caves in the hills above the facility. For some unholy reason, they bonded and crossbred with a colony of nocturnal predators and with each generation, their size increased.

This was the outcome. An Alpha species. A killing machine.

It studied the group. Its lidded eyes flickered with subtle intelligence, and then, with an ear-piercing shriek, it unfolded its ample leathery wings and flapped upwards, its shape creating distorted shadows across the warehouse.

'Go!' The echo of Drake's voice was lost in the cacophony of roaring engines.

The five bikes hurtled into the tunnel, quickly followed by the beast, whose wings spread and propelled it almost effortlessly in pursuit. The tunnel lights flickered and shorted, strobe-like, as the creature ripped at more and more of the fluorescent tubes and cables. As they sped past the hole in the tunnel wall, sensing that the creature was gaining on them, Cliff turned slightly and fired off a burst of gunfire back in its direction. The recoil of the gun and an errant piece of brickwork were his downfall. The front wheel of his bike twisted and the machine slewed sideways into the tunnel wall; the impact threw him, dazed across the floor. In an instant, a clawed foot pinned him down and rows of needle-sharp teeth separated his helmeted head from his body.

Jenna glanced back at the horrific demise of her partner. Anger and despair clouded her judgement and she spun her bike around with a squeal of tyres. Revving the engine, she accelerated towards the beast and raised her machine gun, with the intention to riddle it with a tirade of hot bullets. The gun jammed. Panic took over, and she frantically tried to clear the breach. The precious seconds she took cost her dearly. Too late to swerve, she slammed into the wreckage of Cliff's bike; her body spun forward to land broken and unconscious at the creature's feet, mercifully oblivious to her own immediate death.

Drake, Savannah and Tanis rounded the curve of the tunnel to see the blast doors, a hundred metres ahead of them, begin to swing inward.

'Gillespie's going to seal us in!' shouted Drake.

The engines of the three scramblers screamed with fury as their riders pushed the throttles to maximum power in a desperate race to freedom.

52

LOST

In the overcast light of early evening, the two girls stood on the verge of a long-abandoned quarry pit, and Solli kicked out frustratingly at a few loose stones, which fell as a spray to pepper the glass sheen of a black lake, far below. As they watched a myriad of circles ripple out, a large, dark shape rose from the depths and settled like a stain just beneath the surface of the disturbed water. The girls exchanged uneasy looks and stepped away from the edge.

This was the second disappointment to hit them in the twenty-four hours since leaving Greentrees. The first had been when the scrambler bike ran out of fuel. They assumed the tank was full when they stole away with it.

As darkness fell the previous night, they had taken shelter in a small cave at the edge of the forest, only to sleep restlessly until they unwillingly rose, half rested, to face a dawn that had arrived too soon. The railway line that they planned to come across failed to appear. Instead, they found themselves walking along the bottom of a small gorge, until around midday, faced with no other option, they set out to scale one of its easier cliff faces. What appeared to be a narrow dirt pathway wound its way up and around numerous boulders and outcrops, making their ascent a little more bearable, but still strenuous.

'Goats!' announced Soli as she pointed out the hoof marks in the dirt.

'Let's just hope that's all it is,' replied Beth.

On reaching the top, and after a short rest, they continued walking across a stretch of open grassland that brought them to where they now stood above the quarry.

'Lost. Damn it!' grumbled Beth.

'Minor setback,' consoled Soli.

'How can you call being lost, a minor setback?' asked Beth.

'Well, for one thing, we don't appear to be going around in circles, and the other is that there's a church steeple over there.'

Beth's eyes followed Soli's pointing finger. About a mile in the distance, the unmistakable spire of a church rose up from behind a tree-lined ridge.

'The sun will be going down in an hour or so,' said Soli, 'and we need somewhere to shelter. Also, my drinking water is low, and I don't fancy going down and filling my canteen from that lake, no matter *how* thirsty I get.'

They followed the curve of the quarry, and then dropped down a grassy bank to reach the edge of a small woodland copse. Pushing their way through a barrier of tangled bushes, and into the trees, the sudden, flapping wings of a lone wood pigeon, panicked by their presence, startled them.

'Shit!' announced Beth.

'Bit jumpy, aren't you,' giggled Soli.

'You jumped too,' accused Beth.

'Did not.'

'Did too.' Beth froze. Her eyes locked in on a point just over Soli's left shoulder. 'Don't move,' she hissed.

Soli stood statue-like. Her eyes craned in their sockets in an attempt to see past her line of vision. 'What is it?' she whispered.

Beth slowly reached down and picked up a short stick from the woodland floor. 'Keep still,' she said as she manoeuvred herself around Soli.

Soli swallowed hard. 'Please don't let it be a bug. I hate bugs.'

'It's worse than that,' replied Beth. There was a pause as she savoured the moment. 'It's a twig!' She flicked the back of Soli's neck with the small stem.

'Ha! I bet you nearly wet yourself!' she screamed with delight, before she made off through the undergrowth, laughing excitedly as she went.

For a moment, Soli stood still as confusion turned to realisation, and then to fury. 'Why, you…' Then she was in pursuit. 'Come back here. That wasn't funny. I'm going to kick your ass!'

The noise of the two girls shouting, laughing and crashing through the shrubbery drifted out on the evening breeze, until, quite some distance away, it alerted a group of hunters. Hunters that hadn't eaten for a while, and yearned for fresh meat. Instinct told them to wait for nightfall. Then, in the shadows, they would stalk their prey, strike swiftly for the kill and feed from warm bodies still in the spasm of their death throes.

Solli leapt onto Beth's back; the force carried them forward to tumble out from the tree line and into the long meadow grass at the top of a ridge, where they collapsed in a tangle, their bodies heaving from exertion and laughter.

As they lay there staring up into a slate grey sky, the silhouette of a large, black bird swooped and wheeled high above them searching for its evening meal.

Beth sat up and examined the town below them. Nature had long ago reclaimed its streets. Green tentacles of ivy and wild creeper clung to most of the buildings, disguising their original shape and purpose. Trees reached up through broken rooftops and stretched their limbs across once busy paths and avenues. Now, she could see that only the stonework of the church spire remained defiantly uncovered as it pointed like an accusing finger towards the sky.

With the approaching twilight, shadows deepened and seemed to shift amongst the darkening leaves and branches. Beth craned her neck forward and squinted her eyes. *Was that a movement?*

'What is it?' asked Soli.

'Just on edge. I keep thinking of Crazies,' admitted Beth.

'Slim chance out here, I reckon,' said Soli. 'They stick mainly to the city areas. Anyway, we can't sit here all night,' she said, rising. 'There's more likely to be fresh water down there. We might even find a clue as to our location.'

'Okay. Load up your crossbow,' said Beth, as she swung her own from her shoulder, 'and if anything comes at us, shoot first. If need be, we'll apologise afterwards.'

Soon, the sound of running water attracted the girls, and under a haze of moonlight, Beth and Soli reached a wide stream that ran along the side of an overgrown churchyard. Beth stooped and cupped a handful of cold liquid into her hand. She sniffed at it, and then tentatively sipped at the clear water.

'Tastes like spring water,' she smiled. 'A little on the chalky side, but it'll do for us.'

After filling their canteens, they followed a tall, untidy hedge until they reached an entrance to the churchyard. Ancient yew trees formed a dark archway towards the stone porch of the church. Very little had the chance to grow under the green umbrella of the old evergreens, and the path beneath their feet was relatively clear as the girls crept silently to the porch entrance. A deeper shade of darkness signalled that the church doors were open.

'What do you think?' whispered Soli.

'Well, I guess that we're too late for the service!' Beth quietly replied.

Soli suppressed a childish giggle, removed the safety catch on her crossbow, and stepped forward into the stillness of the building.

Both of them stood by a long wooden pew, allowing

their eyes to acclimatise to the gloom, their senses as taut as the wires on their crossbows.

'Altar,' said Soli, indicating to the far end of the building.

As they moved down the aisle, Soli crossed herself and muttered softly.

'I didn't know that you were religious,' said Beth.

'I'm not particularly; just don't see any harm in showing a bit of respect for beliefs, whether it's Christian, Jewish, Buddhist, Muslim or any of the others.'

'You know that religion has been responsible for more wars than anything else?' challenged Beth.

'Don't want to lecture you, but it's got nothing to do with religion, and everything to do with a lack of tolerance,' said Soli philosophically. 'Anyhow, at the moment, as long as they use candles, I don't mind who they worship!'

With a few flicks of her flint, Soli had orange flames dancing on four dust-grey beeswax candles on the altar. Misshapen shadows were thrown across the empty church, where not even the ghosts of a congregation remained.

'What now?' asked Beth.

'Well. We've still got some supplies, so I suggest that we find somewhere comfortable to sleep and have something to eat. Grab a candle and let's see what's about.'

To the left of the altar was a door to the vestry. It was in here that they decided to bed down for the night, with the comfort of some dusty old seat cushions, and after a meagre meal of bread and cheese, they sat in the candlelight, their thoughts unravelling into conversation.

'Sorry,' said Beth.

'What for?'

'I guess that I got carried away. I should have realised that it wasn't going to be that easy,' Beth reflected. 'We can't even travel more than a day without getting lost. What chance is there of carrying out my plan?' Her mood was sombre.

'Minor setback, that's all,' encouraged Soli.

'What was I thinking?' Beth shook her head. 'Look what Savannah, Tanis and the rest of them went through to get me *away* from Opulence.'

'Look.' Soli reached out and held Beth's hand. 'Revenge can drive people to do some crazy things. Whatever you decide, I'm with you all the way.'

'Oh, it's not just revenge,' admitted Beth. 'I want some excitement. I've got bored waiting around while Savannah's having all the fun.'

'I feel the same with Tanis, so let's just see where this adventure of ours takes us in the morning.'

'Whatever happens,' said Beth, 'I'm not going back to sit and twiddle my thumbs at Greentrees.'

'Okay. Let's sleep on it. Now, give me a hug,' said Soli.

They left one candle burning, just so that if they awoke during the night, they wouldn't feel disorientated. Later, it was to the steady wavering of its flame that Beth slowly opened her eyes. Something brought her out of a dreamless sleep. Not a loud or sudden noise, but a soft snuffling and sniffling. She pulled herself up on one elbow, pushing away the last fingers of drowsiness as she focused her hearing.

There it was, from behind the vestry door. It was definitely animal in nature. Something seeking. Searching. Not with curiosity, but with an urgency, a craving.

She reached across and shook Soli's arm. 'Sol…' Before she could finish, Soli's instinct for survival kicked in. She sat bolt upright, eyes wide open, and reached for her crossbow. The quiver of bolts clattered on the flagstone floor. In the silence of the night, it sounded like a bag of bones being emptied.

'What the hell?!' she all but shouted.

There was a pause, and then the snuffling at the door became frantic, accompanied by clawing and scratching at the woodwork.

'What's going on?' asked Soli.

'Something's trying to get in, and I don't think that it's looking for affection,' said Beth.

The sound of wood splintering was accompanied by a piercing canine howl of urgency.

'What the hell is it?' screamed Beth.

'Dogs!' There came another wild howl; this time it was a hunting call. 'No. Not dogs. Wolves! We need to get out of here, now,' announced Soli.

'You don't say. And here's me missing my beauty sleep,' said Beth, sarcastically.

'Well, you did say that you wanted excitement!' Soli gathered up the wayward bolts, and then the girls were on their feet, bags over their shoulders and crossbows aimed at the now visibly shuddering door. The noise was manic.

There were two doors at the end of the vestry; one

was raised up above a couple of stone steps and seemed to lead in towards the church, the other faced the outside of the building. Soli wiped grime from the glass panels of a small leaded window beside the exterior door. As she pressed her face against it, there was a resounding "thump", followed by more clawing and scratching of wood.

'They're outside as well!' she shouted.

The thin vein of a split appeared in a panel of the vestry door, and several yowls of encouragement rent the air from inside the church.

'This way,' said Beth, as she turned the metal ring handle of the third door. It swung open to reveal a curving upward set of well-worn stone steps. 'I'm thinking that it's to the bell tower,' she voiced. The ascending darkness beckoned them. 'Give me a candle. Quick!'

Soli passed the chunky wax block to Beth; its orange flame flickered in protest.

'Follow me and shut the door behind you. It'll buy us some time.'

They scrambled up the narrow stairway. Soli slipped, cursed and regained her upward momentum. The way was blocked by a trap door, which she shouldered upwards. It flipped away to fold back noisily on the belfry floor, and she pushed through a cloud of dust to clamber onto the belfry platform. In the moonlight, the grey silhouettes of the bells rested silently, waiting to be woken again and send out their peels to summon a long-lost congregation. Beth pulled herself up alongside Soli as another chorus of frenzied howls resonated from below.

'Now what?' she asked, her head swinging wildly

around, searching the darkness beyond the bronze cast sentinels. 'There's no way out. We're cornered!'

'Shut the trap door.' shouted Soli. 'Anything that comes through it gets a bolt in its face!'

'And when we run out of bolts?' asked Beth.

Soli's silence masked her own concerns.

There was a wooden chest, which contained spare pull ropes and wooden staves. The two of them dragged it across the trap door as an added barrier.

'There, they can't get up,' Soli said with satisfaction.

'And we can't get down,' advised Beth.

Soli moved to a small doorway and pushed it open to allow a wide beam of moonlight to spill into the tower.

'We can find a way to escape over the roof,' she said, easing herself out to disappear into the shadows.

Beth followed, anger and frustration gnawing at her confidence.

A narrow parapet encircled the base of the spire with small pinnacles at each corner, and the girls ran round, stopping to lean over at various points. On three sides they were about thirty metres up from the ground, with at least a ten-metre drop to the church roof.

Beth kicked at the stonework. 'We're screwed!'

Below, half a dozen dark shadows emerged from the church door and began to mill around excitedly. Frantic howling echoed into the night.

Soli checked her quiver. 'How many bolts have you got?'

'Fifteen,' replied Beth.

'Okay,' said Soli. 'That's twenty-nine between us; surely that's more than enough?'

Beth looked down at the frenzied pack. 'It's too risky trying to pick them off from here. We'd probably waste more bolts than we can afford to.'

'Only one thing for it then,' confirmed Soli. 'We're going to have to shoot at point-blank range if we've got any chance of getting out of here.'

They climbed back into the tower and made their way to the hatch. Soli dragged the chest to one side. Muffled yowls and barking filtered up from below.

'It doesn't sound as if they've gotten through the vestry door yet.' She tentatively lifted the trap door as Beth aimed her crossbow at the widening slit of darkness.

For no other reason apart from that known to itself, a lone rat leapt from a wide beam and onto Beth's shoulder. She screamed in surprise and the rat responded by digging its claws into her. Even through her clothing, it felt like a dozen tiny, hot needles. In an effort to free herself of the creature, she spun around wildly, swiping at it with her free hand, only to lose her balance and tumble against the wooden chest. The impact pushed the box to the edge of the platform where it balanced precariously until the rat, in an effort to escape Soli's beating hands, chose to leap onto its lid.

The creature's eyes widened as its seemingly insignificant weight proved enough to tip the chest over the edge to collide with one of the bells before it began its descent to the church floor below. The lid of the chest opened up and its contents of bell-ringing paraphernalia became entwined in the bell ropes, which in turn pulled a couple of the great bronze bells from their resting staves.

The noise was deafening. Soli and Beth clasped their hands to their ears in a futile attempt to block out the mind-numbing cacophony.

The peels rang out; their discordant echoes escaped from the bell tower to disturb the moonlit landscape.

Inside the church, the pack of blood-hungry wolves clawed their way through the splintered vestry door, and immediately set their claws and teeth to work on the dry and ancient wood at the base of the stairway. Their numbers were many. Many more, in fact than the amount of bolts in Beth and Solis' quivers.

53

EXODUS

The space between the blast doors seemed to mock them as it narrowed; and aware that Tanis was no longer beside him, Drake pulled back on his throttle and glanced around. About thirty metres back, Tanis was frantically pumping his kick-start in an effort to resurrect the bike from an untimely engine failure. Savannah swung the rear end of her bike around and the scrambler wheeled up like a rearing horse. She shot forward and as the front tyre thudded down on the concrete; somehow, she managed to keep control of the bike as it swerved erratically. As she raced towards Tanis, Drake's eyes focused on the dark shape beyond them, clawing and flapping down the tunnel in its own hellish frenzy to feed on their lifeblood.

He was about to unleash the fury of his Heckler and Kosh at the creature, when he realised that both Savannah and Tanis were certain to be hit by stray fire or ricochets.

Seeing Savannah tearing toward him, Tanis finally let his bike topple sideways. Again, she expertly swung its rear end around in an arc, cutting the throttle to idle and pausing for just a moment to allow Tanis to straddle the rear of the pillion and grab her waist; then with a twist of her wrist, the bike jerked forward. As they neared Drake, he let loose with a burst of machine gun fire, and the creature screeched with pain and rage as bullets tore through one of its leather wings. Still it pursued them with deadly intent.

Savannah and Tanis shot past Drake, who hastily gunned his own bike into action. Both the scramblers plummeted with reckless commitment towards the now seemingly impossibly narrow exit.

The handlebars of Savannah's bike bounced off the steel doors as she and Tanis squeezed through. Ten metres behind, Drake could see that he wouldn't have the same luck, and his instinct for survival kicked in. He slewed his scrambler sideways and allowed himself to slide from the bike, backwards and rigid with his arms across his chest, coffin-style, hoping above all hope that he had judged the right trajectory. His body slid through the last closing gap as the monster's head lunged forward; rows of needlepoint teeth bore down towards him. He closed his eyes and rolled sideways. His head felt the impact as his crash helmet bounced on the concrete floor. The creature's malicious screams fused with the metallic roar of the bike and echoed in his head like an approaching avalanche, then the sound of gunfire brought pain and silence into his world and he lost consciousness.

Disjointed sounds invaded the dark oblivion of his senses. Half-recognised voices dragged him insistently from the sanctuary of unconsciousness and into the wakeful sensation of discomfort.

'Drake! Drake!'

'Is he breathing?'

'Drake!'

'Keep him still so I can stop the bleeding.'

'Drake. Open your eyes.'

Then, a spike of searing pain hit him. With a gasp, his eyes opened and widened with the shock. Faces swam into focus – Tanis, Savannah and Dexter, a trained medic. Members of his team stood behind them, wearing faces of concern, anxious for his survival.

The pain served to clear his head and allowed memories of the most recent event to flood his mind. 'Let me bloody well get up,' he insisted through gritted teeth.

Hands put pressure on his shoulders. A gentler palm pressed softly but forcefully on his chest.

'Stay still and let Dexter fix you up,' said Savannah.

'Where's Gillespie? Where's that ass-wipe Gillespie?' he spat venomously.

'Calm down, Drake. Gillespie's being tended to by a medic,' said Savannah. 'He's in a worse shape than you.'

As he lay there being tended to, and only after being made to take a drink of water, Tanis and Savannah described the event of Drake's dramatic entrance through the doors.

He had been clutching his machine gun, with no safety catch on. As he rolled to escape, he had inadvertently fired off a couple of rounds, one of which had hit his shoulder. It was a clean shot and thankfully gone straight through without doing serious damage.

Gillespie, however, had fared much worse. Ignorant

of the welfare of Drake's group, he was so insistent in getting the blast doors closed that he was pushing against them with his back in an effort to speed up their progress. That's exactly what he was doing as Drake shot through the closing gap like a bullet, followed by the creature's head. In its last vicious act before the doors clamped around its neck and decapitated it, the monster's jaws fastened around one of Gillespie's arms and severed it at the shoulder. Even now, the limb lay at the base of the doors, still held in the monster's bloody, but cleanly separated head.

Prior to the incident, and following Gillespie's orders to close the blast doors, Drake's Diss had tried to intervene, which resulted in a Mexican standoff at gunpoint between them and Gillespie's commandos.

Drake felt no compassion for the man. His was not an act of reasoning, or of panic. As far as Drake was concerned, Gillespie sought to stamp his authority and exercise his arrogant ego with an act of needless sacrifice. His men possessed more than enough firepower to repel the creature and allow Drake, Tanis and Savannah to escape through the open doors. At that moment in his bitter anger, he also, somewhat unjustly, blamed Gillespie for the deaths of Jenna and Cliff. The passage of time and reasoning would allow him to absolve Gillespie of that responsibility, but the sour taste of betrayal would never remove the hatred and loathing that he held for the man.

'You'll live,' announced Dexter, 'but there'll be no using that arm for a while. Sit up and I'll strap it in a sling.'

'I don't want a damn sling,' argued Drake.

'You'll have it strapped up, or I'll have *you* secured to a stretcher for the rest of the journey,' insisted Dexter. His eyes held Drake's with stubborn confidence.

'All right. All right. Just help me up. We need to get this operation back on schedule.' He raised his eyebrows at Dexter. 'I take it that you have no issue with that?'

'None at all. Sir.' The sarcasm in Dexter's voice was undisguised.

Tanis and Savannah helped a slightly unsteady but unshaken Drake to his feet. Adrenalin was coursing through him, and along with the jab of a painkiller that Dexter had administered, it was fuelling Drake's mind and body in a human-style system reboot.

*

Assisted by Savannah and Tanis, Drake had taken control of and organised the convoy's exodus from the tunnels, and an uneventful journey back down the gully, to their eventual arrival at the airfield.

Batten stood ready to greet them, sheepishly, having witnessed the arrival and swift departure of a heavily sedated Gillespie stretchered and strapped on the back of a trailer. Batten had been briefed of the incident by the accompanying commandos, and was more than surprised to see the further arrival of an alert and confident Drake.

Refusing any assistance, Drake clambered out of a buggy. Muttering curses and clearly irritated by the impedance of a strapped up arm, he made directly for Batten.

'Before you say anything, I'd like to get one thing clear,' Batten announced to Drake. 'Whatever reasoning was behind Gillespie's error of judgement, I do not condone or agree with it. Personally, I don't believe in sacrificing or leaving anyone behind in the field of battle. If there's to be an inquiry into the incident, you have my full support.'

Drake studied the man for a moment, and let the statement run through his head. *Okay. The guy's either sincere in his motives, or he's conducting his own arse – covering exercise. Either way, I still don't trust him an inch.* 'Thanks for that,' he smiled. 'Nice to know that I can rely on you. Now, we have about an hour of daylight left and I for one would like to be a long, long way from here before it gets even remotely dark. You take control of the commando squad from here on in and my team will resume their escort duties.'

To Drake's surprise, Batten saluted, 'Yes, sir!' before he moved away and commenced issuing orders at the top of his voice.

'Frightening,' voiced Tanis.

'Why?' asked Savannah.

'He already sounds just like Gillespie!'

Drake spat on the ground. 'Come on; we've got a long journey home.'

54

BASE ONE

The journey back to Ridgeway and subsequently on to Broadway Junction passed without mishap or event, other than running the gauntlet through the expected onslaughts from Crazies. However, it was noticeable that the attacks were muted and seemingly less frantic. There was a flurry of Molotov cocktails, but the physical presence of Crazies appeared less in numbers.

'Something's going on,' observed Drake. 'Either we've caught them off guard, which is highly unlikely, or...' He paused, running options over in his mind.

'Or what?' prompted Savannah.

'Or they're shifting their resources,' finished Drake.

'You mean an organised attack on one of our bases?' suggested Tanis.

'Possibly. Perhaps we'll find out when we meet up with Fairfax,' said Drake.

They didn't need to wait long for that event. As they disembarked from their rail truck at Broadway Junction, a small escort ushered them to the meeting room, where a stern-faced Jean Fairfax sat at a trestle table;

documents and paperwork littered its surface in her own disorganised, but efficient style of working.

'I've had the reports,' she glowered at Drake. 'We'll deal with the Gillespie incident when I get around to it. For the moment, we, and I emphasis *we,* have more pressing issues. Report to sick bay, Drake. I can't have you in the line of fire with your arm in a sling.'

'Not a problem. Ma'am,' said Drake. He turned and let himself out of the room, closing the door behind him.

Savannah glanced sideways at Tanis. Her eyebrows rose. Her eyes widened.

Before another word was said, the door reopened and Drake strode back into the room, minus the sling.

'Reporting for duty, Ma'am.' He saluted with his uninjured arm. 'According to sick bay, the sling was an unnecessary precaution.' He stared stony-faced at a point above Jean Fairfax's head, avoiding eye contact.

She continued to glower at him for a few more seconds, until… 'You're so predictable, Drake. Very well. Have it your way.' She shuffled the small sea of paperwork around until she found a map of Earthland's coastline and opened it out for them to see. 'We're expecting Jago's invasion force to focus on the estuary and then drive their way inland to assault Base One, so this will be our first line of defence.' She tapped at the map in various places. 'As we speak, all of the munitions and equipment are being unloaded and will be distributed across our defence network, of which the majority are now gathering together at Base One and along the coastal regions. However, there is also a chance that he'll send out heavily armed groups to attack some of the countryside retreats, such as Greentrees.'

Savannah turned to Tanis. 'The girls! We need to warn them.'

'Don't worry. I'm sure that all of the compounds have been alerted, and the girls are safe,' Tanis replied.

Jean Fairfax leaned back in her chair and slid the wireframe spectacles from her face. She steepled her fingers to her chin, and exhaled a sigh. 'For some reason, Beth and Soli took it upon themselves to leave Greentrees and go walkabout, or should I say rideabout.

'A few days ago, they took one of the compound's scramblers, and from what we can gather, along with their weapons and some supplies, managed to bypass the compound guards. To say that both anger and concern has been eclipsed by Danny Hench's response would be an understatement! He has assured me that every available patrol is out searching for them.'

Savannah grabbed Tanis' arm. 'We need to go. Now! We've got to help find them.'

Jean Fairfax stood. The legs of her chair scraped on the wooden floor. 'Everything that can be done, is being done. The girls are my responsibility, don't doubt my concern for them; they are, after all, as close as family to me. I need you to be in the right place, so you will be leaving for Base One. The three of you are charged with heading the estuary defence team. You'll be on the next shuttle.'

'But...' started Savannah.

'There's no time for buts,' said Fairfax. 'Jago is coming and from what I can gather, he hopes to bring hell with him. We are all that stands between him and what's left of any hope for a civilised, un-oppressed world. If you want to protect Beth and Soli, you need to be at the front line and meet that degenerate vermin head on. We need to end this thing.'

It was Tanis who spoke next. 'You promise that you'll find them and take care of them?'

'Find them, take care of them, and spank their sorry arses if need be,' smiled Jean Fairfax. It was a brief smile. The seriousness returned to her face like a cloud passing over the sun. 'Here are your orders and your clearance passes.' She handed Drake a narrow brown envelope. 'Get down to the rail shuttle; it closes at the end of the day after all essential personnel have been sent to Base One. I'll be travelling on the last cart and I'll meet you there at 0900 tomorrow.'

'Why are they closing the shuttle?' asked Drake.

'Because we've adapted a fleet of quad bikes to haul arms and munitions back to Base One through the tunnels. The air in them will become toxic after a few runs, so the drivers are being equipped with the few oxygen masks that we have available. After we've finished, the network will be unusable for at least a month. The remaining staff here will relocate over-ground to the countryside compounds. Now, get moving. We'll meet up for a final briefing tomorrow.'

'And an update on the girls,' added Savannah.

'And an update on the girls,' repeated Jean Fairfax.

★

As Drake, Tanis and herself sped through the old underground network, even the clattering of the dolly wheels and the numbness in her thighs could not distract Savannah's thoughts and visions of Beth. A familiar halo of light floated ahead of them; beyond that was the dark domain of rats and green-slimed masonry. For her, the journey was not over too soon. Even if she and Tanis had wanted to talk, the noise would not allow either of them to be heard, and so they had sat holding hands, taking solace in each other's presence.

They spent the night in Savannah's cabin. Old familiar surroundings only deepened their anxiety for Beth and Soli, and woken by unseen images of a restless sleep, they sought comfort in their passion for one another, until, just before dawn, they slept in the tangled embrace of lovers.

0900. A melancholy smile hung on Savannah's lips as she sat with Tanis, Drake and several other Diss commanders. The old grandfather clock stood in the corner, imposing its supposed authority over time. Her thoughts trickled back to the last occasion that she was seated in the room, and poignant memories mingled with recollections of bitter coffee and sweet oatcakes.

The arrival of Jean Fairfax focused her attention on the now. Several of those present began to rise from their seats.

'Don't get up!' It was said as an order, not as a request.

Jean Fairfax was in no mood for formalities. It had been a long night. Even though she was one of that rare breed who could survive on a habitual four hours sleep in twenty-four, her temperament had been tested. She found the circumstances surrounding Beth and Soli's disappearance, frustrating and emotionally distracting. This, along with a prolonged and confrontational meeting with the Commando squad leaders had pushed her to her limits. She had threatened to relieve them all of their positions of authority and take direct control herself, unless they could convince her that Gillespie's disregard for unity within the Earthland Defence Force was an isolated and personal point of view.

It had taken wise and thoughtful words from Batten to repair the perceived rift between Commando and Diss. *Now here's a man who knows how to play chess,* thought Fairfax. *Best I always keep myself several moves ahead of him and a spare Queen in my pocket!* She had rewarded his loyalty by appointing him Lieutenant General of the Commando force and answerable directly to herself. She could tell that he was both pleased and perplexed, but no less loyal.

She seated herself at the end of the table and placed a mug of black coffee and a large brown file down in front of her. Savannah had brief sensations of déjà vu and a recollection of Jago's file sent a shiver down her spine.

'Are you okay?' whispered Tanis.

Savannah gave a nod and a weak smile, and he squeezed her hand beneath the table.

Jean Fairfax looked up directly at Savannah and Tanis. 'You two don't need to be here. Drake and I will finalise your briefing at a separate meeting tomorrow morning.'

Tanis and Savannah looked at each other and then back at Fairfax.

'You… you want us to leave?' asked Savannah.

'Yes.'

'But we have questions about Beth and Soli,' she insisted.

'I'm sure that you'll both find the answers to all of your burning questions sitting in the canteen, enjoying a breakfast. They were brought in by one of the patrols early this morning. You'll find that their ears are still numb from the bawling out that I gave them a while ago. Apart from that, they're fine,' grinned Fairfax.

It took a moment for the message to clear in their heads before Tanis and Savannah scrabbled from the room, making various apologies along the way as they bumped into numerous shoulders and chairs on their way out.

As the door closed, Drake looked at Fairfax. 'That was a bit mischievous, making them wait like that.'

'I know,' she smiled. 'I have to have a little fun now and again. Perks of the job!'

The screeching and laughing of reunion was heard down the corridors as Beth, Soli, Tanis and Savannah embraced each other.

The girls let their emotions show as tears tracked down their cheeks, but Tanis kept a check on his own by masking it with initial anger.

'What the hell were you two thinking?' he voiced loudly. 'You could have been killed.'

'But we weren't,' smiled Soli impishly.

'Right. I want every detail,' said Savannah.

They sat there for nearly an hour while the girls relayed their story, each one interrupting the other and adding their own narrative. They started off by passionately and tearfully apologising for the now self-admitted foolish aspirations of their plan. Only after another round of consoling hugs did Soli begin to relay the details of their venture. The initial seriousness drained from their regaling as fits of giggles burst into the conversation. The recall of a leaping rat and Soli's subsequent ability to dance like an octopus on fire brought tears of laughter to their eyes.

The accidental peeling of the bells was their saviour. An armed Commando patrol heard the clanging from a couple of miles away. They were one of several groups that had indeed been assigned to the task of finding the girls, and they made all haste to investigate the source of the bells. By the time the patrol had reached the church, the wolves were over thirty in their number. Intelligent and organised, half of the pack separated to attack and fend off the Commandos, while the remaining wolves continued their assault on the final barrier to their quarry – the bell tower trap door. Thankfully, for the girls, the Commandos were issued with Sten and Uzi machine guns, which made quick work of dispensing with the majority of the wolves. A lucky few were sensible, and fast enough to scatter back into the landscape and freedom.

As they sat in the safety of the canteen, Soli and Beth agreed that neither of them could decide whether it was the sound of the bells, or Jean Fairfax's voice that was still ringing in their ears!

★

Later that night, as Savannah lay quietly in Tanis' arms, the silence was broken by the whisper of his voice. 'Now the girls are here, you know that they'll want to be part of the fight.'

There was a soft sigh. 'Then we'll all face Jago together,' she said.

It was a welcome surprise for them to find both Beth and Soli seated in the meeting room the following morning along with Drake and Jean Fairfax.

'I've come to a decision,' began Jean Fairfax. 'That the safest place for these two,' she nodded over her glasses at Beth and Soli, 'is alongside the rest of you.'

She had decided that any final confrontation with Jago and Roth had to involve Savannah and Beth at the very least, with Drake, Tanis and Soli as support. At the end of the day, putting aside Jago's fanatical desire to dominate and rule, his demise must be at the hands of those who he had hurt the most, both physically and mentally – his family. It was personal.

'You five,' she continued, 'will operate as a covert group to draw out and confront both Jago and Roth. In a rightful and just world, I would insist that you drag their vile arses back here, and that they stand trial to be appropriately punished for their monstrous activities.' She paused, mentally running over what she was about to say. 'To intentionally take the life of another, unless in self-defence, is unforgivable, but there are some monsters living in the guise of humanity that are not worthy of sharing the air that we breathe. Jago and Roth are such monsters and if you choose to deal with them in a final and absolute way, that's something for all of our consciences to live with. I know that personally, I wouldn't lose a moment's sleep over it.'

55

No Delay

At that same moment, out across a restless sea, Jago stood at the centre of a wide jetty. He was surrounded by several Transportation Commanders, their cobalt uniforms bringing no contrast to the steel architecture of the plaza behind them.

He surveyed the man-made marina and the huge fleet of boats and barges, tethered by chains and anchors, spreading out in either direction, which jostled impatiently like hunting dogs hungry for the chase. The fringe of a storm filled a distant grey and bruised horizon where, in a boiling sky, lightning streaked and thunder rumbled threateningly. Ominously.

A gust of sea air heavy with ozone whipped at the towers of Opulence, and skittered across the jetty to tug at the material of Jago's robes like a petulant child.

One of the Commanders leant towards Jago. The words came nervously from his lips. 'We have it on good advice that the storm will pass in forty-eight hours. Then it will be safe to proceed with the invasion.'

Jago turned to face him impassively. 'Delay? Are you suggesting that we delay?'

The pale, clammy-skinned face of the Commander stammered back. 'On… on the advice of others, my Lord Jago. I am merely the messenger.' He stepped back, willing himself invisible. It didn't work.

'And what is your opinion of this… *advice*?' asked Jago. His eyebrows raised, the curl of a smile on his lips. The Commander shivered inwardly as the tone of Jago's voice revealed that there was no humour behind his smile.

He heard a shuffling of feet as his fellow Commanders eased themselves away from him, and he bowed his head to avoid eye contact. 'My opinion is of no value, my Lord Jago.'

'Damn right it isn't!' snarled Jago. His face reddened. For a moment, the Commander knew that his own fate lay in the balance. Jago breathed noisily in through his nose, and then exhaled, slowly.

The madness of Jago's vision swept away all reason and caution. 'We proceed as planned. The storm shall be an asset. They will never suspect that we would attempt an invasion in such weather. We shall emerge from the tempest accompanied by the fury and sound of hell. We are destined to be victorious.'

A roll of distant thunder rattled out as if in dark approval.

Jago faced his Commanders. His eyes were as dark as the storm clouds.

'Destiny awaits you. You sail in five hours as planned. Take my army to victory. This is a momentous day for Opulence.'

Every one of them stood rigidly to attention and

saluted Jago; however, not one of them dared to look into his eyes, before they turned and hurried away to their duties.

56

STORMFALL

The storm raged throughout the night and into the next day, sitting in the sky like an obstinate and unwelcome guest. The rain fell in torrential bursts; great globs splattered and punched into the ground, creating large puddles and gushing streams across the landscape. Raw power zigzagged in white-hot streaks overhead, seemingly synchronised with a depth of thunder, which left unprotected eardrums ringing after each burst.

In the last forty-eight hours, most of Earthland's defence force were mobilised and deployed. An army of thousands had been amassed from satellite compounds, near and far – pockets of surviving humanity, intent on raising a better world from the wreckage of man's folly and failure, waited to fight and if need be make the ultimate sacrifice, in the battle to put an end to another episode of one man's greed for power and oppression.

'Even the Crazies have gone to ground,' commented Tanis, as the five of them huddled together under the canopy of a derelict shopping arcade that had been set up as a surface command centre. Like everyone else, they were waiting. Waiting for any news of the invasion.

'They've been conspicuous in their absence over the last couple of weeks,' said Drake.

'Suits me fine,' said Tanis. 'One thing less to worry about. We'll deal with them when the time comes.'

'You're sounding very "gung-ho", young man,' jibed Drake.

'We could be waiting for a lot longer,' said Soli. 'Jago would be insane to launch a fleet of boats in this weather.'

'The key word is "insane",' said Savannah. 'It's exactly the sort of thing that he *would* do.'

★

Five miles away, groups of Diss huddled in makeshift shelters spread out along the estuary. A sky of grey and black clouds churned above them; gale force winds whipped the ocean into white shredded waves. From behind the crest of a sodden sand dune, Diss hands gripped a pair of binoculars. Her tired eyes eagerly scanned the horizon, which as she watched, turned silver grey.

'The tail end of the storm's heading for landfall!' she announced as she stretched the stiffness from her back and rubbed a weary eye with the heel of a palm before resuming her vigil.

The black dots bobbed in and out of the waves, mirage-like at first, and then, a ragged hole in the clouds broke through, a shaft of watery sunlight hit the sea, and the dots took shape and form. She lowered the binoculars, frantically wiped both lenses and brought them back up to her eyes again. The dots, now different shapes and sizes, spread out like an unhealthy rash across the seascape. She turned to her comrades.

'Send up the flare! Send up the flare!'

Each group was issued with distress flares. As soon as one was sent into the air, the intention was that it would set off a chain reaction, a domino effect of flares spreading out across the line of defence and back to Base One.

Ten minutes later, an infrared starburst snaked its way across the storm-raked sky and over Base One's command centre.

★

Jago's invasion fleet had fared well despite his reckless venture to travel in the belly of the storm. They had lost no more than a dozen of the smaller boats and their occupants, of which he gave no more than a fleeting thought. Eerily, the wind dropped, but the sea continued to throw the dinghies about as though they were insignificant flotsam. The great barges ploughed forward, propelled by rows of oars heaved by strong-armed men below decks – modern versions of roman troop galleons. It was almost surreal to witness the solar-powered jet skis bouncing in and out of their wake, buzzing like a swarm of aquatic bees.

The line of vessels, more than a hundred without taking into account the jet skis, converged towards the estuary, working their way up the current in an undulating line like a many-spotted water snake. At its centre, Jago's flagship. He and Roth stood side by side on the open deck above the prow. Jago with his white skullcap, and Roth with his long reddish-brown hair and crimson eyepatch. Their black and silver capes flapped around them, tugged and tormented by the persistent sea wind.

A red laser beam streaked heavenward, and on this signal, half of the fleet turned to the shore, while fifty or so jet skis opened their throttles and roared upriver to cause disruption and test defences.

Jago gripped Roth's hand. 'Let us watch them fall and be swept away. The bodies of our enemies shall be a carpet for our victorious feet,' he smiled.

'I have a hunger to take a few lives myself,' said Roth.

Jago put his arm around Roth's shoulder. 'Patience, dear friend. Patience. I have issued orders that Savannah and Beth are to be taken alive. You shall have your pleasure, and we shall savour our revenge – theirs shall be the slowest of deaths.'

Jago drank in a rapturous breath as the first wave of vessels reached the shoreline and his troops massed onto the beach. The grey air was lit with red tracer fire and streaks of white laser energy. His war had begun.

Details of the assault reached the command centre along with reports regarding the armada of jet skis and their passage upriver. Jean Fairfax called Drake and his team together.

'They're looking for a back door in,' she said. 'At the moment we have that covered, but we need to draw Jago and Roth away from the frontline, so we're going to give them a way in, and you are the bait.'

An hour and a half later, having journeyed through the tunnels that had last been witness to Liam's escape, Drake, Savannah and Tanis crouched as safely as they could behind the twisted railings of the ruined bridge. Beth and Soli remained out of sight in the doorway of the concrete bridge support.

Although the storm itself had passed, a gusting wind persisted to batter the bridge and sing around its steel cables. Tanis looked down into the choppy grey waters below, and pulled a black woollen hat down over his dreadlocks, his face a mask of displeasure.

'Remind me why we're doing this,' he said with sarcasm.

'Let's go over it one more time for Tanis' benefit,' said Drake.

'I was joking,' said Tanis.

'Do you see me laughing?' replied Drake. He stared at Tanis, who thought better of responding. 'When we see the jet skis, I'll attract their attention so that we can make ourselves visible enough to be recognised; then, we run back to the tower covering each other as we go. When we get to the tower door, Beth and Soli will briefly make themselves seen before we hunker down and shoot as many of the morons as we can. Hopefully, one of them will turn tail and get news back to Jago that we're pinned down here. All we have to do is wait for the creeps to turn up. Then, it's up to Savannah and Beth how we play this out.'

They didn't have to wait long before a distant gurgling-drone announced the impending arrival of the fleet of jet skis. They zipped in and out of the shallows, searching for suitable landing spaces for the larger boats to eventually discharge their cargo of armed fighters.

'Time to announce ourselves,' said Drake, standing up. The others followed suit, and Drake unclipped one of four grenades attached to his tunic. He pulled the pin and threw the egg-shaped object down amongst the milling jet skis, one of which exploded dramatically, and its rider was catapulted in a ball of flame to disappear amongst the reed beds.

All hell broke loose as white streaks of laser fire hit the metalwork around them, leaving molten red-hot burn marks.

'I think that got their attention!' said Tanis.

'Run!' shouted Drake, and they set off in a frantic pace for the tower as more laser fire spat at the steel bridge supports and cables. When they reached the doorway, they returned a volley of fire as Beth and Solli briefly made an appearance; then, they crowded back into the sanctuary of the tower. Hot streaks of light popped and fizzled against the tower's stonework, loosening and crumbling small chunks of masonry to fall and clatter away.

'How long do you reckon we have to hold out?' asked Savannah.

'I'll tell you in a second,' said Drake. He reached his gun around the doorway and fired off a few rounds, before quickly ducking his head outside and back in again. In that moment, he'd seen the plume of water from a jet ski racing back downriver. 'There goes the messenger, so I'd say at least an hour or so.'

'Is this tower going to last that long?' asked Beth.

'Should do,' Drake replied. 'A shot from those laser guns may be fatal, but I don't think that they've been designed to punch a hole through concrete.'

'I should imagine that they're under strict orders not to harm us,' said Beth. 'And I'm sure that that sicko brother of ours wants to have his sadistic revenge, so I can't see them launching an all-out attack on us anytime yet, at least not until Jago has arrived.'

'Anybody want to stick their head out and test that theory?' said Tanis.

Drake stuck out an arm and a flurry of laser shots peppered the walls on either side of the doorway. 'Ha!' he grinned.

'Obviously, you're expendable,' smirked Soli.

'I'm glad that you've all retained your sense of humour,' said Drake. 'Now, let's get down to the serious stuff. Everyone check their weapons and ammo.'

Soli and Beth, despite their protestations, had been issued with crossbows. They hadn't had any formal firearms training and Drake felt that it was an unnecessary risk to put machine guns into their inexperienced hands. Savannah, Tanis and Drake carried a sidearm each, along with magazine clips and Sten guns.

During the next hour, dismounted jet ski riders made several attempts to storm the tower, which resulted in a serious depletion of ammunition within Drake's group. He had thrown two more of his grenades out as a further deterrent; this added more casualties to their assailants, but not stopped the assault.

Back along the estuary, the message from the jet ski rider was music to Jago's ears. He smiled a reptilian smile. 'Come, my dear Roth. We have an appointment with my family and their friends. Let's not disappoint them.'

'And if they choose not to wait for us?' asked Roth.

'Then we shall, if need be, pursue them to the ends of the earth.'

57

'IT ENDS HERE'

Drake fired off another burst until his gun responded with dull metallic clicks.

'Persistent little sods,' he growled as he reloaded. 'I'm on my last clip. Ammo check. Now!' he shouted.

'Half a clip,' replied Tanis.

'Same here,' added Savannah.

Drake turned to them as another smattering of laser fire exploded across the tower's exterior. 'Right. We have to make a choice. Either we make a run for it into the tunnels and hope that Jago and Roth follow to where we can get some backup, or we sit it out here and lure them in.'

'I'm tired of running,' said Savannah. 'It ends here.'

'Okay. We'll soon be down to handguns. Are you ready for this?'

Savannah and Tanis nodded.

'What about us?' said Beth. 'We have our crossbows.'

'All you've done is keep us in the background,' complained Soli.

Tanis turned and waited for the sound of another

volley of fire to pass. 'You two are here so that we wouldn't be worried about what might be happening to you elsewhere. Savannah and I agreed that if this goes to the wall, you guys have to run. Whatever happens to us, this is about *your* survival.'

Beth bristled angrily. 'That's not fair! It's our fight as much as yours.'

Savannah put her hands on Beth's shoulders. 'Listen! Listen to me, Beth.' Savannah fixed her with her eyes. 'I'm not going to let those monsters get their hands on you again. They killed our parents. Tore a hole in our hearts.' Tears spilled in tiny rivulets down her cheeks. 'I don't want to die knowing that they'll lay their filthy paws on you next. If we fall – you run, and don't look back. Promise. For me. For Mum. For Dad.'

Through her own tears, Beth nodded. 'I love you,' she sobbed. 'I promise.'

Tanis took Soli's hands in his. 'Same goes for you.' He chewed his lip, refusing the tears their opportunity. Soli could not contain hers and she threw her arms around him.

Jago's voice drifted up from outside and broke the silence. 'Savannah. You've been a naughty girl,' he sang, mockingly. 'You and your friends have got thirty seconds to give yourselves up.'

'Go to hell!' she shouted.

Silence was the only response.

'They're going to storm us,' said Drake. 'This is it. You two girls get down into the storeroom and wait for us. If anybody else comes down those stairs, get the hell out of there and don't stop running until you reach the safety of Base One. Tanis, you take the right; Savannah, the left. I'll cover the middle.'

Beth and Soli headed for the stairwell and the others took up their positions just as a barrage of laser fire exploded across the doorway. A spray of hot brickwork ricocheted at Tanis, and he raised his arm in protection, but not before a small chunk sliced across his cheek, drawing a line of blood as it went.

'Son of a…!' He reached for his Sten gun and fired wildly.

Savannah and Drake followed suit until all three machine guns became silent, barren of ammunition. Tanis recklessly stepped forward to assess the situation. Men were clambering up the metal steps and along the walkways from either side. He threw his Sten at an advancing trooper, more in frustration, before he fired off shots from his handgun; killing two of the party and making those behind take whatever cover they could. More laser fire exploded around him.

'A little help out here,' he shouted.

Savannah and Drake emerged from the doorway, firing off volleys, until as the second and final ammunition clips were inserted into their handguns, Drake made a decision.

'Fall back. Get back inside!'

As the three of them crouched behind the scorched and battered doorframe, he addressed Tanis and Savannah.

'It's not quite worked out how we planned, but I think that we can still draw those two assholes in here. From my reckoning, there's only half a dozen or so troopers left. If we can take them out, we'll still have a chance. This is going to have to be face to face.'

'Then what are we waiting for?' said Savannah. She pressed her lips on Drake's cheek, and then she gave Tanis a soft kiss on the mouth. 'Let's do it!'

They emerged from the tower, firing as they went, which was unfortunate for the troopers who thought that it was a good idea to sneak along the walkway – they had nowhere to run and the first explosive shots ripped into them with fatal results. A laser beam found its way through and hit Savannah in the shoulder. Its force threw her back into the tower, and she lay there stunned, her padded tunic smoking.

Drake and Tanis drove themselves forward on either side of the door using their remaining bullets. Tanis' gun fired its final round and the last trooper to face him fell, blood jetting from a fatal neck wound. Back on the walkway, Drake was battling in hand-to-hand combat. The trooper that he had disarmed now had Drake in a desperate stranglehold, and with one mighty effort, Drake heaved him up and over the metal railing. In panic, the man released Drake and scrabbled vainly to grab the railings. Drake, his body infused with adrenalin and anger, stared into his face.

'You picked the wrong side, buddy.' With that, Drake watched as the man lost his hold and his screaming body fell to a bloody impact on the concrete below.

He turned to Tanis. 'Give me your gun, and go see to Savannah.' Then, he picked up his own and Savannah's fallen pistols and walked to the railings. Far to the right, on a rocky outcrop, stood two cloaked figures.

Motionless, waiting like birds of prey.

'That's it,' he shouted. 'That's all we've got.' He threw the three guns out into the air. 'If you want us, come and get us.' He turned to go, paused and then added as an afterthought, 'or bugger off and leave us alone!'

Inside, Tanis was helping Savannah to her feet.

'How are you?' said Drake.

'Okay, apart from the hole in my shoulder, which bloody stings!'

'You'll survive,' grimaced Drake. 'Now it's time to join the girls.'

Time dragged the next minutes into history, until a hooded and robed figure appeared in the outline of the tower's doorframe, a black silhouette against a silver-grey backdrop.

'A little bird tells us that you're out of ammunition,' came Jago's voice. 'You should have brought one of these to the party.' A white streak of laser exploded against the back wall of the room.

'Come and get us, you pathetic psycho!' Savannah's voice echoed from the stairwell.

Jago stepped into the shadowed room and Drake slipped from his hiding place to stand behind him.

'Why would I need one of those, when I have a loaded one of these?' he asked as he jabbed the cold gun barrel of a Sten gun into Jago's neck. 'Now, put your weapon on the floor. Slowly.'

Jago crouched in submission and discarded the laser gun.

'Stay down there,' ordered Drake. 'Now, tell that

buddy of yours to show himself, or I pull this trigger.'

Too late, a sixth sense told Drake that something was wrong. He felt the warm breath of a whisper in his ear.

'Asking after me? How touching.'

The blade of a surgeon's scalpel cut its way across Drake's throat, severing his jugular artery and his windpipe. Blood gushed freely onto Jago's cloak before he could rise and step away, and as Drake's life force drained from him, his body tumbled to the ground. 'I'm coming, Jake,' he whispered.

Roth picked up the gun and pulled out the magazine. It was empty. 'I knew that he was bluffing,' he said with contempt, and threw the weapon to the floor where it clattered away. He knelt down beside Drake's lifeless body.

'Oh! Look what we have here.' He unclipped a solitary grenade from Drake's tunic and handed it to Jago.

They exchanged an evil smile of agreement and Jago pulled its detonation pin before he casually tossed it to rattle down the stairway. There was a load explosion and a plume of smoke drifted up. As it began to clear, Jago and Roth cautiously made their way down into the storeroom. A small fire, started by the explosion, flickered away amongst a couple of crates, the rest of which were scattered and broken. Soli and Beth's bodies lay either dead or unconscious in a corner amongst splintered wood and debris.

'Well. What have we here?' said Jago. Savannah was supporting herself against an overturned fuel drum. Blood streamed down the side of her face from a head wound and a shard of wood jutted from her thigh. A red stain soaked through her combats. Next to her, Tanis struggled to his knees, shaking his head, trying to regain coordination of his senses. His face looked like a battered beetroot, and one arm hung useless and broken.

Jago strode over to Savannah and grabbed a handful of her hair in his fist. She shrieked with pain as he dragged her to the centre of the room.

'Bring lover boy over here,' he said to Roth.

Roth kicked Tanis in the ribs. 'Crawl to her, you little parasite!' he screamed.

At the shock of the kick, Tanis coughed out a mouthful of blood and two loose teeth.

'Move it!' shouted Roth. 'Or you'll get another one.'

Tanis shuffled his way to Savannah, and as they sat, their bodies hunched with pain, Savannah reached out her hand and Tanis clasped it.

'I love you,' he wheezed.

The red dots of two laser guns flickered restlessly on the backs of their heads.

'So, here we are again,' said Jago. 'Those stupid little girls cannot help you. There will be no cavalry coming to the rescue. No last-minute salvation. Your friend is dead. Too quickly for my liking, but dead all the same.'

For a moment, there was silence as Jago and Roth stood quietly; dark imaginings of things to follow drifted through their thoughts.

'What to do. Hmm? What say you, Roth?'

It sounded like two puffs of wind, just seconds apart.

Behind Savannah and Tanis, Jago stood immobile, his back slightly arched. A crossbow bolt penetrated the centre of his shoulder blades. He turned his head to meet Roth's wide-eyed expression. Blood foamed across Roth's lower lip, and just below his Adam's apple, a deadly bolt protruded from his throat. His body fell and folded up, bloody and soiled. In his last moment of life, he knew fear and his lips trembled.

A single sob escaped from Jago's mouth.

'Now you know how it feels to watch someone you love die.' It was Beth's voice. With agonising effort, she loaded another bolt into her crossbow.

Paralysed, Jago's shaking hand tried to reach out for Roth's crumpled shape.

The bolt pierced his rib cage and skewered the largest muscle in his body. Aware that his heart had not reached its next beat, Jago fell, and what was left of his mind went screaming into oblivion.

As Beth lost consciousness, she was aware of concerned voices entering the room, and Savannah calling out to her.

58

EPILOGUE

As soon as word spread that both Jago and Roth were dead, the majority of the conscripted troops turned on the ranks of the Transportation Police and any other hardliners. They took no prisoners; their hatred for everything that Jago and his regime had enforced on them and their families ran deep. With hope that their loved ones would now be safe, they announced their allegiance with the Diss and Earthland's defence force.

In the following weeks, Opulence was seized with little resistance and a process of accountability and justice was introduced against all those who had played a part in the repression and brutality of the Servanti. The class divide was abolished. A new democratic order became established and Opulence was renamed Horizon. The luxurious residential areas and the notorious Transportation Centre were stripped and rebuilt as a research hub and a technology and design institute, their sole purpose to work for the benefit of all.

On Earthland, the mystery of the missing Crazies was solved; their corrupted body chemistry had finally fallen victim to a fatal virus that attacked their immune systems, spreading quickly throughout their population and eradicating the biggest remaining threat to re-establishing a new, safe society.

Humanity had a second chance to redeem itself as custodian of a fragile Earth, and amongst countless others who had taken up the fight for a free and just society, there were five who held a special bond with each other for the rest of their lives.

*

Three days after the tragic events at the bridge tower, Jean Fairfax sat alone in her office. A rarity stood in front of her. "Single Malt Scotch Whisky" read the label. She'd opened the bottle an hour ago and it was now a third empty. Not for the first time, she cursed herself out loud. 'You bloody fool, Jean. You bloody, bloody fool.' Then, she cursed Drake, but mentally. *Damn you, Drake, damn you. How dare you leave me like this.* The tears rolled down her cheeks. They weren't driven by the alcohol. They were driven by love. A love that she had left unacknowledged for so long… and too late.

The final damage to the group read like a car crash.

Savannah. Eight stitches to her head, four to her shoulder and another ten to patch up her leg once she'd gone through the excruciating pain of having the shard of wood pulled from her thigh. Luckily, it had missed the artery by centimetres. She would walk with a slight limp for the rest of her life.

Tanis. Two missing teeth. Three stitches to his cheek.

A broken nose, two cracked ribs and an arm fractured in two places.

Beth. Concussion and ringing in her ears for more than two weeks. Three broken ribs, and her back looked as though she had been stabbed with a porcupine; it was covered in a myriad of cuts from splinters thrown out by the explosion.

Soli. She fared the worst by far. The grenade exploded closest to her and the left-hand side of her body took the force. Her leg was broken just below the knee, and she lost three fingers on her left hand. Her left ear was also gone. She was in a coma for two weeks, and a piece of shrapnel the size of a large coin had to be removed from the back of her skull.

However, the greatest pain that they all had to bear was the loss of Drake.

Every year, on the anniversary of his death, Savannah, Tanis, Beth, Soli and Jean Fairfax would meet at a simple stone cairn in a quiet glade, to join hands and remember him.

Not that they didn't think of him every single day.